Nights of Obedience

RACHEL MAYS

To everyone who fell in love with a bleach-blonde wizard as a preteen and never got over it – this one is for you ♥

Sage Habor

Fort Malck

Murvort

Osavian

Twin
Beacons

Renoa

Dreslen

Lourova

Chapter One

Emilie

My life was over. At least life as I'd known it—the one before my parents traded me like a rare jewel in exchange for the king's benevolence. I'd known it was coming for a while, but now that the day was here...I wasn't sure I was ready.

"Hurry up. We're going to be late." I heard my mother screeching from beyond the bedroom door, signaling it was time to finish getting ready. It had taken all morning to curl my long, brown hair properly, and for what purpose? As soon as we got on the road, the humidity would leave it frizzy and untamed.

I grabbed a powder compact from the mess of products beside the sink and dabbed it over my face. It would help to absorb any excess sweat during our long trip through the desert.

The dress my mother had picked out was impractical, although I had to admit it was stunning. According to her, the dark green accentuated

1

my golden-brown eyes, but I was afraid the pools of sweat left under the long-sleeved dress would offend my betrothed. Honestly, it was the middle of summer. What was my mother thinking?

Could I have chosen my own dress? Sure. But some battles were not worth fighting when it came to my mother. This was an easy one to let slide. I'd wear her chosen dress, but I was sure she'd still find something to criticize.

It was her greatest talent.

I grabbed the pair of beige flats lying beside my wooden armoire. At least I wasn't expected to wear heels.

A knock on the door made me turn my head toward two men—burly and muscular, with dark beards and even darker eyes. They headed toward the stack of trunks beside my bed and began to carry them out one by one.

"Did you pack enough?" my mother asked sarcastically as she followed the men into the room.

"I packed everything I own," I said with a little more attitude than I would've normally let slip. If I was being sent off to be married to some man I didn't know, then I should at least be able to take all of my favorite belongings. There was a strong possibility that I would never lay eyes on this room again. I wasn't about to leave my treasured jewelry behind. Or the books my grandmother had given me before she passed. It was *all* coming with me.

"Is that the dress you're wearing?" she asked, and I almost screamed.

"Yes. It's the one you picked out a week ago. Don't you remember?"

"Oh. I suppose it is. It's a little snug around the hips, honey. I expected it to be more...elegant."

Thank the gods for the extra layer of powder on my face, because my skin turned a furious shade of red as I listened to her critique my appearance. "I can change if you don't like it," I huffed.

"No, no. Your clothes are already packed, and I don't want to be late. That'll have to do. Let's go. Your father is already waiting outside."

My mother sighed as she ushered me out of the bedroom. I took one last glance back. The room looked rather empty now, only drapes and beige bedding. Discolored squares remained on the walls where I'd removed my personal art collection. I had no idea if there would be space for them in my new quarters, but I'd be damned if I left them behind. No one in this castle appreciated art the way that I did.

In its barren state, I could hardly recognize the room I'd spent the entire twenty years of my life in. My sanctuary and safe place. It no longer belonged to me.

It was strange how a place that held such warm memories could turn so cold and desolate. Even as I walked down the halls of our castle, I could feel the walls closing in on me. It seemed like they were eager to get rid of me, too.

My father stood waiting at the front door, reaching out an arm for me to hold as I walked down the steps. It was early morning and already it was scorching hot. The sun reflected off the tan stone steps and cracked pathways.

"I'm proud of you, Emilie," my father said quietly, and I suppressed a laugh.

My relationship with my parents had always been contentious. I'd been bred for a reason. For a purpose. My brother, born two years before me, was the heir. The golden child. He would inherit the Kingdom of Dreslen, which was fine with me. I didn't want it, anyway. Instead, I got to be my parents' chess piece. I was a pawn in their game for power—given to the kingdom with the most to offer in return.

That kingdom was Osavian. I knew very little about Osavian. I'd only visited a handful of times, but what I did remember was the lovely fields of wildflowers and glistening rivers. A harsh contrast to the arid, brown and beige hellscape that was Dreslen. I wasn't sad at all to be leaving my homeland. I just wished that I had been asked about what I wanted. I wished that I'd had a say in my future.

Now I was on my way to meet a man named Cyrus Castelli, the King of Osavian. We'd met before, but I'd been so young I could hardly recall. He'd been previously married, but his wife had passed away and my parents, the vultures that they were, swooped in to form an alliance before her body was even in the grave. Since she'd never had children, I knew without my parents' saying that I'd have to give him an heir.

My life was not my own.

Still, I was determined to make the best of the situation. What my parents didn't realize was that I had ambitions of my own. As Queen of Osavian, I could do whatever I wanted. I would no longer be under their house or their rules. I could take back my life. I would put up with a man twice my age if it meant I could wield power for my own purposes. I wouldn't be my parents' mouthpiece in the neighboring kingdom. They shouldn't have assumed my loyalty.

The prospect of being queen was exhilarating to me. I'd never considered myself to be hungry for power like my parents, but I knew I had it in me to be a fair and just ruler. Someone the people could look up to and would worship and admire. They'd speak my name with love—write songs about me. I would be remembered long after I was six feet under. *That* was my dream.

Wasn't that what everyone wanted? To be loved for all eternity?

I didn't care if that love didn't come from a man. I'd accept it from the world instead.

A carriage awaited us in the gardens surrounding the castle entryway. Calling them gardens was generous. The only greenery that survived in these conditions were the multitudes of cacti. Just as prickly as my mother.

Two white horses, freshly bathed and brushed, were hitched to the wagon. Behind the first wagon was a second, large enough to fit all of my belongings. My father helped me into the covered cart and sat down next to me on the plush bench. A whoosh of air rushed by as the cushion deflated under his weight. Across from us, my mother straightened her skirt as she settled into the seat.

"You look beautiful, my dear," my father said.

I pulled out a fan from the side pocket of the cart and waved it in front of my face dramatically. "That's because the sweat hasn't started yet."

My mother scoffed, but my father let a grin slip before he quickly disguised it. I got my sense of humor from him.

After a few minutes of waving the fan, I got tired and turned to my magic. I concentrated and summoned a breeze through the carriage, sighing with relief.

I was an air wielder. Most mages possessed one of the four common elemental powers: water, fire, earth, and air. Then there were a few uncommon powers, such as healing, light, darkness, and a handful of others.

And even rarer were those with no capabilities who relied on experimental potions and blood magic—something that had been outlawed for decades, but traces of it were all around us. The water that came from our faucets in the middle of a desert. The threads in our clothing that never tore. It was said that blood magic had been banned because those without magic shouldn't be able to create it, yet we used their spells on a daily basis without thinking twice.

It was incredibly hypocritical, but no one wanted to be the one to point it out, lest we lose access to our simple pleasures.

"Are you nervous?" my father asked, interrupting my train of thought.

"Why would I be nervous?"

My parents exchanged a look. "You haven't been to Osavian in at least a decade, and it's been longer than that since you've seen Cyrus. You were little more than a child when you first met."

"And?"

"Well, I expected it might be a bit nerve-wracking to see him again, knowing that you will be wed to him by the end of the summer."

I stared out the window and watched as we rode through the endless desert. Hills of sand stretched as far as the eye could see and today there was a slight breeze that caused swirls of sand to dance in the sky.

"I'm not nervous. It's actually a bit exciting to leave Dreslen behind. I feel like my life is just beginning."

My mother missed the bite in my tone. "That's the spirit. This wedding will be beneficial for both of our kingdoms. Murvort has been silent for far too long. Mark my words—they're planning something."

"You say that every year, darling."

"And every year I mean it. You can't honestly believe that they aren't a threat, can you?"

"I think if they come out of their mountains, we will deal with them as we have every other time. If they're smart, they'll stay hidden in their dark caves."

Murvort was the kingdom in the northwest corner of the continent of Lourova. A mountain range separated them from Osavian in the northeast and Dreslen in the south. I'd never been there, so all I knew about the kingdom was what I'd been told. That it was dark, cold, and wet. The harsh terrain left them with little resources and many died before adulthood.

In many ways, it was the exact opposite of Dreslen. Our deserts also made survival hard, but we had our allies to the north—Osavian. Osavian was a fucking paradise by comparison. The wealthiest of the three kingdoms and our charitable neighbor. If it weren't for them, the citizens of Dreslen would also be starving to death.

Which was why, when King Cyrus's wife had passed away, my parents swooped in to further strengthen the alliance between our kingdoms.

Every once in a while, Murvort made moves to invade the southern countries and every single time they retreated when they were met by Osavian's forces. They were little more than a nuisance. I wasn't sure why my mother was so obsessed with them. She needed a hobby.

The carriage rocked back and forth roughly when we passed over a rut in the road and my mother clasped a hand to her mouth.

"These trips make me sick."

"I know, Nadine. Try to relax. Did you take your tonic?" My father rubbed my mother's leg in a soothing motion.

"Of course. I could never travel without it." She sighed heavily. "Emilie, when you have the king's ear, make sure he sends gold to fix our roads."

I stifled a snicker. "I'll add it to the list."

That wasn't hypothetical. I had a growing list of demands from my parents that got longer by the day. This alliance with Osavian felt very one-sided. They provided a lot of benefits, but the only thing Dreslen had to offer in return was me.

I didn't have a self-esteem issue. In fact, I was a very confident woman. And yet, when I thought of how much our country had to gain in exchange for my hand in marriage, I felt very inadequate. I just hoped King Cyrus was pleased with his *gift*.

The road from Dreslen's capital to Osavian was dull and deserted. Only tradesmen came through these routes. There were no villages to break up the monotonous scenery. It was far too dry and hot for anyone to survive in this part of the kingdom. We only made stops when my mother was about to be sick or when one of us needed to relieve our bladders.

Another reason I hated this dress. Hiking up the long skirt and hovering behind the cart was not an easy task.

The sky darkened after hours of tense silence and weary sighs from my mother. I thanked the gods above that she didn't vomit in this carriage. We slowed down as we reached the border between Dreslen and Osavian. There was a small outpost where two guards strode out to meet our driver. They exchanged a few words and not long after, our carriage began to roll again.

I looked out the window. It was mostly dark now but, in the distance, I could see light. A sign that we were getting close to Osavian's capital city of Renoa.

We crossed over a one lane bridge and my father had to pull me back from the open window.

"Why did you do that?" I asked.

"You were about to fall out."

I shook my head and leaned out the window again, this time with more caution. There was a flowing river below and I counted four baby swans with their mother floating downstream. I recognized them from one of the books I'd been forced to study when I was young. One that listed all variants of fowl and other creatures native to the Lourova.

Another thing that I wouldn't miss about Dreslen. Aside from our horses that were imported, small lizards and insects were the only wildlife that existed. Neither of which I was fond of.

Our carriage came to a halt along the outer wall of the seaside castle. A man in a light beige cloak opened the carriage door and smiled in greeting.

"Welcome. The Royal family is eager to see you. Allow me to escort you. My men will bring your luggage inside." He waved a hand at what I assumed was the second carriage behind us, where his men were working to unpack my belongings.

The moment I stepped out, I was instantly greeted with the fresh breeze off the water and the busy noise of a vibrant city. Everywhere I looked, there were people in beautiful, elegant gowns with smiles plastered on their faces. Music poured out of the building across the street, and I could smell something sweet and fruity in the air. A woman waved at her friends as she ran across the street to meet them. Another man laughed at something his partner just said. It might've been late, but the residents of Renoa were still wide awake and full of energy.

My senses were overwhelmed and before I could take it all in, my parents pushed me through a large archway and into the gardens that led up to the castle entry.

It was every bit as magnificent as I imagined. The gardens in Renoa were nothing like ours back home. Ours were dry and brown, hanging on by a thread, but these were lush and full of color. Bright and beautiful pinks, yellow and oranges. The floral scent hung in the air and infiltrated my lungs, coursing through my veins.

And the castle was a level of extravagance I'd never known. Vines traveled from the ground up to the second and third levels, weaving their way between windows and balconies where warm light poured out. The castle was made of light sandstone, but the vines were like veins that pulsed in the colossal building, giving it a life of its own.

We reached the front steps and four people were there to greet us, standing still and regal.

I took a deep breath.

No looking back now.

Chapter Two

Emilie

"WELCOME," THE MAN IN the center said. He was tall with light blonde hair and looked to be twice my age, judging by the wrinkles on his face and the subtle gray hairs dispersed throughout his beard. He wore dark slacks with an elegant blazer covered in golden decals. I'd bet my best gown that he was Cyrus. I tried not to stare at my future husband, only letting my eyes linger for an acceptable amount of time.

On his right was another man. He was large, even taller than Cyrus, and at least twice as wide. His huge muscles were covered in lightweight armor. Protective but practical. The belt strapped to his waist was fitted with numerous daggers and a sword, and he kept a casual hand on the hilt. While Cyrus looked pleased to see us, this man looked absolutely uninterested. In fact, I'm not sure he was even looking at us, but *beyond* us. Waiting for an unknown threat to present itself.

It seemed unlikely to me.

A third man was on Cyrus's other side. He looked younger, perhaps in his late twenties or early thirties. He was of a similar build to Cyrus but his hair was so light; it was practically white. Actually, in the moonlight, it was more silver. No one had told me that Cyrus had siblings, but I would've guessed that this man was his brother.

And finally, at the end, stood a petite woman. She kept her distinguished blonde hair neatly pulled back into a tight bun, adding to her polished appearance. Her long gown was a midnight blue that contrasted with her pale skin. She was old enough to be Cyrus's mother, but there was a youthful curiosity in her eyes as she looked us over.

"Cyrus." My father stepped out of line. "It's so good to see you again."

Although my mother and I rarely visited Osavian, my father came here frequently to discuss business. He closed in on Cyrus and the large man next to the king didn't move to stop him. Either he wasn't a very good bodyguard or he trusted my father enough to let him get close to the king. My father and Cyrus embraced and exchanged a cordial handshake.

"It's good to see you again, Misha. And Nadine. It's been too long." Cyrus wrapped my mother in a hug and she returned the gesture.

"Thank you for inviting us, Cyrus. You remember my daughter, Emilie," she said with a wave in my direction.

For the first time, Cyrus's eyes met mine. They were a lovely shade of green, and he beamed as he stepped toward me. He took my hand and planted a gentle kiss across my knuckles. My stomach fluttered at the delicate touch. Those nerves I hadn't felt? They made their appearance now. It all hit me and my cheeks flushed a vivid shade of pink. Hopefully, he mistook it for rouge.

"It's a pleasure to meet you, Emilie," he said, and I noticed he held my hand a little longer than necessary.

This wasn't the first time we'd met, but I didn't correct him. No one needed the reminder that our first meeting was actually when I'd been a child and he'd already been a young adult.

"The pleasure is mine," I replied.

Cyrus stepped back and acknowledged his entourage. "This is my brother Ladon and my mother Sophia. And this is my advisor, Hudson."

Hudson gave a curt nod to my parents and me. I extended a hand toward Sophia, but she pulled me in for a warm embrace instead.

"Oh," I said softly. I hadn't expected such an intimate introduction.

"It's so nice to see you again, Emilie. I'm sure you don't remember your visits here as a child, but you were always such a joy to have around. I still remember you splashing in the waves of the sea for the first time. You were the most darling thing. I look forward to catching up." She looked deep into my eyes and I struggled not to fidget. "You've grown into such a beautiful woman. Wouldn't you agree, Cyrus?"

I turned to face the man behind me, and he nodded in affirmation. A soft smile stretched across his face and I found that mine soon matched his.

Maybe this wouldn't be so bad.

Lastly, I greeted Cyrus's brother Ladon. I raised my hand, and he stared at it a second too long before he reached to grab it. He gave me a firm, steady shake with a calloused palm and didn't say a word before dropping my hand and moving toward his brother.

"Nice to meet you, too," I mumbled under my breath.

"Shall we move inside?" Sophia asked. She had a shawl draped over her shoulders, even though it was pleasantly warm this evening. Perhaps I was just so used to the overbearing heat of Dreslen that Osavian's night air felt comfortable to me.

She led us inside and already there were workers making trips in and out of the castle carrying trunks of my belongings and the bags my parents packed. Theirs were much smaller than mine since they wouldn't be staying long. Just a few days while I acclimated.

Cyrus and my father were deep in conversation while my mother clung to them like a parasite. It was embarrassing how desperately she wanted to exert her influence.

I took one look at the stacks of my possessions that were now piling up in the entryway and realized my mother might've had a point. It seemed excessive now that everything was out in the open for all to see. I hoped Cyrus didn't think that I was simply a material woman.

I loved dresses and jewels and fine art, but I also loved to read and learn. Hopefully, he would see there was more substance to me than what these trunks presented.

Ladon watched as each of the trunks paraded past him. He caught me looking at him and his eyes squinted in the tiniest fraction. "Is this all yours?" he asked.

I lifted my head a little higher. It was one thing to be hard on myself, but I would not be shamed by Cyrus's brother for wanting to bring all the comforts of home. "Yes," I responded firmly.

His jaw rippled, and I figured he was holding back a retort. If he was smart, he probably knew it was unwise to insult his future sister-in-law and future Queen of Osavian.

I brushed my hair from my shoulder and strode toward Cyrus and my parents. Ladon scoffed behind me, but I didn't turn around. I refused to give him the impression that his opinion mattered to me—even if it did.

The first lesson in power that I'd been taught was to never let anyone believe they hold any persuasion over you. It was a weakness they would exploit every chance they got.

"I can show you to your rooms now if you'd like. I'm sure you must be tired from traveling all day," Cyrus said.

"If you don't mind, I'd love—"

"Yes, we would love to settle in for the night. Thank you, Cyrus. You are so thoughtful." My mother interrupted me and spewed a load of her usual over-the-top dramatics. She acted as if we'd been traveling for weeks and not hours.

I had just been about to say how much I'd love to see the town—it had looked so inviting as we'd passed earlier—but I supposed I'd be going to bed instead. I took a deep breath, reminding myself I only had to put up with my mother for a few more days.

"I'll be there shortly," Ladon said from a distance, as he turned to talk with the workers who were transferring our belongings.

Cyrus led us to the living quarters of the castle. We hadn't seen much of the castle yet, but I could already tell every corner was dripping in grandeur. From the ornate banisters to the long, patterned rugs that lined the hallways. Every detail was intentional. The marble floors contained swirling lines of black that reminded me of the vines that crawled up the castle's exterior. And I was half-convinced the curtains at the top of the grand staircase were enchanted. They were closed, but they shimmered as if the stars were just beyond the fabric, filling the landing with a majestic blue glow.

Cyrus set my parents up in a suite next to Sofia. Then he took me up a second staircase to another level of suites.

"How many floors does the castle have?" I wondered aloud.

"Three plus the lower chamber."

"Dungeons?" I asked with more interest.

He looked at me with a glimmer of curiosity. "Yes. Is that something that you'd like to see?" He raised his eyebrows in a way that said he found me amusing.

"Call me morbid, but I find dungeons have the most history behind them. My brother used to dare me to sneak into the dungeons when we were kids. He thought that I would be terrified, but secretly I loved it.

I would sit in an empty cell and in the complete silence I swear I could hear ghosts of the men who had died there."

"That *is* incredibly morbid, Emilie."

I shrugged my shoulders. "They didn't scare me. They seemed to be sad souls, wandering as if they'd lost their way."

He continued to stare at me with an odd sort of fascination. Had I shared too much? I had a tendency to do that. My mother would be furious to find that I'd already made a poor impression.

"Sorry. That was an odd thing to share about myself." I tucked a stray hair behind my ear and bit the inside of my cheek. A nervous habit I hadn't been able to shake.

"Don't be sorry. I'd love to know more weird things about you," he said with a chuckle. I studied his face, but there was no trace of deceptive flattery. He was being honest.

"Where is your brother, by the way? I'm surprised he didn't join you."

"Adrien is in Twin Beacons."

Cyrus gave an understanding nod. Twin Beacons was an island off the coast that guarded Lourova from marauders and other unknown enemies. It was a narrow island with two nearly identical peaks on either end. In between, the land was so low that it often disappeared beneath the waters. From a distance, if one didn't know better, it looked like there was a passage between the two peaks. Ships attempted to sail right between them, only realizing too late that they were headed straight for a hidden land barrier. It was incredibly effective at protecting our coastal borders.

My brother had been in Twin Beacons for at least three years, training and building allegiance with the troops stationed there. I rarely saw him, but he had his role to play, just as I had mine. One day, when he took over as ruler in Dreslen, those troops would be fiercely loyal to him.

"I hope he'll be able to join us for the wedding," Cyrus remarked.

"I believe he intends to."

We stopped outside of a slate gray door and I realized that we were completely alone. I swallowed and shoved down the bile rising in my throat. Was I expected to share his suite? Wasn't it improper to sleep in his bed until we were married?

If we were an ordinary couple, I would have no hesitations, but Cyrus wasn't ordinary. He was a king. And a child out of wedlock wasn't an heir. There was no way he'd take that risk. Or at least that's what I told myself.

Could he tell I was breathing heavily? I needed to calm down.

"This is your suite. I figured you might like your own for now. Or even after we're married, it might be nice to have a space to call your own."

"Thank you," I said, trying to mask my sigh of relief. "That was thoughtful."

He offered me another kind smile. "I know this is...uncomfortable."

"Is it?" I teased.

He let out a soft, nervous laugh, and I was stricken by his beautiful green eyes and unassuming smile. Cyrus wasn't at all what I thought he would be. "This isn't my first arranged marriage."

I leaned against the door to my room, feeling a bit sad for the man before me. "I'm sorry about your late wife."

"I appreciate that. Isabella was a lovely woman. Anyway, I know it can be awkward at first, but I'm a good man, Emilie. Or at least, I try to be. And I hope that we will become close. I promise to treat you well, and I hope you feel welcome here."

He seemed genuine, and my heart warmed a little to the idea of marrying him. Even at his age, I could still make out handsome features. I'd never been in love. I'd never felt that emotion that minstrels sang songs about and novelists wrote stories about. But maybe I could learn to love him.

"Thank you," I said again.

"Right. Well, if you need anything else, I'm down the hall. Marjorie, your handmaid, is also on call. She can get you anything from the kitchen or extra linens. Just say the word. Goodnight, Emilie."

"Goodnight, Cyrus."

Inside was a beautiful room, decorated with gold and white and a few pops of my favorite color—purple. A four-post bed with a sleek silk canopy faced the floor-to-ceiling windows. Between the windows was a small sliding door that led to my balcony.

I stepped outside and leaned on the railing, gasping as I laid eyes on the most gorgeous view. Gardens surrounded the castle, and beyond the blankets of red, orange and purple petals, the midnight blue sea shimmered under a full moon. It was a sight that rivaled any art piece I'd ever laid eyes on. No paint could ever mimic the vivid beauty before me. And the *scent*...I took a deep breath of that sweet and salty air and let it calm my nerves and soothe my soul.

For a moment, I thought about raising my arms and dancing in the breeze, but I quickly realized that my balcony wasn't private. Below in the gardens, I saw a few stragglers who hadn't yet gone to bed.

Upon closer look, it was Ladon and a few of the servants. They were carrying the rest of my luggage inside the castle, and I expected they'd be up to my room at any moment.

I walked to the corner of the balcony, hidden behind a tall green bush, and watched as Ladon commanded the men. I couldn't help but notice his dominant stature. He stood straight and his broad shoulders were pulled back. From the backside, I could see how nicely he filled out his black pants. The body and muscles of a warrior.

I couldn't hear what they were saying despite my efforts to strain my ears. I could've called upon the wind to carry their voices in my direction. It would've been a gross, inappropriate use of magic, of course, but...

It was too tempting to resist.

I concentrated and the flower beds that surrounded Ladon and the servants fluttered in the light breeze. Their voices came quietly at first, then louder.

"These are all going to the third floor—the bridal suite. Make sure you take that one to the second-floor guest suite." Ladon turned to another servant who had just arrived.

"The horses are all fed and stabled for the night. Do you need anything else from me, sir?"

"No," Ladon answered. "You're free to go home. Thank you for the help tonight."

"It's nothing, sir."

"It's not nothing. I know you weren't on the schedule to work today. I appreciate your extra efforts and I'll be sure to make sure the additional funds are included in your wages."

"Thank you." The man turned to leave, and the others were already carrying my suitcases inside. Ladon now stood alone in the middle of the gardens.

And then he turned, and I swore he looked directly to where I was hiding behind that bush. But, no—he couldn't possibly know I was hiding up here, could he?

But his eyes were locked in my direction. And then he whispered.

"Emilie."

I gasped and then clasped my mouth.

He dragged a finger over the row of lilies that were still swaying in the breeze—the breeze that I had created.

"If you're going to spy, you need to do better than that."

His words carried as if he were standing right next to me. Like he was whispering in my ear. His voice was calm but I didn't miss the unspoken threat. I allowed the wind to die, but stayed frozen in horror. How did he know?

He plucked one of the red lilies and then stalked back to the castle entry and out of my sight. It was only then that I allowed myself to breathe.

My heart was still racing when there was an abrupt knock on my door.

"Fuck," I shouted and nearly jumped out of my skin.

Please don't be Ladon. Please don't be Ladon.

I opened the door and breathed a sigh of relief. It wasn't Ladon. It was only the servants there to deliver all my suitcases.

"Where would you like these, miss?"

I took a quick look around the room and settled on an empty corner near the bathroom door. "Over there is fine."

They stacked them in a neat pile and I knew I should've started to unpack, but my head was still spinning. I was still thinking about Ladon's voice tickling my ear. The threat in his words had sent shivers up my spine. The horror, knowing I would have to see him in the morning and face his judgment.

How in the world had he known I was listening to his conversation? It chilled me to the core to think he might be some sort of mind reader. My privacy felt invaded, which was ironic considering I was the one that had invaded *his* privacy.

I locked the door and thankfully only had to search through one suitcase before I found my nightclothes. I changed quickly and crawled into bed. It didn't take long at all before I was fast asleep, dreaming of shimmering seas and blooming flowers. Definitely *not* picturing a handsome, silver-haired Castelli brother.

Chapter Three

Emilie

WHEN I WOKE UP the next day, I could see a single strip of light peeking through my violet drapes. I rolled over and hid my face. The bed was too soft and warm to get out of. I could've laid there forever, but a knock on the door interrupted my lazy morning.

"Come in," I grunted loud enough for them to hear. Then I cursed when I remembered I had locked the door last night before falling asleep.

But somehow it opened anyway, and a young woman entered. She looked like she was about my age, with shiny black hair slicked back into a braid. She wore a simple green dress that cinched at the waist, showing off her slender figure. "Good morning, Miss Duval."

"Please, call me Emilie."

"Emilie, it is then. I brought you coffee and a pastry. I brought cream and sugar as well. I wasn't sure how you take your coffee."

"Thank you..." I hesitated.

"Oh, forgive me. I'm Marjorie, your handmaid."

"Thank you, Marjorie." I paused and considered the locked door. "How did you get in?"

"What do you mean?"

"I could've sworn I locked that door last night."

"Oh." She waved a dismissive hand in my direction. "The door is enchanted for me. As your handmaiden, I can always get in. Don't worry, I always knock first."

Odd. I wasn't sure I liked that.

"Does anyone else have a free pass to my room?" I questioned.

"Cyrus, of course. And then Sophia and Ladon."

There was a look of horror on my face which Marjorie immediately tried to placate.

"The entire royal family can gain access to any room at any time. It's how the castle was built. It's enchanted to the bloodline, including spouses. In fact, once you're queen, you can also enter any room you'd like."

She said it like I should've been excited to meander the castle at my will, but all I could think about was the lack of privacy and the possibility that Ladon might come to confront me in the middle of the night. I still wasn't sure what his deal was, but I'd probably find out soon enough. Or not. Maybe the whole disgruntled fiend act was just his entire personality.

I sat up in my bed, and I didn't bother to cover up. My nightgown was thin, and it was a bit cold in my room, but Marjorie paid me no mind. Part of her duties would be helping me to get ready, so we might as well get comfortable.

"Did you get all of your things unpacked?" Marjorie looked to the corner of my room and found all my trunks, hardly touched and still packed to the brim. "Oh, if you need some help, I'd be happy to assist."

21

"That's okay. I'm more than capable of sorting everything out." It felt unkind to make Marjorie unpack all of my clutter. I had insisted on bringing it, so I would be the one to take care of it.

I poured some sweet cream into my coffee and bit into the flaky, triangular pastry. To my surprise, it was filled with fruity gelatin. Citrus, if I had to guess. But there was something red mixed inside as well.

"What is this filling?" I asked.

"Orange and raspberry jam."

"It's delicious," I moaned and Marjorie chuckled.

"I'm glad you enjoy it."

"Can I get more of these?"

Majorie laughed again. "I'm afraid not. Cyrus has breakfast planned. You should actually get dressed now or we'll be late."

I finished the pastry and my coffee and searched through one of the trunks that I was sure I'd shoved my clothing into. Everything was a disaster though, and I struggled to find something I actually wanted to wear. I settled on some soft and lightweight blue pants and a black sleeveless top. Thankfully, I didn't have to look far to find matching black sandals.

Marjorie assured me this was a casual breakfast, but I still felt out of place as she led me to the multi-tier balcony jutting out over the sea. The view was stunning as I walked a few stairs to the upper level. It was absolutely breathtaking; the way the morning sun hit the water. In the distance, I could see a fleet of boats, their sails marked with the royal insignia of Osavian—a black dragon silhouette over a white moon. The sound of seagulls and waves crashing created the most bewitching melody.

At the top of the steps, a table had already been set for breakfast, and seated around the table were my parents, Cyrus and Sophia. I ignored the feeling of relief that Ladon wasn't present, and we wouldn't have to talk about my eavesdropping the previous night.

It only took one look from my mother to know she was judging my attire. I couldn't find it in me to care. Tomorrow she would return home and I'd finally be free of her criticism.

"Good morning, Emilie." Cyrus pulled a chair out for me to sit beside him. "Hope you're hungry. The chefs outdid themselves with this feast."

It was a feast like I'd never seen before. Trays of fruit, toast, meats, muffins, and other items accompanied a centerpiece of fresh flowers from the gardens. I even spotted the jam-filled pastries that Marjorie had brought to my room that morning.

"How did you sleep?" Sophia asked politely.

"Very well, didn't we, dear?" my mother responded, patting my father's forearm. Sophia was likely asking me, but my mother, as usual, was so eager to be the center of attention. It was too early to fight with her, so I allowed her to engage in all the small talk while I filled my plate with fruit and more of those flaky pastries.

Sophia sipped from a glass flute, and I was curious about what she had inside it. She caught me eyeing it and waved over at the server. "How rude of me. Could you bring Miss Emilie a drink as well?"

The server placed a glass in front of me, and I tasted the bubbly beverage. It was fruity with a little bite.

"Do you like it?" Sophia asked. "It's pomegranate and sparkling wine."

"I love it," I answered truthfully. I liked Osavian more and more. And I could tell Sophia was going to be a more tolerable mother than my own ever was.

"It's a little early to be drinking, isn't it?"

I rolled my eyes at my mother's tone, but thankfully she was looking toward Cyrus. His approval was the only one that mattered to her.

He shook his head gently. "I find that sparkling wine is appropriate for all hours of the day."

"And he wouldn't dare tell his mother what she can or cannot do," Sophia added.

Cyrus smiled, and I liked the sight of it. It was warm and friendly, and although we hardly knew each other, somehow it felt familiar. A server placed a glass in front of him as well, and the three of us raised our glasses in a toast.

I knew my mother had to be reeling next to me, but she bit her tongue.

We passed around trays and loaded our plates with a second serving of all the Osavian delicacies. I couldn't tell if this was a normal breakfast here in Renoa or if they'd brought out the best just to impress us.

Either way, I *was* impressed.

A servant filled my glass a second time while I listened to Cyrus and my father discuss politics. Meanwhile, my mother and Sophia talked about the upcoming wedding and I couldn't decide which conversation was the least appealing. All I wanted to do was get out and explore the city. Just as a servant was about to fill my glass for a third time, I heard someone climbing the steps to join us.

"Sorry I'm late. There was a bit of a situation with the northern outpost that I had to take care of," Ladon said.

He glanced right over me without making eye contact. I didn't know if I was mad at his indifference or relieved. As he stepped closer, I realized I'd been holding my breath from the moment I'd first caught sight of him.

"Is everything okay?" Cyrus asked.

"Nothing to worry about. We can catch up later." Ladon surveyed the remaining food. "Right now it's time to eat and enjoy each other's company."

He smiled, but it was unlike Cyrus's. There was an echo of arrogance there. A dangerous coolness that had me sipping from my glass once again just to feel some relief over my heated body.

"I'm afraid I'll have to leave you. I have errands to run in town, and I've got an appointment with the seamstress in an hour. How did it get to be so late?" Sophia carried on as she stood from her chair. "Here, you can have my seat, Ladon."

Sophia placed a soft kiss on her youngest son's cheek and he accepted it politely before sitting down in her now unoccupied seat.

It took all my effort to avoid his gaze now that he sat directly across from me. I started to sip from my glass before realizing I'd drained it. Three glasses of wine before noon. My mother would be so proud.

Speaking of my mother, she stood and grabbed my father by the arm. "We need to be going too, Misha. I planned a full day of activities while we're in town. We'll see you later tonight, honey."

They walked away and I could still hear her going on about dresses, shoes, and bags. All the finer things in life that she could never get her hands on in Dreslen.

And then there were three.

"So what news comes from Fort Malek?" Cyrus asked while finishing the rest of his sautéed potatoes.

Ladon gave me the quickest glance before turning to his brother. "I told you we could talk about it later."

"Don't be silly. You can speak freely in front of Emilie. She should be brought up to speed on matters concerning the court, anyway. Might as well start now."

It made me happy to hear Cyrus's confidence in me. He truly was doing his best to make me feel like I belonged here, and I was incredibly grateful.

Ladon glared at his brother with fierce blue eyes before sighing in resignation. He tilted his chin up in my direction. "Fine. It's not like she won't find out eventually, anyway."

The knowing look he gave me made my cheeks flush. Or maybe they were already flushed from the alcohol, but regardless, the reminder of last night's mishap made me shift in my seat. Ladon was frowning, and I wondered if he ever smiled.

"Two of our scouts went on a mission last week and didn't come back. This morning, one was found."

"That's good news."

"No. His head was found. Severed from his body."

I gasped, and both men looked at me, Ladon with an annoyed expression, and Cyrus looking more apologetic. I didn't want to risk being told to leave, so I quickly composed myself. "Sorry. Continue."

"And the other scout?" Cyrus asked.

"Still missing. The captain wants to send a convoy to look for him."

"And what do you think?"

"I agree. I think it's cruel to leave him to fend for himself. You know how vicious Reyna is. He'll die or worse if we leave him in Murvort."

"Murvort," I said and again both men turned to me. "Your scouts are in Murvort."

Ladon's irritation grew. "Yes."

"I thought Murvort wasn't a threat." I turned to Cyrus for some sort of confirmation. "They've stayed out of our lands for decades."

"Who do you think keeps them in place?" Ladon spat.

"Easy, Brother." Cyrus placed both palms on the table, calm and steady. "Yes, Murvort has been held at bay for decades. We have outposts spread across the border to keep them in place. Sometimes there are clashes, but it's nothing to worry about."

Cyrus did his best to assure me, but the way Ladon's jaw tensed made me wonder if he was being entirely truthful.

He addressed his brother. "I trust your judgment. Let Kalen know we can spare three guards."

"Three?" Ladon asked, his face contorted in outrage. "That's not nearly enough."

"I won't risk losing more men, and I also won't risk breaking our current treaty. It's already fragile enough. We don't need to provoke them by sending in a full squadron."

"I'd say the treaty ended when they sent a head rolling into camp."

"That's enough." Cyrus's tone was quiet but firm. I would've been less rattled if he'd raised his voice. "You can send three or you can send none at all."

Ladon deflated, but he didn't argue. He pressed his lips into a thin line before he spoke again. "Yes, Your Highness."

Cyrus sighed and I could tell he didn't appreciate his brother's mockery, but he let it slide, anyway. I understood. It was the same way I bit my tongue in my mother's presence.

I watched all of this unravel in silence. My head was still spinning after three cocktails and the new knowledge that Murvort was, in fact, a threat. My mother had been right. Gods, if she ever found out, we'd never hear the end of it.

When Cyrus stood, I straightened in my seat. "My attendance is required at a meeting. Ladon, could you give Emilie a tour of the castle? I would do it myself, but I'm afraid these meetings are going to last all day."

Cyrus gave me another apologetic smile, a plea to understand his demanding position as king. But when I looked at Ladon and his scowl, I wondered if Cyrus might reconsider.

I could probably figure out the layout on my own. "It's okay. I don't need a—"

"I'm not your errand boy, Brother," Ladon interrupted.

"No, but you are my family and Emilie's future family. Don't you want to get to know your future sister-in-law?"

Ladon looked at me, and my bones turned to ice. I could sense a dark contempt within him and shuddered to think what he might do if we were alone. He slowly grinned, and I found no comfort in it. "It would be my greatest pleasure."

I already regretted the drinks I'd had at breakfast. As soon as Cyrus left the table, Ladon wanted to get the tour over with, but I insisted on changing into something more practical for walking around the castle's massive grounds.

We were silent the entire way back to my room, and he waited for me in the hall. My head pounded, and I chugged a glass of water from the pitcher Marjorie had left on the nightstand. I quickly applied some fresh powder to my face and some kohl to brighten my eyes. The mirror in the bathroom was cruel and told me just how tired I appeared. Yesterday had been a long day and every fiber of my body would've rather rested in bed than parade around the castle with the angry brute.

I kept my top but changed into the first pair of fitted trousers I could find in my mess of luggage. I swore to myself I'd unpack later if I managed to survive my private tour. I found a pair of gray boots and laced them up over the top of my white cotton stockings. Lastly, I wrapped a light piece of fabric around my shoulders and headed out the door to find Ladon leaning against the wall with a surly frown.

He looked me over and I crossed my arms in front of my chest, feeling defensive for no reason whatsoever. I swore a cool hatred radiated from him that I couldn't figure out. But rather than running from it, I only became more curious.

"Ready?" he asked, as if the five minutes I took to change was the biggest inconvenience he'd face all day.

"I suppose so."

Chapter Four

Ladon

THERE WERE SO MANY other things I could've been doing with my day other than leading the princess—sorry, future *Queen* of Osavian—around the castle. Unfortunately, my brother knew that it was impossible for me to tell him no and he used that knowledge against me any chance he got.

"So..." Emilie started.

She was already a little out of breath, but I didn't slow down. We were on our way to the furthest wing of the castle and I was determined to get this tour done in record time. It wasn't my fault she had short legs and apparently had never done trained a day in her life.

"So," I echoed. The question was right on the tip of her tongue. I knew she wanted to talk about last night. To clear the air. But watching her squirm was more fun.

"What's in this room?" she asked, and I didn't bother to check which door she was waving toward.

"That's what you want to say?"

"No. I guess not. I...could you slow down?" she huffed, but I kept moving. I had told my brother I would give her a tour. I hadn't promised it would be a good one.

"Ladon," she said my name, and I froze, turning on my heel and her body slammed straight into my chest. Her cheeks turned pink, and she brushed the loose brown curls from her face. Because of the nearly one-foot height difference, she had to step back and tilt her head up to meet my gaze.

"Yes?" I asked with feigned interest. The only thing I was really interested in was making her as uncomfortable in Renoa as possible. I knew she and her family were a bunch of leeches, desperate for any crumb of power they could get their hands on. They didn't belong here. My brother refused to see it, so if I needed to be the one to get rid of her, then so be it.

Her shoulders lifted and then settled again after a long exhale. "I'm sorry for listening in on your conversation last night. It was wrong and I shouldn't have done that."

"Okay," I said with as much indifference as I could muster, and then I began to walk again.

"What?" she practically shrieked.

"I said 'okay.'"

"You're supposed to say 'apology accepted' or something like that."

"Am I?"

"Yes." She raced after me and wrapped her hand around my forearm.

I moved faster than lightning. Before she could even blink, I had her pinned against the wall. Her once flushed cheeks rapidly drained of color.

"Touch me again, princess, and it'll be the last thing you do with those pretty little fingers."

I stared deep into her brown eyes and felt a sense of pride, knowing that I was the source of her terror. But the longer I looked, the more her fear turned to anger. She was a fiery little princess. It was amusing to see so much rage inside such a small human.

I backed off and gave her room to breathe. Emilie was still throwing daggers at me with her eyes, and I resisted a smirk. Did she think she was menacing? She could use more practice.

"This tour was a bad idea," she said with a shaky breath. "I can find someone else—maybe Marjorie is free. Or I can figure it out myself. I don't need you to show me around. You weren't doing a very good job of it, anyway."

The insult rolled off of me, but as much as I would've liked to leave her to wander the castle by herself, I had told my brother I would do this. And I didn't break my promises.

"The room behind you is a servants' room. It's for linens. If you'd like to begin the tour there, we can, but I don't think it's the best use of our time."

Color rose in her face again, and I watched the steady rise and fall of her chest. I knew there was another insult on the tip of her tongue, but she swallowed it down. "Fine. Let's continue then."

I carried on with the tour. The next door led to the kitchen. I stopped briefly to show Emilie, though I doubted she'd be visiting very often. Marjorie had the ability to bring her anything she might want.

We made it to the end of the west wing, and that was where our tour truly began. A three-story library came into full view as we entered through a grand double door.

I heard a gasp from behind me.

"Nothing like the libraries in Dreslen?" I asked.

"Not at all. We only have one library and it's mostly textbooks shoved into a building no larger than a shed. I've never seen anything quite like this."

She stepped forward and looked completely enamored by the aisles of leather-bound tomes that lined the walls. The light coming through the floor-to-ceiling windows created a sparkling effect on the marble floors, highlighting the veins of black quartz.

Emilie didn't wait for me before she headed to the right and I followed her from a distance. She skimmed the titles of the books closest to her.

"Looking for anything in particular?"

"Not really. I just want to see what all you have." She ran a finger over the dusty edges and took them in one by one. "Gods, it'll take forever to read all of these."

I huffed a laugh. "Do you intend to read all of them?"

"Of course," she said before grabbing one with a red spine and gold lettering. I snuck a peek at the cover to find it was a history of Osavian.

Interesting.

I could almost recite verbatim every word in that book. The story of three travelers who had first settled in this land. The eldest took care of his friends—fed them, built them shelter, kept them safe. And in return, they tried to take what didn't belong to them.

As more people settled into the lands, the eldest became the leader, but the two younger men were hungry for his power. They betrayed him—tried to take his life—and he was forced to banish them. One to the deserts now called Dreslen, and the other to the snow-capped mountains that we now call Murvort.

While relations between Dreslen and Osavian have improved over generations, I can't deny that treason runs in the princess's blood.

"Can I take as many as I'd like?" she asked.

"Yes." A small part of me was curious about what else she would pick up. I'd read most of the books in this library and found it alarming that the first one she picked up was one of my favorites. I'd bet our similarities ended there.

We continued on through rows and rows of books. I explained that the first floor was stocked with non-fiction—history, biographies, potions, maps, and so many more. Emilie took a few on magical theory and added them to her stack.

The second floor was filled with fiction. Any genre a person could think of, they'd find it there. The castle library had a copy of every book ever written.

I watched as Emilie's cheeks turned a shade of pink before she took three more books from the shelf. She tried her best to hide them from me, using her air wielding abilities to send the books back to the table on the first level and freeing her hands to grab more. But we were in the romance section, so it was easy enough to figure out why she was blushing.

Pathetic.

I'd also read most of the books in this section, too, but more for research than anything else. The stories themselves were completely un-realistic, but they provided good instruction for charming the ladies of Renoa. Unsurprising that Emilie would be interested in these fairytales.

"What's on the third floor?" she asked when we reached the spiral staircase. It was blocked off with a simple black rope. It appeared as though someone could easily get past it, but what they didn't know was that it was enchanted to freeze anyone who tried to trespass without permission. I contemplated whether or not I should tell Emilie that.

She reached out a hand, about to unclasp the rope, and I decided to stop her. I grabbed her wrist, and she startled. "I wouldn't do that. The third floor is restricted. It's where we keep our more *sinister* books. Dark magic, the uncensored graphic accounts of history. You know, the things we wouldn't want just anyone to be reading."

"So I can't go there?" The look she gave me was as if I'd given her an unacceptable boundary. It almost made me laugh.

"No, princess. You can't." It wouldn't have been hard to get her access. I only needed to ask Cyrus and, as the keeper of the castle, he could've given her immediate permission. But I enjoyed seeing her riled up like this.

She tore her wrist from my clutch and gazed longingly up the staircase. When she turned back to me, I couldn't miss the rage in her eyes. It was a good thing she wasn't a fire wielder. She might've set the whole place up in flames with that glare.

"Don't you have enough books to keep you busy for a while?" I asked, attempting to appease her. We still had more of the tour to go and I was tired of the library.

"I suppose so." She sighed, but followed as I led the way back to the first level. I made a brief stop to talk to the librarian, arranging for Emilie's stack of books to be sent back to her room.

Our next stop was the northern wing of the castle. While the southern wing contained the massive mazes of gardens and the pathway to the city, the northern exterior consisted entirely of our training grounds.

Racks of equipment, archery targets, and sparring dummies were scattered across the large barren field of dirt. This late in the morning, the field was already full of soldiers-in-training. We stopped along the exterior wall and sat on the bleachers overlooking the field.

"Is this where you spend most of your time?" she asked.

I gave a noncommittal grunt and noticed her frown from the corner of my eye. I'd told my brother I'd give her a tour. I'd never said I'd make small talk.

I sensed that she was just as entertained by the sparring as she was with the library. Chancing a look in her direction, I found that she wasn't even blinking. The sound of swords clashing made her jump and inhale sharply. There were two warriors training with metal swords. Normally, we practiced with wooden ones, but as they advanced through training, we switched to swords of steel so they could get a feel for the weight and balance of the weapons they'd be using in proper battle.

Emilie smiled as one warrior outsmarted the other, bending to dodge a strike and then tapping the dull edge of their sword against the other warrior's back. A swift kick to the back and the second warrior fell to the ground. Without a moment's hesitation, the first warrior pulled up on the other's neck, blade pressed to their throat, and the warrior tapped out.

It was a matchup I'd seen a million times before, but Emilie was hanging on every movement. Then she nearly jumped out of her seat. She smacked my arm with untamed excitement and interrupted my own trance of watching her reactions.

"What did I say about touching—"

"You let women fight?" She turned to me and the eagerness in her expression made me forget about my promise to break her fingers. I looked back at the field and sure enough, the winning warrior removed her helmet and leaned over to help her partner off the ground, patting him on the back in consolation.

He smiled, and I could read his lips as he offered his congratulations.

"Yes, our armies are made of women and men. Of course, we have to let them train, which includes sparring."

I knew the armies in Dreslen excluded women. I'd hardly call them armies, though. They had a handful of guards for the royal family and some soldiers available for personal hire, but as far as I knew, their army was nothing compared to Osavian's. It hadn't occurred to me they wouldn't even allow women to *train*.

"Have you never..."

She shook her head and frowned again.

"That's a shame. You should know how to protect yourself, even if you aren't on the front lines."

We sat a while longer and watched a few more matchups. A mix of women and men met in the center of the field, and every time I noticed Emilie rooting for the women.

I couldn't help but grin. The training ground was my favorite place in Renoa, too. I quickly wiped the smile off my face, though. Just because we shared something in common didn't mean I approved of Emilie. Or her conniving family. She didn't belong here.

"Are you ready to move on?"

She looked disappointed, but stood to leave anyway.

Most of the other rooms were boring compared to the library and the training field. The only rooms worth noting were the Hall of Heroes—a room dedicated to all the kings of the past—and an art gallery. Emilie took her time studying each of the paintings while I followed a few steps behind.

"I think this one is my favorite," she said, and I crossed the room to stand beside her. It was a dark painting. Mostly black with waves of blue and violet. It was impossible to tell what it was supposed to be.

"Why?"

"It makes me feel something."

I crossed my arms and stared at the painting, trying to see what she saw. I still remembered that deadly winter day over five years ago. My father had gone out to sea with a naval force. It was supposed to be a drill...a routine exercise. It shouldn't have been dangerous. But the blue skies had quickly turned black and none of the ships in that fleet returned. That had been the last day I'd seen my father.

A mind healer had said a creative outlet like painting would help me work through my feelings. It was hard to tell if it actually helped or if time just healed the wounds, but I hadn't painted in years. I didn't know who decided to hang my painting in the gallery.

I took a step back, and Emilie looked toward me.

"Do you feel it?"

"No. It's just a dull painting, clearly created by an artist with no talent. I've seen children with better painting skills."

She practically steamed from the ears before stomping off. With one last glance at that soul-sucking painting, I followed her out of the art gallery.

The last stop on our tour was right outside of the living quarters. On the first floor, past the grand entrance and beyond four white pillars, was a courtyard that opened up to bright skies. Sunlight streamed in and the pink and red roses were in full bloom, surrounding a shallow pool. The water was crystal clear and if we were to dip our toes in, it would've been the perfect temperature. It had been enchanted so that it was unique to each person's preference. It didn't matter if it was winter or summer, it would always feel perfect.

Had we come here at night, it would have featured a bioluminescent glow. Some said the water was healing, but that was only a myth. It was simply a pool. That didn't stop the soldiers from coming in after training to soothe their sore muscles.

A handful of lounge chairs lined the wall, where a couple of our servants gave massages to members of the nobility—people who had nothing better to do than to sit around in the middle of the day being pampered. Emilie should fit right in.

"This is the end of our tour. You're more than welcome to stay here. I can send for Marjorie to grab your bathing clothes and a towel."

Emilie stared at her reflection in the water and I couldn't tell what she was thinking. Or if she had any thoughts at all in that pampered brain of hers.

"Emilie?"

She frowned, still glaring at the pool, and I cursed the gods. *Why* did my brother give me this job? What could she possibly be unhappy about now?

"What is it?" I questioned and made no effort to keep the disdain out of my voice.

"Nothing," she responded. "Thank you for showing me around. And yes, if you could have Marjorie retrieve my things, I would appreciate it."

I gave a quick nod and turned on my heel, thankful the most painful part of my day was over.

Chapter Five

Emilie

I STAYED IN THE pool until my fingers and toes turned to prunes. I'd had my reservations when Ladon first showed me the courtyard spa, but as soon as my feet touched the sparkling water, I knew it was what my body needed after traveling all day yesterday.

It's not that the pool wasn't beautiful. The scent of roses lulled me into a sleepy state only magnified by the warm water, and I was in absolute heaven. But I looked around and couldn't help but wonder if this was the life Cyrus had planned for me. Did he think I wanted to spend my days being pampered by the other wealthy families of Osavian? Did he expect me to be a trophy wife who had little else to offer aside from bearing his children?

This wasn't at all the life I envisioned for myself. I wanted my life to mean something. I wanted to help better the lives of those in Osavian and Dreslen. The poor, the sick, the downtrodden. I had ideas, but I was afraid I'd never get the chance to voice them if Cyrus only thought of me as an accessory.

I stepped out of the pool and grabbed the towel that Marjorie had brought for me. It seemed the pool's enchantments extended to the chair I'd dumped my belongings onto because the towel was a blissful wrap of warmth around my shoulders. It was like velvet sunlight had engulfed my skin.

I couldn't tell exactly how long I'd been soaking in the giant pool, but late afternoon crept up on me. More than half the pool was now cloaked in shadows. My stomach rumbled, and I realized I'd accidentally skipped lunch.

As I headed back to my room, thinking about what I'd like to eat and if Marjorie could fetch me more of those jam-filled pastries, I ran into my mother. Two servants followed behind her with arms loaded full of shopping bags, some of them almost bigger than me. Though I preferred to avoid her, she spotted me immediately and walked my way.

"Successful trip into town?" I asked. I hated to admit I was a bit curious about what was in the bags, but if she sensed it, it would be impossible to get rid of her. She'd be modeling each and every item if she had her way, and the last thing I wanted to do was sit through that.

"Absolutely. I picked up a few things for you as well." She ruffled through the bags, trying to find the ones that were meant for me.

"I don't need anything else, Mother. I've already brought a million dresses, tops and pants. I have everything that I need. *More* than I need."

I thought back to my room and the trunks that were still packed there. It was going to be a nightmare sorting through it all, and I didn't need her to add more to my closet. A small part of me wanted to burn it all. I'd had enough of being treated like a pampered princess for one day.

"Ah, here," she said, handing me a blue striped tote bag. I peeked inside, finding a white gown with an iridescent shimmer. "For tonight."

"What's tonight?"

"Didn't Cyrus tell you? He has a special dinner planned. Just the two of you." She bounced with excitement at the prospect of the king and me spending an evening together. Alone.

"No, he didn't."

"Hmm, perhaps that was meant to be a surprise. Oh well. You should wear this tonight. It'll look stunning on you, dear."

I took the gown, knowing there was no way to convince her I wouldn't be wearing this. At first glance, it did look quite lovely. Still, I would've liked it more if I could've chosen it myself.

Patience, I reminded myself. After tonight, I'd be rid of her.

She grabbed another bag from her multitudes. "Can't forget the shoes," she said, pushing a smaller lilac bag into my hands.

"Thanks," I uttered through gritted teeth. I began to head toward my room before she stopped me again.

"Oh, Emilie, try your best to win him over tonight. This marriage is all but final, but it would go a long way if you could seal the deal, if you know what I mean."

Something lodged in my throat. Had my mother just encouraged me to *seduce* Cyrus? I was on the verge of vomiting. First, because my mother had asked me to make a whore of myself and second, because I'd never seduced anyone in my life. The thought alone made my knees wobble. I wasn't ready for this.

The furthest I'd ever been was with a boy named Weston when I was fourteen. He'd fondled my breasts inside a cloak closet while we played hide and seek with our friends. My brother had caught us and had made me swear to never do it again. I'd agreed because it was the only way to stop him from telling our parents.

I thought Weston must've been upset about the whole thing because later, I'd overheard him telling another boy that my breasts were weird. What the fuck did *that* mean?

"Of course," was all I managed to get out. And then I fled to my bedroom to have a minor breakdown.

I used unpacking as an excuse to take my mind off dinner that night. It took over two hours to sort through my clothing and get it all organized in the cavern of a closet I'd been given. The closet might've been bigger than my entire room back in Dreslen. It was complete with a full-length mirror and a cream-colored chaise nestled between two alcoves. After I finished putting away my collection of shoes, I took a break and sat on the cozy chair.

From this angle, I could still see the stacks of trunks in the corner of my room taunting me. I'd managed to clear at least half of them, but there was still so much to be done. I released a heavy sigh and, rather than returning to work, I laid down and closed my eyes.

*Just a minut*e, I told myself.

A minute turned into several hours. Marjorie knocked on my door and, after I startled awake, I shouted for her to come in.

She was carrying another tray and this time it included a glass of wine and some bread with butter. "Just a little something to hold you over before dinner tonight. I ran into your mother and she told me she spoiled the surprise. How are your acting skills?" she asked.

I frowned. "My acting skills?"

"King Cyrus really wanted to do something special for you. Can you pretend to be surprised?"

"I can try."

Marjorie's eyes lit up as she pulled the gown out of the bag I'd left lying on my bed. I probably should've hung it up when I'd gotten back to my room, but I hadn't thought about it. It didn't matter anyway. The fabric fell to the floor and there wasn't a wrinkle in sight. The seamstresses in Renoa were experts in their field.

Marjorie helped me put on the long, white dress. I realized the shimmer I'd noticed early was actually a pattern of pearlescent shells that covered the entire gown. They looked so real; I thought they might be actual shells but as I felt the fabric between my fingers, I knew they were merely an impressively life-like design. Marjorie pulled the laces on the back tight and tied them neatly in a knot at the top near my neck. They formed a unique pattern that showed off my back in what I hoped was a seductive manner. That uneasiness in my stomach crept back in, and I thought I might be sick.

I grabbed for the glass of wine and took a few sips, hoping to settle my nerves. Was that why Marjorie brought it? No, she couldn't have known. She was likely just used to Sofia's drinking habits.

No one knows you're trying to fuck the king tonight, Emilie.

Another sip of wine.

Marjorie picked out a set of jewelry from my shelves. Aquamarine gems that dangled from earrings and a matching stone that hung from a silver necklace.

"There's a matching tiara," I told her, and she searched through the many pieces I owned. I tried to ignore the trembling in my hand as I brought my glass of wine to my lips. Marjorie returned with a tiara in hand, and I carefully set it atop my brown curls, securing it in place with a few pins.

"You look like a queen already," Marjorie told me, staring at me with glistening eyes. "I don't think I've ever seen someone quite so beautiful."

"You're exaggerating."

Marjorie shook her head subtly. "I'm not." She paused and studied me. More words seemed to be on the tip of her tongue. "You know, King Cyrus is very beloved. He's been very...reserved ever since Isabella's passing. The citizens, those of us who work in the castle, his family—all of us would like to see him happy again. I hope that you'll be the key to that."

My eyes fixated on the pearl-colored flats peeking out from beneath my gown. I'd had no idea there would be this much pressure. I'd thought this was going to be a simple marriage arrangement. Instead, I was both the key to Cyrus's happiness and my parents' golden savior. Suddenly, the dress felt too tight. And the tiara was too heavy.

"Shall we go?" Marjorie asked.

I took one last sip of wine and then nodded.

Dinner was indeed an intimate occasion. Cyrus had chosen a private set up for us—a tiny table in the common area of his chambers. The sitting room was as majestic as the rest of the castle. A golden design embellished the impossibly white carpet. The couches were also blindingly white and arranged in the perfect setup for conversation and friendly gatherings. Books with leather bindings were spread on the center table and fluffy blankets had been tossed in a staged casualness across the backs of the couches. A grand fireplace roared and yet somehow the room was still a mild temperature.

"A specialty of mine," Cyrus said when he noticed me staring at the flames. He flicked his fingers, and the tips burned for a few seconds before fading.

"You're a fire wielder?" I asked.

He nodded. "And you're an air wielder."

We both took our seats at the elegant table in front of a large bay window. Cyrus's sitting room had a beautiful view of the sea and the sun had just set, painting the sky with hues of pink and purple before fading into midnight blue. He snapped his fingers again and a pair of candles lit in the center of the table.

"How did you know?" I asked, draping a napkin over my lap.

"I've done my research." He drew out the words with an effortless smile.

"Oh?" I wondered if I should've done research before coming to Renoa.

He chuckled and tilted his head to the side. "More like your father was eager to share details about you when we were discussing, ah, *arrangements*."

I tried not to wince at the word. If we didn't say it out loud, we could pretend this relationship was organic and not something we'd been forced into.

"What else did he tell you?"

"That you were kind, funny, witty." Cyrus leaned over the table, closer to me. "Beautiful."

"He did not."

"I may have added that last one myself."

I didn't even have to force the smile that formed on my lips. It was nice to be complimented.

"Can you show me something?" he asked.

I racked my brain for some display of magic that would be impressive enough for a king. The window burst open with a gush of air, bringing in the scent of the sea and an array of red and white roses. They circled around us and Cyrus watched with a twinkle in his eyes as I let the petals fall around his room.

He laughed. "You know I'm going to have to clean that up."

Shrugging, I said, "Leave them."

I could tell he wasn't upset at all with the mess I'd made and I hoped that we'd wind up on top of that blanket of roses in front of the fireplace before the end of the night.

"It seems unfair. I hardly know anything about you," I said. "Tell me something I should know."

"Hmm, well I—"

The door to his chamber opened, and two servants pushed a cart toward our table. I could smell the savory food before they even crossed the room, and it made my stomach growl. They set a pasta dish in front of me and I spotted shrimp and mushrooms among the white sauce and noodles. I ran my thumb over my bottom lip to make sure I hadn't drooled.

All good.

We ate in near silence, occasionally taking sips from the light sparkling wine the servants had left behind. I was so lost in the delectable flavors that I momentarily forgot to be nervous.

It was only after the main course and the following dessert had been finished that I realized the evening was coming to an end. I hadn't done nearly enough flirting to seduce this man. We'd broken the ice, but that was a far cry from getting him to rip off my dress and take me to bed.

My heart rate picked up as the minutes ticked by.

"What do you do for fun, Cyrus?" I asked.

The corner of his mouth curled up. "For fun?"

I nodded. "Surely you must do something aside from ruling the country. Something for yourself?"

Cyrus leaned back in his chair and I caught sight of how his dark shirt stretched over his chest. For a man in his early forties, he still looked ridiculously fit. I wondered how often he trained with Ladon.

I blinked a few times, erasing all thoughts of Ladon.

"I rarely find time to sleep these days, let alone take up hobbies. But I guess if I did have spare time, I'd spend it in the kitchens."

"Eating?" I joked, stifling a laugh.

Cyrus grinned, and it was a delightful sight to behold. His eyes practically sparkled with life and joy and passion—all the things I wish I'd had more of in my own life. "Cooking, Lady Emilie."

He stood and moved around the table, closer to me. "Maybe one day I'll cook a meal for you."

"That sounds lovely."

He reached his hand out and I took hold of it, letting him pull me up from my seat. His hands were rough and warm. "Thank you for joining me this evening."

"The pleasure was all mine."

"Can I walk you back to your room?"

I cleared my throat. This wasn't how the night was supposed to end. I needed to do something—say something. "Or...we could stay here a while longer?" My eyes flitted to the door to his bedroom, and I hoped he got the hint.

Instead, his smile straightened. Not into a frown, but something short of disappointment. Had I been too forward? Should I have played it more coy? I was a fool for thinking I could ever seduce a man, let alone a king. Gods, my mother would kill me if I somehow ruined this arrangement already.

Suddenly my lips felt too dry, my palms felt too clammy.

"As much as I'd love for you to keep me company tonight, I think it's best if you return to your own room," he said.

I searched his green eyes for some sense of what he was thinking. Was he upset that I'd asked? Was he not attracted to me? I felt the urge to sprint from the room and hide my embarrassment in the comfort of my own bed.

But Cyrus leaned in and planted a soft kiss on my cheek and even after he pulled away, I could feel the flames on my skin where his lips had been. "I'm very glad you're here, Emilie."

My heart fluttered, and I could see the sincerity in his eyes. He hadn't turned me down out of disinterest. He was just a gentleman.

He walked to the door, and after a moment of hesitation, I followed in his footsteps. He pulled the door open for me, propping it against his hip and giving me space to squeeze past. My shoulder brushed against his chest as I stepped over the threshold.

"I'm happy to be here, too, Cyrus."

And I actually meant it.

Chapter Six

Ladon

Running on sand was infinitely harder than running on any other terrain. It was why I did it every day. To be better than everyone else, I had to train like I was better than everyone else.

I was the High Commander of Osavian's army. But I was also the king's brother. And if I wanted half the respect of other ranking members, I had to work twice as hard. I didn't want them to think I'd gotten here on my name alone. I had to prove I deserved to be at the top.

I'd woken up late. I'd tossed and turned all night and by the time I'd finally gotten some decent sleep in, the sun had already begun to peek through my drapes.

Now I was paying for it because the sun was high in the sky and its rays were scorching hot on my bare back. My shorts stuck to the back of my thighs and each stride took more effort than the last. Each muscle from my calves to my shoulders was tense from the strenuous movement. I felt like my lungs were on fire.

I came to a slow jog as I approached a group of rocks jutting out of the pristine white sand, detached from the nearby cliffs. Treye's Grove, they called it. Three rocks standing taller than any giant—one each for the god of sun, moon and stars. Some thought it was a sacred spot but, for me, it was just a good point to turn around mid-run.

As I reached the gray and white rocks, I stretched out a hand and placed it on the cool side that hadn't yet been touched by the sun. I took a minute to catch my breath, stretching my legs and wiping the sweaty hair back from my face.

Treye's Grove was deserted except for a handful of birds striking the sand with their beaks and searching for a snack. It usually was peaceful when I ran in the mornings, but since I'd woken up late, I worried I might have to deal with the zealots and their daily worship.

Not that I didn't believe in a deity or higher being. But I looked at these jagged rocks and couldn't understand why they'd chosen such lifeless objects as symbols of their faith.

I didn't want to hang around too long in case the beach started to fill in with worshippers. I'd made it to Treye's Grove in twenty minutes. I could probably make it back to the castle in fifteen.

My second favorite thing about running, aside from the physical effects, was the way it cleared my mind. The waves crashing on the beach and the seagulls diving to catch their morning meal provided just enough distraction to keep my mind from wandering. Which was a good thing because ever since the Duval's arrival two days ago, I'd been having a hard time taking my mind off of my brother and his upcoming nuptials.

I'd tried to tell him they were grifters. Misha was nice enough, but the man called himself a Lord for fuck's sake. Truthfully, Dreslen had nothing to offer. They were a cursed people from the very beginning.

Centuries of droughts had left it barren and mostly uninhabitable. If there were anything of substance in that gods' forsaken land, then Osavian would've annexed them in a heartbeat. We all knew there was nothing worthwhile within those borders. Misha could keep his kingdom of treachery and lesser folk.

Lord of Nothing.

And his daughter, Emilie—Lady of Deceit.

I'd bet everything I owned that she took after her greedy mother. I was waiting to see what exactly it was that she wanted from Cyrus. They had everything to gain while we received nothing in return. I hoped when the day came, he would be smart enough to not give into her every demand. My brother had a good heart, but he was easily persuaded by women.

And he wouldn't listen to my concerns, of course. He and Misha had been friends since they were children, so he rebuked the tales of old. Didn't want to believe that his friend was the descendant of a traitor.

I was about to pass the old wooden dock that marks the edge of the royal seaside property when I saw my mother approaching.

"Morning," I said between jagged breaths, coming to a stop. I checked the mage device on my wrist designed to keep time. Sixteen minutes and thirty-two seconds.

Damn it.

"Good morning, Ladon. We missed you at breakfast this morning. Don't you usually finish your run earlier?"

She knew my habits well enough; she shouldn't have to ask. I'm sure she's mostly interested in why I wasn't at breakfast.

"I woke up late," was the only response I offered.

We walked across the beach and onto the rickety dock. My mother leaned against a wooden rail and watched as a small group of ducklings floated underneath us.

I stood next to her and rested my forearms on the railing, still dripping sweat. The water looked so blissfully cool; I could've dived right in just for the reprieve.

"What's on your mind, Son?"

Her voice was sweet and soothing. The same tone she'd used when I was only a child. She still treated me that way sometimes. I guess to her, I'd always be the baby of the family.

I pressed back against the railing and stood up straight. "Nothing."

"I know you better than that. You've been standoffish the past few days. What's bothering you?"

"I'm always standoffish."

She smiled but didn't laugh. "You've always been reserved. There's a difference."

"Just stressed I suppose." It was true. Between the tension on the border and the apprehension over Cyrus and Emilie's wedding, I hadn't had a moment of peace in weeks.

My mother rubbed my back in soothing circles. The sweat didn't seem to bother her. "Cyrus puts too much pressure on you."

"It's fine, Mother. It's my job."

"I'm only saying, just because you're his right-hand man doesn't mean you're invincible. We all need a break sometimes."

I scoffed. The chances of taking a break in the near future were very slim. I'd sent a message to Fort Malek yesterday that we were to send three guards to search for the missing scout. Three. I shook my head, knowing it was a lost cause before we even began. I worried those three guards wouldn't come back either. We should've sent an entire platoon.

"You're drifting again," my mother said, brushing her hand through my white locks.

"One day." I turned to her and patted her other hand before clasping it in my own. "If I take one day off, will you get off my back?"

She looked back out at the sea. "I suppose it's all I can ask for, isn't it?"

I nodded. "Yes."

"Alright then. One day."

We started to walk back to the castle. Now that my heart rate had settled, the sweat on my back and in my hair gave me the chills. I needed a hot shower and some food.

A stone staircase crossed over the sand dunes and led the way to the castle gardens. My muscles burned once again as I took the first few steps upward. By the time we made it to the top, I found my brother waiting for us, sitting on one of the many benches that scatter the gardens. He tilted his chin in greeting when he saw us approaching.

"Hello, Brother," Cyrus said.

"Good morning. I'm surprised to see you sitting out here. Don't you have some important matter"—I swirled my hand fancifully—"to attend to?"

"I do, but I needed to see you first. Hudson said he saw you headed toward the beach this morning, so I've been waiting for you to come back."

I'd been out for a while. I hoped he hadn't been waiting too long. As if he could read my thoughts, he sighed and stood.

"You were out longer than usual."

I sensed my mother's eyes on me, no doubt hoping I'd keep my promise to take a break. But Cyrus clearly needed something, so I'd rest some other day.

"What do you need?"

My thoughts flew back to Fort Malek and Murvort. Maybe he'd decided to send more guards? And he wanted me to carry the message personally? If I packed immediately, I could be there before nightfall.

"Emilie expressed interest in learning to fight."

My mind went blank. "Sorry?"

"She told me how you went to the training grounds and how she's never learned to fight. She said she wanted to learn some basics, so she could protect herself if anything ever happened to her."

My brows scrunched. Still not sure how this had anything to do with me.

Cyrus stood and started to pace. "I agree with her. It would be wise for her to have the fundamentals down."

"I'm sorry, Cyrus, but I don't know why you're telling me this."

"Because I want you to teach her."

I laughed. Not a scoff. Not a huff. A full burst of laughter. He couldn't be serious.

With horror, I realized that he was serious, and my amusement turned to frustration. My lips curled at the thought of spending more time with Emilie. "Why me?"

"Because I trust you with my life, and therefore, I trust you with hers."

I couldn't argue with him there. I was, without a doubt, the most trustworthy person in my brother's life, and even with my reservations about Emilie, I still wouldn't let any harm come to her. I'd dedicated my life to protecting the kingdom, which unfortunately now included Emilie. But it was just training. Anyone could do that.

I told him as much. "Surely there is someone else who could teach her the basics. We have instructors for every level, even a novice like Emilie." Her name tasted like venom in my mouth and I half spat it out.

Cyrus looked at me through squinted eyes. I would've blamed the sunlight, but he was standing in the shadows of the apple trees, so it was pure disappointment written on his face.

"What is it with you and the Duvals?" he asked, not for the first time.

"I've told you; I don't trust them." How could I?

He shook his head. "You have no reason not to. I think this will be good for you, Ladon. It doesn't matter if you like her or trust her or even tolerate her. She's here to stay. But this would be a lot easier if I had your support. I love you, Brother, and I don't want her to become a wedge between us. If you train her, maybe you'll find some things in common. Will you do that for me?"

I bit my cheek. This had disaster written all over it. I would've rather popped my fingernails off one by one than spend a significant amount of time training the pretty princess. But I couldn't say no to my brother. He and I both knew I was about to give in.

"There are a million other things I could be doing, Cyrus. But you'd rather have me babysit your fiancé?"

"It's not babysitting," he said, clapping me on the back. "It's teaching."

Chapter Seven

Emilie

My parents had finally left for Dreslen.

Thank the gods.

Something gnawed at me, telling me I should've felt guilty. That I should've felt lonely now that they weren't here and that I should've missed them. But I only felt *free.*

It had taken everything in me to hold back a squeal of delight as I'd watched them step into the carriage taking them home. An unfathomable amount of weight had lifted from my shoulders as it rolled away from the castle and out of sight.

There was an extra pep in my step as I headed toward the training grounds. I didn't even care that Ladon was the one teaching me. I'd been ecstatic when Cyrus had found me the day before to let me know I'd be getting lessons. So much so that I hadn't even flinched when he'd told me who my instructor would be.

The halls of the castle were bustling. Citizens of Renoa were there to see the king, members of the guard on their way to the training facilities, noble constituents doing whatever it is that they did. I smiled and waved at a servant exiting the kitchen as I walked past and they returned the gesture. Nothing could bring me down.

I was wrong.

I wiped the sweat from my forehead and glared at Ladon from my resting place on the ground. I couldn't begin to count the number of times I'd found myself flat on my back with an ache crawling up my spine.

This wasn't at all what I'd expected training to be like. In hindsight, I should've known when I found out that Ladon would be my instructor that this wouldn't be enjoyable. I just hadn't expected it to be so brutal. It was almost like he wanted to inflict pain.

The first few times I'd found myself lying in the dirt, I had assumed it was because I lacked skill. I'd never had any training, and it was normal that I would struggle. But after the fifth time, I was positive Ladon was doing it on purpose. On the few occasions that I'd looked around the training field, I hadn't seen one other person hit the ground with a sword to their chest.

Ladon removed the tip of the sword pointed right between my breasts and took a step back. I pushed myself up off the ground and stood once more, shaking the dirt from my pants and my shirt that had once been white but was now brown. I noticed a small rip in the fabric where Ladon's sword had been pressed against me moments ago. It was a good thing I didn't like that shirt.

Ladon walked in a slow circle and cracked his neck a few times before turning to face me again. "You hesitate too much before striking. I know what move you're going to make before you even lift your blade."

For some reason, I was mesmerized by the way his muscles flexed and relaxed as he rolled his neck and shook out his arms. He'd started the day with a loose cotton blouse, but as the sun had risen and beamed down on the training courtyard, he'd removed and tossed the shirt aside. Now his ridiculous muscles were gleaming in the sunlight and distracting me from my lesson.

I lifted the wooden sword, and my arm protested against the weight. I'd never been one for working out and that day made it clear how out of shape I was. I didn't want to give him the satisfaction of complaining, though. So I nodded. "Okay."

He licked his lips and gave me a once over with his eyes, like he expected me to collapse at any moment. "Let's move to some hand-to-hand combat for now."

Masking my relief at finally having a break from the weight of the weapons, I leaned my blade against a stone pillar. Just then, an arm snaked around my neck, and I found myself gasping for air.

"First lesson: Don't turn your back to an assailant."

I tapped his forearm, but he didn't release me. His arm was a vise made of stone and I couldn't force it from my throat. He dug into me and my shoes slid against the dirt as I tried to escape his clutch. My eyes watered at the lack of oxygen, and my head began to feel fuzzy. I was losing consciousness. Was he insane?

It took everything I had in me to jam my elbow into his stomach, but it didn't have the effect I wanted it to. He just linked his free arm through mine and when he finally released my throat, it was only to spin me around and pin my hands behind my back.

I sucked in a breath and nearly cried with relief, but my delight was short-lived.

My chest pressed against his, and he looked down at me with a mixture of amusement and disdain. He was so close I saw every speck of silver in his blue eyes and I felt his breath ruffling the loose strands of my hair. He smirked. Like a wild animal that had caught its prey.

At that moment, I knew—I hated him. I'd never wanted to kill someone before, not even my mother, but I could've taken that sword and driven it straight through his chest. Yes, even the wooden one. It would've been grisly, but it would've been satisfying.

My fury only grew when I realized with irritation that while my chest was heaving from the scuffle, his breath was even and controlled. Completely unfazed.

His hold on my wrists began to sting. "You're going to have to do better than that," he said, before finally releasing me and taking a step back.

"You're supposed to be *teaching* me. You haven't taught me a thing all day," I shouted at him, releasing my anger. I'd been bottling it up all morning and I couldn't do it anymore.

Ladon chuckled, and the sound of it made me want to scream. Instead, I let my emotions get the best of me. I couldn't help it. He ignited something in me that I couldn't control. I silently commanded the wind like she was a friend of mine, swirling it around him and building up a vacuum effect.

He didn't realize what was happening at first. The dirt at his feet disrupted, rising in the air. He tried to take a step forward, but he was caught in my airstream now. His face turned red and the veins in his neck pulsed as breathing became more difficult. The air moved too fast for him to inhale. And then his eyes flashed with a wrath I hadn't seen yet, and it was my turn to smirk.

I wondered how long I could keep this up. Long enough for him to pass out? Maybe he deserved a dose of his own medicine. To know what it was like to be completely helpless while someone else enjoyed watching his downfall.

Speaking of downfalls...he hit his knees and grasped at his neck. Like that would do any good.

His hands clawed at the ground, and I thought he might've accepted defeat. Any moment now, he'd probably black out. I didn't even worry about the consequences of my actions. It would be worth it to see him defeated for once. Maybe he'd stop tormenting me if he saw me as a threat.

And then the ground shook beneath my feet. It was a subtle tremor at first, so light I almost thought I'd imagined it. But I hadn't. The rattling grew in intensity, and then the ground burst as an explosion of rock and dust sent me flying across the training pit.

I landed on my back for what felt like the hundredth time, losing control of my magic in the process. It slipped from my fingertips, disappearing in an instant. I grappled for control, but it was out of reach.

The ground rumbled again, and I rolled to my side. Just as I tried to lift myself, something like a wave rippled through the dirt, knocking me off balance again. I was airborne for a moment before slamming back and landing on my hip. That was going to bruise.

I looked toward Ladon, where he'd been on his knees, but now he was standing...and approaching me with a devilish glare. I struggled to get to my feet, but every time, another tremor sent me falling. I crawled on my hands and knees, attempting to put some space between us, but he overcame the distance with ease.

Ladon grabbed me by the shoulders and flipped me so I faced the sky once more. This time the shadow of his face blocked the sunny skies and boy, did he look *pissed*.

I tried to push up using my hips, but he sat...he fucking *sat* on my stomach and I couldn't do anything to remove the weight of him. I went to throw a punch, but he'd trained all his life for this. I was no match for him and he easily blocked it, grabbing both of my wrists and pinning them to my sides. I squirmed, but it was no use.

I huffed, blowing the loose hair from my face.

"*That* is cheating, princess."

His chest hadn't been heaving before, but it was now. Though I didn't think it was from exertion. I was pretty certain it was from pure rage. His hands seared my skin as I tried to wriggle my wrists free. He only tightened his grip.

"I don't know what you're talking about," I snapped.

Ladon smiled, and it was a wickedness I'd never seen before. It radiated from him, dripping all over me. I writhed again, just wanting to escape his hold.

"You shouldn't play games that you're incapable of winning."

"If you would just *teach* me something, I wouldn't have to resort to using magic. What does it matter anyway? We all have natural-born gifts. Why shouldn't I use mine like you used yours?"

I felt a sinking sensation, realizing with horror that the hard ground around us had turned to mud. It slowly swallowed my lower half. My shoulders had already sunk an inch. I peered at him with terror-filled eyes.

He smirked. I swore to the gods I'd erase that smirk if it was the last thing I did.

"Why don't you try that *gift* of yours now?" he sniped.

It felt like a trick. Should I actually summon the wind, or would he berate me if I did? I was still at his mercy and didn't like the thought of testing him as my shoulders sunk further into the mud. I could feel it on my neck now. How much longer until it reached my mouth, my nostrils, and my eyes?

"Go on," he said with a snarl.

I concentrated on my fingertips, but the familiar tingle didn't come. I must've been too distracted. I closed my eyes and pictured it—the sky, the air as if it were a living thing. Dirt swirling as it had before while I'd attacked Ladon. The flags around the training field standing straight as the wind kept them afloat. I pictured all these things, but I felt...nothing.

I opened my eyes to find Ladon looking ridiculously pleased with himself. "What's wrong, princess?"

"You...what did you do?" I sputtered, hating the apprehension in my voice.

His eyes flickered to where his fingers wrapped around my wrists, half covered in mud. I don't know how I missed it before. Where our skin collided, there was a faint warm glow of light. Hardly noticeable until it had been pointed out to me.

"You can siphon?" My voice was little more than a whisper. Like the question was a secret that should be kept between us.

Something sparkled in those silver-blue eyes and I knew I'd guessed correctly. "How?"

Siphons weren't supposed to exist. I remembered from the books I'd studied growing up. Centuries ago, there'd been hundreds, maybe even thousands of them. They had the ability to temporarily drain another of their magic. It wasn't stealing per se; more like drawing one's power to fuel their own. But laws had been enacted to detain or even sentence them to death, since most people didn't want other mages stealing their magic, even if it was temporary.

Today, no such laws existed because they weren't needed. Siphons were extinct...or so I'd thought.

Ladon sneered at me while I processed this information. At last, he released his hold on me, nearly crushing my ribcage as he stood from my body. Gentleness was not his strong suit.

"We're done for today," he said with his back facing me. I didn't have to see his face to feel the disdain in his voice.

The words escaped my lips before I could even process what I was saying. "Why do you hate me so much?"

He turned and I couldn't tell if he thought I was joking or if he was simply amused by the question, but either way, he huffed a laugh.

I tried to stand from the mud pit but the ground had solidified again, forcing me to tug my legs to release them from the earth. Not only was he a siphon, but apparently, he was also an earth wielder. I supposed I should've learned all of his strengths before I'd let my temper get the best of me.

"Don't think I haven't seen the way you look at me. Like I'm little more than vermin to be exterminated. The way you speak to me like I'm inferior to you. I haven't done anything to you, so what is it?"

There were at least a dozen others training in the field with us, and each of them had turned to watch our spat. Ladon's smile faltered when he noticed our audience, but he exited the training arena without so much as a word to me, only reinforcing the idea that I wasn't worth his time.

I followed him into the hall, fully aware that my footsteps sounded like a toddler throwing a tantrum. I hated that he got under my skin so easily.

"Hey," I shouted, grabbing the collar of his shirt without thinking.

In a flash, he spun and pushed me against the wall, my head slamming against the cool stone. Add it to the list of bruises and bumps I'd be covered in tomorrow.

"What did I say about touching me, princess?" he snarled. His nose was close enough to brush mine, and it sent a chill down my spine. The heat of his body pressed against every inch of me, and I didn't know if I was frozen in place or melting into a puddle.

He terrified me.

But for some reason, I reveled in his hatred.

I licked my lips and raised my chin in defiance. "Queen."

Ladon leaned back enough to look down at me, but I met his steely glare with a fire of my own, refusing to let him intimidate me. "I am your future *queen*."

He might not like me, but he would respect me.

He scoffed before stepping back. His eyes turned to slits, and he tilted his head ever so slightly. "Courtesan."

The vile insult was smooth as honey dripping from his tongue.

My jaw dropped. Had he just called me a whore? I was Lady of Dreslen and future Queen of Osavian. Not some peasant off the street, seducing the king to steal his riches and line her pockets.

I was too stunned to speak, and before I could return an insult of my own, Ladon turned on his heel, stalking down the hall and out of my sight.

Chapter Eight

Ladon

SLEEP EVADED ME FOR the third time this week. A blur of onyx swirls and shimmering gold filled my vision as I stared up at the ornate ceiling of my bedroom. I wasn't sure how long I'd been gazing toward the sky. Long enough to make my eyes burn. It didn't matter how tired I was physically. My mind refused to succumb to the drowsiness I felt.

Giving up on sleep, I threw back the emerald green blanket that covered my bed and swung my legs to the side, rolling my neck before standing and walking to the corner of the room.

The servants knew to keep my drink cart stocked, and tonight was no exception. Crystal bottles of navy, maroon, and gold lined the top rack, all in varying degrees of opacity. A slender one with a faded black label called my name, and I filled my glass to the rim, swirling before bringing the fiery whisky to my lips.

I looked around the room, searching for something to distract myself with, maybe long enough to lull myself to sleep before daylight snuck up on me again. Bookshelves lined the wall on the other side of my bedroom. A collection of books that had grown over time, some tales of fiction and others of the more educational variety.

Surely there was one on these shelves that could bore me to sleep. Perhaps one of my father's hand-me-down texts on war strategy. I searched the dusty tomes for the one I was thinking of, surprised by how neglected they all appeared. I hadn't had much time for reading lately. The growing threat of Murvort had taken up most of my attention.

While Dreslen had a more subtle approach in their quest for power, Murvort was more interested in physical force. They were two sides of the same coin.

My thoughts returned to Emilie and our day of training. My blood boiled knowing that she was keeping me from my duties on the border. I'd have another chat with Cyrus about that. He had to know that my strength and leadership would be better utilized at Fort Malek.

I'd read the titles five times and still hadn't found what I wanted. Sighing, I searched for some pants and a shirt to throw on so I could head to the library. I could've sworn the book was in my own collection, but every once in a while, I'd trade books out for new ones and I must've exchanged it without realizing. If it wasn't in my room, then it was definitely in the library.

I was no stranger to the quiet of the castle halls in the middle of the night. After my father died, I'd had trouble sleeping then, too. Although my solo trips into the night at that age usually ended in the kitchens with a piece of pie or sorbet. Sometimes the governess would catch me, but she never told my mother.

The castle was so peaceful at this time. So quiet you could hear a mouse. Magical lanterns floated high in the air, emitting a warm golden glow. Their luminance dimmed behind me as the ones in front of me came to life. It was like my own personal spotlight following along as I wandered the castle corridors.

"I'm surprised to see you up so late."

I stiffened and gritted my teeth. It was usually impossible to sneak up on me. I'd blame it on the lack of sleep.

When I turned around, Cyrus was leaning against a door frame, his arms crossed and a frown on his face. It was the door to his office, so I assumed he'd been working late tonight. Maybe it was the lighting, but he looked older than I remembered. The wrinkles on his face were more prevalent, and his hair was thinning in some spots. Sometimes I forgot the toll that being king took on him, but it had never been more obvious than it was at that moment. He looked as tired as I felt.

"Couldn't sleep. And you?" I asked, curious what matter was so pressing that he was still working in the middle of the night.

He jerked his head to his office, a silent invitation to come in. An invitation that I couldn't refuse, even if I wanted to.

His desk was an absolute mess. I understood his office was the one place the servants wouldn't touch, but this disaster rivaled a pigsty. I took a seat and examined the heaps of papers and maps. A patch of ink had dried in the corner where a bottle still sat, tipped over. A letter dated three months ago looked like it had been used as a napkin. My nose scrunched as I picked up what appeared to be an old banana peel.

Cyrus met my gaze and shrugged his shoulders. "I know it's a mess. I've had a lot on my plate, literally." He gestured at the clutter before us.

I dropped the rotting peel back on his desk and settled into the seat, crossing my arms over my chest. "So, what did you want to talk about?"

"I need a reason to talk to my brother?"

He was stalling, and it only made me more eager to know what was on his mind. "No, not usually. But when those chats come at two in the morning, I do wonder."

Cyrus sighed and leaned back in his chair across from me. "I received a message today from Kalen."

I straightened in my seat. I didn't think the captain of the northern stronghold would get back to us so quickly. It'd only been a few days. "Did they find the missing scout? Is he dead?" My skin went cold and my leg shook with restlessness. I wanted to jump up from my seat and race to Fort Malek myself just to check and see. These men trusted me and I'd failed them twice now. Losing a life under my watch was a feeling I'd never wanted to know.

Cyrus raised his hand to keep me seated, like he knew I was ready to bolt from the room. "Yes, they found him, and he's alive and well."

My brows pinched together. "How is that possible?"

"This is good news, Ladon. Aren't you glad now that we didn't go barreling in with an entire army? Reyna would've had all our heads on a stake." He smiled, but I didn't feel the same sense of relief. Reyna would have our heads regardless if we started a war or not. I couldn't believe he was being so naïve.

"Reyna already took the head of a scout," I reminded him. "Or do you think his head just detached itself?"

His face flinched almost imperceptibly, and I knew I'd struck a nerve. I didn't care if it irritated him. He was smarter than this. Doubting Reyna, the ruler of Murvort, would only lead us to our ruin. "How do you explain the murdered scout?" I asked again.

Cyrus shook his head and frowned. "An accident. An animal perhaps."

Unfuckingbelievable.

I scoffed and clenched my fists until my nails bit into my palms. "You can't be serious, Cyrus. I know you don't want to start a war, but you can't be this blind. You *know* it had to be Reyna and her forces. If you don't respond to her blatant disregard for the treaty, then she will see it as an open invitation to breach our borders and infiltrate our lands."

Cyrus lost whatever trace of a smile he had. "You don't understand. The weight of the world, of our people, lies on my shoulders. I can't lead them into war without due cause. I won't risk their lives unless I'm certain it's necessary. We've been at peace for centuries and I don't intend to end that streak anytime soon."

"You're a fool if you don't think Reyna will end it for you."

"Do not patronize me, Brother. You may be High Commander but *I* am King," he said in a tone that sounded foreign—too powerful and mismatched to the kind, gentle brother I knew.

"Then act like one." The words came out louder than I'd intended and it only served to highlight the silence that followed.

He eyed me with a burning temper. I spotted the flames of his power flickering in his pupils, but he kept them at bay. It was a dance we'd been doing since the day our father died and Cyrus had been forced to fill his role. I tested his patience, and he gave me the leniency I didn't deserve. Thinking it would somehow make up for the fact that he sat where our father should've.

It never did. No amount of coddling would ever bring back our father. And it wasn't Cyrus's fault that he so quickly had to place that crown on his own head. A fact I'd told him over and over again, but it never seemed to sink in. He still felt some sense of responsibility for my pain.

The silence was suffocating and when I could no longer take it, I moved to stand. "Is that all, then?"

"No."

The agitation written on his face was enough for me to take a seat again. I got the feeling that whatever he was about to say was worse than the news of his indifference toward Murvort.

"I saw Emilie today."

Fuck.

I remained silent. I wasn't sure what she told him, but I wasn't confessing anything until Cyrus admitted what he knew. Tension lingered in the air as we waited to see who would break first.

Cyrus did, as I knew he would.

"You are supposed to be training her to fight, Ladon. Not using her as a personal punching bag to take out your aggression."

Lifting a finger, I defended myself. "I never punched her," I said, but he acted as if he hadn't heard me.

"I asked you to do this because I thought I could depend on you."

"You can." I shook my head and rolled my eyes. Something he caught and offered a scolding gaze in return. I murmured under my breath, "I can't believe she told you."

Cyrus raised his voice. "She *didn't* tell me. The bruises on her arms and *neck* were enough for me to figure out for myself. What were you thinking, Ladon?"

"Does this mean you'll find someone else to teach her?" I asked, trying not to get my hopes up. Even with his unwavering guilt over our father, Cyrus wasn't the type to change his mind. If anything, what I did would only make him dig his heels in further. He confirmed that a second later.

"Absolutely not. You will do as I commanded you. And you're not to lay a hand on her again, Ladon. Do you understand?"

Glancing at the floor, I mumbled again, "How can I train her if I can't touch her?"

"Ladon," he roared.

I forced myself to meet his gaze. "I understand."

I did my best to keep my interactions with Emilie and Cyrus to a minimum over the next few days, just to give myself time to cool off. It turned out to be surprisingly easy since they were both busy with wedding planning. The entire castle had gotten wedding fever overnight. I couldn't walk down a hall without passing a servant carrying cake samples, floral arrangements, or color swatches for linens.

I overheard a woman and a man speaking as I passed, talking about the songs they'd play during the wedding reception. Gods, I couldn't wait to get this entire ordeal over with, return to my post at Fort Malek, and move on with my life.

Rounding the corner of the corridor, I slammed straight into my mother, nearly sending her tumbling to the ground.

"Are you alright?" I asked, wrapping my hands around her elbows to keep her steady.

"Yes, yes." She looked flustered as she gently swatted my hands away. "Oh, good. I was looking for you. Lunch has just been served on the balcony and—" she paused when she caught my grimace. "Don't you make that face with me, Son. You haven't eaten with the family in three days and I won't have you missing one more meal, so come on."

I placed my hands on my hips as she turned to head for the balcony overlooking the sea. It would've been comical how she treated me like a child sometimes if it weren't so irritating. Swiping a hand through my hair, I worked to come up with an excuse. "I can't, Mother. I have to—"

Spinning in place, she didn't even allow me to fumble through a lie before she was in my face, pressing a finger into my chest. "If you don't come with me, I will spend the entire evening sharing every embarrassing moment you've ever lived through with anyone who will listen. I mean it. I'll go to the middle of the town square and tell them about the time we went to the beach, and you picked up a crab—you remember—and its little pincers grabbed ahold of your—"

"Okay!" I shouted. A shiver ran through my body, recalling the pain I'd felt that day. I'd rather have kept that story between us. "You're scary sometimes."

I meant it as a compliment and she knew me well enough to pick up on it.

She tossed me a winning smile before turning with her arm outstretched expectantly. I looped mine through it and together we walked to lunch.

"Ah, there he is," my brother said the moment I stepped into his sight.

"Here I am," I repeated, mystified by his excitement to see me. I would've thought after our last conversation that he'd still be annoyed with me. And seeing as I hadn't spent any more time training Emilie, I'd expected him to be even more upset with my disobedience than before.

Speaking of the princess, her arms were crossed and I could see with perfect clarity the marks on her skin in the shape of my fingers. Apparently, I was a little rougher than I'd meant to be. Still, she deserved it. No one went through training without a scar or two.

"I was about to tell Emilie the good news."

There was a grating scrape of wood against stone as I pulled out a chair to sit next to my brother. Meanwhile, my mother filled the seat to my left. From the corner of my eye, I caught Emilie glancing my way before returning her gaze to Cyrus. "Go on then," I said with what little enthusiasm I could muster.

"I received another message this morning from Kalen," Cyrus started. My ears perked at the captain's name. Two messages in one week?

"What did it say?" And why hadn't he addressed me? I was his superior.

"Just once again reassuring me that everything was calm on the northern front. In fact, he suggested that I come to visit to see for myself and I couldn't agree more."

Emilie leaned forward in her seat, eyes lit with excitement. "May I come along?"

"Absolutely not," I said at the same time my brother shook his head.

From the look she gave him, I knew she expected him to side with her. My refusal, however, didn't faze her.

"I'm sorry. The outposts really aren't suitable for you. It's nothing like Renoa. Very dirty and filled with rougher folks than you're used to."

I grinned, feeling pleased that she'd be staying behind. I'd already had enough of her constant presence.

Emilie frowned. "I can handle myself. I'm not as delicate as you think I am. I want to be included, Cyrus. Please reconsider?"

He looked pensive as he stared at her. She fluttered her lashes, and I almost lost my shit. "You've got to be kidding me."

"I didn't say anything," he said to me.

"Your face says it all, Brother."

He sighed and placed his hand over Emilie's on top of the table. "I'll think about it."

Already he was caving into her demands. It didn't take long for *Queen* Emilie to have him wrapped around her finger. And she knew it, too. Looking across the table, I found her glaring at me with her pink lips pressed into a deceitful smile. I curled my fists so tightly under the table that I left little crescent indents in the center of my palms.

"So, when will we be going?" I asked.

"Two weeks. The evening of the full moon."

The lunar cycle was sacred to the religious nuts in Osavian. Luxurious balls and fancy dinners often fell on the full moon in our kingdom, as it symbolized new beginnings.

I nodded my head, still fuming that he was even considering allowing Emilie to come along. And I still wasn't sure why Kalen hadn't contacted me directly, but I couldn't deny the desire to see for myself how things were going at Fort Malek.

"Perfect. Can't wait."

Chapter Nine

Ladon

I FLIPPED THE PAGE of the latest book on war strategy I'd chosen to keep myself entertained. This one detailed the battles that had occurred on the Murvort and Osavian borders many centuries ago. The people and weaponry might've changed over time, but the landscape hadn't. If there was anything in that tome that we could use to our advantage, I'd be happy to study it day and night.

So far, I'd already learned of a tunnel of caves hidden in the mountains. The people of Murvort used them to evade a blockade of resources during the Battle of Endless Night. It was only briefly mentioned and fables of these supposed tunnels had never reached my ears before, but it was worth checking out.

"Are you even paying attention?" My eyes fluttered closed at the grating sound of Emilie's voice. After a moment's hesitation, I peered over the top of my book. Ten feet away from me, Emilie stood with one hand on her hip and another hand holding a small throwing knife. Many yards beyond her was a target with black and white lines.

I huffed a laugh when I noticed she hadn't hit the target once. Not *once* in the forty minutes we'd been out there under the scorching morning sun.

"Are *you* even paying attention?" I taunted.

Her face reddened, and I smirked, infuriating her further. I knew she hated it. The fury in her hazel eyes gave her away every time.

She made an indiscernible noise when my eyes flitted back down to my lap and I turned the page. It sounded something like a wild hog, and I had to hold back a laugh.

It didn't take long before a shadow descended on the pages of my book. When I looked up, Emilie's lips were pursed and her hair was a frizzy mess, a visual representation of the wild frustration trapped inside her.

If she was waiting for me to break the silence, then she was going to be waiting a long time. It was a challenge to see which of us would blink first, but I met her determined gaze with an endurance of my own. The slivers of green danced amidst a pool of bronze in her eyes and my pulse quickened.

The air felt thinner, and I questioned for a moment if she was using her magic, but I didn't sense its tendrils swirling around me. No, it was just her very essence that made me feel dizzy.

"How will I ever learn anything if you won't actually teach me?" she huffed.

My eyes went back to my book, making my boredom apparent. "*Someone* went and told my brother about our last lesson and now I'm not allowed to touch you. You'll have to figure it out yourself."

The sound of her steps retreating was accompanied by the disappearance of her hovering shadow. I flipped another page, sighed, and then returned to the start of the chapter. I had not digested a single word on these pages, too distracted by Emilie.

I tuned out the world around me and focused on the discolored pages, some of the letters fading from time. I had just read an interesting tidbit on the oversized bats with venomous fangs when a flash of metal whizzed by my ear.

There was a thud, followed by a lingering echo, and the din of the rest of the training field faded away. I pried my eyes from my book to find a small metal knife buried in the wooden wall behind me, no more than ten inches from my forehead.

I slammed my book shut as I stood from my chair. Counting my breaths to remain calm, I tugged at the blade and pulled it free from its resting place. Slowly, I turned to face Emilie.

"Are. You. Fucking. Insane?"

There was a mix of fury and regret in her eyes, battling to see which would win. I was curious to see as well. Which would it be, princess? Would her rage win out? Her bubbling contempt for me that was nearing its tipping point? Would she let go of that sweet façade?

Or would remorse prevail? I secretly hoped it wouldn't. If she tried to apologize now, I'd likely be sick at the depths of her insincerity.

Own it, Emilie.

"I...I—" she stammered while I took a creeping step toward her.

Don't start games you can't finish, Emilie.

The closer I got, the more she seemed to shrink. I could practically feel a shudder roll through her body as I closed the space between us. Each deliberate step sparked excitement in my own veins. I felt the hairs on my neck stand straight as our eyes locked.

Towering above her, I watched her throat bob as she swallowed. I had to give her credit for at least not shying away. She stood her ground even when I invaded her personal space. A wave of floral and citrus hit my nostrils and my calculated steps faltered.

Emilie looked up at me through thick lashes and in an instant, I knew which one she would choose.

She seethed. Her only regret was that she'd missed her mark.

"Next time, it'll be your heart. If one even exists under that armor of yours."

My heart pounded in my chest, a foolish insistence that I *did*, in fact, have a heart. I didn't know why it chose that moment to spring to life.

I made a pointed glare at the target beyond her, the one she'd missed repeatedly. "I highly doubt that," I said in a low whisper.

She huffed, the warmth of her breath brushing across my neck. My stomach tightened. The tension between us was magnetic. Pushing and pulling me at the same time. Getting under her skin was a high unlike any other. I waited eagerly for her next move in this game we were playing. And maliciously plotted my turn in response.

Then something odd happened. Her fingers lightly grazed mine, the delicate touch throwing me off guard. Not at all what I'd expected. Before my brain had a chance to catch up, she wrapped her hand around my knife's handle and tugged it from my grasp.

When she backed away, I regained my composure. I was an expert at guessing adversaries' next moves, and yet I hadn't been able to guess her complete shift in demeanor. I hated that it only made me more curious to see what she'd do next.

Emilie's shoulders relaxed, and the fire in her eyes simmered. She closed her eyes, and I counted to three before she opened them again. "Teach me," she said, this time with more desperation, more of a plea.

It occurred to me that if she'd been any other person, I would've caved to her requests right then and there. If she'd been anyone else, I would've taught her from the beginning. But I couldn't do it. Call it pride. Call it stubbornness. Whatever it was, I was certain that my initial assessment of her had been correct. She was a leech, a parasite, and the sooner we got rid of her, the better.

I ground my teeth as I considered the many women of Renoa that my brother could've chosen. Why had he chosen Emilie of all people? I stared at her with her untamed brown hair, hazel eyes, freckles sprinkled across her nose and cheeks, her pink lips—I wanted to believe that she was ordinary, nothing special. But even I had to admit, she had a rare natural beauty.

My jaw tensed, the realization sinking in that I would never be able to get rid of Emilie. We were in for a long journey, with her as the Queen of Osavian. The idea of submitting to her made me want to throw something.

A tray of knives stood to the side, practice blades with dull edges and tarnished handles. I grabbed the one closest to me, noticing a chip in the side, just below my thumb, which I traced with fascination.

I set my eyes on the furthest target, the smallest circle merely a speck. But as I concentrated, that small circle became clearer, almost like it was growing in size. When I pulled my arm back and flung the blade forward, I knew with absolute certainty that it would find its mark.

A dull thud rang out through the field as the blade lodged inside the small black circle.

Emilie inched closer to me, and when I turned, I noticed her features arranged in a look of awe and longing, her mouth parted slightly.

"The trick is to pretend the target is something—*someone* you hate. Something that drives you mad enough to destroy. Let that repulsion flow through you and release it with the dagger." I shrugged. "I just pictured you."

Her mouth snapped shut, and I strolled past her, toward the field's exit. I called back to her, "I think that's enough training for today."

I chose a spot in the far corner of the pool to ease my tension. I hadn't done much physical training today, but I still felt drained from the time spent teaching Emilie. It was probably the most mentally exhausting job I'd ever had. And I'd had a lot of taxing positions.

It took so much gods' damned effort to not throw her over my shoulder and dump her outside the city's gates. I cupped water in my palms and splashed it over my face, wiping sweat and dirt as I ran my hands over my skin.

I leaned back against the marble edge of the pool, soaking in the sun and perfectly tempered water. Warmth permeated my body, and I slowly began to relax. I even closed my eyes for a bit while I listened to the water trickling into the pool from a small fountain.

I'd ended our training session early enough that no other soldiers were here to disturb my peace. Only three older women laid on the lounge chairs across the room. By the way they hadn't moved since I'd arrived, I assumed they were fast asleep.

I might've dozed off too if it weren't for the sound of a towel billowing and something else clunking as it hit the floor. I sighed. Was it too much to ask for a moment's peace?

I squinted and peered out beneath one eyelid. Then I sighed heavier. Of course, it was Emilie. The gods hated me. They knew I wasn't a devout worshipper and so they'd chosen me to punish for all eternity. That was the only explanation.

It was no use pretending I didn't know she was there. She glared at me as she dipped her toes in the water. She had changed into black bathing clothes. The bottoms were modest but the top was merely a thin piece of fabric that dipped low enough to see the curves of her breasts.

It was impossible not to notice her long legs and toned torso. For someone who had never trained, her body didn't show it. I chalked it up to youth and good breeding.

"Don't you have any place better to be?" I growled.

Emilie sank further into the water, relaxing against the side like a mirror image of myself. She gave me a pensive look. "No. This life of pampering and uselessness is apparently all I was made for."

Chapter Ten

Emilie

CYRUS WALKED ME THROUGH the gardens late in the afternoon. The enormity of the castle grounds never ceased to amaze me. We wandered through hedges and groves until we found ourselves under the largest pergola I'd ever seen.

Lush green vines climbed the trellises, deep purple grapes hanging from above our heads. There was just enough space between the plants to allow glimmers of light to peek through, decorating the sandstone floor with a majestic glow.

My steps faltered, and Cyrus slowed beside me. "What do you think? I thought we could have the wedding reception here."

Tables had been arranged in a circle around the patio, leaving a space in the center for a makeshift dance floor. As I looked around, I noticed each table had been decorated differently. Different floral arrangements, different linens, different accent colors. A plethora of options for me—for us—to choose from.

"It's stunning. I can't imagine a more beautiful place to celebrate." I could picture it already. The sun setting in the distance. A cool breeze blowing through the open sides while people danced and drank. Myself in a flowing white gown, perhaps with an open back, and Cyrus guiding me back to his room well past midnight.

My cheeks flushed at that last thought.

"Good," Cyrus said cheerfully. He placed his hand on the small of my back and led me forward into the center of the reception area. Across the patio, a plump man with a white coat was racing back and forth, tampering with an array of plates and directing his assistant, a woman with brown hair pulled back in a bun, to fetch a serving utensil.

He didn't see us approaching until he turned around and, with a shocked expression, greeted us warmly. "Welcome! You're early. I sent Dani to grab some utensils to serve the cake. I brought everything you asked for and then some. And this must be Emilie!"

The man bounced back and forth on his feet, his energy too much to contain. He was a few inches shorter than me, his wrinkled skin flushed from the heat of the afternoon. And up close, I could see smudges of frosting and dye on his otherwise white coat.

"Yes. Emilie, this is Ivan. He is our baker here in the castle. One of the most talented men you'll ever meet. Ivan, this is Emilie." Cyrus wrapped his arm around my shoulder as he introduced us, pulling me close to his side.

I held my hand out. "It's nice to meet you, Ivan."

"Likewise." Ivan waved an arm at the long, rectangular table. "I've brought six different cakes for you to try. As soon as Dani gets back, we can dig in."

Cyrus and I moved closer. Each cake was labeled with a small white note card. There were the basics—vanilla and chocolate. And then there was also red velvet, salted caramel, double fudge, and a zesty lemon. They were all decorated uniquely, yet still stately enough for a royal wedding.

The vanilla had white roses, while chocolate had shaved swirls of dark chocolate sprinkled on top. Red velvet was covered in fondant with a red and white marble pattern. They were all so beautiful, I almost felt guilty for digging in.

Almost.

When Dani returned with a serving knife, I was nearly drooling. She effortlessly sliced into each cake, serving two sample sized pieces for both me and Cyrus of each flavor.

"They're all so incredible. I don't know how to pick," Cyrus said as he went back to the zesty lemon for a second taste.

"I think my favorite is the salted caramel. What frosting is that on top?"

"It's a caramel and vanilla swirl with toffee bits," Ivan answered. He exchanged a look with Dani. "And a surprise ingredient."

"Bourbon," she said with a wink.

My eyes rolled in the back of my head. "That is amazing."

"That settles it, then. We'll go with the salted caramel." I appreciated Cyrus's desire to appease me.

"Excellent choice," Ivan said. Dani took out a small notebook no larger than the size of her palm and jotted down our preference. "Next up are table centerpieces. The interior decorators have set up a variety of options for you. I'm sure you've already noticed them."

The cake decision had been easy for me, but the décor was a different story. Every table was so beautiful, with expertly chosen complimentary colors and flowers. We'd stop at one table and I'd determine it was my favorite. But by the time we made it to the next table, I'd changed my mind and decided *that* one was my favorite.

I finally gave up. "I can't decide. Do you have a preference?"

Cyrus rubbed his head and sighed. "I've got to be honest. I don't know what half of these flowers are and I can't tell the difference between the eggshell and cream tablecloths."

I laughed. "Me neither. Can they just surprise us?"

"Let me see." He searched for Dani with her notepad and then waved her down.

I barely overheard them discussing options. Based on Dani's facial expressions, she was confused by our lack of decision. I read her lips. "You want us to surprise you?" she asked with a raised brow.

I stifled a laugh. She looked to be about my age and I felt a tidbit of remorse for making her responsible for an important detail of our big day. She was probably mortified that she might choose the wrong thing and upset the King and Queen of Osavian. Poor girl.

"We'll go with this one," I said, my voice loud enough for Cyrus and Dani to hear. I pointed at the table in front of me—a mix of turquoise and golden flowers paired with ivory satin linens. The light teal napkins were wrapped with a golden metal decal that matched the plates and silverware. Simple but elegant.

"Does that work for you?" I asked Cyrus.

He nodded in agreement, and Dani visibly sighed with relief.

That evening Sophia showed up at my bedroom door with three other women whose names I didn't know. Sophia took all of five seconds to introduce them—Adelaide, a woman in her late sixties with gray hair and a look of permanent exhaustion on her face, and her two helpers, Emma and Daphne, who I immediately observed were twins. They were mirror images of each other, with short auburn hair, bright blue eyes and matching blue cotton dresses. Emma's hair was pulled up into a half ponytail and Daphne's was left down, the only way I was able to tell them apart.

Adelaide and Sophia moved into my room without an invitation, chatting in hushed tones like two young girls sharing secrets with their best friend. Emma and Daphne both followed, their arms full of white fabric wrapped in clear plastic coverings.

It wasn't hard to tell what they were carrying. Wedding dresses.

A loud popping noise pulled my attention away from the piles of dresses, finding Sophia pouring sparkling wine into two glass flutes.

"For you, bride-to-be," she said, pushing a glass into my hand.

"What is all this?" I asked. Of all the wedding planning events, I'd been looking forward to dress shopping the most. I thought we'd go to a boutique in town. Surely, they had more than one to choose from. I'd been stuck inside this castle for two weeks. I was dying to see the city, and it felt like my one chance to get out had been taken from me.

I was being dramatic, of course. I had the rest of my life to stroll the streets and visit the shops, but that didn't ease my disappointment.

Sophia took a drink from her glass and opened her arms wide. "We're trying on dresses! Well, you're trying on dresses. I'm going to watch and tell you how gorgeous you look while secretly wishing I was still young and beautiful."

Sophia was my favorite of the Castelli crew.

Emma magically conjured a rack out of nowhere. Or maybe she was hiding it under that stack of dresses. She and her sister began to hang the dresses, and I watched the rack go from empty to overflowing in a matter of seconds.

How many dresses did they bring? Did I have to try on all of them?

The room buzzed around me and I took a drink of the fizzy beverage to settle my nerves. Adelaide was sifting through the dresses now, with Sophia looking over her shoulder.

"Excuse me, Miss." Daphne tapped my arm and prompted me to lift them while she circled me with a tape measurer. She rattled off numbers, and Emma wrote them down.

When she finished taking my measurements, Daphne stepped out of the way so Adelaide could approach. She held two dresses in her hands and alternated holding them up to my neck, envisioning how they might look on me.

"Try this one first," she said, thrusting a bundle of tulle into my outstretched arms.

"Umm," I murmured. "Can I—"

Adelaide had already turned her back to me and focused her attention on a bag of veils and tiaras. Sophia was still browsing through the racks of dresses while Emma and Daphne discussed something on a clipboard. No one paid attention to me at all.

I sighed, but headed toward the bathroom to change into the gown.

"Where are you going?" Adelaide asked with a worried expression.

"To change," I said, lifting the dress in my hands to emphasize. Wasn't that what she had just asked me to do?

She waved her hand frantically and whipped her head back and forth. "No. No. Do it here. No need to be shy. We've so many dresses to get through. You'll just waste time if you keep going to the bathroom. Here, Emma or Daphne can help you."

I stared, completely dumbfounded. I was used to handmaidens helping me dress and undress. Marjorie and I had already become comfortable in that way. But I'd never had anyone force me to do so. It made my skin crawl to have the choice taken from me.

But after twenty years of living with my mother, I was used to stifling my own thoughts and feelings for the sake of others. So I awkwardly lifted my blouse over my head and unbuttoned my pants, tossing them carefully onto the beige velvet stool beside me.

Emma held the first dress for me to step into, pulling it until I slipped my arms in. Then she carefully laced the corset back. I regretted all the cake I'd eaten earlier when she tightened it more.

I lifted the skirt of the dress and made my way to stand in front of my mirror. I startled myself when I saw my reflection.

A fucking horror.

The first dress was a *lot* of fabric. So much fabric, I felt lost in it. It was a gigantic heap of frills and over-the-top detailing. I wanted to vomit and, quite frankly, I thought a mess down the front might've actually *improved* the dress.

The sleeves were bulbous and larger than my head. The top half of the dress hugged my body closely, thanks to the corset, but the bottom flared out into a dome of a skirt, easily twice as wide as my stance.

I was speechless. I couldn't even think of the words to describe this atrocity. I slowly turned to face the others. They'd stopped what they were doing now and were waiting to see the first option.

I immediately felt relieved when a collection of jaws dropped and eyes widened. Sophia even brought a hand to her mouth in shock. Adelaide's cheeks turned pink and Emma and Daphne exchanged a look, a silent conversation that normally only twins would understand, but it didn't take a genius to know what they were quietly conveying.

And then Sophia laughed. All that wine had gotten to her head. She sputtered into her hand and then apologized. "I'm so sorry, Emilie. That is *not* the dress for you. I will not allow my future daughter-in-law to look so atrocious on her wedding day. No offense, Adelaide. I'm sure that dress would look lovely on someone else."

I caught her eyes, noticing the gleam in them that said she didn't believe *anyone* would look beautiful in this monstrosity. But she didn't want to hurt her dear friend's feelings.

Adelaide let out an exasperated sigh. "How about we give the next one a try, then?"

The next few hours felt like a never-ending cycle. Dress off. Dress on. Dress off. Dress on. The monotony was only interrupted by grimaces and looks of horror. After the first dress, I thought it would only get better.

But I was wrong.

Somehow, each dress I tried on only got worse. I was on the verge of tears and drowning my sorrow in a fourth glass of wine. My tear-filled eyes and rosy cheeks didn't help matters. I looked like a downright mess as I tried on the fiftieth dress of the night.

This was a complete disaster.

"Let's take a break," said Sophia, giving me a pitiful look. "More sparkling wine, anyone?"

At this point, Adelaide and the twins had also begun drinking. I needed some fresh air. I didn't bother taking off the latest fiasco of a dress. I didn't have the energy for it. The doors to my balcony swung open and the cool night breeze swept over my hot skin. Thank the gods this dress didn't have a corset so I could inhale and exhale deep and slow.

The gardens below were quiet tonight. No lingering princes to eavesdrop on. Which was definitely a good thing because if he could see me in this dress, he'd ridicule me till the day I died. Oh gods, this was a nightmare.

I leaned against the railing and dropped my head into my hands. I was so tired and mentally drained. I just wanted to call it a night and perhaps we could try again tomorrow.

The thought of returning to the room made my head pound, but I knew I couldn't hide out here forever. As I returned through the open balcony doors, my eyes caught on a slim white satin dress. Unlike the others I'd tried on so far, this one was simple and modest. But something about it drew me in.

I reached for it as I came back inside. It was soft and felt like water gliding through my fingers. The fabric glimmered in such a way that I almost wondered if it was laced with magical properties. Like the way light reflects on waves at the surface of the sea. It was beautiful.

"What about this one?" I asked, but no one seemed to hear me. From the little conversation I picked up on, they were bickering over how to resolve this nightmare of a situation. Why hadn't they given me this one to try?

Even Emma and Daphne were involved in the discussion. I guess a few glasses of alcohol had loosened their lips. It was the most they'd spoken all night. So without their help, I removed my oversized ballgown and slipped into the slim, fitted dress that had caught my eye.

I didn't even have to see myself in the mirror. The moment I put it on, it just felt right. Still, I picked up the fabric around my knees and let the train follow me as I went to stand in front of the mirror again. My dismal frown was immediately replaced with a tentative upward curve of my lip.

The dress had thin straps and the neckline dipped in an elegant v-shape that highlighted my cleavage. It was tight enough to accentuate my curves, but unlike most that I had tried on, I could still breathe in it. Although it hugged my stomach, I didn't see the bloat from a day's worth of wine and cake. Again, I questioned the dress's magical properties.

The bottom half of the dress flowed to the floor, its long train trailing behind me. There was no lace, no beads, no tulle or patterns. And yet it was stunning. It was hands down the best dress I'd tried on all night and, better yet, I felt like a bride for the first time. I felt beautiful.

My slight grin turned into a full-blown smile and my eyes were once again glistening, this time with happy tears.

I was met with silence when I turned around, but this time was nothing like the first dress. Looks of awe and pleasant surprise adorned their faces when they noticed me waiting for their attention.

Rather than sputtering, Sophia's eyes glistened, and she placed a palm across her chest. Emma and Daphne exchanged another look. This time I understood it as acknowledgement that the dress was perfect. Adelaide looked confused, and I wasn't sure why until she spoke.

She muttered softly, "I don't remember bringing that one."

I wasn't sure how to respond, but thankfully I didn't have to. Sophia moved forward to embrace me in a hug. "Well, thank the gods you did. She's stunning. Oh Emilie, I can't wait to welcome you into our family."

Sophia held me close, and I patted her on the back awkwardly. I wasn't used to this physical affection that she loved so much. Her glass flute tilted in her hand and the twins gasped while Adelaide ran forward to grab it from Sophia's hand.

Thankfully, nothing touched my perfect dress. Sophia's tears of joy only landed on my bare chest. She was a blubbering mess and as we stood in an embrace, I started to tear up too. And then I laughed at how ridiculous we must've looked. But it was nice to have a mother like Sophia.

A knock on the door made us separate.

"Am I interrupting?" Ladon asked.

The sight of him left me breathless. I hadn't seen him in a week. It had been that long since our last training session. After which, I'd decided not to go back. Miraculously, I hadn't run into him in the halls or anywhere else in the castle. I was becoming quite accustomed to the lack of his snarling presence.

Right on cue, his focus landed on me and I thought I saw his nose twitch. Like he'd caught a whiff of a foul odor.

Fuck him.

"What did you need, sweetheart?" Sophia asked her son.

I stifled a laugh at the nickname. Ladon was far from a *sweetheart*. Perhaps his mother had permanently suffered some brain damage from her drinking habits.

He tore his eyes from me and focused his attention on Sophia instead. "Cyrus wants to see you. Mentioned something about the Driash family complaining about taxes again. He needs you to help smooth things over."

Sophia sighed and explained. "The Driashes. They were my neighbors growing up. I was really good friends with their daughter and once I married Ezra, they started looking for favors. I've told them a million times they won't be receiving any preferential treatment, but they won't take no for an answer."

"But Cyrus is king now. Why would they still seek you?" I asked.

She laughed. "That makes it even worse. They think I have even more influence now because he's my son."

Then she leaned in to whisper conspiratorially. "Don't tell them, but they're right."

She set her empty glass on the bar cart. "Anyway, I should go take care of this. Come on, Ladon. Stop staring at the beautiful bride and escort your dear mother."

Horrified, I looked toward Ladon, still perched next to the door. His cheeks flushed red.

Had he been staring?

Chapter Eleven

Emilie

I HEARD A KNOCK on my door, and before I could speak, Cyrus walked in. He was wearing his night clothes—soft and loose-fitting black pants with a thin gray shirt.

I sat up in bed, holding the blanket to my chest. I'd gone to bed without clothes and my skin tingled while Cyrus looked at me, like he could see straight through the blanket. The way his pupils dilated made me wonder if he actually could.

"What are you doing here?" I asked.

"I had to see you," he said, stepping closer to the bed. "I couldn't stop thinking about you. About our wedding. About you...as my wife."

He was so close now; his hand was resting on the top of my comforter.

"Is that so?" I asked. My voice was shaky...breathless. Warmth radiated from between my thighs.

"Yes, Emilie. I was having a hard time sleeping. And I think if you were sleeping next to me, I wouldn't have that problem." He tugged at the edge of the blanket, and I scooted over to make room for him to slip in beside me. My chest felt tight, my body rigid.

Was this really happening?

Cyrus wrapped an arm around my waist and pulled me close, my naked body pressed against him and I could feel something hard pressing against my thigh. Instinctively, I threaded my fingers through his wavy hair, wrapping one leg around him.

"I've been thinking about this nonstop, Emilie. What it would be like to have you in my bed." He rolled on top of me and the weight of his body between my legs had me breathing heavily. My body was on fire and I knew it had nothing to do with his flame wielding abilities.

I rolled my hips. I wanted his shirt off, his pants off. I wanted to feel his skin against mine. As I clawed at his back, his hands roamed my bare chest, cupping my breast and brushing a thumb over my sensitive nipple.

My brain was going haywire. Torn between uncertainty and lack of experience while also being overwhelmed with pleasure. I thought I must've blacked out for a moment because Cyrus's shirt came off in a heartbeat and then his bare chest was covering mine.

He lowered his mouth, brushing his lips across my neck and making me shiver with anticipation. He paused, looking toward the bedroom door where another figure stood. "Stop staring at the beautiful bride, Ladon."

I bolted awake, my heart pounding out of my chest. I ran my hands frantically over my body. The feeling of silk pajamas didn't do anything to slow my racing heart or my rapid breathing.

It was just a dream.

I reached for the glass of water I knew I'd sat on the nightstand next to my bed. The water helped to relieve the burning ache that still lingered in my core. My forehead was sweaty as I pushed back the tangled hair from my face. I was a complete mess.

The moon was high in the night sky, peeping through a crack in my curtains. It couldn't be more than a little past midnight. I fell back against the mattress and sighed.

Tomorrow was the start of our trip to Fort Malek. I should be sleeping. Gods knew I'd need the rest before the journey, but I was too excited. And too disturbed by the dream I'd just had.

While my heart had stopped pounding and my breathing steadied, there was still an aching sensation between my thighs. A warm, wetness that was hard to ignore, no matter how much I tossed and turned.

I tried to think of Cyrus, of what his body had felt like under my fingertips. It hadn't been real, but that didn't mean it wasn't vivid. If I closed my eyes and concentrated hard enough, I could almost feel his breath on my neck. I slid a hand down my stomach and slipped it under the hem of my pajama shorts.

A soft moan escaped my lips and for a second I froze, irrationally worried that someone might've heard...that someone knew what I was doing under the cover of darkness. That was silly, of course. Everyone else in the castle was fast asleep.

I bit my lip as my fingers brushed against my clit, and then down to the pool of arousal I knew I'd find waiting for me. I pushed a finger inside, dragging it out slowly before pressing in again. With one hand, I worked myself into a frenzy, while the other hand toyed with my nipple. Rocking my hips against the palm of my hand and arching my back off the mattress, I chased that feeling of bliss. I was desperate to have it, sure that once I found it, I'd be able to rest again.

My legs shook, but I found myself distracted by the image of Cyrus hovering over me. I furrowed my brows, frustrated by how elusive orgasms always seemed to be. I thought the fantasy of my future husband would've helped, but I only felt that high slipping away, dissolving into nothing.

Damn it.

I took a deep breath and tried to clear my head. Attempted to focus on just the pleasure from my fingers slipping inside my pussy, stretching me wide as I bucked my hips.

Closer...closer...closer. Once again, I conjured an image of Cyrus. I fantasized about the way he might fuck me. Would he be sweet and tender? Or would he be forceful and rough? My insides were wound tight, pressure building in my abdomen. I was so close; I could hardly breathe as my muscles tensed.

My vision of Cyrus turned fuzzy. His blonde hair lightened to white. The wrinkles on his forehead smoothed and his eyes transitioned from green to a silver blue.

Right before my eyes, Cyrus morphed into Ladon. A warm smile vanished and was replaced with a wicked sneer. And that was the moment my body betrayed me.

With the mental image of Ladon pressed against me, his hand wrapped around my throat, my cunt pulsed around my fingers, and my entire body trembled uncontrollably. It felt like an earthquake rumbling through my bones, and I only clenched harder when I thought about the way Ladon *could* manipulate the earth.

Shit, I should not be thinking about Ladon and his magical abilities while finger fucking myself.

My muscles relaxed as I unraveled from my high. I sat up and quickly went to the bathroom to clean myself up. I felt gross. Like the essence of Ladon was covering my skin, and I needed to wash him off.

But when I hopped in the shower and scrubbed my skin, Ladon's presence sank into me like ink from a tattoo, permanently marking me. My skin crawled at the thought of him...at the thought of experiencing him in such an intimate way. I wished I could burn the image from my brain, but it lingered no matter how hard I tried to erase it.

As I left the bathroom and headed back to bed, I stopped at my door. I heard muffled voices from beyond, somewhere within the halls. I moved closer, pressing my ear against the hardwood. I could make out the voices of Cyrus and Ladon, but their words were too distorted by the thick, sturdy door.

Carefully, I twisted the knob and opened the door just a crack. Their voices carried inside my room, unaware that I was listening.

"We've been over this a hundred times, Ladon. I'm getting tired of having the same conversation repeatedly. You either trust my ability to make decisions for myself or you don't." I could hear the anger in Cyrus's voice.

"It's not that I don't trust you. I know you, Brother. You want to see the good in people, but I'm telling you, the Duvals do not have your best interest at heart."

"And you do?"

Someone, I guessed Ladon, scoffed. "Of course I do. I always have. I'm offended you would suggest otherwise."

"You're right." The rage in Cyrus's tone had simmered. There was a pause before he spoke again. "What is it going to take for you to accept Emilie into this family?"

"I don't think it's possible."

My eyes burned as tears swelled. I ground my teeth as I imagined all the things I'd like to do to Ladon. I'd never done anything to him. Or at least nothing that would warrant this kind of hatred.

He spoke again, and I listened attentively. "They have nothing to offer you." Cyrus tried to speak, but Ladon interrupted him. "Dreslen is a wasteland. Misha may have been your friend once upon a time but he and his wife and children are only after your power and your money. You're letting a parasite into this family. She'll never love you."

"Sometimes marriage isn't about love."

"No, but I know you, Cyrus. You believe in love. You loved Isabella, and she loved you. You can't honestly tell me that you could love that harlot."

"Enough!" Cyrus roared, and I shuddered. I quietly pressed the door closed. I'd heard enough.

Tears began to fall as I let Ladon's words sink in. I wasn't after money or influence. I wasn't after anything. My parents arranged this whole ordeal without ever considering what I wanted, though I suppose money and power were *exactly* what my parents were after. I was only trying to make the best of the situation. Ladon's anger was misguided.

I tried to take solace in the fact that Cyrus had stood up for me. He'd make a great husband, but I couldn't extinguish the overwhelming desire for Ladon to accept me too.

Chapter Twelve

Ladon

MY HEAD THROBBED WITH each footstep as I took my morning run. I had to wake up extra early to get a workout in before we set off for Fort Malek. I could've skipped it, but it was going to be an all-day journey and I knew I'd get restless if I didn't release some of this pent-up energy.

I'd stayed up too late last night, fighting with Cyrus over the same old thing. Time was running out for him to change his mind and I felt my chances slipping away. But I wasn't letting Emilie within an inch of the throne. I'd have to find a different approach if my stubborn brother wouldn't listen to reason.

I finished my run and showered quickly. An empty trunk lay open on my bed, and I hastily tossed clothes and shoes and other necessary travel items inside. It was a chaotic mess, but it would suffice. I fastened it shut with ease. I'd always been a light packer, and I didn't expect to be there long. Even though I'd be happy to stay there permanently, I had to come back with the rest of our entourage for the big day.

My mother was waiting for me in the hall near the castle entryway. She wrapped me in a hug as soon as she saw me. "Try to relax a little. And be safe."

A genuine smile made an appearance as I thought about leaving Renoa and Emilie behind for a few days. "I'm honestly thrilled to be out of the castle and have some time alone with my brother for once."

When I pulled back, my mother's face was fixed into a confused grimace. "He didn't tell you?"

"Tell me what?" I could feel my blood pressure rising. "Tell me what?"

"I think Cyrus should tell you himself," she said, nodding her chin past my shoulder.

I turned and sure enough, Cyrus and Emilie had rounded the corner, smiling and laughing like two old friends. I felt the tips of my ears turn red, but I bit my tongue.

Behind my brother and his betrothed were two of the castle's workers, carrying multiple trunks. Pretty princess couldn't even carry her own fucking luggage.

"Ah, good morning. Perfect weather for traveling, don't you think?"

"Is there something you'd like to tell me, Brother?"

He straightened the lapels of his jacket and responded without even bothering to give me his full attention. "Do not start with me, Ladon. It'll be fine."

Anger bubbled inside me. I didn't care if it would be fine. I cared that he was siding with Emilie over me. I cared that he was already letting her influence his choices, and not for the better.

Emilie had the good sense to leave his side and head for the carriages, giving us a chance to speak alone.

"Promise me that you'll at least *try* to be civil to her on this trip. You haven't given her a fair chance. Maybe if you did, you'd see she's actually a very kind person, and she doesn't deserve your hostility."

The thought of being even remotely cordial to her made my skin crawl. I shook my head, unable to form the words.

Cyrus fixed me with a harsh glare—the kind he used when he was giving a command, not speaking to his family. "If you can't fall in line, you will be staying behind."

I could count on one hand the number of times my brother had addressed me in such a fashion. I knew he'd had enough of me and his threat was serious. And I couldn't let them go to Fort Malek without me.

"Fine," I bit out.

"Say it."

"I promise I'll *try* to be nicer."

He didn't miss the inflection in my voice, but my vow seemed to be good enough. He clapped me on the back as he followed Emilie out of the castle. I had to count to ten before I trailed them both.

We filed into the covered carriage while my brother's guards occupied the one in front and the one in the rear, protecting us on both ends. It was only a precaution. The roads through Osavian were extremely safe, but it was proper procedure nonetheless.

Cyrus and Emilie sat on the bench facing forward while I took the seat across from my brother. Cyrus took off his dress jacket and wrapped an arm around Emilie's shoulders. She leaned into him and gave him a wistful look that made me want to vomit.

As the carriage began to roll, I focused my attention on the passing scenery. There was a mist hovering over the royal gardens and many citizens had lined the streets of Renoa to wave goodbye. I gave them a polite nod and, from the corner of my eye, I noticed Emilie waving and smiling.

To my dismay, the people seemed to love her. They called her name and wished her well. Cyrus beamed next to her and played with the curled ends of her hair.

My leg began to shake with irritation. This was going to be a very long ride.

"How much longer is it going to be?" Emilie whispered. My eyes were closed, so they thought I was sleeping, but really, I just didn't want to feel obligated to socialize.

The carriage jostled, but I remained relatively still, listening to all their conversations, which were honestly boring. For some reason, I'd expected more than the awkward questions and stiff responses. It was painfully clear that these two were not meant for each other.

I released a small sigh. Cyrus had dismissed my last attempt to persuade him. I didn't think there would be another, especially now that he was flaunting Emilie around the country.

"It shouldn't be too much longer. Maybe an hour or so," Cyrus guessed. The carriage was dark enough that I didn't need to open my eyes to know that night had fallen. His guess was as good as mine.

"It'll be pretty late when we get there, I guess," Emilie said.

"Yes, we'll probably head straight to bed. Tomorrow we can do the introductions and all that fanfare."

"Hmm."

I tried not to laugh at how forced the conversation was. It was unbearable. It felt like Cyrus tapped my shoe once or twice, but I successfully ignored him. I had no interest in alleviating some of his discomfort. He should've listened to me and sent her packing several weeks ago. In fact, he never should've invited her to Renoa in the first place.

The carriage slowed to a stop, and I finally opened my eyes. Cyrus gave me a disgruntled look, but I ignored it, sitting up straight and stretching my arms over my head.

Rain came down as I peered out the window, distorting the stronghold before us. Through the downpour, I could just make out the outline of a guard atop the watchtower. Two lanterns lit the path to a large metal door, the only opening to Fort Malek.

It creaked open slowly as someone pulled a lever from the inside, allowing our caravan to pull through the gate. Beyond the walls was an open, square courtyard. On the far side were three tall arches which connected the outdoor opening to the greeting hall inside. On either side were matching arches—the ones on the right led to the lodging, while the ones on the left were reserved for meetings and offices of the other high-ranking members.

Something didn't feel right. As I looked around the opening inside the stronghold, it was eerily quiet. Aside from the sound of rain hitting the rooftops and the wind blowing against a broken shutter, the outpost felt abandoned.

Cyrus noted the same. "Guess everyone is inside, hiding from the storms."

"I suppose so," I murmured. Though an unsettling feeling crept up my spine. I'd feel better once we were inside.

The guards in the carriage ahead of us leapt down into a massive puddle in the center of the opening. Water came to their ankles as they splashed toward us, then pulled open the carriage door.

One man helped Emilie out first. Cyrus held his jacket over her head and I followed behind them. We walked quickly to the center arch and once we were under cover, I shook my hair out.

I entered the greeting hall first and froze as soon as my eyes adjusted to the light. I felt the blood drain from my face. From my entire body. Bile rose in my throat.

I was no stranger to death. To gore and all the horrors that come with battle. But nothing could've prepared me for what I'd stumbled upon.

I stepped over one body, the head detached and nowhere to be found. A pile of mangled limbs lay beside him. The next body still had a head, but his face had been removed, leaving only cartilage and bone.

My breath came uneasily. Bodies were piled everywhere, and the floor was slick with blood. I leaned down and closed a woman's eyes. Her shirt had been ripped open, and she'd been gutted.

The smell was enough to make me sick, so I tried to take shallow breaths. I was dizzy from the rancid scent of decay and the sight of all my soldiers brutally murdered and left for me to find.

Worst of all, at the front of the hall, a man had been dismembered. Each piece of him—his torso, his arms and legs, and his head—had been rearranged and pinned to the wall with large spikes.

Kalen.

He hadn't sent that message. Someone else had. Someone who wanted to set a trap.

I whipped around, my boots sliding in the crimson puddles. When I turned, I found Emilie, her face pale and eyes frozen in shock. Cyrus didn't look much better.

"Who...who would do this?" Cyrus asked between shaky breaths.

Emilie looked as if she might feint. They needed to get out of here.

"Take her. Take her and leave. She doesn't belong here and you need to get back to Renoa. Tell the captains at the other outposts—"

A shout and the clank of metal interrupted my commands.

Cyrus and I wasted no time running back from where we'd come. It had to be less than ten steps to the arches, but by the time we ran out into the rain again, the courtyard was full of masked fighters. They swung wildly, untrained, unlike my armies. Our four guards held them off easily, but their numbers grew as more spilled out from the side arches.

Anderson, the oldest guard, was taking on four at once while Braden and Clarence fought three a piece, slicing through their foes with deadly precision. On the other side of the carriage, Lee was engaged in combat. His sword clashed against another masked soldier's, but two were approaching from behind.

"Lee!" I shouted, running toward him and drawing my sword as I went. I slashed through the first's chest with little effort, and he hit the ground with an anguished scream. Then I brought my sword up and went for another fatal blow. The second heard me coming and turned just in time, blocking my sword with an old, dented shield.

It clanged, the vibrations rippling up my arm. I planted my feet and took another swing, this time aiming for his thigh. He quickly brought down his own blade, which clashed with mine at the last second. He twirled in a move that was more theatrical than practical, and I thwarted his attack. We danced back and forth until Lee surprised him, jabbing his sword into the soldier's back while I took the fatal blow to his chest.

It was my first chance to look around the clearing. Somehow, there were even more soldiers than before. It was like a tidal wave of enemies and there was no way we could continue to hold them off.

"Cyrus!" I shouted, swinging my blade and massacring our enemies as I made my way toward him. He was surrounded by six more soldiers, and I could see the strength draining from him as he fought valiantly. I paused and took a deep breath, sending a shock wave through the ground.

The soldiers were unprepared and thrown from their feet while Cyrus was able to get away. The moment it took for me to focus my magic cost me. Someone attacked from behind, slicing the back of my thigh. I roared and clutched at the gash, blood covering my hand in a matter of seconds.

Cyrus rammed his sword through the assailant, giving him an extra kick in the chest for payback. As the man fell to the ground, I heard Braden shouting and I whipped my head in his direction. Clarence was lying face down, blood spilling from his abdomen. Braden sank to his knees beside his brother. Even though Clarence had stopped breathing, Braden protected him from further violence. He fought and fought, but after a few minutes, our enemies buried him and his brother, swarming over them like flies on a rotting carcass.

I tried to find Anderson in the chaos, but he was nowhere to be found.

"Get back to the carriage!" I yelled at Cyrus. With Clarence and Braden gone, and Anderson missing, our odds of getting out of here alive were dwindling.

"Where's Emilie?" Cyrus shouted back at me.

For fuck's sake, had he not been watching after her?

I searched the bloody battlefield, dodging and cutting down soldiers as I did. Just as I was about to give up, I spotted her behind one arch, her hands outstretched as a magical barrier kept our enemies at bay.

Fuck, I really should've taught her proper self-defense. She couldn't hold on to that power forever, and judging by her faltering stance and pained expression, she was going to give out soon.

Cyrus took a step in her direction, but I stopped him with an outstretched arm. "Get to the carriage. I'll get her."

He seemed conflicted, his eyes flickering between Emilie and me. There were few instances in which Cyrus allowed me to be in charge, but in the heat of battle, he listened to my commands. Lee was next to us now, tugging on Cyrus's arm.

"Let's go, Your Highness," Lee said, and Cyrus reluctantly followed him.

I sprinted toward Emilie, thrashing through the crowd of masked menaces, and prayed to gods I didn't believe in.

Emilie's wall of wind broke just as I reached her, and the horde crowded around us.

"Ladon," she cried. Terror laced her voice and painted her face. She reached for me and I fought my way through a blur of bodies. But they closed in, swarming faster than I could keep them at bay.

Emilie's hand wrapped around my arm, and this time I didn't throw her off or snarl at her touch. I felt for her blindly as my blade flashed, reflecting lightning from the sky above. My hand was sweaty when it clasped around hers.

Suddenly, she was ripped from my grasp. She screamed, and I pivoted to find her being dragged away by one of the masked fighters. She struggled, kicking and clawing at their arms, but they were stronger than her.

"Emilie!" I shouted, reaching for her desperately.

And then a blunt object struck me in the back of the head.

Everything went black.

Chapter Thirteen

Ladon

MY HEAD POUNDED AS I pried my eyes open. I was lying on cold, hard ground, like the first frost of the winter. Fog swirled around me, making it impossible to see the sky above me, while tall hedges lined the sides of my vision.

It was dark—perhaps dusk?

Where are we? Where are we? A voice inside my head whispered.

I blinked, trying to clear the haze from my vision. The world was spinning, and I felt as though I might be sick.

Where are we? Where are we?

That voice in my head grew louder. I tilted my head, my neck cracked as I worked out my stiff muscles.

"Emilie?" I spoke softly. She was lying on the ground, her face frozen in terror. Eyes wide open yet unseeing.

"Where are we? Where are we?" she repeated.

"Emilie." I crawled on my hands and knees to her, shaking her from whatever trance held her captive. "Hey, it's all right. Snap out of it."

Her lips stopped moving, and her eyes focused on my face. Then her brows furrowed. "Ladon?"

"Yes, it's me. Are you injured?" I asked, scanning her body briefly. She appeared to be physically unharmed, other than a scratch across her forehead and a bruise forming on her cheek.

"I...I think so...I..." She looked around in confusion. "How did we get here? What is this place?"

"I don't know," I said, rubbing the back of my head. I flinched when I came across a wet spot. When I pulled my hand away, my fingers were covered in sticky blood. "I blacked out. I don't know what happened. You don't remember anything?"

She frowned, and tears welled in her hazel eyes. "I remember you coming for me, right before my magic gave out. But then I don't remember what happened after that."

I took her by the hands and pulled her into a sitting position.

She gasped. "What are those?"

Her hands trembled in mine, and when I followed her line of sight, I found our hands intertwined with black vines crawling up our fingers and wrists.

I jumped back and landed on my ass. With my fingers outstretched, I stared in horror at the black that tainted my skin. I rubbed it with my thumb, but it didn't smudge. The markings were permanent.

Emilie stared at her hands as if they didn't belong to her. Her face drained of color. I understood the feeling.

I rose to my feet and brushed the dirt from my chest and back. We were nestled between two walls of dark green bushes, like the hedge gardens back home. Except I couldn't see the end of the row through the hazy mist.

I shivered, looking left to right, wondering which way to go. "We should move."

Emilie stood, brushing her wild hair from her face. "Which way?"

When I didn't respond, she raised her hand, her eyes narrowing in on the dense fog. Her power of wind might've been able to lift the haze and clear our path.

She stood frozen for a moment, summoning her magic, but then she crashed to her knees, throwing her hands to her temples and screaming.

I rushed to her side while she continued to cry in agony. I tugged at her hands, unsure what was wrong with her. "Emilie, what is it?"

Whatever pain she was enduring was internal. There was nothing I could do.

Finally, after what felt like hours, she slid her hands over her face and let them fall to her lap. She looked exhausted and was breathing rapidly. She whispered, "My magic...it's gone."

"No." I shook my head and backed away. "No."

The echoes of her screams made me hesitate for a moment. But ultimately, I directed my power to the ground a few feet in front of me. I concentrated on the dirt, what it would be like to melt it into mud, for it to sink and flow like a river.

It didn't take long for a searing pain to shoot through my head. Lightning dashed across my mind, electrifying every one of my senses. My vision went white and I couldn't feel anything other than the burning flames licking at my fingertips.

Oh gods, what was this?

My intestines felt like they were being dissolved by acid and my ribs were being cracked in half, one by one.

When it finally ended, I was in the fetal position, my stomach still reeling from the violent experience. I squinted. There was no daylight to be found, but even the white fog was too much for my blinding headache.

"Are you all right?" Emilie asked. I caught her feet moving toward me out of the corner of my eye.

"Obviously not," I spat. Her feet retreated.

My skin was still on fire, though the cool mist helped to ease my suffering. I heard Emilie moving to my left.

"Where are you going?"

"I don't know."

"Gods, you're insufferable," I muttered under my breath. She shuffled her feet farther away from me. "Wait."

I stood on shaky legs, not fully recovered yet. But I couldn't let her wander off on her own. We still had no idea where we were. Where were the masked soldiers? Where did this path lead?

Following her lead, I headed down the left side. It was a fifty-fifty shot to nowhere. We walked slowly; my ears perked for any noise of an oncoming slaughter.

Perhaps this was a game? They wanted to sneak up on us like they had at Fort Malek.

Something in my gut churned. The attack...did Cyrus make it out? Was he here somewhere?

A sense of urgency washed over me and I picked up my pace, Emilie right beside me. I was keenly aware of the fact that all of my weapons had been removed. If we came across any of our enemies, we'd be completely defenseless. Even our magic was no use.

A howling noise came from behind us. We both turned toward the sound, Emilie's eyes wide and frightened. I was more angry than terrified. Angry that we'd ever gotten into this situation, but not stupid enough to think we weren't in danger.

We were *very* much in danger.

"Run," I said.

And we sprinted along the dirt path. The towering hedges next to us were endless. For all I knew, we could've been running straight into a trap, but what other option did we have?

The howling from behind us grew closer, and I could differentiate multiple pitches. More than one beast...

A wall of green vines appeared through the fog and we skidded to a halt. The maze allowed us to choose left or right, so I pivoted to the left without much thought, grabbing Emilie and pulling her alongside me.

I had to go with my gut.

Another hound-like sound erupted.

"What is that?" Emilie gasped.

"Don't think about it. Just keep running."

We stumbled upon multiple openings, and multiple dead ends, moving endlessly without knowing where we were going. Was there even an end to this maze? Were we moving in circles until our bodies gave out and the beasts overcame us?

I wiped the sweat from my brow as we stumbled on another dead end.

"Fuck!" I roared.

Emilie cursed and threw her hands into her hair. She was on the verge of tears.

I was about to head back the way we'd come when two beasts rounded the corner. Two identical hellhounds, their eyes beady and burning with a ravenous desire for our blood. They had to be at least seven feet tall, more if they stood on their hind legs. They probably weighed a few hundred pounds, too.

Emilie shifted until she was behind me, her hands trembling as she gripped the fabric of my shirt. I blocked her as the beasts moved closer, though I had no idea how I'd protect her.

They were going to pounce. It was only a matter of time. They prowled; the sound of their heavy paws was like a pounding war drum.

"Come on, you filthy mongrels," I muttered under my breath. The anticipation, the uncertainty, was always the worst. "Just do it already."

Behind me, Emilie was pulling me backwards, trying to put as much space between us and the hellhounds as possible, but there was only so far we could go. I reached behind me and grabbed her waist, keeping her close.

The beasts were drooling, their rancid dark silver saliva dripping to the ground. The one on the right was pawing at the dirt while the one on the left stood at attention. They were waiting for something.

"Ladon..." Emilie's panicked tone disturbed me. The protector, the High Commander, in me was failing.

Suddenly, the sky lit up. A bolt of lightning shot across the sky, reflecting off the beasts' slick fur, and illuminating the unending hedges. The hellhounds snarled before shooting forward, barking and snapping their teeth ferociously.

I felt frantically for a sword that I knew wasn't there. Muscle memory took over and I held up my arm, but there was no shield to protect me from the teeth that tore through my flesh. A blinding pain coursed through my veins, but I fought off the urge to pass out.

Adrenaline kicked in and I pushed the beast off me. The second was darting around me, looking to attack Emilie. I side-stepped and threw a punch, which did very little aside from agitating the hound. It shook its head in surprise before lunging forward again.

Emilie screamed, and I turned to find the first hellhound ripping into her ankle. It tugged, and she fell to the ground, dragging behind the beast as it retreated backwards.

I tried to grab her hand, but as I scrambled to reach her, the other beast sprung forward and landed on my back. I crashed to the ground, landing face first and hitting my chin and scraping my palms.

Before I could scramble to my feet again, teeth clamped around my ankle and dragged me across the cold, hard dirt. I couldn't see her, but I could hear Emilie still screaming as the two beasts carried us off to an unknown destination.

My heart thundered in my chest. I tried to grab something, *anything*, but there was nothing to save me. The flimsy leaves from the hedges ripped to shreds in my fingers. My nails bled as I clawed at the ground. Even if I had been able to grab ahold of something, the beast would've torn my limbs from my body.

This couldn't be how it ended.

We flew through more than a dozen pathways, twisting and turning too quickly for me to memorize the way back. The hellhounds knew the way, as if they'd run the maze a million times.

It felt as if the skin around my ankle was being torn from my bone. I didn't even want to know what it looked like. Of course, if they chose to eat us, I may never know how badly my body had been mangled.

Suddenly, my body was being dragged down a set of stairs. White marble, I discovered once I was able to focus enough. The bump as my face hit each and every step made my head spin.

We slowed and eventually came to a stop. Beside me, Emilie was whimpering. Her hair was even wilder now, tangled with leaves and twigs while scratches covered her face. Mine likely looked the same.

A bright white light flooded the area around us, and the two hellhounds relinquished their hold on us. Slowly and painfully, I pushed myself up and twisted to find the source of the light.

The light was blinding, and I could only make out the dark outline of a figure standing atop a platform made of stone. A woman, based on the curves of her body and the dress-like shape flowing out from her waist. The platform was about ten feet tall and the stranger came slowly to the edge to stare down at us.

"Sit," she commanded, and her two faithful pets gathered at the edge of the platform and sat, facing Emilie and me. The woman took another step forward, and I held a hand up, attempting to shield my eyes from the light's intensity.

Her body blocked the source of the light, and I could finally make out her features. Black hair. Sharp, cat-like eyes that sparkled orange. Maroon lips and white, almost translucent skin. She wore a simple black gown that covered everything but her neck and face. Even her hands were covered with black gloves.

"Reyna," I hissed. Of course, this was all her doing. Who else would've been so bold to attack one of our strongholds. "What have you done?"

She smiled with sinister sweetness. Then she took a seat on the ledge of the platform, crossed her legs and rested her chin in her palm. "So good to see you too, Ladon. Though I must admit you're looking a little rough."

I struggled to rise to my feet, putting most of my weight on my good ankle. I took half a step forward before the hellhounds stood at attention and bared their teeth. There was no chance they'd let me anywhere near their owner.

I glared at her, thinking of how I'd like to knock her off that pedestal and rip her to pieces. The urge to rattle the ground, split it open and let her be swallowed whole crossed my mind before recalling my loss of magic. I peered down at my hands and the vines that covered them before staring at her again.

"Ah, do you like those?" she asked. "Your body was so beautiful, so pristine and untarnished. I couldn't help but add a little décor. Now every time you go to use your magic, you'll think of me."

Rage coursed through me, begging for release, but I had no outlet. No power. No weapons. No way to break through her hellhounds and wrap my hands around her tiny neck.

Emilie coughed. I'd almost forgotten she was with me.

Reyna eyed her with annoyance. "Ah, yes. You know, I was hoping for a pair of brothers to play with. Such a shame Cyrus was able to get away, but my soldiers brought back this pretty creature. I can think of some ways to have fun with you, too."

Emilie trembled, her clothing cold and wet from the mist.

"Let her go," I snapped. She never should've been at the outpost. I'd told Cyrus a million times. I'd told him that she didn't belong with us at all. She should've been safe at home in Dreslen.

"Afraid I can't do that, Ladon." Reyna redirected her attention back to Emilie. "And who might you be, pretty thing?"

Lie, I thought.

"Emilie," she said softly, and I pressed my eyelids shut. Even if Reyna didn't recognize her face, she'd recognize the name. Word spread like wildfire that Cyrus was to remarry a woman, Emilie of Dreslen. Reyna would've heard and she would put two and two together.

Reyna huffed a laugh. "Are you kidding me? *The* Emilie? Well, we *are* going to have some fun."

Chapter Fourteen

Emilie

I FELT NUMB. I could see where my clothes had been tattered and my ankle had bite marks around it, but I didn't feel any of it. I shivered—not because of the cold, but because this mysterious place chilled me to the core. Because of the woman staring down at me like I was her next meal.

She was strikingly beautiful. I'd expected her rotten soul to be reflected in her appearance, but that wasn't the case at all. The air was still, but somehow her long wavy black hair fluttered around her round face. Her ruby red lips were bright against her pale skin. And she had an ever-present smile that whispered of her malevolence.

Beside me, Ladon was fuming in a way that I'd never seen before. Which said a lot since he'd never looked at me with anything other than disdain. I watched as his fists clenched and relaxed repeatedly, like some sort of coping mechanism to deal with his rage. He was breathing through his nose with his lips sealed shut.

I locked eyes with Reyna, who was now tapping her lips with her index finger. She squinted her eyes, and I dreaded whatever torture she had planned for me.

"What do you want?" Ladon's voice was low, barely audible. I swallowed, then crossed my arms, running my hands over the goosebumps present there.

I wasn't sure if it was better to let Ladon take the lead. Clearly, there was a lot of history between the two of them. I imagined all the feeble attempts at keeping an alliance between their borders. The way he'd spoken about her before made it obvious he didn't trust her.

For good reason.

Reyna looked at him with devilish delight. There was something about her demeanor that was unhinged. She wasn't just evil. She was crazed. Which made her even more dangerous.

A sane person would kill us. Or torture us for information before tossing us into a cell to rot. Somehow, I didn't think that was what Reyna had planned.

"I want Cyrus to abdicate his throne and bow to me. For too long, you've kept us in these dark and cold mountains, waiting for us to perish. I want the prosperity that Osavian has enjoyed for centuries, leaving Murvort to fend for ourselves through famine and droughts."

She had a point there. Wasn't that why I was sent to marry Cyrus? To gain his favor and help my people back home in Dreslen?

She continued. "I want to see you and your brother on your knees. I want to see you beg for mercy."

Ladon scoffed. "It's a good thing you're used to failure, Reyna. You'll never be a queen, and you'll never see me beg."

Reyna rose to her feet with a scowl. Lightning cracked in the sky and it occurred to me that perhaps her power manifested in the stormy weather. The looming fog. The sunless sky. The electricity in the air was as wild and chaotic as she was.

She snapped her fingers, and thunder boomed. I watched with terror, waiting for something to happen. She stared down at us through her long dark lashes. The corner of her mouth turned up in a feral, terrorizing grin.

Just when I was beginning to think nothing was happening, that her command had gone unanswered, I heard something moving behind me. Something rustling the twigs and loose soil. I looked over my shoulder and my eyes went wide as I shouted in horror.

A large black snake slithered from the hedge maze, down the marble steps, making its way closer to Ladon and I. I jumped to my feet as best as I could, putting distance between myself and the latest arrival to this party of lunacy.

The snake was at least twenty feet long, and the thickest section of its torso was larger than my waist. It could crush me in a matter of seconds if it chose to. If Reyna commanded it to.

It inched its way toward the platform, slithering right between Ladon and I. I took another step back for good measure. Ladon didn't show any fear, just an uneasy bob of the throat as he swallowed. As for me, my icy tremors turned to beads of sweat.

Even the two hellhounds looked apprehensive. One whined but halted immediately when Reyna shot it a look of malice. It drooped its head after being silently scolded by its owner. I almost felt bad for the creature until I remembered how it had terrorized me.

"Do you like my pets?" Reyna asked, and I realized her attention was once again focused on me. "Nova and Nox are still puppies. Bred them myself with starlight and things that hide in the depths of the mountains. Things that make even *my* skin crawl."

She bent down and scratched one hound behind the ear. "They're very energetic and their eagerness makes them hard to tame at times. But they're learning."

If those things were puppies, then I didn't want to know what a fully grown hellhound looked like.

"But Vessina, my viper, I've had her for decades. She's well trained. Patient. She knows how to extend the pain without completely incapacitating her prey. She's cool and calculated. Much like me. I'm sure you can appreciate the similarities."

Reyna paced back and forth on the platform and, oddly enough, Vessina swerved back and forth in time with her master. Her black scales matched Reyna's dress and her beady eyes had a sliver of orange down the center.

"So...you don't intend to play nicely, Ladon? What a shame. I don't think you're going to like Vessina's games. Vessina," she pointed her finger to the snake and then flicked it toward Ladon. "Play."

The snake reacted quickly, turning from the platform and coming straight for Ladon and I. She closed the distance in a matter of seconds, rearing her head to strike. The shadow of her massive figure swallowed us entirely. Vessina hissed and bared her venomous fangs.

Something foreign tugged at my core, unwilling to let Ladon endure the assault. Gods knew he didn't deserve my consideration or my interference. But I darted in front of him anyway, and rather than attacking Ladon, Vessina drove her fangs into my shoulder.

Those sharp ivory teeth cut through my skin with such ease. She latched on while her venom surged into me.

I screamed. The pain was blinding. A million times worse than the damage the hellhound had done to my leg. Like a thousand tiny shards of glass had been injected into my veins. They multiplied and shredded my very soul as they spread through my body.

I shook violently, but Vessina didn't let go. She kept her fangs buried deep into my skin and muscle. The pain was so excruciating; I wondered if she'd pierced the bone, too. I felt her everywhere, even in my mind. She was all I could see. My heart pumped wildly, seemingly fighting against the intrusion, but it backfired as the venom spread.

I was faintly aware of Reyna laughing in the distance and Ladon's hands grabbing me from behind. He didn't pull or try to rip me from the viper. Likely knowing that if he tried, Vessina would only dig her fangs in deeper. Ladon simply held me up. He kept me grounded, whispering something that sounded like *hold on, Emilie.*

"You stupid girl," Reyna said with a shrill laugh. "Vessina, release her."

The viper pulled her fangs from my shoulder, and cool air whipped around the puncture. Two gaping holes were left behind and what should have been a relief was more like salt on a wound. I gritted my teeth and tried to breathe through my agony.

My body slumped against Ladon, and I felt myself being lowered to the ground. He held me in his lap, against his chest. There should've been warmth where our bodies met, but I just felt cold.

"Hold on, Emilie," he said again. I didn't have the energy to respond. It took everything in me to keep my eyelids open. My head lolled to the side, resting against his shoulder.

"What are we going to do with you now?" Reyna asked with an air of amusement. Like my impending death was no more consequential than a spilled glass of wine. The disposal of my body would be a mere inconvenience for her.

I licked my lips—parched. I'd give anything for a glass of water right now. My body was shriveling up. My eyes hurt and I considered if it would be better to just close them.

Ladon shook me gently. "Don't you dare give up. Do you hear me?"

Reyna chuckled. "How sweet...it doesn't really matter how hard she fights, though. The venom will kill her eventually. If only there were an antidote..."

Through my blurred vision, I watched Reyna dip her hand into a pocket and pull out a small glass vial with a cork stopper. The liquid inside was black and thick like syrup.

"I don't want to play your fucking games," Ladon snarled. "If that's an antidote, then give it to me now."

"Ladon, Ladon. I'm not sure where you get your insolence. Look around you." She paused for dramatic effect. "Does it look like you're in any position to be making demands?"

I felt his heavy breathing against my back. I heard his heart hammering with rage. The rapid rhythm grew louder in my ears. I realized my other senses were growing stronger while my vision went entirely black.

The end drew closer, and I panicked. "Ladon..."

"It's going to be fine, Emilie," he said softly.

"I wouldn't make promises you can't keep," Reyna said.

He huffed. "What do you want? What will it take for that vial in your hands, you wretched bitch?"

"For starters, I'm going to require that you never call me that again. You may call me Reyna, or you may call me your beautiful queen. Either will do."

"You're not a fucking queen and you never will be, *Reyna*."

"Look at that," she exclaimed. "He obeys. What a good dog. I'll have you trained like my hellhounds in no time."

Ladon was vibrating with wrath. If Reyna didn't stop taunting him, he might explode. I couldn't see his expression, so I reached for his face. I felt his ear first, then the stubble on his cheek. He leaned into my palm in an oddly compassionate move. One I never would've expected from him.

Tears rolled down my face as I struggled to breathe.

"Please," he pleaded, his jaw rippling under my fingertips.

"And what will you give me in return?" Reyna asked.

"Whatever you want."

"Anything?" Her tone expressed her delight.

"Anything."

There was a pause, and then Ladon jerked. I couldn't see, but it sounded like he'd caught something—the vial.

He pressed it to my lips. "Drink."

The sludge poured into my mouth and down my throat, almost making me gag. I didn't have time to worry if it had been a trick. If there had been no antidote and only more misery to be found at the bottom of the vial. Reyna clearly loved to play games, but drinking the concoction was my only option.

I felt it travel down my esophagus and my stomach churned as it settled there. I coughed and sputtered, but did not expel the contents.

Slowly, the feeling in my fingertips returned. My vision was no longer black, although it was incredibly blurry. I could only make out shapes and colors like I was looking through clouded glass.

I found the strength to sit up on my own, but pain lanced through my spine. My face contorted with anguish, and Ladon cradled me once more.

"You said it was an antidote," he growled.

"I did," Reyna replied. "I never said it would be pleasant, though. It'll take a while for the potion to dissolve the venom in her body. Vessina had her fangs in for quite some time, so I imagine there's a lot lingering in poor Emilie's veins."

I hated the way they were speaking about me, as if I couldn't hear. I tried to voice my frustration, but another blast of pain surged through me and my eyes rolled in the back of my head. I seized, and Ladon held me tightly.

After the tremors passed, I slumped again. Every last drop of my energy had been used up in those moments. Survival seemed impossible.

"You're in for a very long night, I'm afraid," Reyna said.

Chapter Fifteen

Ladon

Reyna grew bored with her games while Emilie writhed in my arms. Her eyes were unseeing and glazed over. They flitted from side to side, seeming to search for something. I couldn't help but blame myself for what had happened. It was my duty, above all else, to protect, and I had failed.

"Get up. Pick her up," Reyna said.

A mystical power coursed through my veins; a power that wasn't my own. It seemed to stem from those tattooed vines wrapped around my wrists, and now I realized my ankles as well.

Despite how badly I wanted to disregard her demands, my body began to move. Whatever magic stemmed from those vines had taken root, had dug its way into my nervous system and maneuvered me like a puppet.

I rose to my feet with Emilie's limp body lying across my arms.

"Follow me." As soon as Reyna spoke, the platform shifted and a steep staircase formed down the center, leading up to her. It was a sign of her confidence in her magic tricks that she allowed me to approach. She knew as well as I did that these mystical binds had anchored.

I carried Emilie up the steps while Reyna moved inside an enormous oak door. I studied it as I entered. Symbols decorated the edges in an old language I couldn't understand. They glowed a blue light once I passed, and I had the sinking feeling of being trapped.

Reyna led us through passages, up and down flights of stairs. The hallways were dark and disorienting. No distinguishing features to help me make sense of the route we'd taken.

We finally stopped outside a bedroom on a lower level. It reeked of grime and mold. Puddles of water lay stagnant on the hard floor in front of the bedroom door. When Reyna opened it, she gave me a sinister smile.

"I hope you like it. I've been waiting for over a decade to let someone use this guest room." She chuckled cruelly.

The *guest room* was a cell, ten feet across and ten feet wide. The walls and floor were made of a black stone that seemed to suck the light from the room. There was one small opening on the ceiling covered by a grate with small slats, the only source of light the room had to offer. Unfortunately, it also provided dripping water, which landed in a metal bucket.

Clang. Clang. Clang.

It was enough to drive me mad.

A single mattress sat in the corner of the room. It was thin, barely five inches off the ground, and a worn, dirty white sheet was the only blanket atop it.

"How generous of you," I said quietly.

"What was that?" Reyna slid a finger down the back of my arm and I shivered, fighting the urge to break her hand.

"Nothing."

I lowered Emilie to the mattress and covered her with the sheet. She was still twitching and making little whimpering noises. It was probably for the best that she remained unconscious. It was clear from Reyna's warning that it was going to be a painful experience getting rid of the venom in her body.

The door creaked, and I turned to find Reyna slowly closing it. The corner of her mouth rose when our eyes met. "I'll be back when I have use for you. Have a good night."

The latch clicked shut, and I heard the clatter of locks turning on the other side of the door. If I had my magic, I could've blasted through it easily, but I'd have to get creative instead.

I looked down at the vines weaving between my fingers and crawling up my forearms. Was I imagining it, or had they spread?

It was a magic I'd never seen before. I examined them, the way the inky black melted into my skin. There was no way to remove them aside from cutting my limbs off. Could I use my siphon abilities on them? They were a source of magic, after all.

It was worth a shot.

I focused on the familiar pulling feeling, on absorbing the magic into my veins and bending it to my will. Inhaling it in like oxygen to empty lungs.

Needles pricked at my temple, and I doubled over coughing. The same pounding headache from when I'd first tried my magic returned to me now.

I rubbed my temples and prayed for it to cease. "Fuuuck."

"Ladon..."

Emilie stirred in the bed, looking around in confusion. There were tears in her eyes, but she wasn't grimacing in pain. At least not for now.

"How are you feeling?"

"Not great...I think I might throw up."

I didn't doubt it. Her face was paler than usual. "Let me see if I can get you a glass of water."

She nodded with her hand pressed to her mouth.

On the left side of the room, a rectangle hole had been cut out. No door, only a tall opening that led to a dark and dirty bathroom. In the corner was a shower with no curtain. The metal fixtures were rusted and the tile floor looked like it hadn't been cleaned in years. Next to it was a single toilet with a closed lid. I didn't even want to look inside to see what horrors lay beneath. And on the wall was a white ceramic sink with a murky mirror above it.

There was also a cabinet, and when I peered inside, I found a handful of raggedy towels, washcloths, half-empty bottles of soap, a couple of toothbrushes, and a few other simple hygienic items. Miraculously, there was also a small cup, just large enough to rinse your mouth after brushing, but it would have to do.

I turned the faucet on, and the water came out crystal clear. I almost moaned in relief. The stream was slow, so I waited with the cup held under the faucet, watching Emilie in the mirror.

She was laying down, curled in a ball. It was hard to assess her pain levels. How much was she letting me see, and how much was she trying to hide? She wiped a shaky hand over her brow and sighed.

I didn't want to watch anymore. I was still furious that she'd been invited to travel with us. She had no one to blame but herself for the predicament she was in.

No, I didn't believe that.

It's true she would've been safe right now if she hadn't come with us, but the blame should lie solely with Reyna. Heinous bitch.

I pinched the bridge of my nose as I shut the faucet off.

What were we going to do?

The one thing that gave me hope was knowing Cyrus had made it out. I hoped he'd made it home safely and had gotten messages to the other outposts. He could round up our troops and storm Murvort. Even if he thought Emilie and I were dead, he would surely retaliate. Right?

I wasn't entirely sure where Reyna had taken us, but I assumed we were beneath her castle in the mountains. The black walls appeared to be made of the natural stone of the Murvort mountain ranges.

Emilie straightened as I knelt down beside the bed. I pressed the cup into her trembling hands. "Here."

She drank with caution, barely making a dent in the glass I'd poured for her. "Thank you. Are you...are you okay?"

"I'm fine," I said without giving it any consideration. I didn't have any other options but to be fine. Someone needed to keep it together and make sure we made it out of here alive.

Emilie sighed and placed the cup next to the bed. She settled in, crossing her arms over her stomach again.

"How much pain are you in?"

"I'll be okay."

"That's not what I asked."

Her eyes fluttered closed. "Maybe an eight out of ten? I don't know. I feel like my insides are disintegrating, but it comes in waves."

Eight out of ten? She sure was handling it well. "Try to get some sleep."

She opened her eyes and stared at me. "What are you going to do?"

I shook my head. What was there *to* do? We were locked in a tiny cube with the bare necessities. I could shower, but I didn't have any clean clothes, so the thought of putting dirty clothes back on prevented me from doing so.

I sat, my knees drawn in and my back pressed against the damp wall. Everything felt damp and dismal here. "I'll be sitting here."

She seemed to hesitate for a moment. Then she slid till her back was pressed against the wall. "There's enough room for both of us."

I looked at the tiny mattress. She was already taking up half of it and she was much smaller than I was. There was no way we would both fit without touching.

"I'll pass."

Emilie rolled her eyes and then rolled over so her back faced me. "Suit yourself," she mumbled.

I leaned my head back and closed my eyes, but I doubted I'd be getting any sleep. Water continued to drip into the metal bucket. Already, my muscles felt stiff from the day's travel, from the battle at Fort Malek, and then from Reyna's nightmarish hedge maze.

Reyna was hard to figure out. I'd always believed that she wasn't quite right in the head. Her methods for getting what she wanted never made any sense to me. She'd rather play games and mess with people's minds than just get straight to the point, which is probably why she'd always failed to get what she wanted.

But it also made it tricky to predict her moves. What twisted schemes did she have planned for us next?

I shivered. Our room was like an ice chamber. My attire was prime for the moderate weather of Osavian, not the frozen depths of Murvort.

I eyed the mattress with a twinge of jealousy. The thought of lying down and using the blanket, no matter how thin, did sound nice.

"Emilie," I whispered.

No response.

I crawled to the bed and climbed in, removing my shoes as I went. The mattress was so thin it hardly had any room to shift with my weight, so I didn't have to worry about waking Emilie. She didn't move at all while I pulled the sheet over my legs and up to my shoulders.

If I slept on my side, then our bodies wouldn't touch. So I turned away from her and closed my eyes.

I woke when a body collided with mine, shoving me forward and tumbling across me. Emilie scrambled to her feet and fled to the bathroom. I was still half asleep when I heard her retching.

"Gods, kill me," I murmured while rubbing my eyes. I rolled out of bed and walked toward the bathroom to find Emilie on her knees, hair pulled back and bent over the toilet. "Do you need more water?"

She cursed between a few unintelligible words. I assumed that meant yes.

I retrieved the glass of water from beside the bed, topped it off, and returned it to her. She flushed the toilet and leaned back, and I was delighted to find that the pot didn't look nearly as horrendous as the shower did.

Emilie took a sip of water and sighed.

"How are you feeling?"

"I've felt better." She took another sip and stared into the cup. "Do you think she's poisoned this?"

I shook my head, sliding to the floor next to her. "I doubt it. That would be too easy for Reyna. She'll have a much worse demise planned for us."

I locked eyes with Emilie, who looked at me with a pathetic vulnerability. If she didn't toughen up, she wouldn't make it out of here alive.

She tucked a curl behind her ear. "What are we going to do?"

We. I didn't like the way the word sounded on her lips. A grating reminder that we only had each other here.

"First, you need to get better. You'll never get out of here if you're still doubled over in pain, hurling into a toilet."

"You wouldn't leave me, would you?" Her voice raised an octave, and I whipped my head back in her direction.

"When did I fucking say that?"

"You didn't. You just—"

"Do *not* put words in my mouth, princess."

"I didn't mean to. I thought—"

"I could, you know. I could leave you here. It wouldn't bother me in the slightest. You don't belong in Renoa. You don't belong with Cyrus."

I stood. Anger rising in me again. Fury at the fact that we were trapped in a dark room under the mountains. Pissed that Cyrus hadn't listened to me. And livid that of all the people I could've been stuck with, Emilie was the one sitting on the floor beside me.

Emilie looked as though I'd slapped her across the face. She stood and moved close; her head coming just below my chin. She glared up at me with fiery brown eyes. When she prodded me in the chest with a single finger, I took a step back.

"*What* did I *ever* do to you, Ladon Castelli?" She punctuated certain words with a sharp jab to my sternum. "Were you born with a gigantic *stick* up your ass? Have you been *knocked* on your *head* one too many times during training? I would say you didn't get enough love as a child, but I know Sophia and Cyrus too well to think that could be true. So what is it? Huh? What is *wrong* with you?"

133

"What did I say about touching me?" I grabbed her by her slender shoulders and slammed her against the wall. "Nothing is wrong with me. The only thing wrong is that I have to share this space with an insufferable brat like you. I fought in Fort Malek to protect *you*. If it weren't for you, I wouldn't even be *here*."

I shook her a little, my fingers digging into her flesh, but she seemed unfazed. She only pushed me off and stormed out of the bathroom, back to the bed on the floor. "Oh, *poor* Ladon. I've *ruined* your whole life, haven't I?"

Her tone was anything but sympathetic. I didn't expect her to be, but I also didn't think she'd have such an attitude with me. She huffed and pulled her hair back into a bun.

"What are you doing?" I asked, watching as she tossed the blanket aside and crawled back into bed. She spread out, not bothering to make herself seem small. She didn't leave any space for me.

"I'm going to bed. You can sleep on the fucking floor."

Chapter Sixteen

Ladon

THE SOUND OF METAL scraping across the floor made me pry my eyes open. I'd slept in the corner of the room opposite of Emilie. Perhaps it was my own fault that she chose not to share the bed after our spat, but I'd never been good at controlling my temper. Something about Emilie always made the heat rise in me and if I didn't release it, I'd explode. My neck cracked as I turned toward the source of the noise.

Emilie had overturned the bucket and now stood on top, reaching toward the grate on the ceiling. She grabbed it and shook and the thing rattled, but remained in place. Meanwhile, the bucket she stood on slid an inch in the puddle of water that was now on the floor.

"Have you lost your mind?" I mumbled.

She smacked her hand against the grate, in a move that I was sure had to do more damage to her palm than it did to the metal bars. "Maybe. I can't just sit around doing nothing like you."

"Beg your pardon," I said, sitting up now. "What the hell do you mean by that? We've been here less than a day and you spent most of that time incapacitated and heaving over a toilet."

"And you did nothing." She flung her hands above her head, exasperated. "I expected the *almighty* Ladon to have had us out by now. After all, you can do no wrong. You're *so* perfect and everyone else is beneath you."

I rolled my eyes and mumbled under my breath. "I'm glad you're coming to that realization."

"What?" Her eyes widened. She looked more crazed than I'd ever seen her and a part of me wanted to laugh. Gods, it was so easy to get under her skin. But I also knew if I let out even the smallest chuckle, she'd probably throw herself across the room and slam her tiny fists into any part of me she could reach.

I massaged my temples. I was too exhausted to start the day like this. "Listen, we need to get along if we're going to get out of here alive. Can we not start the day with arguing?"

The noise that came out of her was manic. Like releasing a screech and simultaneously trying to hold it back. It sounded a bit like an animal in heat and once again I had to stifle a laugh. My shoulders shook a little, but she didn't notice.

She took several deep breaths before speaking again. "Fine. We can call a truce. Now would you help me try to open this grate?"

There was no point, but I stood to humor her anyway. She pushed and pulled at the metal bars while I took the few steps across the room to her. All it took was one misstep, one toe over the edge of the bucket's flat surface, and the thing went sliding across the room.

And Emilie fell backwards.

Instinctively, I reached out my arms to catch her, but she'd caught me so off guard, we both went tumbling to the floor.

My back crashed into the hard black stone, and the weight of Emilie slamming into my chest took my breath away. Her forehead collided with my chin and I bit into my lip. I could taste the blood almost immediately.

Emilie struggled against my body, one of her lean legs creating friction between my thighs. She pressed her palms into my chest, her pelvis pushing into mine. Her top was disheveled and I could see the curves of her breast with unsettling clarity.

"Emilie, please," I said between gritted teeth. She continued to move clumsily over me, failing to right herself. I grabbed her by the waist and forced her to remain still. If she wiggled against me any further, I might not be able to control my body's response.

She pushed her hair back from her face before finally managing to sit up. My heart thudded at the sight of her perched on top of me, looking flushed and on edge.

She seemed to realize her position after a few seconds and leaped off me. I stood as quickly as possible and turned my back to her. I could feel the heat in my own cheeks and didn't want her to see me flustered.

How was it possible that someone as unbearable as Emilie could have *that* effect on me?

No, she couldn't. There was no way. It was simply my body betraying me. A physical reaction and nothing more.

I swiped my hand through my hair and then turned around after regaining my composure.

Emilie was staring at me like she was waiting for me to combust. A fair concern, considering the way I'd reacted every other time she touched me.

"Ladon, I'm so—"

The sound of a key rattling in the door made Emilie pause, and we both straightened. I headed for the door, Emilie not far behind me, and it opened at the same time I reached for the handle.

"Step back," Reyna said with a finger pointed at the center of my chest.

Despite having no intention of following her directions, the vines encircling my wrists and ankles burned with the need to obey.

I stepped back and Emilie did too, with a look of horror. I realized this was the first time she'd experienced the strength of our magical bindings. Her arms were pinned tightly to her side. It was as if the magic sensed her struggle and fought harder against it.

I kept that in mind as I allowed the vines to guide me where they wanted. Reyna moved further into the room with two of her minions behind her, dressed in all black with face paint distorting their features. Beneath the paint I could see scarred, mangled flesh. I wasn't entirely sure that they were human.

"I have a job for you to assist with today. If I'm going to give you free room and board, the least you could do is help me prepare for a party this evening. The dining hall will need a deep clean as well as the drawing room. You can follow me."

We didn't have the chance to deny her. Reyna exited the room first, while Emilie and I followed mindlessly. The two henchmen trailed behind us.

Reyna again took us on what I suspected to be a roundabout path to the dining hall and kitchen. I tried to tally the turns and memorize the marks on the walls, but they all blended together.

Eventually, we came to a chamber filled almost entirely by a dark walnut table adorned with a black and turquoise floral arrangement in the center. A dozen chairs were spaced evenly around the table and a plush black and emerald rug was laid underneath.

There were no windows in the dining room, giving it a stifling atmosphere. It smelled like dust and damp, mountainous rock. A fireplace roared, and I embraced the warmth of its flames. Golden candelabras lined the exterior walls, flickering softly despite the still air.

Reyna pointed toward a sponge and bucket. "These floors will need scrubbed, and the mantle needs dusted. Once you're done with that, the furniture in the drawing room has some stains that need tidied up. I want all of it sparkling clean by the time my house guests arrive this evening. That should give you about...seven hours," she noted after checking the clock above the fireplace.

Emilie and I shared a suspicious glance. This couldn't be all that Reyna wanted from us. Her big evil plan was to imprison us as housekeepers?

"And if we don't?"

She sneered. "Then Luther and Tristan have my permission to punish you as they see fit." She looked toward her guards and they nodded in understanding.

The skirt of her black dress swirled behind her as she left the dining room. Her two wardens stayed behind, guarding the open door to the hallway and another closed door, which I suspected connected the dining room to the kitchen.

"Well, you heard her. I guess we should get started," I said.

Emilie didn't move. I could see the wheels turning in her mind, though I wasn't sure what exactly she was thinking. She whispered so the guards wouldn't hear. "This is absurd. We shouldn't be scrubbing her floors. We should be looking for a way out. Aren't you supposed to be a war god or something?"

I huffed a laugh. "You're living in a fairytale, princess. In the real world, things don't work that easily. I don't have any weapons. I don't have any magic. And I don't have my armies. What is it exactly that you think I can do?"

"I don't know. Can't you take out the guards? If we get their weapons then we can find a way out of here and run back to Osavian."

"Do you know the way, princess? I didn't realize you were familiar with the layout of this prison." I couldn't help the sarcasm in my tone. Emilie seemed to bring out the worst in me. "And what happens once we've escaped? *If* we escape? We'll likely starve to death or die of extreme cold out in those mountains. No, it's best to stay here and keep our heads down until we have a solid plan."

Emilie looked indignant. "Fine. I'll dust. You scrub."

She flicked her hair over her shoulder as she headed toward the fireplace.

I couldn't remember the last time I'd scrubbed a floor. Never, perhaps? I was pretty certain that usually there was a mop involved, not a tiny sponge, barely the size of my hand.

I knelt before dunking the sponge into the soapy water, which had cooled to room temperature, and began to work on the spotted floors.

"What the hell is this?" Emilie asked. I looked to find her dragging a rag across the velvety arm of a sofa.

I shrugged. "Wine?"

She sat back and flung her hands into the air. "Wine isn't going to come out. This is pointless." She looked around the room as if she were trying to make sense of it all.

Much to my delight, the drawing room was the one place we'd been taken so far that had a window. I tried to inch closer to see where it led, but everytime I did, the guard moved toward me. Eventually, I gave up. It was nearing sunset, and the light cast a cool glow over Emilie's freckled skin.

"Are you getting anywhere?" she asked me.

The entire day had been plagued by Emilie's pestering and attempts to make small talk. I just wanted to be left alone with my thoughts. To think of other ways to escape or outsmart Reyna.

"Did you hear me?" she asked, her mouth pressed into a thin line.

"I heard you."

When she realized I had no intention of answering her question, she rolled her eyes and began scrubbing again.

By the time Reyna returned, my back ached from being hunched over all day. My fingers were pruned from scrubbing floors and furniture. I clutched at my stomach, hoping to silence the continuous growling noise.

Reyna's eyes shone with delight when she caught my movement.

We hadn't been fed all day, but I chose not to say anything. I didn't want to give her the satisfaction of thinking she'd somehow bested me.

"Something wrong, dear?" she asked with feigned concern.

"Just a little nauseous at the sight of such a heinous creature."

The color drained from Reyna's face. She looked as though she'd tasted something foul herself. She snapped her fingers and her henchmen appeared at her side. "Luther, take her back to her room. I have plans for this one."

I ground my teeth, but watched in silence as the taller man escorted Emilie away.

Reyna spoke without turning away from me. "Tristan, will you go make sure my hounds are fed?"

Tristan grimaced but nodded and left the room.

Just Reyna and I now. I would've loved to wring her neck, but I knew the vines across my skin would stop me before I got very far.

Reyna let out a long breath through her nose.

"I always knew you were the more stubborn of the Castelli brothers." She stepped closer and began to circle me, dragging a fingertip down my arm that made me shudder. Then she leaned in close, close enough for me to feel the heat of her breath on my ear, and whispered, "I can't wait to break you."

"Why are you doing this, Reyna? What's your plan? You wanted to bring us here to clean your floors?"

"Well, if you must know; my initial plan was to kill Cyrus obviously and take Osavian for myself," she stated rather matter-of-factly.

"That's ridiculous. They'd never follow you. There'd be a rebellion and our people would burn the kingdom to the grown before they'd see you with a crown."

"That's where you'd come in. As long as I can make you submit, they'll follow your lead."

I laughed. "Well, that's even less likely to happen."

She smiled as her eyes roamed my body. "We'll see. Follow me, Ladon. I've got quite the surprise for you."

I found myself following her despite my unwillingness. Step one of whatever plan I concocted would need to revolve around removing these markings on my skin. I wouldn't get anywhere while Reyna still had a leash on me.

We turned a corner and then another. As High Commander, I'd practiced making mental maps on more than one occasion, but I wasn't prepared for the mazes of Murvort.

The hall began to slope downward, slightly at first and then more steeply. I stumbled to keep up with Reyna. My movements didn't quite feel my own while under her command. They were stiff and awkward, like my limbs could feel my mind's resistance.

Reyna smiled and winked at me when we reached our destination. One side of an iron double door was propped open. She extended an arm and gestured for me to step through the open archway.

Inside was a...bathtub? A huge rectangular tub that could fit a dozen people at once. I'd expected a torture chamber full of sick devices meant to inflict pain and suffering. Instead, steam rolled off crystal blue waters. A light emanated from the bottom and illuminated the two steps down into the tub. On the far end, a ledge for soaking was visible.

I looked back at Reyna, and she was a vision of depravity.

She returned to that cat-like prowl she'd demonstrated before. "I like to come here sometimes to relax. To sit, think. Maybe even find a little *pleasure.*"

My skin crawled, and I tried to look away—at the ceiling or toward the pile of linens in the corner. My eyes caught on a counter with wine and bite-sized appetizers before Reyna's fingernails grazed my cheek.

To my horror, she'd stepped out of her dress and now stood completely naked before me. Reyna was less than a decade older than me, and she had a lithe figure with smooth porcelain skin. But there was no part of me that wanted to look down. She was a horrible excuse for a human being and no amount of beauty would make up for it.

"What—"

She silenced me with the tip of her finger across my lips. "Where are my manners? Look at you. You're filthy. That's no way for any guest to stay at my home. Let's get you cleaned up."

My mind was humming, and my throat constricted. The steam in the air clouded my vision and felt unnatural in my lungs. Between the lack of food and sleep, I was feeling lightheaded and unable to truly comprehend what was happening.

Reyna sauntered to the steps and walked down into the tub, trailing her fingers across the top of the water. It rippled, and tendrils of steam rose around her. I waited as she moved to sit on the ledge and turned to face me again.

I froze while she watched me expectantly. "You can't get in the bath with your clothes on, silly. Take them off."

It took more effort than usual to swallow. My lip twitched, but my hands obediently pried at the hem of my shirt, untucking it from my pants and pulling it over my head.

Reyna smiled as she took in the hard ridges of my abs and the curves of my shoulders and biceps. I was fuming, but there wasn't anything I could do. I was her plaything, a puppet, while she dangled the strings.

When her eyes fell to my groin, I wanted to vomit. But I unbuttoned my pants anyway, just as she knew I would, kicking off my shoes and socks in the process. My pants fell to the floor along with my undergarments, leaving me completely exposed.

Her eyes roamed my body, and she bit her lower lip. "Get in the water."

Chapter Seventeen

Emilie

I TRIED NOT TO think of where Reyna had taken Ladon. It was unlikely he'd be worried about me if the roles were reversed. But sitting in our quiet, empty room made me miss his presence for the first time. Or maybe I just didn't want to be alone.

The grate in the ceiling was dripping again, so I replaced the bucket beneath it. I decided to take a shower to help pass the time, and because I felt disgusting. My clothes were still dirty from the attack and the maze, and now they also smelled like fabric cleaner from scrubbing upholstery all day.

Even though I hoped he'd return soon, I wanted the opportunity to shower on my own. Since the bathroom had no door, only a rectangle cut into the wall, privacy was severely lacking around here. The shower didn't even have a curtain. Only a half-wall that came up slightly above my breasts.

I stripped and set my clothes on the closed lit of the toilet, then turned the knobs inside the shower. Thankfully, the water was warm. I quickly scrubbed and used the provided soaps to wash my hair, face, and body. Even though I knew it wouldn't do any good, I also took extra time to scrub at the black vines on my skin. Had I imagined it, or had they spread even further?

Stepping out of the shower, I grabbed a towel to dry off, my eyes catching on the clothes I'd set on top of the toilet. They were now clean and folded in a neat pile. Thank the gods for that magical kindness, because I was dreading putting them back on.

The bedroom was still empty, and with nothing else to do, I decided to lay down on the bed.

I hadn't expected to fall asleep, but the next thing I knew, Ladon was stepping into the bedroom as the door slammed behind him. I startled and sat up, expecting him to tell me where he'd been—what had happened.

But he immediately headed for the bathroom without a word to me. The shower turned on and I settled back into bed. I'd gotten my moment of privacy, so he should get his as well. He could fill me in once he finished.

Except...the water continued to run. I waited and waited...and waited. And he'd accused me of being a pampered princess. I didn't think I'd ever known someone to take such long showers.

Once I'd lost all patience, I stepped out of bed and tiptoed to the bathroom.

"Ladon?" I called out to him before peering around the corner. I didn't see his head or shoulders above the dividing wall, though the water was still running. "Ladon?"

I edged closer to the shower, worst-case scenarios running through my head. He'd been poisoned like I'd been. He was now dying—or was already dead.

What I found felt worse somehow.

He was sitting with his knees pulled to his chest, his head bowed down, with his hands threaded through his hair. Was he...crying?

I reached across him to shut off the water. He hardly moved at the disturbance. Even when I knelt next to him, he didn't acknowledge me.

"Ladon, are you hurt?" I asked, gently touching his shoulder.

His head snapped up, and he growled, "Don't. Touch. Me."

If his words hadn't frightened me, then the look on his face would've. His eyes were dark, swallowing all of the striking silver-blue that I'd come to know so well. His face appeared to be drained of life entirely, his skin pale and showing all the jagged edges of his jawline and cheekbones.

"What happened?"

"Nothing," he said quietly.

I could've pressed him further, but it was clear he was in no mood to talk. So, I stood and grabbed a towel from the cabinet.

"Here," I said, extending it out to him.

He looked at it for a moment, his eyes still vacant. Then he slowly stood, and I had to look away quickly. Ladon's naked body was more than I was prepared to handle. What little I saw of him was lean and sculpted and still dripping wet. It was enough to make my cheeks flush.

Ladon wrapped the towel around his lower half and combed his fingers through his sopping hair.

"If you won't tell me what happened, can you at least tell me that you're okay?"

He gave me a curt nod before striding past me into the bedroom. I watched as he crawled into bed, still wrapped in only a towel. "I'm not sleeping on the floor again."

I was stunned into silence. Once I finally found my ability to move, I crossed the room to join him in bed. Ladon was turned on his side so his back faced me and I lay on my back, staring at the ceiling. I couldn't tell if he'd already fallen asleep or not.

"Are you awake?"

"No."

I smiled despite myself. "Do you think your brother is looking for us?"

Ladon sighed, his irritation evident. "Probably, though I don't know if they'll find us here."

"What do you mean?" The panic in my voice was unmistakable, but he made no effort to comfort me.

"No one in Osavian has ventured this far into Murvort. At least, no one that's still alive. The only place we've been invited to in my lifetime is the settlement near our outpost. The mountains themselves could disorient the most seasoned hiker. Who knows how far we've traveled inside them."

So there was no hope then. The entire army of Osavian could be scouring the country and there was still a chance they wouldn't find us. It would be entirely up to us to save ourselves. No one was coming.

I swallowed, and tears pricked my eyes. I whispered, "I don't want to die here."

Ladon rolled over and I met his gaze, his face startling close to mine. "We're not going to."

A light pierced through the thin skin of my eyelids and woke me from my restless sleep. Somehow, the light from outside had managed to find just the right angle to stream in through the open grate.

My eyes fluttered open, and I inhaled a sharp breath. At some point in the night, I had turned and now faced Ladon, who was a mere inch from my face. I tried to scoot back, but a heavy arm pulled me in tight. *Oh shit.*

There was enough space for me to observe our lower halves—legs tangled together, Ladon's towel hanging low on his hips, a trail of fine hair leading from his belly button to the bulge pressed against my thigh. *Oh shit.*

I let out an involuntary whimper, but thankfully, Ladon didn't stir. His chest rose and fell with shallow breaths and his lips parted slightly. His usual guarded demeanor was nowhere to be found.

Digging his fingers into the small of my back, he let out a low hum. I held my breath, fearful that any noise or movement might wake him up and there was no telling how he'd respond to this predicament.

I gently lifted his arm—enough for me to slip out from his grasp. He mumbled again, and I moved slower. Like prey escaping from a dragon's nest. Every inch was torturous.

Finally, I managed to roll off the mattress and onto the floor. While ordinarily I would hate how low the mattress sat, this time I was thankful to not fall clumsily out of bed.

I snuck to the bathroom and tried to freshen up as quietly as possible. When I returned, Ladon was still sleeping peacefully. I almost hated to wake him, but it had to be late morning by the way the sunlight was falling into the room.

He'd been so broken and lifeless the night before. I didn't know what had happened with Reyna, but something in me wanted to give him a little bit more time to dream without worry. To rest without despair.

Just a few more minutes, I thought.

If only we'd been given paper or something useful in this bare box of a bedroom. I sat with my back against the wall, listening to the soft sounds of Ladon breathing. My eyes fell to my hands, and I was tempted to test my magic again, but feared the consequences.

Part of Reyna's plan must've been to drive us crazy with boredom because after five minutes of staring into the void, my fingers tapped restlessly against my knee.

A knock at the door relieved me from my misery. I shot to my feet while Ladon finally stirred.

"What was that?" he mumbled.

I reached the door, which I realized was pointless right around the time it swung open. I couldn't have opened it even if I'd tried. One of Reyna's burly guards, Luther, stepped forward with a tray in his hands.

"Back against the wall," he commanded.

He waited until my back pressed against the cool black stone and then he sat the tray on the ground. He kept his eyes trained on me until the door closed once more.

I sprinted forward to see what he'd brought. It smelled enticing, and I allowed myself to hope that it might be something appetizing. Once I was close enough, I could see two plates of eggs, bacon, and toast. In addition, there were two glasses of juice.

I fell to my knees and thanked the gods. It had been over a day without anything to eat and only water to drink. My uncertainty kicked in like an unwelcome house guest and my shoulders slumped.

"Well, what is it?" Ladon asked from behind me. I looked up, and he was still clutching that white towel around his waist. I hated the way my skin grew warm.

"Do you mind putting on some clothes?"

He ignored me entirely and bent down to examine the tray. I could still smell the rose-laced soap from the shower emanating from him.

Ladon grabbed a piece of toast and took a bite.

"What if that's poisoned?" My voice came out a higher pitch than I'd expected and he stared at me while he chewed and swallowed.

"You've already been poisoned once, princess. Do you really think Reyna would torture you without making a spectacle of it? Eat."

I huffed, but he didn't need to tell me twice. I dug into the eggs while Ladon went to put his clothes on. He returned, and we sat on the floor, eating our breakfast in awkward silence.

"So, are you going to tell me what happened yesterday?" I asked.

"No."

I shook my head, but secretly I was grateful that he had mostly returned to his usual grumpy self. This was the version of Ladon I knew how to deal with.

"Have you thought any more about how we might get out of here?"

He sat his cup down. "I was thinking about the tunnels."

"The tunnels?"

"Yes, I've read about a network of hidden tunnels in these mountains. Though I don't know much about them other than the fact that they exist. I know they are gods-made. They can appear and reappear in the blink of an eye. But I don't know where one would even begin to look for them."

"So you have nothing."

"Well, what's your brilliant plan then, princess?"

Steam rose from my ears. He was right, though. I didn't have any more of a plan than he did. "What about your siphoning abilities?"

"What about them?" He took a bite of his bacon before pointing at mine. "Are you going to finish that?"

"I suppose not. Can't you use them to—I don't know—drain the life force from these bindings?" I lifted my arms where the black vines were clearly visible in the daylight. They looked ghastly against my freckled skin.

"I've tried." He continued to chew his food without further explanation. I wanted to strangle him for his lack of regard for the situation.

"And?"

"Nothing happened. Well, that's not true. My head felt like it was splitting in half but"—he lifted his left wrist where vines still covered him too—"nothing happened."

"Damnit," I said, slamming my empty plate onto the tray.

"You need to keep a clear head. You have to keep your composure."

"Says the man who came back here last night and sulked for hours."

Ladon's eyes went pitch black as he scowled at me, and I regretted my words immediately. If Reyna didn't kill me, Ladon still might.

His voice was quiet, commanding all of my attention. "Don't speak about things you know nothing about."

There was an almost imperceptible shudder when he spoke to me. What in the hell had Reyna done to him? The more he thwarted my questions, the more curious I became. I didn't think it was possible to rattle Ladon like this.

We stared at each other while tension built between us, waiting for the first to snap, until the second knock of the morning rattled the door. Before we had a chance to rise to our feet, Reyna stepped inside.

She wore her usual black gown that shimmered and sparkled as she moved. This one had lace sleeves that resembled cobwebs, and when she moved a certain way, it looked as if there were actual spiders crawling along her limbs. It had to be a trick of the light. Then again, she was a psycho. They were probably more of her *pets*.

She tossed me a flippant look before sizing Ladon up. Perhaps it was my imagination, but I thought I saw Ladon's body go rigid before he settled into the calm and collected stature of a High Commander. He looked so determined not to let anything get to him.

"I hoped you enjoyed your breakfast. It was such a sacrifice for my people to offer you food this morning. I hope you appreciate it and really think about the toll you've taken on our community," Reyna droned on.

Her ridiculous pleas for gratitude wouldn't work on me. "You could always set us free. I wouldn't want to be a strain on Murvort's resources," I said with the same faux civility she'd shown us.

She smiled. "Nonsense, Emilie. I wouldn't dare prematurely toss out my guests. Especially not Osavian's finest."

I half expected Ladon to correct her. To inform her that I was Dreslen filth, but he remained silent.

Her eyes slid to Ladon, and out of the corner of my eye, I noticed him shift back and forth on his feet. He looked seconds away from tackling Reyna and strangling her to death.

"What is it that you want, Reyna?" I asked, drawing her attention back to me.

"I'm glad you asked. I'll need your help today sorting out the Scholars' Cavern. You see, we had a little quake a few weeks ago and all that shaking brought down shelves upon shelves of tomes. It's an absolute mess."

There were worse ways to be punished, I thought.

Chapter Eighteen

Emilie

CALLING THE SCHOLARS' CAVERN an absolute mess was an understatement. It was similar to a library, but one that had been demolished. Massive piles of books stretched farther than the eye could see. It was as if every tome had been pulled off the shelves and dumped into the middle of the cylindrical cave.

Speaking of shelves, nearly every single one had been toppled over. Some still stood on the main level of the cavern, fastened in place to the wall. But as I looked up, balcony after balcony had been damaged by shelves falling over the railings.

The cavern was stories high, with a staircase that spiraled up the circular walls. It stretched toward the sky and disappeared into blackness. It was impossible to tell how tall the cavern was. Stalactites hung haphazardly from the occasional stone that jutted out of the walls.

When Reyna first took us into the cavern's opening, we could hardly take more than ten steps before stumbling over mounds of books. Some of them appeared to be torn with cracked spines. Others looked like they had water damage from the cave's moisture. An assortment of pages littered the floor with no clue as to which book they belonged to.

Reyna looked around with her lip curled in a snarl. She winced.

"Like I said, an absolute mess. I'm sure this should keep you busy for a while."

She turned, and I watched as an invisible seal rippled behind her. Even with the vines on our wrists depriving us of our freedom, she didn't trust us enough to leave an open door. She hadn't left her henchmen behind, but I questioned whether the bats hanging from the balcony railings also reported to her. One ruffled its wings like it was insulted by the mere thought.

I've got my eye on you.

Ladon laced his fingers through his hair before placing his hands on his hips. He looked overwhelmed by the destruction and I felt the same way. He pointed toward a toppled shelf. "Help me lift this."

After hours of sorting through endless heaps of books, it looked as if we'd made no progress at all. We'd cleared out a five-foot square, but most of it had just been moved to a second pile that we'd started for disposal.

About halfway through the day, Luther stopped by and within the blink of an eye, vanished the pile of books that were unsalvageable. It created a little more space for us to sort through the endless stacks.

I wiped sweat from my brow while Ladon placed books on the top-most shelf. He'd been abnormally quiet while we worked. He hadn't even taken a moment to taunt or scold me.

"That one's upside down," I said.

He looked at me first and then stared at the row of books with a puzzled look. They were all right side up.

I laughed. "I'm just kidding."

"Ha ha," he deadpanned. I was happy the silence had finally been broken.

"Have you come across anything interesting?" I flipped through the pages of the book in my hand, a theoretical study of elemental magic. Dull, but potentially useful. Would it be possible to sneak it back to our room?

"This one is full of images of mythical creatures fornicating. A gryphon, a ghoul, a sea witch…"

"What?" I yelled, closing the distance between us. "You can't be serious. Let me see."

The corners of his mouth pulled up into a grin, and then he huffed a laugh. "I'm just kidding, princess."

My mouth fell open. His smile was disarming. I was so used to the annoyed looks and hateful words he threw my way that I was entirely stunned by this moment of jest.

He shook his head while he placed the book on the shelf. "My, my, do you have a tentacle kink or something, Emilie?" he teased.

I smacked his arm with the book in my hand. "No."

"It's okay if you do. Don't be ashamed."

"Stop it," I said, but giggled, nevertheless.

"I mean, I personally would never, but if you're into it—"

I prodded his side, and he laughed like he might be ticklish there. It dawned on me that this was the first time he'd allowed me to touch him without threatening my life in return.

"Unbelievable," I said, turning back to a messy pile of books. But out of the corner of my eye, I saw him still smiling. It was a breathtaking sight to behold.

We went back to working in silence all afternoon, though the air around me felt lighter somehow. I didn't realize how badly I needed the distraction but I'd never admit to Ladon that he helped in a way.

There was a stack of seven books that I wanted to take back to our bedroom, but I realized I'd have to pare it down. The most I could slip under my shirt without it being obvious was two.

"*The Power of Your Mind* or *Murvort's Mysteries*?" I asked Ladon, holding up two thick leather-bound books, one green and the other a mustard yellow.

"What is Murvort's Mysteries?"

"I think it's supposed to be a child's fictional tale, but I figured it wouldn't hurt to know some of the folklore around here. Dreslen's children's stories are often rooted in truth. Maybe there's something useful."

"Why not take both?"

"I can't. I can only take two and there's no way I can leave behind the *Medical Studies of Suppression and Neutralization.*"

He rolled his eyes as if I were being unreasonable.

"Here," I said, thrusting one into his hands. "You put it in your shirt."

"Emilie," he sighed, pushing away my hands as I tried to press the book against his abdomen. I pinched the fabric of his shirt, hoping if I could just lift it a little, I could slip it in myself. "Emilie."

His hand closed around my wrist, and we were right back where we started. His eyes filled with an ice storm and the heat of his palm spread like wildfire across my skin. I should've known our truce wouldn't last.

"Sorry."

He loosened his hold before releasing me altogether. "It's fine. Give me the book."

He took it from me and then slipped it beneath his shirt, tightening his belt to secure it.

It wasn't long before Reyna and her guards showed up to take us back to our room. I crossed my arms over my chest, but thankfully, she did not notice the extra baggage on my front side. Her eyes were too focused on Ladon.

It was like she was obsessed with him. Whenever they were in a room together, she stared at him in a way that made my stomach coil. I couldn't explain why her gaze made me so uncomfortable. While half of me felt sorry for him, the other half was thankful that she wasn't focused on me.

A fresh meal of beef stew and bread was waiting for us back in our room. Steam rose from the bowls of soup, so I knew it must've just been delivered. Once again, lunch had been skipped, so I was starving.

"I'll be back in a couple hours," Reyna said, pausing at the door. "I have another *task* for you, Ladon."

The 's' rolled off her tongue like the snake she was.

When I turned to look at Ladon, his face was drained of all color. He removed the book from under his shirt, then moved to the bed and laid down with his hands behind his head.

"Aren't you going to eat anything?"

"I'm not hungry."

That seemed impossible. I knew his aversion to food had everything to do with Reyna's parting words, but I couldn't find it in me to press him again. Not when we had finally gotten along for twelve hours.

I sat on the floor, wishing we'd been given a proper table with stools. I ate my soup quickly, mopping up the last dregs with the loaf of bread. I thought about eating Ladon's, too. If he wasn't going to eat it, then someone should. It wouldn't be any good if it sat much longer.

It was almost as if he had read my mind. When he heard the clink of my spoon against an empty bowl, he turned to me. "You can have mine, too."

I waited for him to change his mind, but when he returned to gazing at the ceiling, I pulled his bowl toward me. I grabbed the second loaf of bread and tossed it across the room, where it landed on his stomach.

"At least eat the bread. You're no use to me if you starve to death."

He gave me a half-smile before pulling off a small piece and popping it into his mouth. I smiled back.

As promised, Reyna came back a short while later to collect Ladon. He held his head high as he left the room and the door closed behind him, leaving me alone once again.

At least this time I had books to help pass the time.

This happened routinely, day after day, week after week, until a month had flown by in the blink of an eye. Ladon and I would spend the days carrying out various chores for Reyna, and at night, Ladon would disappear at Reyna's request.

Every time, he came back with haunted eyes and hunched shoulders. It was as if she was draining the life from him and I was helpless to stop it. He still wouldn't tell me what was happening, no matter how hard I pressed. My imagination jumped to the wildest conclusions, and I wished he'd just tell me so I could stop fearing the worst.

I sat under the pale moonlight coming in through the grate, attempting to read another chapter on suppressive magic. I'd been hoping that the studies would cover the necessary requirements to remove the magical shackles Reyna had fitted us with. But most of what I'd read so far dealt with defensive techniques. Things like stopping the spread of contagious ailments or stifling unwanted magical outbursts that children were sometimes susceptible to. Nothing to help with my mission to get rid of the vines wrapped around my wrists and ankles.

With every passing day, my hope drained. I was exhausted and beginning to feel like we would never escape Reyna's grasp. Like we'd been abandoned. Ladon said it would take time for Cyrus and the Osavian army to find us, but I had to admit, I didn't expect it to take this long. I thought we'd be rescued within a week. Now that we'd been enslaved for a month, I was doing my best not to spiral into despair. Falling apart would be no use. I had to keep myself distracted with the mundane day-to-day tasks and the endless supply of texts to consume.

I rubbed my eyes. Ladon wasn't back yet, and it was later than usual. I hated the idea of going to sleep when he hadn't yet returned. We might not have been the best of friends, but we're all each other had in this dismal hell. Plus, it was hard to sleep without the warmth of another body. The room was far too cold for comfort.

Closing the book, I laid down on the stiff mattress, wrapping myself in the thin blanket. I could hear the wind howling over the opening in the ceiling. At least the water wasn't dripping in tonight. I could only listen to that pestering rhythm for so long without losing my mind. Before I could doze off, I heard the sound of footsteps in the hall.

The door creaked as it opened, and Ladon stepped inside. Without a word, he headed toward the bathroom. I could hear the groan of the pipes as the shower turned on.

This was also part of his routine every night when he came back. I allowed him the time and space to rid himself of the hidden stains on his heart, mind, and soul. After that first night, he typically came to bed without my persuasion.

The mattress shifted with his weight and his wet skin pressed against my arm. He wore only his pants and his chest was still warm from the shower.

"Are you okay?"

He nodded.

I knew better than to ask what happened. I decided to try a different approach this time. "Tell me something honest."

His eyes reflected the soft moonlight as he turned to face me. "Like what?"

I shrugged. "I don't know. Something—anything—that's on your mind. Something I don't know."

"You don't know anything about me."

"Then start with one thing."

I saw his tongue dart out across his bottom lip while he appraised me. I shivered a little and brought the blanket further up over my shoulders, though I didn't think it was the chill that caused my body to tremble. I was pretty sure it had more to do with his proximity.

Even when he hated me, Ladon looked at me like he really *saw* me. Other people either paid me no attention or only reluctantly did so because they knew I was of noble lineage. Not Ladon. His eyes had always pierced right through to my soul, even if he didn't like what he saw.

And experiencing it now while he was only inches from my face...I shivered again.

"My favorite color is green."

I snorted.

"What?" he asked. "You said to tell you something honest, and I did."

"I somehow imagined you might've shared something more substantial. Like a favorite memory or something you're proud of."

"And I bet you're so willing to share personal details with me?"

I blinked a few times and racked my brain. I could've chosen something easy, like how much I enjoyed my brother's company and how I missed him when he left home. But there was one truth that landed on the tip of my tongue and demanded to be let out. "I wanted you to like me."

"Why?"

"You know I didn't have a choice. I was sent to marry Cyrus without ever being asked what I wanted. I know your hesitations. That you think I'm more of a liability than an asset. That I'm a poison seeping into your kingdom. That because of my lineage, I'm somehow inferior to you. And I won't argue that my mother isn't a power-seeking, money-hungry, conniving woman. It's why she didn't think twice about sacrificing her own child. But I thought...I thought that at least I'd find a family in Renoa, one who cared for me more than my own. And Cyrus and Sophia are loving and generous, but Renoa will never be home so long as one of the members of the Castelli family wants me gone."

Ladon stared at me, attempting to digest the weight of the truth I'd given him. His throat bobbed as he swallowed. By the way his jaw rippled, I assumed he was grinding his teeth. I braced for an angry retort, but what he said next surprised me.

"Perhaps I was quick to judge you, princess."

Chapter Nineteen

Emilie

THE NEXT DAY, REYNA had us scrubbing the dog kennels. It smelled like something had died and then I realized, something probably had. Who knows what she fed those vicious beasts. At least she'd taken them out for some exercise while we worked.

Ladon held a shovel, flinging piles of shit into a wheelbarrow to dispose of. I had the great displeasure of working on my hands and knees, scrubbing blood stains from the stone floor. An impossible task, but Reyna seemed to enjoy handing those out best.

By midday, my hands were covered in brown muck. I tried not to think about what lay beneath my fingernails. If I didn't consider it too much, I could trick my brain into thinking it was simply dirt.

A creature under Reyna's command stopped by to deliver lunch. She was a half-human, half-bird sort of creature with black feathered wings and talons on her feet. She didn't say anything as she laid a tray on top of a wooden barrel.

"Thank you," I said. She peered at me with owl-like eyes, widened with trepidation.

She opened her mouth, but nothing came out. Her cheeks flushed pink, and she scuffled through the door.

"Was that a harpy?" I asked once I assumed she was too far to hear.

"I think so."

"Hmm, the ones I've seen in books were more bird than human." I'd never seen one myself. To my knowledge, harpies weren't native to Lourova. In fact, most mystical creatures belonged to the continent of Moridia.

"I wouldn't put it past Reyna to be dabbling in breeding."

I shuddered at the thought. Gods knew what other creatures she had stored in this mountain.

The afternoon passed in the blink of an eye. Ladon finished early, so he offered to help me scrub the rest of the grimy floor.

"I never want to clean another shit or blood-stained floor ever again."

Ladon chuckled. "Not used to manual labor, are you?"

"Oh, please. I'm sure you've never had to clean up after yourself either, as a precious prince."

"Maybe not, but I have contributed in other ways."

"And you don't think I have? You think I spent my days in Dreslen lounging about?"

"Well, kind of."

I threw the sponge in my hand at his head and it made a comical slapping noise as it struck his cheek.

He froze, taking a moment to process what had just happened. I knew I was testing his limits, but in our time in Murvort, we'd managed to move from loathing to tolerance to reluctant companionship. It was bound to happen when we only had each other to rely on.

Ladon looked at me with a mischievous twinkle in his eyes. "You'll pay for that, princess."

He leapt across the room, grabbing his own sponge as well as mine. Within seconds, he had me pinned to the floor with his thighs trapping my torso, squeezing the excess water from the sponges over top of my chest.

"Stop! Stop!" I said, while struggling to catch my breath. I couldn't help but laugh while swatting at his arms. The whole thing was so silly, but a welcome moment of levity in our dire predicament. Somehow, he knew I needed it. And maybe he needed it just as much as I did.

When there was no water left to be wrung from the sponges, he dropped his hands and they rested lightly on my stomach. He was as breathless as I was, and his chest rose and fell while he stared into my eyes.

His gaze tended to make me feel vulnerable. Insecure.

"What?" I breathed out.

He shrugged. His disheveled white hair fell in loose strands, catching on his eyelashes. I reached up and brushed them from his face, not wanting to miss a single sparkle in those silvery eyes.

His body tensed, and I realized what I'd just done. I quickly pulled my hand back.

"Sorry."

He quirked a brow, but before he could respond, the sound of heels clicked against the stone floor, accompanied by Reyna's voice. "Well, well. What do we have here?"

I could hear Ladon grinding his teeth before he slid off my body and came to a stand. I sat up and though it did no good, I brushed at my shirt, now damp and splotched with muddy water. Ladon reached out a hand and I took it, letting him pull me up to stand beside him.

"Did I not give you enough to do? I thought for sure cleaning out the kennels would keep you busy today, but clearly not if you had time to roll around in the muck. I guess I need to work you harder."

She held a pointed nail to Ladon's chin. "Ladon, why didn't you tell me you wanted to play with the dogs? I could've left Nova and Nox behind."

Her laugh was sinister. It made my blood boil, but I kept my clenched fists at my side. She scraped her fingernail down the side of his neck, leaving a streak of angry red skin behind.

Something in me snapped. "Leave him alone," I shouted, stepping in between the two of them.

Ladon stirred behind me, but I held my ground. Reyna tilted her head back, peering down her nose at me. A smile spread across her thin lips, sending a chill down my spine.

"You're a foolish girl."

"Reyna," Ladon growled. I felt his hand on my back and leaned into it. Maybe I was foolish for provoking Reyna, but I couldn't stand by and watch anymore.

Whatever she was doing to him was draining the life from him. We'd both lost weight since our arrival, but Ladon's loss was more visible. The dark circles under his eyes never disappeared, even on the rare day we had off and he was able to sleep in.

I could see it in his eyes. I felt it in the way he stirred in the middle of the night. She was killing him, slowly and painfully.

Reyna took a step forward, her chest practically touching mine. She was only a few inches taller than me, but I felt so small next to her. I bumped into Ladon's chest as I took a step back.

"So far, you've been such a delightful *guest*, Emilie. Staying out of my way and completing your chores without complaint." She began to walk in circles around us and I turned my neck to follow her. "Perhaps I've been too lenient with you. I've allowed you to think that you have an inkling of power within these mountain walls. That won't do."

She stopped circling, and with a twist of her hand, Ladon fell to his knees, clutching his stomach.

I reached for him, but as soon as I pivoted, I felt the magical threads pulling my limbs to her desire. I stood tall while Ladon writhed on the floor. Even the tears that welled in my eyes were beyond my control.

"I think I'll give you a break tonight, Ladon. Since Emilie is so intent on coming to your defense. She can take your place tonight."

Ladon stopped writhing and looked up from his spot on the floor. His eyes were filled with fury and he struggled to speak amidst his panting. "Do not touch her, Reyna."

She laughed, aware that his threat held no substance.

Then she tapped her fingers against her bottom lip and hummed. "Maybe I won't touch her. But I could think of a few who would like to."

Ladon's eyes widened and before I could comprehend her statement, a heavy blunt object collided with the back of my head. In an instant, the world turned black.

When I woke, the room spun. I felt a warm sticky spot on the back of my scalp and found dark blood on my hand when I pulled it away. I sat up and forced the nausea reeling inside of me back down. I suspected I might have a concussion.

I cursed under my breath. I'd been stupid and look where it had gotten me.

Where had it gotten me?

I was alone in what appeared to be a spa room. Crystal clear water filled a sunken basin in the center of the room. The air was thick with humidity and a soapy scent.

My head swiveled, searching for Reyna hidden in one of the corners of the room, but I was truly alone. I stood on shaky legs and headed to the door. I wasn't surprised when the iron door didn't budge.

My hands curled into fists, and I pounded on the steadfast barrier. I screamed until my throat ached. The noise all seemed to absorb into the dense air. I wasn't sure if anyone could even hear me.

I fell to my knees and sobbed, uncertain of how much more I could take. I was tired, both physically and mentally. I missed my family, even my mother and her snide remarks. I missed the comforts of Renoa, though I had only known them for a brief time. At that point, I would've settled for the overbearing heat of Dreslen. I was tired of being cold and damp all the time.

Using the back of my hand, I wiped the tears from my eyes.

Get it together, Emilie.

I stood and surveyed the room. Aside from the pool, there were a few cabinets full of towels and soaps. Two robes were hanging on a rack on the back wall. A bar cart in the corner caught my eye.

As I approached, I noticed fruit and cheese and bread. My stomach rumbled at the sight. I was also sick of being hungry all the time. The meals we'd been fed were enough to prevent starvation, but they weren't meant to fill our bellies.

Despite my hunger, I didn't trust the assortment of snacks. There was also a glass jug full of what I suspected to be water. My tongue felt dry as I weighed the potential risk.

An echo of Ladon's voice whispered in my ear. *That would be too easy for Reyna. She'll have a much worse demise planned for us.*

Fuck it. I brought the jug to my lips, not even bothering to search for a glass. The thought of Reyna's disgust at my mouth on her pristine water jug made me smirk.

As if she was summoned by my thoughts, the door rattled, and Reyna entered the chamber. I carefully set the jug down and folded my arms across my chest.

"Ah, you're awake."

"Yes, I've recovered after you knocked me out."

She ignored me and gestured to the cart behind me. "I'm glad you were able to get some refreshments. It's going to be a long night for you."

Every word she spoke made me burn with anger. Her act of being a gracious host was unbearable. On top of everything else, the phony performance really got under my skin.

I audibly sighed and rolled my eyes. Whatever she had planned for me, I would grit my teeth and bare it.

Reyna sneered when she took in my obstinate stance. She whistled and two figures emerged from the shadows beyond the iron door, dressed head to toe in long black cloaks. Their movements were feline as they headed in my direction, soundlessly gliding across the floor.

"Ladies, please make sure Emilie is prepared for our guests tonight." She winked and turned on her heel. I watched, frozen in place while she exited the room and the door thudded shut behind her.

Her two assistants eyed me with disinterest. When one placed a hand on my shoulder, I pushed her away. She didn't speak. Didn't show any signs of a fight. She merely reached to touch me again.

"What are you doing?" I asked in a frantic tone. I cleared my throat. No need to panic yet. It was just that the unknown was always somehow worse than anything else. I wanted to know what Reyna had in store for me.

Her maidens were speechless, exactly like the harpy had been. I half wondered if their silence was mandated, like the vines that directed my movements, or if their tongues had been removed altogether. Then I noticed a vine peeking out from the top of the first's cloak collar, running up the side of her neck and disappearing into her hair.

Would that happen to me? Would these vines continue to grow until they consumed me?

A shiver rolled up my spine, and I did my best to erase the thought.

She'll have a much worse demise planned for us.

Curse Ladon for not telling me what she had done to him. I could've been prepared for tonight. Would she torture me? Play mind games? Would I be forced back into the hedge maze, running from her hounds until my legs collapsed?

The two women had their hands on me once again. One was pulling at the sleeve of my shirt while the other unbuckled my pants. I tried to step back, but they loosened and sank to the floor. It was hard to move with them tangled around my ankles. She grabbed me around the calf and forced me to step out of them.

"Please," I said. "What does she mean to do with me?"

The one kneeling before me looked up, and I noticed for the first time a scar running down the right side of her face. Her right iris was white and glassy and I was fairly certain she couldn't see out of that eye, even though her pupil stayed fixed on my face.

She pointed to the bath.

"You want me to get in?"

She nodded.

Her features gave away nothing else. There was no fear. No anger. She was like a shadow of a human being. It made me pity her. I couldn't help but wonder who she used to be.

My empathy for her made me more compliant. The other maiden had removed my blouse and bra. My underwear came off in a swift motion too. I tested the water with my toes first, and after finding it to be pleasantly warm, I finished walking down the steps and sat on a ledge beneath the water.

Now what?

Both of the maidens removed their cloaks, and I gasped. Their entire bodies were covered in vines. Black and so thick that I could hardly see a patch of skin.

They moved through the water with that same grace they'd had on land. The water seemed to part for them so they could gravitate toward me effortlessly. I straightened.

The one without the scar pulled me from the ledge and made a move to dunk my head. Despite the furious beating of my heart, I sank enough to wet my hair and then came back up.

They washed my hair and bathed me in soaps that smelled of vanilla and some flower I couldn't put my finger on. They scrubbed my skin and rubbed my body with some creamy concoction. I gasped when the hair under my armpits and along my groin disappeared entirely.

Once they finished, they pulled me out of the water and dried me off with one of the lush towels. If I hadn't been a hostage in enemy territory, it would've been a pleasant experience, but my nerves returned and I swallowed the lump in my throat.

Why had they made me presentable?

I started to pick up my clothes, but the one-eyed maiden stopped me. She shook her head and held out a chain of gold. No, not one chain. Many chains linked together, drooping in half circles with rubies dangling on the ends.

"What is that?"

She motioned for me to turn around. My knees trembled as I obeyed her wishes. Her arm reached across my chest and she clipped something together behind the nape of my neck.

I looked down, and the sight horrified me. The chains fell over my chest while my bare skin peeked through. Even my nipples were only half-covered. My jaw dropped before I whipped around to face her. "*This* is what I'm wearing? This isn't clothing. This jewelry hardly covers me. You can see"—I gulped—"everything."

She only nodded. There was no sympathy in her eyes. I wanted to take back the pity I had for her earlier.

"No. I won't do this."

She held my gaze, and I jolted as the other maiden fastened a similar garment around my waist.

I closed my eyes and counted to ten before I looked down. A pathetic whimper escaped when I saw the chains falling around my hips, stopping well above my knees. From the breeze, I knew my ass was hardly covered either.

While I was still frozen in shock, they made quick work of my wild hair, slicking it back and pinning it with ease. When they were done primping me and preparing me, the iron door swung open again. Almost as if they shared some magical brain frequency with Reyna.

Maybe if the vines were given enough time to sink in, that's what would become of us—just an extension of Reyna.

Her eyes lit up, delighted with the way I'd been decorated like a prize possession. My powers rumbled inside me, begging to be released, begging to strip the air out of her lungs. But I kept them in check. I couldn't handle the blinding headache that would accompany any attempt at using my magic. Instead, I had to deal with the burning rage inside me.

More than anything, I wanted to cover up. It was humiliating standing before her almost entirely nude. The body jewelry was a poor excuse for attire. But hiding felt like admitting defeat. I held my head high instead.

I was only vaguely aware of my surroundings as I followed Reyna through the dark halls. The dainty chains around my body chimed like bells, like one of her fucking pets.

The sound of chatter in the next room caught my attention. We were standing outside of her drawing room that we'd cleaned that first day. I hadn't been back since. It hadn't occurred to me that she actually used it to entertain guests. Who in the right mind would want to visit with Reyna?

I paused and her twisted smirk only grew more sinister.

"What's the matter, Emilie? I thought you might like some company this evening. It must get rather dull with only Ladon to talk to. Or maybe you prefer him over dear Cyrus."

Her laugh was reminiscent of a hyena.

"Don't speak about him," I snarled.

"Which one?"

She laughed again and opened the door. "Welcome, everyone! I've returned with our entertainment for the evening."

She waved a hand at me and those treacherous vines pushed me forward into the drawing room. I held my breath as a small crowd stared me down. Heat washed over my chest and cheeks. My eyes burned as well. I wanted to run. To scream. But I couldn't move.

Reyna paraded me through the crowd of onlookers. Two women sat on the chaise lounge I recognized from the hours I'd spent scrubbing stains. Their faces were shaped in a scowl as they gaped at my bejeweled torso.

Behind the couch, a triad of women swirled their glasses, filled to the brim with dark red wine. One with long bluish-black hair and a pierced brow took a sip. I tried not to meet her gaze over the top of her glass.

To my left, a group of gentlemen appeared to have just ceased their conversation. They now gawked at me with slack jaws. One raised a cigarette to his lips and took a hit. An illicit substance, if I had to guess. Smoke filled the room, hovering like a cloud above us.

So this is what Reyna did with her spare time? Alcohol and drugs and parties with a group of...truth be told, I wasn't sure what to call them.

From their elegant attire—embroidered gowns and fitted jackets—I could've sworn they were upper class socialites.

But that couldn't be. Murvort was as poor as Dreslen. Even more so if the stories were true. How could they afford luxurious evening parties? It didn't make sense.

Yet even their posture reeked of wealth. The men were plump, like they'd never starved a day in their lives. And the women had jewels hanging from their earlobes and necklines.

And now every single one of their eyes were on me. Like I was a rare new jewel to be collected.

I swallowed, wanting more than anything to cross my arms and cover my bare skin. But the vines on my wrists kept them pressed to my sides.

"Well, Reyna. Please introduce us to your newest pet," a man said. His voice was seductive as he took a step forward. He had dark, wavy hair and soulless brown eyes. There was a harsh angle in his nose, like it'd been broken one too many times. His eyes raked my body as he waited for Reyna's response.

"Her name doesn't matter. She's yours to play with."

She shoved me in the back, right between my shoulder blades. I fell forward a few steps, into the crooked-nose man who'd been eyeing me with desire.

He twisted me around, one arm crushed against my breasts while the other hand made lazy movements across the gold chains dangling above my groin.

"Just remember the rules," Reyna said. She didn't clarify, and I was left to wonder what rules she'd set in place.

It was as though she'd unleashed a pack of hounds. In an instant, I was dragged across the floor. The man who held me flopped against a plush chair and I fell on top of him.

I squirmed and panted. "Stop. Let me go."

His hold was exceptionally strong. "We've got a fighter," he said, and the entire room laughed.

"What will you do with her?" one woman with dirty blonde hair asked. I stared deep into her eyes, begging her to do something. To step in and stop this. But I realized she wasn't asking out of concern. She was brimming with excitement and curiosity.

No one in this room was going to help me.

I struggled against his hold again, not caring that the body jewelry was jostling and showing bits of me I'd never shown to anyone. I didn't have time to be ashamed. I needed to get free.

Regret sunk in, and I wished I'd paid more attention during those lessons in Renoa. Maybe Ladon had been on to something about fighting without magic.

Ladon. Was this...was this what he'd been going through every night? I couldn't think about that right now. Not while I was being pawed at with calloused hands.

I tried to elbow the man in the gut, but he only chuckled. My resistance only turned him on, it seemed. As I writhed, I felt the unmistakable prod of his hard cock near my ass.

I froze, and he took the moment of hesitancy to slip a hand beneath the golden chains. He pinched my nipple, and I cried in pain.

"Shh," he said in my ear. The heat of his breath made me tremble. Everyone was staring. And I was on the verge of tears.

I found Reyna on the opposite side of the room, smiling while my lips trembled.

"Please," I said softly.

The guests were quietly chattering, but Reyna's voice carried through the room. "You really should've considered your actions before. Now you'll pay the price."

From the corner of my eye, I saw the woman with a pierced brow sit on the arm of my chair. Her cold and delicate fingers wrapped around my thigh and she pulled my leg toward her, opening me for the room to see. Eyes narrowed in on my core and I thought I was going to be sick.

My heart thundered in my chest. "Please."

She ran her finger over my slit and the man holding me growled with pleasure. Meanwhile, I was too terrified to move. Shock had left me immobile. My brain was working in overdrive, trying to comprehend what was happening. She slid one finger inside me and I gasped.

Others were drawing closer now, wanting their piece of the prize. Wanting their turn with the new toy.

Hands were all over me, grabbing at me from above, from my side. Lips were on my neck. Fingers digging into my skin, sliding into my core, tugging at a spot that should've elicited bliss but only brought forth more tears.

"Please," I said again, knowing no one was listening. "Don't."

At the end of the night, my body was left discarded on the floor. My body jewelry was disheveled, twisted, and tangled. I'd been prodded and kneaded, touched and tasted, all for the pleasure of others.

It was endless. It was unrelenting. It was violating.

There were a few times I thought my shame would reach its max. I'd bordered on shuddering with pleasure, but Reyna was somehow acutely aware of my condition at all times. She only needed to snap her fingers and it all stopped, leaving me breathless and mortified that I wanted more. She kept me close to that edge but never let me fall over it.

That must've been one of her rules.

A second rule, I'd surmised—no penetration, at least not with any of the males. Fingers and tongues were fair game, but at no point during the night were any of them allowed to fuck me. A small mercy I couldn't muster the energy to be grateful for.

I closed my eyes, wishing it would all fall away. Retreating footsteps sounded, vibrating where my ear pressed to the carpet. I wanted to disappear.

I felt her approach and come to a stop above me.

"Well? Did you learn your lesson, Emilie?" Reyna asked. There was a hint of that fake concern in her voice. Like this had been a tragic accident, and she was simply an innocent bystander. Her voice mocked me. *If only I could've stopped this*, it said.

But I couldn't find the strength to bite back. My body was lifeless on the floor.

There was a thud as my regular clothes landed next to my head.

"Do not test me again."

Chapter Twenty

Ladon

THE ROOM FELT TOO small while I paced back and forth. It didn't feel too small; it *was* too small. Each time I made my way across the stone floor, I counted my steps.

One, two, three...

I hoped it would help pass the time, but as I looked at the door again, I realized nothing would help. I fidgeted, cracking my knuckles and running my fingers through my hair.

As I made my way back toward the wall attached to the bathroom, I noticed my disheveled hair in the mirror. I looked like an absolute mess.

It felt like hours had gone by and Emilie still hadn't returned to our room. Reyna wouldn't be so cruel as to touch her, would she?

Sure, she'd taken advantage of me time and time again. Using my body for her sick fantasies and sharing me with her evening guests. But she wouldn't do that to Emilie. She couldn't.

An involuntary shudder rippled through my body. It wasn't hard to imagine what Emilie might be going through. I'd lived it every night for weeks.

The first time, I'd thought I was in some sort of nightmare. That it couldn't be real. But every time I closed my eyes, I could feel Reyna's hands on me. I could feel the weight of her body on top of me, grinding into me while an audience watched with fascination.

I'd been the High Commander of Osavian's armies for over a decade. I'd seen a lot of horrible things. Soldiers tortured and disemboweled. Entire villages burnt to the ground. Nothing would ever compare to the atrocities that Reyna devised. It was a level of sinister that I hadn't been prepared for. And now she had Emilie.

Bile rose in my throat, but I choked it down. I needed a shower.

I turned to pace in the opposite direction, rolling my neck and scratching my skin. Lately, I was having a hard time feeling like myself in my own skin. I wanted to rip it off. Shed it and be born anew like some reptile.

Without Emilie, I realized just how much of a distraction she'd provided. I was locked in a room, but even worse, I was locked in my head with my own thoughts.

I couldn't stop thinking about Reyna. Her vicious smirk and sick desires. The things she had done to me. And was now presumably doing to Emilie.

Once again, I'd failed to protect her. I'd consistently been failing in my duties as High Commander.

As I motioned to turn and pace in the opposite direction, the door clicked open. I froze while Emilie took a few steps forward, arms wrapped around her body, and the door closed behind her.

I reached for her. "Emilie?"

Slowly, her eyes rose from the spot she'd been examining on the floor and she met my gaze. Tears glistened in her eyes and I immediately felt a tug in my chest.

She pulled back when my fingertips grazed her elbow. "You...she's been doing this to you? The whole time?"

I swallowed the lump in my throat and inhaled sharply. Although I'd suspected this was coming, I hadn't mentally prepared to talk about it...to share those invasive experiences with Emilie.

"What did she do?" I asked, diverting her attention instead.

A tear fell down her cheek, and she looked around the room as if she were lost. Hopeless. Again, I reached for her and she allowed me to step closer, to grab her by the shoulders. She stared at my chest rather than my face, unable to meet my inquiring gaze.

"I suspect you already know," she murmured.

I shook my head. I didn't want to believe it. But even in my heart, I knew it was true. I tilted her chin up to find her face full of despair. "I'm so sorry, Emilie."

She released a shaky breath. "She...she made me attend this *party*. And the guests..." She gulped. It was clear she was struggling to relive the past few hours. She shivered as she carried on. "They *touched* me. They *violated* me. I...I—"

"Stop. You don't need to tell me. I don't need to know the details."

Pain was etched in every freckle, every crinkle in her forehead, every glistening wet eyelash.

"And she's done the same to you?"

I nodded, unsure how much she wanted to know. Sighing, I decided to tell her the truth. "That and more. I've...she's used me in many ways. She's used me as her personal sex slave, I suppose you could say. Those guests of hers love a show."

I tried to make light of the situation, but it came out fractured and tormented. Emilie saw right through it. She wrapped her arms around my waist and pressed her face against my chest, momentarily catching me off guard.

"I'm so sorry." I heard her muffled speech against my shirt. "You should've told me."

How could I have? I was taught to be strong. To be unafraid, lest those around me become fearful. Soldiers looked to me as a pillar of hope. Of bravery. But as she sobbed, I considered that maybe Emilie didn't need an unwavering warrior. Maybe she needed a friend. A confidante.

I brought a hand up to brush the back of her head in soothing strokes. "You have nothing to be sorry for. None of this is your fault."

I felt something like a huff against my chest. And then another as I realized she had just laughed. She leaned back to meet my gaze. "You specifically said that this *was* my fault. That if it weren't for me, you could've gotten out of Fort Malek. And it was my fault that you were caught."

I furrowed my brows while she smiled despite the tears. The events of the evening must've taken their toll on her for her to show such erratic behavior. But then again, Emilie had always felt her emotions fully, at every end of the spectrum. Whether she was tossing daggers at my head or admiring artwork, she laid it all bare.

I rolled my eyes. "I don't recall saying that."

"Ladon Castelli, you are a liar."

"If you're expecting me to say I was wrong, you're going to be waiting a long time, princess."

She chuckled again, but as my lip curved in a reluctant grin, hers turned upside down. Her face scrunched in anguish and she trembled, tears falling freely down her face. A moment of teasing could only pause the pain for so long.

So I held her close, cradling her against my chest and resting my chin on top of her head. It was the only thing I could do.

Chapter Twenty-One

Ladon

EMILIE KEPT TO HERSELF for the next several days. I could tell she was trying to put on a show. To pretend like she was okay. But I heard the desperation in her silence. She wasn't nearly as unfazed as she pretended to be. In the middle of the night, I could occasionally hear soft sniffling while she tried to hide her tears.

It killed me that there wasn't more I could do for her. For us.

The books she'd taken from the Scholars' Cavern had been a dead end. There wasn't anything useful that might help us escape this prison. Nor were there any instructions for destroying the magical vines wrapped around our bodies. Each day I racked my brain trying to think of new ways to solve our problems, all the while entertaining Reyna each night.

At least my presence was enough for her. Gods, what I would do to her if she ever touched Emilie again.

Strange how Emilie had driven me mad before. I'd wanted to strangle her, to tear her down. Still did most days. But the second anyone else laid hands on her, I went into protective mode.

"Can you hand me that one?"

Emilie was standing on top of a stepladder, placing books on a nearly full shelf. Today we were back to working in the library. Of all the jobs Reyna had us doing, this one was the least horrible. It didn't involve dog shit or mystery stains. The only downside was the bats that occasionally stirred and flew down from above.

I grabbed the closest book and handed it to Emilie, reading the title as I passed it. "*How to Train the Untrainable.* Guess we know how Reyna keeps all her pets in line."

"I'm sure you're right. How else would she tame all these beasts?"

"Did you just say, 'I'm right?'" I smirked.

Emilie smacked my arm with the book. "Don't let it go to your head."

A noise down another aisle made us both freeze. No one else was supposed to be in the library. Even Reyna's henchmen had stayed outside the cavern.

Emilie stepped down from the ladder as quietly as she could while I peered through piles of books, searching for movement.

"Maybe it was just a bat," Emilie whispered.

The look I gave her conveyed my skepticism, and she fell behind me, following in my footsteps as I went to investigate.

The Scholars' Cavern was still a disaster, despite the days we'd spent organizing. The massive mounds of books were taller than I was, making it difficult to see.

Emilie's hand clasped around my bicep, squeezing a little too tightly. I gave it a pointed look before lifting my eyes to her face. She let go immediately, pink staining her cheeks.

"Sorry, I didn't mean to...I know you don't like to be touched."

"That's not it." I shook my head. A part of me was in disbelief, realizing all those threats hadn't been for nothing. That she finally got it through her head not to touch me. Except now, her touch was the only one that didn't feel like an assault on my body. "Just not so tight."

I reached back and grabbed her hand, and she stared for a moment, stunned. Her hand was small—delicate—in mine. Her soft skin was icy, and I brushed my thumb over the back of her hand in an attempt to warm it. She shivered and nearly pulled her hand from my grasp, but I tightened my hold.

Returning to the task at hand, I rounded a corner and then another, following the sound of soft footsteps. I could practically feel Emilie's pulse in my palm. I squeezed, letting her know I was here. That I'd protect her, even though I'd failed her so many times already.

At last, we turned down a dark aisle, and at the end, the harpy stood facing us with a somber expression.

I jerked my chin in her direction. "What are you doing? You're not supposed to be in here."

Emilie pushed in front of me and I looked down at her wild brown hair. She turned around to face me. "You'll scare her."

"Excuse me?"

Emilie didn't respond. Instead, she faced the harpy again. "Do you have a name?"

The harpy looked back and forth between the two of us. Then she nodded her head.

"Can you tell us?"

The harpy shook her head and looked down in dismay.

This seemed utterly pointless to me, but Emilie was on some sort of mission. Perhaps my company was no longer enough for her. She needed to make friends with the other creatures of the mountain.

"Let's just go," I said to her, snaking a hand around her waist. I didn't like how the harpy was looking at her.

The harpy took a step forward. She had a look I couldn't quite decipher. Somewhere between terror and bravery. Like she too had a mission.

She placed her hand on a patch of wall left uncovered by the many shelves. She gently tapped the wall several times, as if she were trying to show us something.

"I don't think she can speak," Emilie said to me.

The harpy nodded.

Emilie sighed and inched closer, close enough to see whatever it was that the harpy wanted to show us. I stayed right behind her in case the harpy had any bright ideas. In case this was all a trick.

As I got closer, I could make out a set of runes that had been etched into the stone. Runes that I didn't recognize.

"What does it say?" My patience was wearing thin. At any moment, Reyna might come back and I doubted she'd be pleased to find us fraternizing with the harpy.

The harpy shook her head almost violently. Her own irritation matched mine. What did she want me to do? Magically learn a language that I couldn't even identify? I sighed, but Emilie practiced more patience.

"Maybe you could show us? With your hands? What does it mean?"

The harpy threw her hands in the air.

"Great." I rolled my eyes. "Very descriptive. Thank you."

Emilie smacked her hand against my stomach.

The harpy brushed past where we stood, then turned and stared back at us.

"I think she means for us to follow."

"Lead the way," I said, motioning for Emilie to go first.

We followed the harpy, who took us through the first floor of the library and then headed up the spiral staircase to another floor. And then another. And then another.

My legs were on fire by the time we came to a halt. She was searching through a shelf of books which were, oddly enough, already organized. Had she been doing some work of her own in the Scholars' Cavern?

She moved with such certainty that I had no doubt in my mind. She was not new to the library and all the knowledge it held. Her bony hand grasped a blue spine and pulled it from the shelf. Then she moved to the end of the aisle where a small table stood, dropping the book and flipping quickly through the pages.

Emilie and I moved to read over the harpy's shoulder. She stopped on a page with similar markings to the ones we'd just seen on the wall. She tapped them repeatedly, and Emilie furrowed her brow. She studied the runes and seemed to glean more than I could.

The harpy pointed at individual runes and then pointed out their corresponding letters. Meanwhile, Emilie sounded out a translation.

"Here. Opens. Here opens. Here opens what?" she asked.

The harpy sighed and flipped a few more pages, repeating the same pattern she had before.

"T-U-N-N-E-L-S. The tunnels? There's a door to the tunnels here? In the Scholars' Cavern?" Emilie asked with growing elation. Optimism bloomed in my chest.

The harpy nodded.

"Impossible."

Except it was entirely possible. I had no idea where the openings to the tunnels were in this mountain. I only knew that they existed, not where.

The harpy eyed me, unblinking. It was unnerving, and I shifted back a step.

"How do we open them?" Emilie asked.

The harpy took Emilie's hand and tapped her fingers.

"Magic," she said. My optimism deflated as quickly as it had swelled.

"You've got to be fucking kidding me," I snorted.

"Shh," she said. "Is there any other way? There isn't a key or some other talisman we could use?

She shook her head and again tapped at Emilie's fingertips.

Great. We were no closer than we had been before. There was no way we were getting our magic back anytime soon.

"I don't suppose you know of a way to remove these vines?" I asked the harpy, holding up my wrist. I knew she'd shake her head before she even did.

I tried not to let my frustration show. Emilie sensed it anyway. After being together for so many weeks, she knew how to read me like a book. And I did her as well.

"It's okay. We'll figure something out. Thank you. You have no idea how much this helps."

The harpy bowed her head and then headed back down the staircase.

"Now what?"

Emilie picked up the book that the harpy had been utilizing. I had a feeling I knew what her next nighttime read would be. "We'll keep working on the tattoos. And we'll try to find out if there's another way to open the tunnels. We can do this, Ladon."

Her voice was soothing and so was her gentle touch as she brushed her fingers over my arm before sliding past me.

"We should get back to work."

Our luck extended into the evening. For the first night since we'd arrived, Reyna did not show up at our room to take either of us. I could've shouted with joy, except every time I made a sound, Emilie shot me a look of annoyance.

She poured over the new tomes she'd stolen from the library, desperate for some miniscule drop of information that could help us.

"You could help, you know."

I was lying near the edge of the bed, alternating between rounds of sit-ups and push-ups. Anything physical to keep my body in peak condition. I was used to entire days of conditioning. Being holed up in that room was wreaking havoc on my strength.

"I am helping. This is me helping."

She snorted. "Distracting me with your sweaty chiseled abs and grunting noises is *helping*? How do you figure?"

I stopped abruptly, propping myself up on my elbow and studying her for a moment. "Did you just call my abs chiseled?"

"No," she said, completely monotone.

"Yes, you did."

"I don't know what you're talking about."

I moved to my feet and stood over her, resting my hands on my hips. "Emilie, look at me."

She reluctantly did so, pinning me with a look of disdain. She couldn't fool me. I heard the words clear as day. Her eyes flickered to my bare chest and then back to my face. I smirked, and that really seemed to get under her skin.

Emilie huffed. "Gods, Ladon. Would you put on a shirt?"

I grabbed a plain grey cotton shirt, one of a dozen clothing items we'd finally been given. About time too, since my old guard uniform had been tattered and torn to pieces.

After dressing, I took a seat next to Emilie. I picked up one of her books and flipped through the pages. They were all written in that same foreign language. "So, how can I help?"

Chapter Twenty-Two

Emilie

IF I KEPT MY eyes closed, I could pretend I was somewhere—anywhere—else. Through my eyelids I could see night was fading, and the early sunlight was shining into our cold, damp room. But as long as my eyes were closed, I could imagine I was back home in Dreslen. Or back in Osavian with the sound of waves crashing on the beach, my drapes catching the salty breeze off the sea.

I squeezed my eyes closed, almost willing it into existence.

There was a sharp intake of breath and my head rose half an inch. I grumbled before opening my eyes. The bed was warm for once. The thin mattress was soft and pliable against my cheek. I snuggled into it, wishing to fall back asleep. To take solace in my dreams and avoid reality.

The gray mattress rose and sank before my eyes. Slowly. Steadily. In a rhythmic pattern that matched the sound of soft thumping. A heartbeat.

I shot up.

"Morning," Ladon said, smirking, with an arm tucked behind his head. How was he making such a casual position so...sultry. His voice still held that husky morning rumble. "Sleep well?"

My cheeks flushed. I'd fallen asleep with my head resting on his chest. If I wasn't mistaken, there was a small spot of moisture darkening his gray shirt and I prayed to the gods that it was not my own drool.

I tucked my untamed hair behind my ear. "I slept fine."

"Mmhmm."

"And you?"

He stifled a laugh. "I slept well. Thanks for asking. Do you plan on removing yourself from my thigh anytime soon?"

I looked down and, sure enough, when I'd bolted upright, I'd managed to straddle his upper thigh. I tumbled off his body and on to the floor, standing as quickly as possible and brushing dirt from my clothes. An embarrassing squeak slipped out of my mouth and I rushed to the bathroom, not wanting to face Ladon and the taunts he held on the tip of his tongue.

Breakfast arrived, and we ate in silence, occasionally catching each other's gaze. He had a teasing glimmer in his eyes that made my skin hot. What was happening to me? I felt like I was going mad. Was this what happened to people in prisons? I'd heard inmates sometimes lost their mind due to isolation, but experiencing it firsthand was unnerving.

I shook my head, but it did little to clear my thoughts. Ladon still occupied every corner of my brain, to my dismay. I gulped down a glass of water to cool my heated skin.

"Scholars' Cavern or scrubbing floors?" Ladon asked.

"What?"

"Which one? I'll make a bet with you."

I was torn between curiosity and suspicion. "What does the winner get?"

He pondered for a moment. "Pride."

"That's not a very good prize."

"Says you," he said with a smirk.

I sighed heavily, twirling a stray strand of hair around my finger. I wasn't the betting type, but with nothing on the line, it seemed best to humor him. "Fine. I bet it'll be scrubbing floors today."

"You seem pretty sure of that answer."

"Working in the library isn't all that bad. Therefore, I think it's the least likely chore we'll have today."

He nodded in agreement. "Well, I hope you're wrong. For pride's sake."

We were both wrong.

Reyna didn't come to our room to retrieve us that morning. She sent Tristan instead. He greeted us and when Ladon asked about Reyna, he grumbled before snapping at us to get moving.

I surmised through words unspoken that Reyna may not be in the mountain. That she might've been traveling elsewhere. Probably the reason why Ladon was spared from keeping her company the past few nights.

The thought alone was enough to make my stomach twist and turn. That night kept playing in my head every time I closed my eyes. When I looked at myself in the mirror, I saw the eyes of every guest boring into me. Every draft was a harsh reminder of foreign lips on my neck. A piece of me died that night.

It felt like my entire world had been shattered. I'd been living under the delusion that we'd be safe. That we would make our way out of

Murvort unscathed. Maybe a few minor bumps and bruises, but *whole*, nonetheless. But all along Ladon had been shouldering this heavy weight alone. And now that I knew—now that I'd experienced it myself—I'd never be the same.

I didn't think either of us would ever be whole again.

Tristan led us down winding hallways, up two staircases and through a courtyard with a glass atrium. We dove back into the dark mountain and after three left turns and one right, we made our way back into the light again.

I squinted. How long had it been since I'd seen the unfiltered sun?

Beside me, I felt Ladon turn to stone. As my eyes adjusted, I realized where we'd been taken—the hedge maze.

We were standing on top of the platform where I'd first met Reyna. My blood turned to ice coursing through my veins. It was as if a shadow of the poison I'd once been infected with still flowed freely beneath my skin.

"You'll be trimming the hedges today," Tristan stated. He then conjured two very dull shears and handed them to Ladon and I. He took a seat on the platform and stretched his legs out in front of him, staring at us expectantly.

We'd likely be here for a while.

Ladon led the way down the steps and into the path we'd once ran through. It was hard not to think of that day, though it didn't look as if anyone had cared for the hedges since our arrival. They were overgrown and thick roots erupted through the dirt, forcing us to watch our step.

"Do you think we can make a run for it?" I asked beneath my breath.

Ladon pursed his lips. "I doubt it."

The thought of bolting through the hedges was so tempting, but I knew he was right. Tristan would stop us in a heartbeat and the punishment that followed would be unbearable. I winced as I recalled the pain of Vessina plunging her fangs into my body.

As we plunged into work, sharp thorns sliced at our hands and arms. Each time I reached for an out-of-place branch, another rip in my skin appeared. Of course, Tristan hadn't bothered to give us gardening gloves. By midday, my hands were a mangled mess.

We were allowed a break for lunch, during which I painfully held a sandwich to my mouth.

"Here, let me see." Ladon set his sandwich down and pulled my wrists towards him. I winced at the sharp pain. Dark red mingled with the black tattoos. His own hands were scraped as well, but he hid his discomfort better than I could.

After examining them for a moment, his lip turned up in a grin. "You'll live."

I rolled my eyes. But then he was tearing at the sleeve of his shirt, making thin strips. He tipped his water canteen, rinsing my cuts while I hissed. He worked diligently, wrapping my hands with the torn pieces of his sleeve until they were completely bandaged.

"Thank you," I said quietly. "Would you like for me to do yours?"

"That's okay."

He simply rinsed his hands and flicked the excess water off. Without his sleeve, I was able to watch his muscles ripple with each movement. Such strength and power...

I diverted my eyes and quickly finished my sandwich. The wrapping helped immensely, but by the end of the day, even they were torn to ribbons, too.

As the sun set, I looked around and realized how little we'd accomplished. We hadn't even finished one entire row of hedges. And there were so many more to be trimmed.

A groan escaped my lips as I thought back to the library. The nice, quiet, sometimes dusty library. With unending knowledge and hidden doors. I whimpered.

Ladon appeared beside me. "It's going to be fine. We'll get through it."

And so we did. For days, we came back to the hedge maze, trimming the treacherous thorns. For days, I wanted to cry while they continued to rip apart my skin.

After the second day, Ladon finally broke down and wrapped his hands, too. And every day after that, we both preemptively wrapped our hands, hoping to protect them at least a little bit.

At the end of our tenth day, I held my hands under freezing water back in our bathroom, tears spilling over as I watched the blood run down the drain. By my estimates, we'd be working with the hedges for at least three more days in order to finish. I wasn't sure if I could take it.

Just when I thought it couldn't get any worse, Reyna returned from her trip. She showed up without warning one morning, taking the guard's place to watch us from the platform.

All day long, she mocked and ridiculed us. Made light of the mangled flesh on our hands. Laughed at our pain. Smiled at our despair. While the physical pain never seemed to affect Ladon, Reyna's presence caused a stark shift in his demeanor. He hardly spoke when she was around, and his eyes frequently flickered to where she stood.

I didn't think there was a person in this world crueler than Reyna. She didn't just inflict pain and suffering. She basked in it.

We returned to our room that evening and Reyna once again made it clear that she'd return later for Ladon.

He'd grown pale and stoic. He laid down on the mattress and stared at the ceiling—his typical routine on a night when he was summoned by her. I wanted to scream. I wanted to throw something at the wall. Unfortunately, I couldn't even hold a spoon without grimacing.

"You're pacing," he said quietly. The pain in his voice was so clear.

"I just...what if we—"

"Don't bother, princess. There isn't anything you can do."

A knock on the door had us both stiffening. My heart raced as I looked from Ladon to the door. It hadn't been that long since Reyna had left. Surely, she wasn't back already.

The door quietly swung open, and the harpy came inside. How was it that she could roam so freely in this fortress?

She dipped a hand into her pocket and pulled out a tin can, extending it to me. It was about the size of my palm and didn't have any label.

"What is it?"

She merely tilted her head toward it as if to say, *open it*.

I unscrewed the top. The mixture inside was a pale purple, almost white. It smelled like lilacs and eucalyptus. I dipped my finger in cautiously. I trusted the harpy, despite the fact that she could not speak. She'd shown us the entrance to the tunnels and given us the key to translating the runes. I doubted she would harm either of us.

For a moment, I wondered how she'd wound up in Murvort. If she was born here or bred here. If she was abducted from another continent. How long had she been under Reyna's rule? I contemplated these questions while rubbing the oily substance between two fingers.

Warmth and relaxation spread from my fingertips. I watched as the skin turned pink, like a newborn baby. The dirt under my fingernails disappeared. A spark of hope ignited within me.

I spread the oil further along the back of my hand and watched as the cuts began to heal before my eyes. The thin red slivers disappeared, and the gashes filled with brand new skin, not even leaving a scar.

Ladon appeared over my shoulder, watching with curiosity. As soon as he saw what the salve could do, he dipped his own fingers in greedily and spread it across his palms and then the back of his hands, lathering it on thick. A sigh of pleasure rumbled in his throat and I echoed the sentiment. We both needed this.

"Thank you," I said to the harpy. "I don't know how you got this or how you were able to get in but thank you. Thank you so much."

Words seemed inadequate to express my gratitude. I wrapped my arms around her shoulders and pulled her in for a hug. She stiffened, but didn't push me away.

When we separated, she gave me a small nod and then exited the room.

Unfortunately, our relief was short-lived. Not long after, another knock sounded and Reyna entered the room.

"No," I whispered.

Ladon tilted his head toward me, but said nothing.

Reyna hooked a finger in his direction, beckoning him forward. "It's time, Ladon."

"No," I said again, a little louder this time. I grabbed his hand.

Ladon shook his head and whispered my name like a warning. "Emilie."

It wasn't fair. It wasn't right. I had to do *something*.

"I'm growing tired of your insolence, Emilie," Reyna said. "I thought we had come to an understanding after the last time. Perhaps not?"

She stepped closer and wrapped her hand around my wrist like a vise, pulling my hand from Ladon's. "Maybe this time—"

Something caught her eye—something that infuriated her—and I trembled when I realized. She was staring at my palm. My *healed* palm. Her eyes widened as she turned my wrist, examining my hand. "What is this?"

"I'm not sure what you mean."

"Do not lie to me, girl. How did you heal these wounds?" Her voice was panicked. Frenzied and a small part of me exulted in her hysteria. While another part of me wanted to retreat from the manic expression on her face.

She searched my hands and wrists, trailing her bony fingers along the tattooed vines. It was enough to make me question whether they were as foolproof as we'd thought. She seemed to think we'd healed ourselves with magic. That our tattoos had failed.

When she realized they were still intact, she dropped my hand and huffed.

"Tell me, or else," she said, circling around Ladon like a huntress to her prey.

Ladon's head moved a fraction. He didn't have to warn me. I wasn't going to tell her a thing. She'd punish us regardless.

Reyna stood behind Ladon, resting her chin on his shoulder. He turned his face away, but his body went rigid. I could tell from his unnatural stance that he was held in place with those wretched vines.

I instinctively moved towards him, even though I couldn't do anything to help, but those same vines around my ankles and wrists stopped me in my tracks. I froze, watching as Reyna dragged her spindly fingers down his arms.

Ladon shuddered, breathing through gritted teeth. He was seething, and so was I. My hands were balled into fists at my sides.

Reyna traced the protruding vein in Ladon's neck with her tongue. He snarled and stared at a spot behind me, somewhere in the corner of the room near the ceiling.

"What are you doing?" My voice was broken. Barely more than a whisper.

She turned to look at me and smiled. "Don't worry, Emilie. He likes it. Don't you, Ladon?" Her hand traveled down his stomach and she splayed her fingers over his groin, slipping her hand between his thighs and massaging him over his pants.

"You don't have to do this."

"Oh, I know I don't. But I want to. And Ladon wants me to. You should feel him growing harder in my palm. Can't you see the way his breathing has stopped?"

She was right about that one thing. It was like he was holding his breath, grinding his teeth. His face had an unexpected flush to it. But I knew better than to think he wanted anything to do with her. He was struggling against those magical bonds. It was etched in his eyes. Written in his pursed lips.

I was horrified as those same vines held me in place, forcing me to watch as Reyna continued to rub her hand over the fabric of his pants. He didn't move aside from the rise and fall of his chest and the ripple of his jaw. I could hear each breath he released, breathing through his nose.

It was so quiet. And the blood rushing in my ears was so loud.

Reyna brushed her fingers against his cheek, and a growl rumbled in his chest. She eased her other hand into the band of his pants, sliding down and cupping him.

She continued to stroke him, and his body twitched. Muscles flexed and relaxed. Fighting against that twisted magic and being forced to succumb.

Why was she doing this?

Removing her hands from his body, Reyna stepped back and raked her eyes over Ladon. Like a beast ready to devour its dinner. Ladon looked anywhere but her face.

My heart ached for him.

She circled around to his front side, toying with the hem of his shirt before pulling it over his head. His arms reached toward the sky, not of their own accord, I knew. My lip trembled as her hands moved to the button on his pants.

His eyes caught mine for a brief moment before he looked away. I wanted to convey my deepest sympathies for him. To let him know that he wasn't alone. I'd be there for him when all was said and done.

I felt his shame. I felt his emptiness. His defeat.

Reyna slid his trousers to the floor, and I vowed not to look down. Not to take my eyes from his face.

But Reyna had other plans for me.

"Come here, Emilie."

My mouth went dry as I took a few steps forward, something tugging at my ankles, drawing me closer to her. To them.

Reyna circled behind him once more, running her hand down his bare chest. I tried not to follow that path. Tried not to think about what the slow movement of her arm meant.

My legs trembled the closer I got.

"On your knees," Reyna commanded.

"Wh...what?"

"On your knees." The words came in a staccato rhythm.

I had no choice but to obey. I was a puppet to her whims. I slowly knelt on the floor and looked up, still refusing to look at eye level. Ladon glanced down and his eyes darkened, seeing me on my knees before him.

I'm so sorry.

"Taste him," Reyna said.

My stomach clenched. It was impossible to swallow. I pulled my eyes from Ladon's gaze and finally stared straight ahead, trying not to panic.

Reyna stroked him lazily. He was hard and bigger than I'd expected. I'd never seen a man so utterly exposed. I'd never done anything like this. And for a moment, I was angry with myself. Reyna was playing these sick games with us and here I was, thinking about how inexperienced I was.

It was selfish.

But I had to remind myself that I was her victim, too.

I'm sorry, I thought again as I inched closer. I rested my palms on his thighs and felt his muscles tense at my touch. Wrapping one hand around the base of his cock, I closed my eyes and extended my tongue, tasting him.

His whole body jerked back, but Reyna held him still. Running her hands along his arms, up and down his chest, violating every inch of him.

"Again," she said. "Taste him like you mean it this time."

Tentatively, I grazed him again with my tongue, then wrapped my lips over the tip of his cock. For all the gossiping I'd heard amongst the ladies in my hometown, I'd expected him to taste worse. What surprised me even more was the warmth and weight of him in my mouth. It was unlike anything I'd ever experienced.

I swirled my tongue around him, feeling veins and the smooth skin of his shaft. I was so focused on not grazing him with my teeth that my jaw began to hurt after only a few seconds. Forcing myself to relax only made things worse. It allowed me to take more of him inside my mouth. I felt him at the back of my throat and almost gagged, immediately pulling back.

"Keep going," Reyna demanded.

I leaned forward again, hearing Ladon exhale a shaky breath.

Relax. Relax.

I repeated the words in my head like a mantra, bobbing my head in tune to the chant. I wasn't sure what I should be doing with my hands. Reyna hadn't given any specific instructions. So I kept one hand on his thigh, squeezing, using my touch to comfort him when words weren't an option. The other I kept on his cock, guiding him inside my mouth.

Ladon's legs began to quiver, his strength dissipating. I looked up, wondering what Reyna was doing to him now. He moaned, and I realized she wasn't doing anything. *I* was doing that.

Again, he tried to pull away, but Reyna stood behind him, eyes aglow with malice. She smiled down at me and chuckled.

Moments later, hot liquid exploded, covering my tongue and coating my throat. I swallowed before I could think. Then I sat back and coughed, wiping my mouth on the back of my hand.

I couldn't believe I'd done that. That I'd tasted him. That I'd made him...

Reyna's cackle reverberated in my bones, sending a chill down my spine. She strode to the door, her skirt breezing past where I sat. "I think you've had enough fun for one night. I'll see you tomorrow."

Chapter Twenty-Three

Ladon

WATER SLID DOWN MY back, swirling in a circle before it disappeared into the drain. I sat on the tiled floor in the shower, ridding my body of the filth I felt. Ridding my mind of the cursed images.

Reyna's hands on my body. *Emilie on her knees.*

I wanted to disappear. I don't think I'd ever been so mortified in my life. I thought I could handle this. The endless torture Reyna subjected me to—I could've gotten through it. But having Emilie present? Having her *participate*?

I didn't think I could ever look at her the same.

I tucked my head between my knees and rested my arms over the back of my head. The water turned colder the longer I sat, but I didn't want to move. I wanted it to turn freezing, to numb my body.

At least some part of me could be numb to the pain.

"Ladon?" Emilie's voice was quiet, almost indiscernible through the sound of the shower.

I jerked my head up, expecting to see her, but she was out of sight. Giving me my privacy, I suspected. I heard what sounded like her body sliding down the wall, on the other side of the small wall that separated the shower and the rest of the bathroom.

"Are you okay?" she asked.

I didn't know how to answer that. If I admitted I wasn't okay, then I felt weak. But if I said I was okay, then I was unfeeling. And then there was Emilie. How did *she* feel?

The number of times I'd failed to protect her was becoming too much to count.

"I'm sorry," she said, and I heard a faint tremble in her voice.

It was enough to make me stir. To slide across the floor from my spot in the corner and lean against that shared wall opposite her. I could sense her just on the other side.

I swallowed the knot in my throat. "You have nothing to be sorry for."

"I feel...I feel disgusted. I did things...*assaulted* you."

My stomach lurched forward. "You didn't have a choice. We didn't have a choice. This isn't your burden to bear."

"It isn't yours either, Ladon."

Logically, I knew she was right, but there was still a large part of me that blamed myself for everything that had happened since we'd left Renoa. The title of High Commander felt like a joke, a mockery of what I'd become.

There was a shuffling noise and then the sound of retching over a toilet. I sighed, turning off the water and picking up my discarded pants and quickly pulling them on. I couldn't hide here forever, no matter how much I wanted to.

Emilie was heaving into the basin. I poured a glass of water and gave it to her. "Are you okay?"

She looked up at me with tear-filled eyes, and I knew the answer immediately. I knelt so I was on her level and held her chin between my thumb and forefinger, my eyes darting back and forth between hers. "Don't you dare blame yourself for this."

"I feel"—she searched for the word, her bottom lip trembling—"violated."

I slouched to the ground, leaning my head on the cabinet under the sink. Emilie followed suit and sat with her arm pressed against mine. I didn't snap at her. I'd grown used to the feel of her skin in the past several weeks. Although, the feel of a different touch, her hand around my cock, her lips...

Fuck, I was not ready to think about that. I wasn't ready to think about what it meant...that although it had been against my will, I'd enjoyed it. The sight of her on her knees looking up at me through dark lashes...I hated myself for even picturing it. That was a memory best tucked into the deepest corners of my mind.

I reached for her hand, gently trailing the black vines etched in her skin. The ones that matched mine and dictated our actions. A tingling sensation coursed through my fingertips. She shivered too, as if she'd felt it.

"Tell me something honest," she said, leaning her head on my shoulder. Her warmth sank into me, battling the icy cold numbness I'd sought in the shower.

"I'm scared," I admitted. "I'm scared to hope. The odds are against us, and even if we do get out, I'm scared of who I'll be once we're free."

She shifted closer, wrapping her arm around my bicep. She rubbed my arm and even though it brought heat to my skin, I still broke out in goosebumps.

"You are Ladon Castelli. Revered High Commander of Osavian's armies and pain in my ass. Always have been and always will be."

I chuckled, and her hair brushed against my cheek. "And you are Emilie Duval, annoying, spoiled princess that I can't seem to shake."

"Queen," she said softly, and a new wave of panic rushed through me. I didn't dare meet her gaze as she spoke. "I'm supposed to be Emilie Castelli, Queen of Osavian."

My chest tightened at the sound of my last name next to hers. But she wasn't mine. In all the chaos, I'd forgotten that one little detail. The woman who'd touched me, tasted me...my brother's betrothed. I wanted to forget it again.

Her fingers tangled with mine mindlessly, and I didn't want to let them go. Didn't want to lose her touch. She stirred and began to pull away, but I laced my fingers firmly between hers. Emilie stared at where our hands connected for a moment, motionless.

"Ladon—"

"Please," I pleaded. I couldn't stand to let her go. I needed her presence to keep me sane. "Don't leave me."

It was more than a physical request. Mentally, emotionally, I needed her to get through this. We could deal with the consequences later—if we ever made it out alive.

"It's not that. It's...look at your hands," she said.

I followed her line of sight and studied every point where our hands connected—her palm against mine, her fingers grazing my knuckles, my thumb tracing the vine on the back of her hand.

The vine around her wrist...it was...*glowing.*

I gasped and sat up straighter. "What the..."

Suddenly, she was beaming with excitement.

"Ladon, I think you're...I think you're siphoning." She huffed a laugh. "Do you feel it?"

I'd felt the tingling earlier on but hadn't thought anything of it. Just a physical reaction to a tender touch. But as I watched the vines glow along her hand and wrist, I knew she was right. I was siphoning.

"How is that possible? Am I not hurting you?"

Her face showed a lot of emotion but pain wasn't present.

"I don't know how, but no, you're not hurting me. Maybe...maybe the magical vines are only restrictive of our own magic. Maybe it's possible to tamper with someone *else's* tattoos. Gods, Ladon. You can siphon. Do you know what this means?"

I knew exactly what it meant. Hope. It meant we could stand to hope again.

Siphoning was like refilling an empty cup. My own magic source had been depleted by the vines, but if I could borrow Emilie's... After drawing out the magic laced in those vines, Emilie withdrew her hand. "Do something," she said.

I chuckled. "Bossy little thing, aren't you?"

She tilted her head with irritation.

Not wanting to test her, I focused my attention on the dripping grate in our bedroom. After many weeks of not using my magic, it felt foreign to me. I channeled everything I had, which wasn't much, into carving that mountain to my will. There was a groaning sound as the mountain shifted. Several rocks fell through the cracks into our room, and then it went silent.

"What did you do? Did it work?"

I stood and walked until I was standing under the grate. Holding out my palm, I turned to look at her and smiled. "No more dripping."

I'd focused on bending the ground on the other side of the grate, molding it so the water ran in another direction, rather than falling into our room in an unpleasant cadence.

Emilie jumped to her feet, took four large strides from the bathroom to where I stood and wrapped her arms around my shoulders.

I froze. The weight of her body against me was a shock I wasn't prepared for. My head spun and my heart raced, but she held me tightly. Slowly, I relaxed and wrapped my arms around her waist.

She released me sooner than I'd have liked.

"What about you?" I asked. "Do you feel any different? Did it lessen the binds?"

If I could temporarily steal the magic from the vines, could she use her power too?

Emilie stretched her fingers and then closed her eyes. She inhaled deeply, and then the space between her eyebrows pinched together. She gasped and her knees buckled, hands flying to her forehead.

I was there to catch her as she fell.

"I take that as a no."

She shook her head, and my shoulders sank. When she peered up at me, she still seemed so full of hope, though.

"It's okay. This is a good thing, Ladon. You can practice, get stronger. Maybe even store some magic up to use on a grander scale. We have *options* now."

Her smile was wide and bright. One might even call it beautiful. The optimism she carried was contagious, and I found myself imagining the possibilities. A day where we'd blow through this mountain and escape home.

Emilie leaned forward, and her lips brushed against my cheek, leaving a blazing impression on my skin. It was like fire melting through my frozen body. Cold. I'd been so cold in this mountain, under Reyna's control, but that touch.

I gently touched the spot where her lips had just been. "What was that for?"

Her cheeks turned crimson, and I hoped she didn't regret it. I didn't regret it. She brought her hands up to her mouth and released a soft laugh. "I'm sorry. I was just so excited."

I stared at her, surprised by how carefree she seemed. After all, we were still in a dark, dingy cell of a bedroom. We were still being held captive. And we had done unspeakable things. There was a lot to weigh us both down.

But her eyes twinkled, and I fell into a trance. She dropped her hands while I continued to stare...at her rosy cheeks, at the freckles sprinkled across her nose, at those pink lips. I stupidly wondered what they might taste like.

"It's okay." She didn't need to apologize for touching me. Never again.

After another moment, she reached her hands out to me, and I held them, ignoring the spark that ignited when we touched. It was nothing. Just magic being siphoned.

Her smile was something that couldn't be ignored, though. Bright and beautiful. She leaned in closer, so our foreheads were almost touching, before she spoke once more. "Do it again."

Chapter Twenty-Four

Ladon

SLEEPING NEXT TO EMILIE turned out to be more difficult than it had been before. Even with our backs pressed together, I kept wondering about the touch of her skin. About the taste of her lips. That image of her on her knees made me shiver. The burning desire was quickly replaced with overbearing shame.

I knew it wasn't right to think of her that way. But it was as if a box had been opened that could not be closed. It tormented me, taunted me with her proximity. With the scent of her. It didn't help when she'd occasionally turn my way in the middle of the night, wrapping an arm around my waist. I knew she was doing it unconsciously, but that didn't stop my stomach from tightening. Nor my heart from thundering.

What had she done to me?

It was like a spell had been cast on me. For one moment, as I stared at her sleeping peacefully, I wondered if it was a spell. If it was something Reyna had concocted. But as far as I knew, no such magic existed.

Whatever vile thoughts I had bouncing around my head were my own doing. Just another personal failure to add to my growing list.

As I stared at the ceiling during another restless morning, Emilie shifted, swinging her leg across mine. I swallowed, feeling the entire weight of her thigh over top of me. Her fingers moved across my abdomen, twisting in the fabric of my shirt.

It took my breath away. I lay motionless, torn between not wanting to disturb her and needing to get away before I returned that delicate touch. Before I ran my fingers through her hair. Her hand unclenched my shirt and she exhaled, slow and content.

As sunlight began to creep into our room, I gave up on sleeping entirely and quietly slipped out of bed.

It was almost a week later before we had another chance to work in the Scholars' Cavern, during which we'd split our time between cleaning the kitchen and scrubbing toilets. At least we hadn't been forced to trim hedges again.

Emilie beamed as Luther led us to the cave. I kept throwing sideways glances her way, hoping she'd get the hint to knock it off. If they thought we enjoyed this work, they'd never let us see the library again.

Thankfully, she understood my message about halfway through the halls and masked her excitement. It was almost comical the extreme change in her demeanor. I tried not to laugh at her emphasized frown.

Luther hung around the cave for an abnormally long time, much to my displeasure. Emilie's patience grew thinner with every passing minute. She practically threw books onto the shelves between throwing menacing glances at the guard.

I couldn't figure out what he was looking for. He kept circling the exterior of the room, weaving in and out of aisles. Emilie and I had made a lot of progress and the first floor was now almost entirely put together, leaving us to tackle the second level.

"Where are you going?" Luther asked when I began to ascend the stairs.

I pointed nonchalantly. "To the next level."

He humphed, but seemed to realize there was little left to do on the first floor. Emilie quickly followed behind, dodging into the first row of books and pulling me in with her.

"Oy, what's wrong with you?"

She peered over my shoulder and then whispered, "Will he ever leave? Gods, it's like he's breathing down our necks."

"I didn't think it was that bad."

"He won't stop *looking* at me. It's creeping me out."

I stiffened. I didn't like that he was making her so uncomfortable. "Do you want me to threaten him?"

"No...what? No, that's unnecessary. Oh, I think he's leaving now." She wiped the hair out of her face and visibly relaxed.

The first thing she did when we were left alone was practically sprint to the hidden doorway to the tunnels. I sped walked to catch up with her.

"I didn't realize you had such an affinity for cardio, princess." My voice cracked and I immediately second guessed my choice of words. All the usual taunting and teasing we'd done before seemed out of place now. It felt wrong, somehow. Like there was a forbidden undertone that I needed to keep to myself, lest she see right through me. I cleared my throat, but she didn't seem to notice anything strange.

I watched while she traced the runes with her fingers.

"Magic is key. Here," she said. "Try to use your magic here."

Inching closer, I flattened my palm against the wall. I felt utterly silly. Emilie had been studying the runes in one of her books every night, but according to her, the instructions for opening the door were lacking. *Magic is the key*, it said, but it didn't explain beyond that.

I pressed against the wall, concentrating on the space between my hand and the stone. Focusing all my power on where the surfaces met. I sent a tremor through the stone, hoping something would echo back to me. Some sign of what I needed to do. But nothing came.

I shook my head, and Emilie frowned. She was determined, though. "What if you try to siphon?"

I'd never siphoned in this manner before. Wasn't sure it'd even work like this. For all I knew, the door held no magic of its own. Magic was the key, but was the door magic?

Before, I had exhaled power. Now I inhaled it. I pulled at the magic like a cord, tendrils expelling from my mind and reaching toward the unknown. Like searching for a light in the dark. I searched in every crevice, every crack in the stone, but came back empty-handed.

Again, I shook my head, feeling the weight of Emilie's disappointment.

"It's okay," she said. "We'll keep trying."

I was surprised when she reached out to hold my hand. She moved with such certainty. There was no hesitation. She wasn't struggling with the same inner turmoil that I was, it seemed. I couldn't shake that night from my mind. Did she even think about it all?

She held my gaze while running her fingers over my wrist, and I flinched. Not because I didn't enjoy her touch. Because I *did* enjoy it.

"What are you doing?"

She shrugged, eyeing me curiously. "How does it work? Siphoning?"

"I don't know how to explain it. It's like inhaling, but with your whole body. I can sense the magic like a physical touch, and I...absorb it. I feel it in my veins and it becomes my own."

"When did you find out you could siphon?" she asked, still tracing the vines on my skin.

I huffed a laugh. "When I was a kid. My brother and I"—I briefly paused, waiting for her to react at the mention of Cyrus, but she showed no emotion aside from the devoted attention to my story—"we were goofing around during a summit. All of the highest nobility around the kingdom had come to Renoa to discuss various political matters. My mother wanted us out of the castle, out of the way, so we wouldn't embarrass our father."

I smiled, recalling the way she'd shooed us out into the gardens. "We went into town, to this little gelato shop that Cyrus used to love. His favorite was caramel. He'd done something to piss me off that day—I don't even remember what—but I was desperate to get back at him. So I took the last of the caramel gelato. He was so pissed.

"I tried to exit the shop with it, but he grabbed hold of my wrist. I know he didn't mean to, but he accidentally singed my shirt. He burned through the fabric and then he began to burn my skin, too. I screamed, but within seconds, his power disintegrated. The red marks on my skin all but disappeared. Cyrus's jaw dropped as he stared at my arm. I think he was likely horrified that he'd burnt my skin, but he was even more horrified that his magic was gone.

"Neither of us really understood how it happened. I didn't bring it up to my parents that day. We were too afraid we'd get in trouble for fighting in town. But after a few more similar incidents, I eventually had to talk to someone. Turns out it runs in the family on my mom's side. There's been a line of secret siphons in our family tree, unbeknownst to the rest of the world. It skipped my mother and my grandparents, but my great grandfather was a siphon."

When I finished speaking, I realized Emilie was still dragging her thumb over my wrists. I shivered, and she stopped. She flipped my hands over and rested her hands in mine. "Do it again."

I knew she was under the impression that I could store the magic. That if I siphoned daily, maybe I'd have enough to move a mountain, or at least blast through one. But I'd never tried that either. I'd never had reason to.

"There isn't a lot known about siphoning, Emilie. Those who have the capability keep it to themselves. There are no texts to study or scholars to learn from. Everything I've learned has been from experience. I don't know if it'll be any use, siphoning like this daily."

She seemed unfazed, and I turned my focus to the magic laced in her tattoos. "We can try. What else are we going to do in our spare time?"

There was nothing remotely impure about the comment, but I instantly thought of several things I'd rather be doing in our spare time.

Gods help me.

My hands shook, but she didn't seem to notice. I needed a distraction. "I've shared a story. It's your turn to tell me something honest."

Her face went slack, thinking of something she could share in exchange for the story I'd provided.

"My brother is three years older than I am. The day of my fifteenth birthday, I caught him sneaking off with a girl. Some blonde woman I'd never seen before. She was quite beautiful, though, and she was laughing at something he'd said. I followed them and before he was able to duck into a closet with her, I'd called out his name.

"He turned around and scolded me. Told me to go back to my room and to mind my business, but I warned him. You see, I knew if I'd never met her, then she couldn't be nobility. She wasn't suitable for him. It's what our parents had repeated over and over again. The expectation for us to marry someone with standing. He was supposed to be king, after all."

I scoffed. It was well known that those in Dreslen liked to make up titles for themselves. The only king in Lourova was Cyrus. Emilie's brother Adrien was a lord at best.

She rolled her eyes but continued. "I told him not to make this mistake. His response was a cynical laugh, something I'd never heard from him before. He stalked over to me and put his hands on my shoulder, and I'll never forget what he said to me. He said, 'Emilie, you're in for a lifetime of pleasing other people. The best you can hope for is to have some fun along the way.' He practically skipped to meet that girl hiding in a closet.

"My brother had followed every single rule in his life. I'd never seen him so much as break a curfew. But here he was, taking a chance for a secret rendezvous with a beautiful young woman.

"Later that night he came to my room, looking...frazzled." She laughed. "He sat on the edge of my bed, looking much more somber, and asked me not to say anything to our parents. He looked a little bit nervous, actually.

"I asked him why he'd risk so much. If she was worth it. And he said that she was the love of his life. And it broke his heart that he could never be with her. It really hit me in that moment. That my future would be completely and utterly loveless."

My hands paused the slow circles I'd been tracing on her wrists. I tried to meet her eyes, but she was staring at the floor blankly. Waves of tragic longing rolling off her.

"It doesn't have to be that way," I said quietly.

She shrugged and finally met my gaze. "Cyrus is a good man."

I nearly choked on a sharp inhale, deflating a little. "He is. He'll be good for you."

I dropped her hands, no longer feeling up to siphoning. "I think that's enough for today."

Chapter Twenty-Five

Emilie

THAT EVENING, LADON AND I ate in silence. It wasn't the usual ominous quiet that preceded his private encounters with Reyna. Instead, it was a comfortable, peaceful quiet. The kind that two friends might share on a spring day, basking in the sun near the sea. There was no call to break the silence. We were able to just...exist. To cohabitate.

So when the knock on the door came, right as we finished our dinner—pork, rice and a brown sauce—we both startled. I watched as Ladon swallowed, his throat bobbing. He stood and donned that statuesque, unfeeling mask he wore so well, and waited for Reyna to enter.

This evening she wore a maroon garment, something akin to a robe. It draped across her chest in a deep 'v' and tied together with a satin bow in the front. The slit to the side exposed a long, lean leg, paler than the moon.

She might've been beautiful if it weren't for the vicious scowl on her face. If it weren't for the darkness that lingered in her eyes.

"Glad to see you're ready for me, Ladon. Is it possible you're looking forward to our evenings together?" She flashed him a flirtatious smile, and I wanted to gag. Then she turned to me. "I require your company this evening as well, Emilie."

Panic aggressively spread through my body. Reyna had never requested me unprovoked. Had I been foolish to think I was safe?

I looked at Ladon, and his brow was furrowed slightly, like he was wondering the same thing.

"Hurry up. I haven't got all day," Reyna said.

I stood on shaky legs, and together, Ladon and I followed her out of our room. I felt his hand on my back, then his breath on my ear as he leaned in close enough for me to hear.

"It's going to be okay. We will get through this."

I didn't know if he was trying to convince me or himself. I could hardly swallow, my throat had gone so dry, and my heart felt like it was going to pound right out of my chest. Somehow, knowing what awaited us was even worse than when I hadn't known.

As we passed the hall that would've led to the drawing room and dining area, Ladon and I exchanged a look. I assumed he was thinking the same thing as I was—that being taken to a new area in the mountain was suspicious. Danger lurked in every corner of the mountain and I could only imagine the ways that it could get worse than what we'd encountered so far.

We rounded a corner and then up a staircase, walking along a long, narrow corridor before we made it to our destination. Luther stood outside a dark double wooden door which was decorated with vines that looked eerily familiar to the ones on my wrists and ankles. She nodded to the guard, who opened the door. Then she ushered Ladon and I inside, following closely behind.

It was a bedroom. A four-post canopy bed took up half of the room, decorated with black fur blankets and tasseled pillows. The canopy itself was made of a thin lace rose pattern. Opposite the bed were two chairs centered around a towering fireplace, where a small crackling flame glowed in the night. It was the only light source in the room, except for...moonlight.

The wall across from the door had three grand windows, arched at the top and devoid of drapes. The view from the room was stunning. From this vantage point, I could see how high up in the mountains we were, and this room opened up to a black night sky. Nothing interrupted the view for miles. It was only the moon, some clouds, and endless stars.

Reyna poured a glass of wine before she sat in one of the chairs. It swiveled until she was facing the bed. Neither of us moved while she sipped from her glass. She gestured toward the bed. "Sit."

Ladon led the way, his courage helped me find my own. He sat on the end of the bed and, before I could sit next to him, Reyna barked at me. "Not you, Emilie. You can come sit next to me."

She patted the chair next to her. It felt like a betrayal to leave Ladon's side. But I didn't have a choice. If only Ladon's siphoning power had nullified the vines that submitted me to her will. I sat in the chair and she poured a second glass of wine, extending it to me.

I stared at it. And then stared at her. She was watching me. Waiting for me to drink.

"Oh please, Emilie. I didn't *poison* it." She laughed. "Although I can see why you thought I might."

Her laugh was unnerving. Reyna was the worst kind of villain. The kind that isn't completely sane. Whose actions and words don't make sense. Who acts on every impulse and thinks about the consequences later. She was unpredictable and terrifying.

I took a small sip, just so she would look anywhere else but me.

Finally, she returned her attention to Ladon. "I suppose you're wondering why I brought you here today. No dinner party this evening. My friends had other engagements preventing us from meeting tonight."

Ladon snorted at the word *friends*. I wished he wouldn't push her. But then again, he'd never been the type to hold back. She thrummed her fingers on the side of her wineglass, glaring at him.

"Take off your shirt, Ladon."

His jaw clenched before he reached over his head and pulled his shirt off in one smooth motion. He tossed it on the ground right in front of Reyna's feet.

I knew he meant to anger her, but I think his attitude only excited her more. She turned to me. "Isn't he a sight to behold? All chiseled and hard. The gods blessed him with that warrior body."

She gossiped like he wasn't there. Like I was one of her friends, and not her prisoner. I frowned and took another sip of wine, just to have something to do with my hands.

"I asked you a question, Emilie."

I swallowed my wine. "Um, yes."

Reyna seemed delighted with this response. "What is your favorite part of him?"

I hated her games. I hated them so much. I sighed and reluctantly raised my head, my cheeks burning. Ladon, meanwhile, was the epitome of calm and collected. Aside from the venomous look he was giving Reyna, he seemed completely at ease with the situation.

There was no way that wasn't a façade. I didn't believe for a second that it wasn't affecting him.

Reyna cleared her throat, urging me to answer the question.

My eyes raked his body in the politest way I could manage, never lingering too long on any one feature. I knew what it was like to be put on display and I didn't want to subject him to the same torture.

I went with the safest answer I could think of. "His hands."

Reyna was in the middle of taking a sip of wine when she paused, her glass in midair. "His hands? Hmm...you're absolutely right. I've never noticed how delectable they are. How...big..."

She stared for a while as if I wasn't even present. Her eyes lingering on him like she would devour him at any moment. His returning glare wasn't as kind. The animosity in the air was thick and suffocating. I was simultaneously waiting for someone to break the silence and worried about what might happen when they did.

"Emilie, why don't you go stand in front of Ladon?" She swirled her wine in the glass, contemplating her next steps.

I felt the unmistakable pull to follow her requests and walked over to the bed where Ladon sat. He broke his angry gaze, only momentarily to flick a glance in my direction, and as I stood between his legs, he finally seemed unnerved.

"Undress her, Ladon."

My stomach dropped, and I felt lightheaded. I swayed in place and felt Ladon's fingers wrap around my thighs, holding me steady. When his eyes met mine, there was a silent plea—an urgent request to forgive him for what he was about to do.

I swallowed and gave him a small nod.

My body felt foreign. It was as though I was living a dream—or a nightmare. The things happening around me were real, and yet they seemed...hazy.

"Breathe," Ladon whispered, as his fingers latched on to the bottom of my shirt, and he gently pulled it up over my chest and then my head.

I shook my head once my shirt was gone and my hair fell in loose curls over my shoulders.

He looked like he didn't know what to do next. To remove my bra and expose my chest. Or unbutton my pants which felt intrusively intimate.

I inhaled sharply as he gently caressed my waist, fingertips dancing along my stomach to rest below my belly button. I clenched my thighs. *That* reaction was unexpected.

Ladon didn't notice, though, and he slowly undid my top button, then the second and third. He tugged my pants over my hips and I had to hold his shoulders to keep myself upright.

He tossed them aside and looked into my eyes again. Such sadness there. Such need for assurance. To know that I was alright. That *this* was alright.

This was so far from alright. But it wasn't his fault. I gave him another encouraging nod, and he reached up behind me, unhooking the clasp on my bra and I let it fall in front of me.

Gods, I don't think I'd ever felt so self-conscious. Even in front of a group of strangers. Those people meant nothing. If I ever made it out of Murvort, I'd likely never see them again. Never have to *think* of them again.

But Ladon...

He was looking at the floor where my discarded bra had fallen, doing his best to give me privacy, even if we both knew it wouldn't last long.

Reyna had been awfully silent and chose this moment to squawk with glee. Her sinister laugh made me snarl, turning a fraction of my shame into pure hatred. Funneling my humiliation into a thirst for vengeance.

Ladon's eyes fluttered closed, steeling himself for what he needed to do next. It almost appeared as though he was more nervous than I was. He tentatively reached toward my black panties, slipping his fingers under the band. My breath hitched as he began to slide the thin material down my legs.

He was hardly breathing, staring at my feet as I stepped out of my underwear. Slowly, ever so slowly, his eyes traveled up my body. He licked his lips as he took in the sight of my bare pussy. That movement, that moistening of his lips, made my body tingle. Heat coursed through my veins and an ache I'd never known before settled in my core.

I heard him swallow roughly before continuing his study of my body. He clenched his jaw upon seeing my breasts. I didn't think he was blinking at all. And neither was I. I was too entranced by his every movement. The little details of how his body reacted to the sight of me. Like the way his pupils dilated. I wondered if mine were too.

If Reyna hadn't been in the room, I wondered if he would've tossed me on the bed and ravaged me. The hunger in his face said he might've. But I must've been imagining it. He was only doing this because Reyna was forcing him to.

I heard Reyna stand and move closer to the bed. A better position to watch us, I supposed. The mattress sank as she took a seat on the side, swirling that damn glass of wine. I should've drunk more to forget what was happening.

"You look so stressed, Emilie. Ladon, why don't you help her with that?"

Ladon has been fixated on a spot in the corner of the room behind me, but he looked over his shoulder when Reyna spoke. He tilted his head in question, which Reyna was all too happy to answer for him.

"You know...lay her down and *please* her."

A small cry slipped past my lips, and I cursed. I'd been so determined not to let her know she was getting to me. Ladon whipped his attention back to me with a raised brow. Gods, it was so difficult to swallow under his gaze.

I took a deep breath and moved so he wouldn't have to do it for me. I sat next to him and laid back. The blanket made of fur was heavenly against my skin, and I hated to admit it comforted me. I scooted back on the bed, and Ladon moved to kneel beside me.

Reyna huffed. "Gods, you both are so boring. Act like you've pleased a woman before, Ladon. I know you have."

I shot her a distasteful look without hesitation. How dare she throw that in his face? How dare she taunt him with the things she'd made him do? Especially while she was forcing him to do them to me now?

My thighs pressed together. Reyna hadn't allowed any of her guests to penetrate me. At least not with their cocks. Did that same rule apply to Ladon?

My heart was beating wildly in my chest. I was truly terrified. I'd never slept with anyone. I sure as hell never imagined my first time would be with my nemesis-turned-cordial-roommate while my abductor watched.

What if it hurt? What if I bled? My thoughts were racing, and I almost laughed at how ridiculous it was that I was thinking about losing my virginity when the real panic should've been over being assaulted. Maybe it was okay to be frantic about both.

"She looks eager for you. Or maybe nervous? Here. Have some more wine, Emilie."

Reyna held out her glass, but before the red liquid could reach my lips, a small amount trickled onto my chest. She poured it on me intentionally, and as my mouth fell open in shock, Reyna bent down and licked her way across the swell of my breast.

She looked at me once she'd finished. "Oops. Clumsy me. Ladon..." She made a hooking motion with two fingers and my eyes shot to him. He understood her instructions perfectly, judging by the look on his face.

226

Absolute horror. And maybe a tinge of disgust? I couldn't help but wonder if it was directed at me. If he didn't want to touch me. Did he still consider me to be beneath him, even after the weeks we'd spent together? My shame intensified.

Ladon's hand slid from the inside of my knee, up my thigh, and came to a stop inches away from my pussy. I was still clenching my thighs together and he couldn't move his hand any further without prying my legs apart.

He wrapped his other hand around the back of my knee and slowly pulled. My legs turned molten, and he was able to position me any way he wanted. I let out a shaky breath while he bent my knee and pushed it toward the side, splaying me wide. He settled between my legs and I stared at the ceiling, unable to look him in the eyes.

Just the touch of his fingers was enough to set me into a frenzy. So warm on my cold skin and so delicate but strong, too. Feather light touches with a steady hand that had me rolling my hips forward as he inched closer...closer...

Oh gods, I was *aroused*. And he had to know it, too. From the way I was on full display for him, he had to see the glistening moisture between my legs.

I gasped and almost jumped out of my skin when his finger finally brushed over my clit, dragging down over my folds. My fingers twisted in the soft fabric of the blanket beneath me. I didn't know if it was worse to tease me first or to just get it over with.

His finger slid up and down my slit with ease, and I wondered what he thought of how wet I was. Was he aroused, too? Or was he judging me for it? The more he teased at my entrance, the harder I found it to breathe.

My mind and body were at odds—half of me wanting to feel him inside me and the other half that couldn't see past how *wrong* this was.

I writhed beneath his touch, deciding in that moment to quiet my thoughts and listen to my body. I could regret it all later. Right now, I only wanted him. His fingers inside me. His mouth on my skin.

I was wound so tight; I was on the verge of combusting before he even pushed a finger inside. He was still circling that bundle of nerves and teasing me with my own arousal.

I hadn't had the courage to look into his eyes, but as he pressed one finger into me, my head jerked up and I found him staring at me with immense fascination. Biting my lip, I let a whimper escape and his upper body tensed.

Slowly, he withdrew his finger and then pressed in again. I watched as he worked my body in ways I'd never experienced. Each stroke had me clenching around his finger, desperate for more.

Ladon pulled his finger out entirely, rubbing my clit again before he inserted a second finger. If it weren't for the other hand holding my legs wide, I would've trapped his hand between my thighs, grinding against those heavenly fingers.

He stroked my inner walls with such precision and expertise. It was like he knew my body, knew every spot that would send me spiraling. He stretched me—filled me—in ways that I had only imagined, pressing against a spot that had me levitating. My legs quivered, and I felt the pressure building. Unbearable need. I moved my hips in time with his hand, meeting him thrust for thrust.

I was so close, so gods damned close.

"That's enough, I think," Reyna said. And I had forgotten she was even watching. Ladon glanced at her quickly, and then he was pulling his fingers out. I grasped his wrist. I didn't think I could stand to lose the feeling of him inside me.

I *needed* that release. And Reyna knew it. She laughed as Ladon removed his hand from my grip and pulled the rest of the way out.

The emptiness in my core was devastating. Even more so when the lack of stimulation forced me back to reality. Back to this dark room, trapped in a mountain, doing unthinkable things with Ladon. Guilt hit me like a wave.

Ladon wouldn't look at me, and my eyes welled with tears.

As if Reyna couldn't get any worse, she spoke to Ladon again. "I wonder...Emilie has tasted you, Ladon. Aren't you curious how she tastes?"

His lip curled in a snarl before he casually brought his fingers to his mouth and sucked on them. He took his time licking his fingers clean, and when he finished, he licked his lips too.

"And?" she asked.

"Delicious," he spat. I knew it was only to enrage Reyna, but I could've died from embarrassment. My cheeks had never burned so bright.

Reyna smirked. "Emilie, it's time to go."

For a moment, I thought I heard her incorrectly, but when her eyes snapped to me, I jumped into motion. I crawled to the edge of the bed and gathered my clothes, rushing to put them on.

I sprang for the door, but before I could open it, I looked back to where Ladon was still kneeling on the bed. His shoulders slumped, and he looked every bit as tormented as I felt.

Reyna jabbed a finger into his shoulder, and he rolled over on the bed, facing the ceiling. He closed his eyes as she straddled him, untying the knot that held her robe together. The fabric fell around her hips and I couldn't watch anymore.

I opened the door and snuck out quietly. Luther was still standing there, waiting to lead me back to my room in silence.

Chapter Twenty-Six

Ladon

ONE COULD ONLY DESCRIBE this feeling as numb. I was numb.

I stared unblinking at the ceiling, only catching minor glimpses of the black hair that sprawled over my chest. Reyna's leg was strewn across my hip, her robe only partially covering her naked body. Her chest was warm against my side, and yet I felt completely and utterly cold.

I felt like I had died. My body was lifeless. My blood had stopped flowing. I cursed each breath of air because it reminded me that this was real. That I was still alive, and this nightmare hadn't ended.

I'd lost count of the days. We had to be nearing two months beneath the mountains' peaks. Two months of being used and discarded. Two months of being little less than a pet. Reyna's plaything.

I peered down at her. She was lazily drawing circles on my chest. A vein pulsed in her throat and I silently questioned what it would feel like to slice it open. To bite down until her blood ran freely, running down my chin while I watched the life drain from her eyes.

If I did that, all the beasts of the mountain would kill me in an instant. Actually, they'd probably take their time. They'd probably kill Emilie first and force me to watch. Then they'd slowly torture me to death, too.

My heart stuttered as I imagined what they might do to Emilie. I didn't have to imagine her look of fear. I'd seen it already. I'd caused it.

I knew what it was like to be used. And now Reyna was forcing me to use Emilie. She'd had my cock in her mouth. And I'd had my fingers inside her. I was disgusted with myself. As much as I wanted to leave Reyna's bedroom, I was scared to face Emilie again.

I could see so clearly the look of horror on her face when I pulled my fingers out of her. The pained expression that I had caused.

I sighed and Reyna paused her movement against my skin. She sat up and peered at the moon beyond her windows. "I suppose it's time for you to be getting back to your own room. After all, I'm sure you'll have a busy day tomorrow."

She patted my upper thigh, fingers edging dangerously close to my cock. It drove me crazy, the way she pretended like this was all normal. Like Emilie and I were merely *guests* and we should be *grateful* for our luxurious stay.

None of this was normal. And she was fucking demented.

She gathered her robe and pulled it over her shoulders, tying a neat knot across her stomach. I stumbled to the end of the bed to retrieve my own clothes. She ran a hand down my back as I buttoned my pants, making my skin crawl. I couldn't wait to hop into the shower. I needed to feel the burn of the hot water scalding my skin and removing every trace of her.

Reyna stood on her tiptoes and pressed a kiss to my neck, right below my ear. I shuddered and took a step away from her. The sound of her laughter filled the room.

"Don't pretend that you don't like our little arrangement, Ladon. I feel the way your body responds to me."

"I cannot control the things you force from me. You're not special," I grumbled. "Do you also feel the way I flinch? Do you see the nauseous look upon my face?"

She slapped me across the face, leaving my skin tingling. I preferred the pain over everything else she subjected me to.

"I'm not special?" she shrieked. Her pupils were dilated and again, I questioned her sanity. It was my turn to laugh.

"No. You're a wench who's incapable of seducing a man on your own, so you resort to rape. You disgust me."

Reyna moved with rage, grabbing me by the balls and, as badly as I wanted to fight, I found my wrists strapped to my sides. She tightened her fist, and I bit my tongue to keep from releasing a yelp.

"Careful, Ladon. Believe it or not, there are worse things I could do with your cock. Feed it to the dogs, perhaps?" Her eyes blazed with what I could only describe as madness. "You think I'm so vile? I wonder what your precious Emilie thinks of you?"

I furrowed my brows before quickly replacing my expression with nonchalance. "What does Emilie have to do with this?"

She clicked her tongue. "It's quite obvious the way you look at her. Only...I think she finds you equally as vile. Poor little Emilie almost ran out of here crying tonight. Haven't you done things to her too? Against her will?"

"*You* did those things." I clenched my fists, but still could not move them otherwise. How dare she insinuate that I was at fault.

"I most certainly did not. I merely requested them and you acted. Did you feel a magical tug on your hands today, Ladon? Or did you move them of your own accord?"

I wanted to vomit. Night after night, Reyna had forced me to do things. And every night, I couldn't fight her. Every night I had to obey while internally screaming. At some point, I'd stopped resisting. Had she made me move tonight? Or did I do that on my own? Everything was such a blur.

Reyna laughed again, and I wanted to wipe the smirk from her face. "I'll see you soon, Ladon. Have a good night."

Back in the room, Emilie was asleep facing the wall. She didn't stir as I entered and quietly closed the door. I immediately headed to the shower and stripped out of my clothes. Turning the knob as hot as it would go, I lathered my body in soap and scrubbed till my skin turned raw.

Then I sank to the floor and closed my eyes. Reyna's words echoed in my mind, accusing me. And I honestly didn't know if she'd been telling the truth. It was enough to drive me mad.

I remained under the hot water until it turned to room temperature, and then to freezing cold. Then I stayed a while longer until my teeth began to chatter and my skin went numb. I welcomed the lack of feeling.

The pipes groaned as I shut the water off and dressed in loose fleece pants and a cotton shirt for bed. I tried not to wake Emilie as I slid under the cover, but she immediately rolled over to face me.

I could see the light reflecting in her eyes, and my heart pounded. There were many things I wanted to say and yet, none of them felt quite right.

"I didn't mean to wake you," I whispered, choosing the easiest words to mutter.

"You didn't. I was waiting." She sighed and slid her hand under her cheek. I rolled on my side, mirroring her with my head resting on my bent arm. "I'm sorry."

I scoffed. We were not about to have this conversation again. "Please, do not apologize to me. You have absolutely nothing to be sorry for."

Something lodged itself in my throat. All I could think about was Reyna's last words to me. The guilt I felt was overwhelming, and I didn't know how to express my regret. Emilie pressed her palm to my cheek, and I realized I was shaking.

"Neither do you, Ladon."

I shook my head. "Yes, I do. I never should've...I can't live with myself knowing that..." My tongue felt swollen and heavy, making it very difficult to speak. "Reyna said—"

"I don't care what she said. Don't let her fill your head with lies. Don't you see? She wants to hurt you in any way possible."

Gods, she wasn't going to let me confess. Little miss know-it-all. I snapped. "Please. Let me speak. I need to say it."

She pulled back her hand and pursed her lips. There was something so familiar about the reaction. It took me back to our first few days in Renoa and, for a moment, I felt completely normal again.

I took a deep breath. "Emilie, promise me you won't hate me."

A flicker of a smile crossed her cheeks. "Of course, I won't."

"I mean it. What I need to tell you...I feel sick."

She had the decency to look a little worried. "Go on, then."

"Reyna said something to me before I left. She said...she said that she didn't force me to do anything. She didn't use the magical binds. She said I did everything myself. She said that you...you...that I was just as vile as she was."

That isn't what I'd meant to say. I'd meant to question whether or not she found me as repulsive as Reyna had said, but my fear of rejection got the best of me. Of course, Emilie was repelled by me. She was betrothed to my brother, for gods' sake. It was never supposed to be me. And asking her to deny it? That felt incredibly selfish.

"Ladon, this is the last time I'm going to say it. You are not to blame, either. I don't care if she didn't force your limbs to move. She has other methods of persuasion. If you hadn't listened to her, she would've forced your hand. Or she would've tortured you for your insolence. I could say the same for myself. She did not force me to...to *enjoy* it."

I was rendered speechless. It was so quiet; I could hear her swallow. She had enjoyed it? No way. I didn't believe that for a second. Her face had been full of agony as I'd removed my hands from her.

I cleared my throat. "You looked rather upset."

Even in the dim moonlight, I could see her cheeks turn slightly pink against her otherwise pale skin. "I was...frustrated."

Something pounded inside of me—a primal beast wanting to be released. This was dangerous territory. Really fucking dangerous.

"Oh," was all I could manage to say. "Right."

Now I could picture that moment even more clearly. Except instead of seeing her pained expression, my mind was buzzing with the fact that I'd left her unsatisfied. Dangerous indeed.

She inhaled deeply and exhaled slowly. The small space between us felt infinite and miniscule at the same time. I didn't know if I wanted to scoot closer or jump out of bed and hop in the shower again. Some magnetic force was pulling me in, desperate for our bodies to connect. For our souls to connect.

I wanted to show her what satisfaction felt like.

Her gaze bounced back and forth from my lips to my eyes, and when her tongue darted out to moisten those pink lips, I wanted to cover her mouth with my own. To be tangled in the very essence of her.

I raised my arm, hoping to wrap it around her waist and pull her body against me, when a flash of lightning lit up the room. We both jumped. Thunder rolled and the sound of rain could be heard beyond the small grate in the ceiling. Whatever fire that had been building between us was doused.

Emilie rolled away from me, my skin immediately mourning the lack of her warmth. "Goodnight, Ladon," she said quietly.

I had to admire her self-control, even though I hated it. Gods knew I had none at that moment. "'Night."

Chapter Twenty-Seven

Emilie

LADON SPENT THE FOLLOWING week seemingly avoiding me. At least, the best he could while also being trapped in the same room as me. He dodged my attempts at small talk and, aside from our daily sessions of siphoning, he avoided touching me, too.

I'd thought for a brief moment that he might actually be attracted to me. That I'd been wrong, and he wasn't disgusted by me. He seemed so close to kissing me that night after our *moment* with Reyna.

Clearly, I was wrong. He obviously still saw me as inferior to him. Repulsed by the very thought of me. It was for the best, anyway. I had no business getting caught up with Ladon while engaged to his brother.

His brother...every time I thought of Cyrus, my spirits fell. Not because I missed him. I missed the life I'd been promised. I'd been so angry with my parents for not giving me a say in my future. Now I had no future at all. I should've been grateful for everything I had.

What a stupid girl I'd been.

I took my time in the shower, not wanting to *burden* Ladon with my presence. His behavior was so juvenile; I couldn't be bothered with it. I lathered my hair with shampoo twice and considered a third time before deciding that would be wasteful.

I turned the water off and stepped out, wrapping my towel around my chest and tucking it to stay put. In the cloudy mirror, I could make out the gaunt features of my face. Gods, I was so pale and sickly. I'd give anything to feel the sun on my skin again. The Dreslen heat suddenly didn't seem so unbearable.

My hair was a tangled mess, and I had to carefully run my fingers through it before even attempting to comb it. If I had known I was going to be kidnapped, I might've had it cut. I chuckled a little at the thought.

Perfect. I had made it to the state of hysteria in my captivity.

I caught a glimpse of Ladon staring at me through the mirror. He quickly looked away when he realized he'd been caught. I suddenly felt too exposed in my towel and reached instead for my clothes. Dressing in silence, I wondered what horrors Reyna had in store for us today.

We returned to cleaning the drawing room for that day. Even being in the room made my skin crawl, though it looked so different in the middle of the day. The lights were bright rather than the deep reddish mood lighting Reyna set for entertaining guests.

These mage lights were bright white and highlighted every single speck of dust and mark upon the furniture, making it easier for us to clean up.

Ladon started to scrub the floor using a handheld sponge, while I retrieved the fabric cleaner from a supply cart. I didn't have to wonder what the stains were this time. I'd been there when one of the guests spilled her wine. I'd seen another use the arm of a chair to extinguish his cigarette.

I'd only been summoned one time during the past week, but Ladon...he'd been taken nearly every night. Some nights he didn't return until well after I'd gone to bed. Those nights I felt more enraged for him than myself. He didn't deserve this. Neither of us did.

I returned to the supply cart to grab a rag and bumped into Ladon as our paths crossed.

He brushed a hand through his white hair and returned to his work.

My patience reached its breaking point. "Are you just going to ignore me for the rest of our time here?"

He stared at me with a blank expression. "What do you mean?"

"You've hardly said a word to me in the past week. You can't even say 'excuse me' or 'sorry for bumping into you?'"

His lip curved into a smirk. "You're excused."

I let out a shrill cry of frustration and threw the rag at his face. He caught it with minimal effort and laughed. "Gods, princess. If you wanted my attention so badly, you could've just said so."

I was going to murder him. If Reyna wanted to kill him, she'd have to get in line. I shoved him and he stumbled a couple of steps back, peering down at me with surprise.

"What is wrong with you?" he asked.

I shoved him again and his lower legs hit the edge of the couch. He was close to toppling over. So I shoved him again. He grabbed my wrists and snarled.

"Have you lost your mind?" he growled.

"Yes, yes, I have. I'm losing it here and you've abandoned me. You've mentally checked out." I tugged at my wrists, but he held them tight. "How dare you?"

His hold softened, as did his expression. "Emilie." He said my name softly and slowly, like a prayer. Like a desperate plea. "I'm still here."

"You're not. You're not here. Not really. Not like I need you to be. We're supposed to be in this together."

"I'm here," he repeated. Then he brushed a thumb over my cheek and I realized I'd begun to cry. My breath hitched, and I attempted to retreat again. This time, he let go and allowed me to take a step back.

He stared at me with a look that felt too invasive. I was vulnerable, completely naked, even though I still had all my clothes. I tugged at my sleeves uncomfortably. I needed something to shield myself from that look. From that gaze that could see every bit of my heart and soul. The things that terrified me and the things I desired. I wasn't ready for him to see it all.

Ladon looked at the floor, seeming to contemplate something. Then his eyes returned to me. "Tell me something honest, Emilie."

I sniffed and shook my head. My eyes still burned with fresh tears. "What do you want to know?"

His throat bobbed as he swallowed. His voice was hoarse. "When I touched you, what was going through your head?"

My breath halted altogether. My heart ceased its beating. I was certain my chest was red as could be underneath my shirt. Thank the gods this top had a high neckline.

"No," I said.

"*No?*"

"Ask me something else." How could I answer that question when I was still trying to sort through my feelings myself? What if I told him I'd wanted more of him? Would he mock me? What would that mean if I wanted him? That I was a sick person? That I'd betrayed Cyrus, precisely like Ladon had expected me to? Was it a trick?

"I'll tell you what I was thinking," he said, taking a step forward. I stepped back again, maintaining the distance between us.

"Please, don't."

He stilled, and I thought a look of disappointment darkened his face. Surely, I'd imagined it. "Right," he said.

He idly played with the sponge in his hands before turning back toward his task. Kneeling to the ground, he began to scrub again. I took that as my sign to return to work, too. This conversation was over, and we were no better off than when we'd started. I still felt isolated…deserted.

"I used to paint," he said, and I paused. "When I was younger, after my father died. My mother and mind healer had encouraged it. I'm not very good at expressing myself. I keep a lot of things bottled up. Mum says I'm a lot like my father in that way. Art was my outlet."

He sighed and tilted his head toward the sky. "What I mean to say is that I haven't abandoned you, Emilie."

I watched as he turned to face me again, looking utterly defeated. Tortured, even. I had to fight the urge to kneel beside him and wrap him in a warm embrace. My breathing was shallow as I waited for him to continue.

"I have no intention of ever leaving you. You and me…we are in this together. I'm sorry if I've let you feel otherwise."

I knew his confession couldn't have been easy for him. I mustered the courage to tell him something honest in exchange for what he'd given me. "I was thinking…I was thinking that I wish Reyna weren't in the room. I was thinking that I wished it was real."

Immediately, I questioned my sincerity. If Ladon would throw it in my face and use it against me. But he blinked a few times, his mouth parted slightly. I thought I saw a tinge of pink stain his cheeks. "You're going to be the death of me."

Falling asleep that night was harder than it had ever been. There was something freeing about confessing to Ladon. About laying it all bare for him. There was also something terrifying about it, and that was what kept me up.

He hadn't scoffed at me. Hadn't told me that I was sick or twisted. He hadn't reprimanded me either. I thought...I thought he might've felt the same. It was confusing and my mind wouldn't stop racing.

I also couldn't stop thinking about the arm around my waist. Ladon had fallen asleep with his chest pressed against my back, keeping me warm on a particularly chilly night. It was as much for his benefit as it was for mine. Body heat was the best way to ward off the cold air.

I didn't stop him when he draped his arm over me and pulled me in tighter. In fact, I might've nestled in closer, relishing every touch we shared. Every point of contact sent energy coursing through my veins. Delightful to experience, but terrible for trying to sleep.

When I finally did fall asleep, my dreams were even more tormented. Reyna haunted every single one of them. Over and over, she taunted me. Made sure I knew how insignificant I was.

He'll never want you. You foolish girl.

She stripped him of his clothes, and seconds later, their bodies connected. He was all over her and I could only watch, frozen where I stood. He released her lips long enough to join in Reyna's heckling.

You must be an idiot to think I could ever be attracted to you. Look at you. You are nothing.

Wind blasted through my mind and their images swirled like shadows, reforming with Ladon kneeling on the ground and Reyna standing over him. She cackled while he writhed in pain.

Look what you've done, Emilie. You're killing him.

No. That wasn't possible. She needed to stop. I needed to stop her. He was dying, blood spilling from his eyes and ears. I lifted my hands to make her stop, and his cries worsened.

My hands...my hands were glowing white. Black vines still decorated my wrists and stretched all the way to my fingers. Something dark and evil was flowing from them.

I *was* killing him.

His screams were unbearable. I heard the sound of bone snapping and his arms and legs bent at odd angles. He curled into a ball on the blood-soaked floor.

Make it stop. Make it stop.

Ladon looked at me, face contorted in agony. His skin was burning and peeling off in flakes, like ashes falling to the ground.

Make it stop. Make it stop.

I didn't know what to do. There was nothing I *could* do. Reyna's laughter filled the chamber. What did she want? I'd do anything to stop her. To stop myself.

Make it stop. Make it stop.

"Make it stop! Make it stop!"

"Emilie. You're having a nightmare. Wake up, Emilie."

Rough hands were on my cheeks. A dark figure bent over me.

"Stop! Please stop! Don't hurt him."

"Hurt who, Emilie? No one is here. It's only me. It's Ladon."

"Ladon?"

"Yes. Look at me."

My vision began to focus. The cloudy haze of sleep began to fade, and I was able to take in my surroundings. Back in our room, with Reyna nowhere to be found. Ladon was hovering over me, studying me with concern.

"Ladon?" I said again. He didn't feel real. I reached out to touch his face, and he cupped my hand with his, leaning into my palm.

"Yes, Emilie. I'm here."

"It felt so real," I whispered. But there he was—skin, muscle, bone—all intact. No sign of the blood spewing from his insides.

"It wasn't." He brushed my hair back, and I shivered. It felt like a part of me had been left behind in that nightmare scene.

Ladon laid down next to me and cradled me in his arms. Slowly, the shivering subsided. My fingertips trailed down his bare chest, to a patch of fine hair on his lower abdomen. He inhaled sharply.

I wanted so badly to continue moving my hand, but thought better of it. I looked up and caught him staring right back at me, stealing my breath away.

"Thank you," I said.

He smirked, alleviating some of the tension between us and his voice was feather light across my cheek. "Anything for you, princess."

Chapter Twenty-Eight

Ladon

"What if you try—"

"Emilie," I groaned. We'd been tampering with that gods-forsaken entrance to the tunnels for hours now. Despite every attempt I'd made, the wall hadn't budged.

"I know you're tired, but who knows the next chance we'll get. We need to make the most of it."

She was right. Our days in the Scholars' Cavern were getting lesser and lesser.

"Give me your hands," I said.

She didn't hesitate to place her palms in mine. It was a position we'd grown accustomed to. Sometimes in the mornings, before we'd even got out of bed, I'd lazily play with her fingers, tracing the black ink on her skin. The rush of excitement I got from it went beyond siphoning the magic in those vines.

I pulled at the magic, absorbing every bit of it I could. She'd been right about one thing; I could store it. It took a while before I began to notice it, but I could feel the magic building up inside me. Like a muscle I'd been training over time. It was easier to wield my power now than when we'd first been abducted. I was getting stronger.

After a few more minutes, I released her hands. "We should probably get some work done, or Reyna will think we're not doing anything here."

"You're probably right."

I followed her as she made her way down the aisle and up the stairs to the second floor. We were almost done organizing this level, and then it was just a few more to go.

"Let's take our time though," I said. "Leave some work so we have to come back again."

Emilie nodded in agreement.

"Have you done any more research on the runes?" I asked, sliding a book onto its proper shelf.

"There isn't much more to be done. The runes are pretty clear. 'Magic is key.' But it doesn't specify what magic. Is it a certain incantation or do you need a relic? At this point, it's a guessing game."

She sounded frustrated; her brows furrowed as she huffed. I knew it was driving her mad, not having the answer. In the time I'd watched her studying the various books she'd stolen, I'd come to learn that Emilie was incredibly intelligent. And she hated not knowing everything.

We continued to work throughout the afternoon, keeping a slow and steady pace as we made our way through the second level. Unfortunately, the higher we went, the less damage there was to sort through. I surveyed the third level, quite certain it would only take a matter of hours if we were to go at our best pace.

I glanced at Emilie, and she seemed to deduce the same thing. She bit her lip and frowned.

"What if we just pushed a few shelves over?" I asked, and she smiled.

"That will definitely get us in trouble with Reyna."

I sighed and prepared to dig in when I noticed eyes peering around the corner of a shelf in the distance. I narrowed my eyes and stalked in that direction. The creature dashed behind the shelf and disappeared from my sight, so I picked up my pace.

I heard Emilie's footsteps behind me. "What are you doing?"

She must not have seen it.

"Shh," I said. For once, she listened to me without arguing.

I rounded the corner where I'd seen it, right as it slipped down another aisle. But I'd caught a glimpse of its black wings—the harpy. Why was the damn thing running from us?

She veered left and then took another turn right. Her knowledge of the cavern worked against me and eventually I lost her trail altogether. I slid my hands through my hair in frustration while I worked to catch my breath.

"What the hell was that?" Emilie asked.

"You didn't see her?"

"Who?"

"The harpy. Why's she got us chasing after her like that?"

Emilie rolled her eyes. "You probably frightened her."

"Ridiculous. I didn't even say or do anything."

"Except run after her like a crazed man," she said, finding her way to the end of the aisle and peeking in row after row, expecting to find the harpy in one of them. "She's a bit skittish. Haven't you noticed?"

It was my turn to roll my eyes.

Emilie finally found what she was looking for in the next-to-last aisle. I watched as she approached the harpy with an outstretched hand—a peace offering.

When she noticed me, the harpy stared with wide eyes and it hit me that Emilie was probably right. I'd accidentally frightened the damn thing. How was I supposed to know she was so cowardly?

Emilie spoke, and the harpy finally moved its gaze to her instead. "You're okay. He won't harm you. I'm sorry if he startled you."

The harpy gave Emilie a small nod.

"Were you looking for us?"

Another nod.

"You have something to show us." It wasn't a question so much as a revelation. A hope that the harpy had discovered something else that might help in our quest to escape. "Will you show us?"

The harpy again looked at me with suspicion in her eyes.

"Apologize to her," Emilie said.

"What?"

"Apologize, you asshole."

I scoffed. "I didn't do anything."

The look Emilie shot me was nothing short of fury.

"Fine." I held my hands up in surrender and then turned to the harpy. "I apologize for scaring you. I didn't mean to. I didn't recognize you at first and then you ran and I assumed the worst. You have nothing to fear from me."

The harpy blinked once. And then twice. I assumed that was the best I'd get in return. She did seem less rigid as she glided past where Emilie and I stood and led the way to an empty corridor that branched off from the main hall—empty save for a small wooden desk and a filing cabinet.

On the desk was a worn leather-bound notebook. Much thinner than any of the other tomes in the cavern. It wasn't even wide enough for a title down the spine.

The harpy picked it up and held it out to Emilie, keeping it open to a specific page. I couldn't help but notice that it was handwritten.

Emilie held it carefully as she read. Her expression went from curiosity to excitement to shock and then to horror. "Where did you get this?"

"What is it?" I asked.

She ignored me and took a step toward the harpy, holding the notebook up with one hand. "*How* did you get this?"

The harpy stared blankly, unable to offer any explanation. I was still very confused.

"What does it say?" I asked again.

Emilie flipped back open to the page she'd been reading. "It's a journal. This entry here...it describes the creation of the tunnels. They believed the mountains themselves were alive, and the tunnels were a living thing created by the gods, too. Since they seem to have magic of their own and can appear and disappear at will. Civilians kept getting lost within the series of caves and tunnels."

"And?"

"And the person who kept this journal...they sealed the entrances to those tunnels to prevent more losses...using blood magic. We need *blood* magic to open them."

"What does that even mean? Whose blood?"

"It's an outdated practice. Most mages find blood magic to be barbaric. It requires a sacrifice—blood, which I'm sure you could've guessed. Not only that, but typically when magic is bound in blood, the spell or enchantment wears off in death. Whoever sealed these doors must've had a lot of expertise to keep them intact after death."

"Or they're still alive?"

She shook her head. "I doubt it. You said you read about the tunnels somewhere?"

"Yes, in an old war strategy book from Renoa. Our soldiers came across them during the Battle of Endless Night."

She frowned. "That was over a hundred years ago. There's no way this mage is still living."

"So then how would we open it?"

"Blood of an heir would be the next best thing."

Emilie closed the journal again and flipped it over. On the back, a name was engraved. "Remi Lemaire."

I groaned as soon as she spoke the name.

"What is it?"

"Lemaire...that's Reyna's surname."

"You can't be serious."

"I'm afraid I am."

Emilie stared into space for a few moments, weighing our options. "Well, I guess we'll need to get a sample of her blood."

I huffed a laugh. "You've actually lost your mind. How do you propose we do that? Walk up to her and give her a bloody nose? That'll go over well."

Emilie fidgeted. "Maybe...during one of your *encounters*."

My jaw dropped open before she continued.

"If you could...I don't know...bite her or something. Make it appear as if it were in the moment." She froze when she saw the look of indignation on my face. "Never mind. Forget I said anything. There's got to be another way to open them."

It took a moment to regain my motor skills. To absorb what she'd said...what she'd suggested. As much as the idea horrified me, she was on to something. It was likely the best way to take a small amount of blood from Reyna without her giving it much thought.

I didn't even want to think about how Emilie came up with the idea. Had someone done that to her in the past? Suddenly, my head was filled with images of me biting Emilie's shoulder while she pleaded in my ear.

I sighed.

"You're right. How much blood do we need?"

Her face brightened. "Just a few drops. Enough to spread over the runes."

"And where will I be putting these drops?"

She looked around the room and then navigated to the cabinets. She opened the top drawer, rummaged around for a few seconds, and then opened the middle one. After digging through the junk, she excitedly pulled out a small ink vial.

She opened it and tipped it upside down, not bothering where its contents landed.

"Emilie," I gasped.

She shrugged, but only a few drops emptied from the vial. "It was almost empty."

"If we're forced to scrub that stain in a few days, I'm blaming you."

Emilie smiled at me as I shook my head. "Ladon, if we have to remove that stain, I will personally make sure it is done. Gods forbid you have to clean up my messes."

She put the stopper back in and pressed the vial into my chest. My hand snapped up to cover hers, clutching the vial between us. I held it there longer than necessary and her eyes met mine.

She gave me a questioning look before I pried the vial from her fingers and placed it in my pocket. I took a step back.

"Think you can handle it?" she asked.

"Of course."

The one night I actually wanted Reyna to show up to our room was the night she chose not to. I didn't question her reasons. I focused on being grateful for having one night of peace.

Emilie didn't seem very put out by it either. As much as she wanted a few drops of Reyna's blood, she wanted to keep me from harm too.

I began a set of exercises while Emilie went back to her books. We both had our ways of dealing with boredom in captivity. I preferred physical exertion while she preferred mental stimulation.

After my fourth or fifth round of the same circuit, I peeked over at her. She was staring at an open book, her chin propped on one hand. It had been a while since I'd seen her turn the page.

"Is everything alright?" I asked, sitting up.

She looked at me and I enjoyed the way she eyed my abs for one long moment before answering me.

"I think you should train me to fight. The first time…in Renoa, I mean…I don't think either of us took it very seriously. If something happens to you, I should at least know the basics of self-defense."

I stood and moved until I was hovering over her. "Nothing is going to happen to me, princess."

"You don't know that." She closed her book rather abruptly and then chewed on her bottom lip. "Tell me something honest."

"What do you want to know?"

"Why do you call me princess?"

I raised a brow. Of all the things she might want to know, that was the one on her mind?

"Because it bothers you."

She rolled her eyes, evidently not in the mood to play. "You know as well as I do that I'm no princess. My official title in Dreslen is Lady."

"Do you want me to call you Lady, then?"

"No," she said through gritted teeth.

"What then? I don't want to hear another word about you being the future *Queen* of Osavian."

Even if it was true. It irritated me that one day she'd be above my ranking. She was from fucking Dreslen, of all places. And everyone knew that Osavian was superior to Dreslen.

Or at least I thought I knew that. Spending time with Emilie had me questioning what I believed about their people. If I'd been wrong about her, was I wrong about all of them?

She saved me from having an existential crisis with three words. "Call me Emilie."

Chapter Twenty-Nine

Emilie

IF TRAINING IN RENOA had been awful, then training in Murvort was akin to living hell. The one advantage I'd had during our first training sessions was my anger. My hatred for Ladon fueled me to work harder. My aggression made me lethal.

Now that we'd broken through some of our barriers, I was more distracted than ever. I was hyperaware of every hand placement—both his and mine. When he grabbed my arm to demonstrate a move. When I touched his chest so he could fix my aim.

Ladon was—for lack of a better word—bewitching. He'd always been handsome, but this...I was having a very hard time focusing. It didn't help that he chose to train me without a shirt.

And when I cursed him and told him it was distracting, he grinned and slyly suggested that I could take mine off if I wanted to even the playing field. And just like that, my panties were wet.

So fucking distracting.

It also didn't help that every time I was taken to be Reyna's plaything, she made it her sole mission in life to make sure I was robbed of every orgasm I came close to. And now my thighs were clenching together as Ladon's breath danced across my ear.

"Are you even trying? You might be weaker than I originally thought," he murmured, and I summoned enough frustration to jab my elbow into him, slide a hand under his arm and twist out of his hold the way he'd shown me a hundred times.

"Better, but if I'd actually been trying to hurt you, you would've been done for."

I crossed my arms over my chest and sighed. "I'm not as strong as you. I don't have all those muscles," I said, waving a hand at his physique. A vein that snaked down his forearm and blended in with the vines was particularly distracting at that moment.

"You don't need to be as strong. You just need to be strategic. Let's practice again from the ground."

I lay down with my back on the floor while Ladon straddled my stomach. I could tell he wasn't putting his full weight on me. He didn't think we were there yet.

"Ready?"

I nodded.

He threw mock punches, and I looked for the window of opportunity, dodging punches and waiting for the right moment. There—I crunched up and wrapped my arms around his middle, pulling him down toward me. He struggled, though not with his full strength, while I dug my heels in and pushed off the ground, flipping us both over so Ladon was on his back now.

"Not bad," he said. It had only taken me fifty tries. The first time, I could hardly lift him, which is why I was certain he was making it easier for me. My thighs hadn't gotten that strong in a matter of days.

"You're holding back," I said.

"I'm teaching you like I would any beginner. You can't skip ahead five steps."

"We don't have the same amount of time you would've to teach a beginner. I need to learn these skills *now*."

"And you will," he said, sitting up and grabbing my chin with one hand. He stroked my skin with his thumb and gods, I forgot everything I was supposed to be learning again.

My breath hitched, and his thumb stilled. He dropped his hand as well as his gaze and nervously cracked his neck.

"Let's take a break."

I wanted to keep training but my mind was so erratic, a break to clear my thoughts would be beneficial.

We didn't have time to practice again until after our chores were done for the day. Reyna's guard dropped by earlier than usual and took us to clean the kitchens.

Once we returned to our room, Ladon settled into his usual routine of staring at the ceiling and waiting for Reyna's return. At least these days he was eating before he laid down.

I didn't interrupt him. If this was how he needed to prepare, then I wouldn't interfere. I only wished there was something more I could do.

Like clockwork, Reyna came to retrieve Ladon a little after an hour. He made an excuse to use the bathroom before he went with her. I figured he was making sure the vial was in place and wouldn't be discovered over the course of the evening.

Reyna stared at me while she waited. And I stared right back.

Heinous bitch.

"I have quite the evening prepared. It's too bad you can't join us, Emilie."

My eyes narrowed to slits.

"Nothing to say for yourself?"

I was pretty sure she was baiting me. Hoping I'd slip up and she could use it as an excuse to take me along, too. Not that she needed an excuse. She could take me this evening too and I'd have no say in it.

But I was convinced she was only interested in Ladon. For every evening she summoned me, she summoned him ten times more. She was so transparent in her lust for him.

I, on the other hand, was just a thing to be humiliated.

Reyna's mouth curved into a forced grin. Like she'd sucked on something sour and was trying to smile through it. "You are quite the insolent little—"

Her eyes narrowed. She was looking at something over my shoulder. I didn't want to turn to see what it was, but it sent nervous energy through my body.

What could it be? The bed? The blanket? My stomach did a flip and then twisted itself inside out. A book?

She moved closer and pushed me aside. I panicked, wishing Ladon would hurry up. Reyna bent down and pulled out one of the tomes I'd stolen. Thankfully, not the journal. The corner was just barely peeking out from beneath the blanket.

"And where did you get this? Surely you did not steal this while you were supposed to be working in the Scholars' Cavern?"

Words failed me. I couldn't form a single excuse or explanation for what I was doing with that book. My only saving grace was the fact that it was the children's fairytale book, and not one of the more substantial texts.

"I took it," Ladon said, suddenly reappearing in the room. I wasn't sure how much he'd heard, but it was enough to realize I was in trouble. He shrugged his shoulders. "I wanted some light reading before bed."

She narrowed her eyes and seconds later, Ladon crumpled to the floor, hands wrapped around his stomach in agony.

"What are you doing?" I shouted. "Stop!"

I knelt beside him and his body was humming with electric currents, zapping my fingertips when I tried to put my hands on him.

His face went from stark white to fiery red, and then a purplish tint began to blossom on his cheeks.

"Stop, you'll kill him." I screamed, reaching for Reyna. My hand closed around her wrist and her concentration was momentarily halted. Ladon took a deep breath, but Reyna's eyes still flashed with a dangerous current.

She swung her arm and backhanded me across my face. I felt with my finger a small trickle of blood where one of her rings must've dug into my skin. She raised her hand again, ready to make a second blow, but my defensive lessons with Ladon had vastly improved my reflexes.

I ducked to the side, and in two smooth steps, I was at her backside. I jammed my heel into the back of her knee and she stumbled forward. Ladon had regained some of his composure, and he tripped her with an extended leg.

Reyna crashed to the floor with an animalistic cry. Tangled in the long skirts of her black dress, she struggled to stand. I threw all my weight on top of her, flinging my fists at whatever piece of her I could reach.

I wrapped my wrists around her slender throat and squeezed with all my might. I'd never killed before, and as I stared at my fingers tightening around her neck, I wondered if I even had it in me.

And then Ladon was by my side. He was saying something, but I couldn't hear him over the pounding in my ears. Reyna's shoulders shook with silent sobs. She knew it was the end for her and that only fueled me further.

Ladon moved out of the corner of my eye, and then a shadow was towering over me. Suddenly, powerful hands were wrapped around my neck. I gasped and then realized just how little I could breathe. Ladon...it was Ladon cutting off my air flow.

What was he doing?

Reyna's shoulders shook again. But she wasn't crying...she was laughing. She choked out words through gritted teeth. "You...stupid...girl."

I released her and clawed at Ladon's hands instead. I couldn't breathe. My chest ached and the edges of my vision began to shrink. The more I struggled, the harder he seemed to squeeze.

Reyna straightened up and dusted off her dress. "Have you forgotten who is in charge here? I could have him snap your neck if I wanted to. Get rid of you once and for all. No...I think I have a better idea for you, sweet Emilie."

She snapped her fingers, and Ladon released me. I fell to the floor, coughing and massaging my neck.

"Emilie," Ladon rasped. "Emilie, I'm so sorry. I didn't...I couldn't..."

"Silence," Reyna roared. "I've had quite enough of both of you this evening. I was only going to require Ladon's services tonight, but I think you're both in need of another lesson or two. I will break you the same way I broke all of my pets."

I never thought I'd miss the dainty golden chains Reyna had put me in that first encounter with her dinner guests. Until I was only given a leather collar with a sapphire stone dangling in the front. Nothing else to cover my bare body.

One of the guards led me from the bathing chamber to the drawing room where guests had gathered. I swallowed when my eyes met Ladon's across the room, and I quickly diverted my gaze.

He was *dressed* in a similar fashion. A simple studded collar and nothing more to hide behind. Reyna was taking the 'pet' analogy quite literally this evening. He was standing between two armchairs, the one on his left occupied by a blonde woman in a green velvet gown, while the woman on his right wore a shimmering silver dress that matched her graying hair.

I couldn't help but notice the way the blonde woman's hand crept up his backside.

I was directed toward an ottoman in the other corner of the room, planted in the middle of a circle of men. I kept my head held high while men and women alike gawked, consciously aware of every sway of my hips and bounce of my breasts.

I sat on the ottoman, crossed my legs, and kept my arms across my chest.

"Oh, don't be shy now. Come, sit with me." An older man grinned, and I noticed a fake golden tooth where his canine should've been. He didn't wait for me to respond before scooping me up and sitting me on his lap. The prod against my ass was unmistakable.

He wedged my legs open with one of his knees and slid his hand between my thighs. I bolted upright at the rough scrape of his fingers on my clit.

I hated being touched, but the humiliation was even more dehumanizing for me. The way everyone watched while he poked and prodded at my entrance. The way they laughed when he pinched a nipple.

He played till he got bored and then passed me off to the next person. Some of them allowed me to take sips of their wine. And I never turned it down. I wanted to dull the pain and forget everything when morning rolled around. Some offered me a smoke from the cigarettes, though I avoided that because I wasn't sure what drugs they were using.

One man attempted to unbutton his trousers, arm wrapped tight around my torso. "I bet your cunt feels so delightfully tight."

I struggled against him, but I was fairly certain it only turned him on more. I looked around the room, for once desperate to find Reyna. I knew she wouldn't allow this.

The man stroked himself and tried to force his way between my thighs. "Get off me," I shouted.

He tossed me around like I weighed nothing and, with my face pressed against the back of the couch, I finally caught sight of Reyna. She furrowed her brows and walked toward us.

"What are you doing, Vero? You know the rules."

Vero paused with a hand still trapped between my thighs. I refused to open them.

"Oh, come on, Reyna. Just one fuck. How much longer will you make us wait? Cyrus clearly isn't coming for her. There's no need to keep her pristine."

Reyna snarled. I wasn't surprised she was saving me as a bargaining chip for Cyrus, even if it was foolish. Ladon mattered more to Cyrus than I did. She should've kept him untouched, not me. Regardless, I was glad she had.

"Don't make me send my dogs for you, Vero," she spat.

"What if I pay? How much for one load?" he joked, and I nearly vomited in my mouth.

"She's not for sale," Reyna responded. Vero grumbled and I could sense Reyna's frustration. She was losing control of the situation. "Maybe next time."

Tears welled in my eyes while Vero rejoiced. He tugged his hand free and went to find another companion to fuck, since I was off limits.

Halfway through the night, I found myself sitting in a chair across from Ladon. Two women were draped over him, kissing his neck and dragging long nails up his thigh.

I did my best not to look any lower than his chest, but the evidence of his assault was clear, even in his face as he gritted his teeth. In his neck as his vein pulsed erratically. In his chest as he inhaled deeply.

He flashed me a sharp look that I understood to mean *don't worry about me. I'll take care of myself*. Still, it was hard not to reach out to him and offer my comfort.

Ladon was right, though. I needed to worry about myself. I was sitting on the lap of the younger man with the crooked nose, who happened to be the worst out of all of them.

While the older ones were often clumsy and the women seemed more or less curious, that man...he knew what he was doing. He didn't just want to embarrass me. He wanted me to hate myself.

He started slow and sensual, rubbing his finger through my folds. He forced me to lick his fingers before he swirled them over my clit. It was always the same with him. He wanted it to feel good so I could be even more humiliated as I tried to fight off the growing need in my belly.

His patience was maddening. It didn't matter how long it took; he always waited until I was aroused before pressing a finger inside me. I jolted, and the sudden movement made Ladon look up.

I watched his throat bob as he looked to where the man had his finger inside me. Ladon snarled, and I could see the anger rising in his silver eyes. But his hatred was nothing compared to mine.

I writhed against the man, trying unsuccessfully to prevent him from touching me in a way that made my toes curl. He held me down and thrust his fingers inside me over and over again until my legs were shaking.

I bit down on my cheek. Despite how close I was to falling over the edge, I knew it wouldn't last. Right on cue, he removed his hand from between my legs and pinned my thigh open for those gathered to see how wet I was.

"Look at the glistening cunt. Such a pretty thing you are." His breath was hot in my ear and I grimaced.

It was Ladon's turn to look at me with compassion, only I wanted him to comfort me. I wanted him to hold down the man so I could skin him alive. And then I wanted him to hold me, so I could crumble in the safety of his arms.

Ladon gave me a curt nod, like he understood everything I was thinking. *One day, we will be free. And we will kill them all. You and me.*

The rest of the night passed in a blur. More bodies. More loud laughter and smell of smoke. More spilt wine. I did my best to drown out everything around me, meeting Ladon's gaze whenever I could. The only thing that kept me upright was his solidarity.

As the guests began to leave and Ladon and I were dismissed, Reyna pulled me to the side.

"Here," she said, thrusting a small vial into my hand. For a second, I thought it was the one we'd stolen from the library office, but this one had more of a copper tint than the empty glass vial we'd taken. The contents inside were dark and a similar consistency to the cream I put in my coffee.

"What is it?"

She shrugged one shoulder. "Drink it and find out."

I hated Reyna and her games, but there was no denying her. If I didn't voluntarily drink it, she'd force it down my throat or inject it into my veins.

I downed it in one gulp. I'd expected something more bitter, but it was light with notes of citrus.

"Now will you tell me?"

"A contraceptive. You'll be required to take them weekly from here on out."

She took the empty vial from my hand and shoved me toward Luther. I followed him back to our bedroom, still in shock.

Chapter Thirty

Emilie

I DISAPPEARED INTO THE bathroom as soon as I got back. Ladon had returned a few minutes before me and had already showered, judging by his wet hair and rosy pink skin.

Once I finished, I settled into bed next to him. My mind still raced with thoughts of impending doom. I'd swallowed the tonic Reyna had given me without a second thought. Clearly, my luck had run out. Things were only going to get worse from here. Very, very worse.

"You're restless," Ladon said rather matter-of-factly.

I sighed. I couldn't lie to him. But the thought of telling him the truth was equally terrifying. It was a vulnerability that I'd yet to share with him.

"Tell me something honest," I said instead, hoping for a decent distraction from both my whirling thoughts and the aching between my thighs.

Ladon repositioned, turning on his side to look me in the eye. "I know you're avoiding something, but I'll play along."

The warmth of his skin was a minor distraction in and of itself.

"I worry about you. And not just because I'm supposed to be this grand protector. Your pain"—he tapped his chest—"I feel your pain in my chest, like it's my own. Your fear is my fear, Emilie. When I saw you tonight...it killed me. I worry about you because I'm terrified of losing you."

I forced myself to swallow and found myself unable to speak for a few very quiet moments. "I worry about you, too. Even more than I worry about myself, if that's even possible. I think...I think you might be the person I care about most in this life."

His mouth twitched into a semi-smile. "Is that your truth?"

I shook my head, and he narrowed his gaze intently.

"I want you to have sex with me," I blurted before I could second guess myself.

His eyes went wide and his mouth hung open, and gods did I hate myself for wanting to taste that beautiful bottom lip. To trap it between my teeth.

My heart was racing, but I carried on before I lost momentum. "Reyna gave me a contraceptive today. I think...I'm certain that things are going to escalate."

Speechless, he gave me a look that said to carry on.

My hands trembled. "I've never...I've never had sex. And if I'm going to be forced...well, I want my first time to be mine. I want control over that much, at least. I don't know how much more humiliation I can handle and I just need...I need this to be my own. And of course I realize that you're involved in this too. I don't want you to think that I'm not considering your position in all this. And what you might be thinking or feeling. And you've been stripped of things too, so obviously you can say no—"

"Emilie." His voice cut into my endless rambling. We stared for an endless moment, during which I regretted everything I'd spilled. "Yes."

"Yes?"

"I will have sex with you."

"Oh," I said and then nodded like it was a nervous tic. Like I couldn't stop myself from bobbing my head like a brainless bird.

Again, that heavy silence sank between us. "Now what? I mean, what...what do we do?"

Gods, I'd imagined my first time in many different ways, but I never imagined I'd be a nervous wreck who could barely string a sentence together. I also never imagined it would be with Ladon, but I'd been wrong about that too.

I could hear him struggle to swallow. Like it was painful for him, too. Had it been selfish to ask this of him? Was it too late to take it back?

"This contraceptive...you took it already? And it's...effective?" he asked.

I nodded and bit my lip. "I think so, yes."

In return, a low torturous rumble caught somewhere in his throat. He looked me up and down and I was certain my heart was going to pound out of my chest.

"Okay," he said, shifting his weight till he was propped between my legs.

His proximity, the full essence of him covering me, caused me to suck in a sharp breath. My entire body was shaking.

"Relax," he said. And if that was not the most unrelaxing thing he could've said. He huffed a laugh, like he could read my thoughts. And then his fingers on his right hand interlaced with mine. He squeezed lightly, and I squeezed back.

"Should we..." he toyed with the loose fabric lying over my belly and I shook my head fiercely.

"Can we keep that on?" The idea of being exposed...it made my anxiousness unbearable. I'd been stripped bare for too many people.

He gave me a quick reassuring nod and then fumbled with the button of my pants. For a second, I almost believed that he was as nervous as I was, but that couldn't be. He'd done this before. What did he have to be nervous about? He smoothly unfastened my pants and pulled them down over my hips.

It never ceased to amaze me all the ways I could worry about inconsequential things in the midst of catastrophe. How terrible the shampoo was...how bland the bread was...the complete and utter lack of sex appeal of my undergarments...

Rough fingers skimmed the skin above my hips, dipping down until they hooked under the elastic band.

He pulled them down a fraction of an inch and my chest came off the mattress. I couldn't breathe. Was this what hyperventilating felt like?

"Emilie," he groaned, sliding a hand beneath my shirt and splaying it over my stomach. He gently pressed me back to the bed, rubbing his thumb against the underside of my breast. "Are you sure about this?"

"Yes, yes. It's only going to be worse if I have to do it for Reyna's entertainment. Please. Please do this for me."

He tilted his head in a way that told me he clearly wasn't convinced. His thumb kept stroking, kept drawing deep and slow breaths from me, until I realized the pounding of my heart had returned to a somewhat normal rate.

When he was satisfied with my more relaxed state, he returned his focus to my panties. This time, I let him slide them off in one fluid motion.

The rumble that sounded in his chest was pure animalistic. It ignited something inside me and made me want to run my hands over him. To see if I could make him repeat it.

He shifted his weight toward the end of the bed and lowered to his forearms, his head poised right above my bare cunt.

He licked his lips and his breath was hot against my throbbing clit.

"What are you doing?" I asked frantically.

His shoulders shook with a chuckle, and his head fell to rest on my hipbone. "Emilie." He drew my name out like it pained him to say it. All I could do was bite my lip and stare, waiting for him to do something. Something other than resting his head, that beautiful head of white hair, on my hipbone. I shifted a bit nervously.

When he lifted his head again, his eyes were filled with lust as they bore into me.

Keeping his eyes on me, he used one arm to lift my leg over his shoulder, brushing it with his chin in a move so intimate I was hearing color and seeing sound. My senses were heightened in an unnatural way. I shivered when he turned and, rather than his chin, his lips skimmed over my inner thigh.

I grasped at the sheet beneath me and his eyes returned to meet mine. "If we're doing this, we're doing it right."

Slowly, and with his eyes still locked on mine, he lowered and pressed a gentle kiss to my clit. My head rolled back, his delicate touch overwhelming my senses and simultaneously making me crave more.

He moved his mouth with more ferocity, alternating between soft, tender licks and soul shattering suction. I propped myself up on shaky elbows to watch while he devoured me. My legs trembled even more viciously as I watched him move.

His tongue flicked over my clit before he pressed it flat against my folds. He traced the rim of my entrance with the tip and then slid up again to close his mouth over that throbbing bundle of nerves.

"Oh, gods."

With one hand wrapped around my hip to hold me in place—despite my persistent writhing—he reached to grasp my breast underneath my shirt. I arched into him and his fingers squeezed my thigh so brutally I was sure it would leave bruises.

My entire body was consumed by him. He was the air I breathed and the blood flowing through my veins. There wasn't a piece of me that he hadn't claimed.

He continued to suck on my clit until I was on the verge of combusting, and then he paused just long enough to slide one finger inside me.

"Fuck," he said slowly. Drawn out, full of hunger and longing. And need.

He slid his finger in and out. In and out. In and...my toes curled and I felt like I was about to free fall over a ledge. With one finger still hooked inside me, he used his thumb to rub circles over my sensitive bud.

He kissed the inside of my thigh. And below my belly button. And above my clit. He left the trace of his lips all over me, still using his finger to stroke my inner walls.

I was panting and moaning, completely unashamed of the sounds coming from my mouth and from where his hand was thrusting inside me.

And then...it was all gone.

I almost screamed in frustration. This was no better than all the times Reyna had tortured me before. To have that sweet, relentless release torn from me...I would kill him.

He sat back on his heels and pulled his shirt over his head, and all murderous thoughts evaporated. I wanted to feel his chest. To feel his hot skin against mine. And the pressure of his body weighing down on me.

He unfastened his pants and tugged them down, his cock springing free and twitching with need.

He was already aroused. And big.

I was suddenly very thankful for how attentive he'd been. It occurred to me that I wasn't apprehensive about how big he was. Wasn't anxious at all because I needed him...to feel him inside me.

I wanted to know what Ladon's cock felt like inside me. I wanted to know the faces he made while buried inside me. And the sounds he made as he fucked me. I wanted it all.

He knew it too and wasted no time wrapping his palm around his length and giving his shaft a couple of languid, sensual strokes.

I ran my foot along his rib, and he flinched, pinning me with a devilish glare. His lazy strokes became firmer.

And then he lowered his body over me, lining the tip of his cock with my entrance. I felt the nudge of him and squirmed while he dragged his cock over my folds, lubricating himself with my arousal.

He was moving painfully slow. Like this was somehow harder for him than it was for me.

"Please," I begged. Enough teasing.

He groaned as he thrust forward, sliding into me in a way that burned and stretched and made me gasp for breath.

"Fuck," he said shakily. He paused long enough to look me in the eye. "Are you okay?"

"Yes. Keep going."

He huffed a laugh again and his white bangs fell over his eyes. I reached up to brush them away just as he slid in a bit further.

He kissed the inside of my palm before I cupped his cheek.

"You feel so fucking amazing. So fucking perfect."

I clenched involuntarily around him, and his eyes rolled back in his head. I could get used to this.

He moved slowly, inching forward while I adjusted to the intrusion. The throbbing ache gave way to something more blissful. Before long, he was fully sheathed inside me. And then my hips were moving in time with his. And he was pulling my knees up. And the angle was *everything*, and he was everything.

And this moment—this joining—it was everything.

I was fighting to take in every shuddered breath, and every whispered praise he had. Fighting to keep conscious and not die from the agonizing, insatiable euphoria that was building inside me.

More. I needed more of him. I didn't know how much more he had to offer, but I wanted it all.

I locked my ankles behind his back, and he drove into me with unbridled want.

He thrusted deeper inside me, filling beyond what I thought I was capable of. He ground against my clit and sank his teeth into my shoulder. The pain mixed with pulsing pleasure and I dug my nails into his back, shattering completely.

Waves upon waves of searing bliss crashed over me and I fluttered around his cock repeatedly. Squeezing him and digging my knees into his sides. I trembled as the waves kept coming and just when I thought it was done, more tremors wrecked my body.

Ladon's hips rocked slower, and he put all his force into driving deeper and coaxing a seemingly endless orgasm from me.

"I can't," I panted. "I can't take any more."

"Yes, you can, princess." Each movement of his hips sent electric pulses through my body. He managed to nudge that sensitive bundle of nerves with each thrust, leaving me reeling each time he slowly pulled out.

"Oh, gods..." Another orgasm ripped through me unexpectedly. My muscles spasmed, and I cried out his name.

"Ladon, please."

I lost all control of my body, and Ladon drove into me one last time, moaning as he came undone with me.

His quivering subsided, and he pulled out, the space between my thighs now painfully empty.

Without a word, he left the bed and headed to the bathroom—I assumed to take his routine shower.

What we'd just done...the weight of it hit me all at once. I shivered, my bottom half still exposed. No amount of rubbing my arms could make me feel warm again. Without Ladon by my side...

I didn't expect him to cuddle or anything like that. After all, we weren't exactly romantically involved. But to leave me so abruptly...

Did he regret it? Did sex with me make him feel dirty the same way Reyna made him feel? Hot tears pricked my eyes.

I felt alone and abandoned. And a little disgusted with myself for using Ladon like that. But I couldn't bring myself to regret it. It was good. Better than I could've ever asked. But apparently, he did not feel the same.

I covered my face as the tears began to fall.

"Emilie?" Ladon's voice was filled with surprise. The mattress sank beneath his weight and I uncovered my eyes to find him looking at me with a soft expression on his face.

He held a wet washcloth, and I sucked in a sharp breath as he gently pressed the warm cloth between my legs.

Ladon shook his head. "I knew this was a bad idea. I'm sorry. I never should've agreed to it."

I choked on a sob. He hadn't abandoned me. He wasn't disgusted with me. No—he'd gone a step beyond to ensure I was cared for. I found my voice again and assured him. "I'm fine. This is what I wanted."

"You're crying."

"I thought…I thought you might've regretted it. You left so quickly…"

He tilted his head, still clearing the traces of him from between my legs. Then he smirked, comforting me in a way only Ladon could. With his inexplicable charm and mesmerizing lure. "I don't regret it. I don't regret it in the slightest."

Chapter Thirty-One

Ladon

I HAD SEX WITH Emilie Duval. Good sex. Hot sex. The kind of sex I wouldn't forget about anytime soon. The kind of sex I'd like to repeat in the future.

As I laid awake listening to the sound of Emilie breathing, curled up next to me in nothing but a thin, oversized shirt, I couldn't stop thinking about it.

Just the memory of her pussy clenching around my cock had me seeing stars. I tightened my hold around her waist and breathed in the scent of her hair.

In this cold and damp prison, Emilie was my one beacon of hope. The reason I hadn't completely given up yet. She gave me purpose, fulfilled my sense of duty and obligation to protect.

But now, we were verging on something more. Friendship didn't seem quite right. We had an unbreakable connection—our clashing personalities melted under the heat of hardship, blended together through shared suffering and solidified with trust, compassion, and affection.

I needed her like I needed air, which was incredibly frightening for someone who had never relied on anyone but myself. And even more dejecting to know that one day, if we ever escaped, I'd have to set her free.

She was my pillar to lean on, but I wouldn't be hers. Couldn't be hers.

It gutted me to know that I had betrayed my brother. Would I even be able to look him in the eye if we ever saw each other again? If he knew the things I'd done, would he want my head on a stake?

I nestled closer to Emilie, seeking comfort in the soft curves of her hips, letting my fingers trace the skin under her breast. She made a soft, drowsy noise of approval, but otherwise did not stir.

I wished more than anything that we'd been given a different life. One in which I was her betrothed and we could spend lazy mornings in bed like this, without the threat of Reyna darkening our days. That alternate life would've been nice.

By sunrise, I'd nodded off again. When I woke, Emilie was already out of bed, the shower running in the next room.

I yawned, stretching as I sat up. Our breakfast was already sitting on a platter near the door, steam rising from two identical bowls of porridge. My stomach grumbled at the mere sight of it.

When Emilie returned with wet hair and flushed skin, I'd finished the entire serving and half of the fruit we'd been given as well. I looked up with a mouth full of berries, searching for any hint of what she was thinking. Or feeling.

She shifted her weight from foot to foot, running her fingers through the tangled mess on top of her head.

She bit her bottom lip before speaking. "So, do we talk about it or pretend nothing happened?"

"Definitely not the latter," I blurted out without hesitation. That was an impossible ask. At the moment, I could hardly go ten minutes without thinking about sex with Emilie.

"Okay," she said, licking her lips and staring around the room. Like it might provide some sort of relief for the awkward tension between us right now. "What do we do now?"

"For starters, you should probably have some breakfast."

"I'm serious, Ladon."

"What makes you think I'm not?"

"I...I don't know."

"You're adorable when you're flustered."

"I am *not* flustered." The rosiness in her cheeks darkened, and I stifled a laugh. Then she quirked her head to the left. "Did you just call me adorable?"

It was my turn to flush. I hadn't meant to let that slip.

"I didn't mean it like that."

"How did you mean it?" she said with a sly grin.

"In the condescending way."

"Liar." Her grin expanded until the top row of her teeth was visible. Her eyes twinkled, and I found myself getting lost in them.

I couldn't dispute her claims, so I only shook my head and rolled my eyes dismissively. Feeling as though she'd won, she retrieved her breakfast and began to eat with a grin of satisfaction.

I smiled too. Even though it hadn't been my intention, I'd managed to resume our familiar banter and ease the tension. If she still felt any lingering awkwardness, she wasn't letting it show.

That evening, I was called to Reyna's room alone. Without the presence of her guests, it was the first opportunity I had to draw blood. Though now that Reyna had found a book in our room, it was unclear if we'd be allowed to return to the Scholars' Cavern.

Still, we had to try. Just in case.

I'd slipped the empty vial into my pants pocket, hoping that it wouldn't be too far out of reach at any given moment.

When I arrived, Reyna was sipping from her glass of wine, lounging in her chair in front of the fireplace. Her black satin robe was parted so I could see one leg crossed over the other. Her eyes flicked toward the chair next to her and I took a seat, following her silent command.

"And how are you this evening?"

I rolled my eyes, but in the dim light, there was no way for her to notice. "Your games are tiring."

She scoffed. "My games? What? Am I not allowed to check in with my *favorite* guest?"

"I'm feeling fantastic, Reyna. I'm far from home. My family likely believes I'm dead. And every night I'm forced to lie with a woman I despise. There. Are you happy?"

Her long spindly fingers tapped on her glass as she glared at me. "I should've cut out your tongue on the first day."

"Why didn't you?"

"Because I thought you might have *other* uses for it." Her smile was wicked. I wanted to crawl out of my skin. "I'm bored. Entertain me."

She flicked her wrist, and I immediately felt an unnatural tug on my limbs. A will that wasn't mine guided my movements. I twisted in the chair so the arm didn't block Reyna's view and unbuttoned my pants.

An angry growl rumbled inside me, but there was nothing I could do to stop it. Despite all the siphoning I'd been doing with Emilie, my earth wielding was no use against the vines wrapped around my wrists and ankles. We hadn't figured out a way to nullify them yet. Even when I siphoned from Emilie, the magical bonds I stole from reforged within minutes.

So I was helpless against Reyna's desires. I slid my hand into my pants, beneath my underwear, and grabbed my cock. Swallowing the bile in my throat, I began to stroke myself.

Rage and resentment made it difficult to force myself into a state of arousal. The problem was, whenever Reyna grew tired of waiting for me, she usually resorted to some other form of sick torture.

Breaking fingers. Burning marks onto my thighs and back. Slicing the skin right off of my arms. Then she'd heal me just to do it all over again. Giving her a show was the much better option.

So I closed my eyes and swallowed. Desperately thinking of anything other than the dark room I currently occupied with Reyna. I didn't think of the smell of her fire crackling or the sound of her wine bottle refilling her glass.

I pushed myself to a different time and place. A beautiful pool, glistening in the sunlight in the castle of Renoa. An even more beautiful woman sitting across from me in sensuous bathing clothes that hugged her delicious curves.

I sighed, and my cock stiffened in my palm. Reyna's robe made a soft swishing sound, but I distracted myself with the thought of Emilie saying my name. The way she had in bed the night before.

The image of the pool returned, and Emilie swam through the water. Her head dipped below the surface and when she rose out of the water, her clothes had disappeared. Droplets traveled down her breasts, rolling over her perked nipples.

She continued to glide through the water toward me until her knees bumped into mine. Then she licked her lips and ran her hands over my shoulders, interlocking her fingers behind my head.

I groaned, feeling moisture at the tip of my cock. My grip tightened as I thrust into my hand. In my mind, Emilie sat in my lap and kissed my neck, sucking on the skin above my collarbone. She gently bit and I squeezed her ass, pressing her hard against me.

I continued rocking my hips, thinking only of Emilie's cunt sliding along my shaft. My breath was unsteady, and I imagined hers would be the same. She leaned back far enough to look me in the eye while she sank down onto my cock. Her mouth parted, and I held the back of her head, pulling her in to kiss her. To taste her while she moaned in my mouth. Her lips vibrated with the sound of it.

Gods, I wished it were real.

The weight of reality pressed into me and I opened my eyes to find Reyna perched in my lap, just as I had been picturing Emilie. I hissed through gritted teeth.

I opened my mouth to speak, but Reyna pressed a finger to my lips.

"Shh," she said. "You don't have to say anything. I know you want this just as badly as I do."

She wrapped a hand around mine and together we stroked my cock. I snarled, but her lips crashed into mine and the wine that lingered tasted like venom. Bitter and acidic.

She bit my lip, hard enough to draw blood, and I broke the kiss. "Don't flatter yourself. This isn't for you."

Quickly, she reached with her other hand and squeezed my balls, and I writhed in pain.

"All of this is for me, Ladon. Don't fool yourself. You *belong* to me."

Her grip on my balls loosened. She caressed them while stroking my shaft. Harder. Faster. Before long, I was spilling into her hand.

She pierced me with a menacing look. "*All* of this is for me."

After she stood, she pulled me up by my wrists. It didn't take much effort on her part since I couldn't fight it. She led me to her bed and once she disrobed, she sat on the end and leaned back on her elbows.

She nodded toward her bare cunt, and I knew what she expected me to do. Like she was in my head and feeding me cues.

I sank to my knees and grimaced. Even though I physically couldn't fight against the magical bonds, my mind still loathed all the things she'd made me do.

My hands wrapped around the back of her knees and I pushed her legs open. She watched with a lust-filled gaze. I stalled the best I could while still obeying the vines that controlled me, kissing the inside of her thigh.

I could still taste the blood from where she'd punctured my lip.

The blood...

There was a vial in my pocket. I'd almost forgotten about it. As luck would have it, my pants were still hanging loosely off my hips. Carefully, I slipped one hand into my pocket and pulled out the empty vial. With one hand, I skillfully removed the stopper and avoided losing it in the process.

The plan fell together quickly in my mind. I continued to place teasing kisses along her thigh. Let her think that I was enjoying this as much as she was. I started with a tentative graze of my teeth—just to test it out.

Her eyes were wild with desire when they met mine.

I bit down, gently at first. I sucked on her skin and soothed the angry teeth marks I'd left. Her head rolled back, and I took the opportunity to clamp down hard, tasting blood the moment I pierced her skin with my teeth.

She jolted and her head flew back up, but I ran my tongue over that spot again, luring her into a false sense of security. After a few moments, she relaxed again and let her head drop back.

I sucked on that spot, drawing as much blood as I could into my mouth. While her head was still tilted back, I quietly spat into the vial and replaced the stopper, then slid the vial back into my pants.

Before she could question the brief pause, I slid a finger inside her and she sighed with relief.

Chapter Thirty-Two

Ladon

"DARE I ASK HOW you got this?" Emilie asked, dangling the vial of Reyna's blood between two fingers.

"You don't want to know."

"Is that...saliva mixed with it?"

"You don't want to know."

"Right. Well, however you did it, I'm impressed."

I smirked. "Did you think I wouldn't be able to?"

Kneeling next to the bed, Emilie tucked the vial into a pair of socks. After Reyna had unexpectedly found her book, she'd hidden all of her items amongst her clothing.

"I didn't doubt you. I just didn't expect you to have it done so quickly."

"Now we need another workday in the cavern."

Emilie looked up at me with a troubled frown. We both knew how unlikely that was. Our luck had run out in that department.

"Do you think there are other openings to the tunnels?" she asked.

I ran a hand through my hair, damp from the shower I'd just stepped out of. "There has to be. Finding them though...that won't be easy. We only found the first one because the harpy knew of its existence."

I sank to the mattress and rubbed my temples. We'd been locked away for what had to be months now. I'd lost count of the days weeks ago. I was pretty sure Emilie was still keeping track. I could've asked her, but confirmation of our timeline would likely only frustrate me more.

A hand ran up my spine and I turned to find Emilie looking at me with a kindness I didn't deserve. I'd treated her so horribly in Renoa. She should've hated me, but her compassion was unending.

"Tell me something honest." My voice came out hoarse.

"I've never met anyone quite like you, Ladon."

It was quiet enough to hear the sound of my swallowing. My mouth and throat felt too dry.

I shook my head and a couple loose strands of white hair fell over my eyes. Emilie drew circles on my back, and goosebumps sprouted on my skin. With her other hand, she traced the vines on my wrists and then the lines of my palm. It tickled, but I liked it.

"I'm nothing special."

"Take that back," she whispered.

It seemed as though she were moving closer. Her face appeared nearer than before. The warmth of her body was more encompassing than before.

"Take it back," she said again. Her hand moved up to cup my cheek. She leaned forward and her forehead pressed against my temple. It took everything in me not to toss her on the mattress and kiss her. Run my lips over her skin softly and slowly until neither of us could keep our hands to ourselves.

"Emilie…"

Her lips whispered against my skin. "You have no idea how special you are, Ladon Castelli."

I wanted to believe her. To believe that she thought I was anyone worthy of her affection. But I was no one. How could I compare to my brother, King of Osavian? In what world would she ever choose me?

"Tell me," I said, desperate to hear her say it again. That I was special. I needed to know what she saw in me.

"You're protective. Loyal. Sensitive." With each word, she stroked her thumb over my cheekbone. My eyes fluttered closed as I leaned into her touch. "You're strong. Smart. Charismatic."

A brief pause and then, "Handsome."

That last word took my breath away. When I opened my eyes again, she was staring at me with a look so tender, so full of curiosity and longing, I could hardly stand it.

My heart raced, and I was sure she could hear the thundering in my chest. Her hand came to a rest there, and I knew she felt it. It felt like an eternity passed, each of us waiting for the other to make a move. Each of us hoping the other would.

We'd crossed a line. I'd convinced myself that having sex with Emilie was practical; that I was doing her a favor. But I was lying to myself. I'd wanted it even more than she had. And I wanted to cross that line again now.

Her eyes were hazy and filled with lust, and I ran a hand over her hip, wrapping the other around her waist. She was on her back in an instant while I hovered over her, pressing kisses down the center of her chest. Even through her soft shirt, I could feel her body's response to me, shifting and arching against the mattress.

I lifted her shirt and kissed below her belly button, too. Her soft whimpers and fingers grasping my hair drove me mad.

"Ladon," she sighed.

My only response was a moan against her skin, and I hitched her legs around my hips.

A knock had us both shooting up straight, rigid and flustered. A moment later, the harpy entered the room. She carried two small glass bottles along with a book in her hand, which Emilie took and expressed her gratitude.

"*Daily Defense: An Everyday Guide to Winning.*" She smiled at the harpy. "Thank you. This will be incredibly useful."

I watched her as she examined the bottles next. They each had a blue label with letters too small for me to read from my vantage point. Emilie tucked a strand of hair behind her ear and I noticed her cheeks were still stained pink.

Damn that harpy.

If it weren't for her, I'd be balls deep in Emilie, hearing her moan my name over and over again. I'd be calling her mine.

Mine.

I tried not to make it too obvious as I adjusted my aching cock in my pants. Thankfully, the harpy was more focused on Emilie than me. She didn't seem to like me much and I could hardly blame her. Everyone in this mountain was facing their own trauma, and it wasn't a surprise that she'd be so untrusting.

Something about Emilie had managed to disarm the harpy. An experience I understood myself.

Emilie blinked once. Then twice.

"What is it?"

"It's some sort of sleeping solution." She looked to the harpy for confirmation and she nodded once. "It's supposed to calm your mind, ease your muscles and warm your body."

"Well, that's not very vital is it," I murmured.

Emilie smacked my arm with the back of her hand and gave me a reprimanding look.

I responded with a look of my own, raising my brows as if to say, *tell me I'm wrong*. A mere warming concoction didn't seem like a good enough reason to interrupt Emilie and me. And even though I was certain Emilie appreciated the book, reading theory was less effective than physical practice.

Emilie studied the harpy again. "Thank you. We appreciate this. Don't we Ladon?"

She turned to me, and I caved under her demanding glare. I cleared my throat. "Um, yes. Thank you for this."

The harpy turned and started for the door.

"Wait," I shouted. The harpy froze, startled by the loud noise. She barely peeked over her shoulder. "Do you know where we might find another entrance to the tunnels?"

She turned around fully and tilted her head to one side, as if in question.

"The tunnels. You showed us the doorway in the library. It's unlikely we'll be back there anytime soon. There must be more of them. Do you know where we could find one?"

The harpy's eyes looked tearful. Large orbs, black as night and glistening like glass. She shook her head, and I sighed. Beside me, Emilie did her best not to let her disappointment show, lest we hurt the harpy's feelings.

"It's okay," she reassured her. "We'll figure something out."

After the harpy left, a thick silence hung in the air between us. The heat of the moment was long gone and yet I couldn't stop thinking about it. Couldn't stop looking at Emilie.

Her head snapped up as she felt my gaze and I couldn't tell what she was thinking. Was it regret? Embarrassment? Bashfulness? Whatever it was, it was clear that we would not be picking up where we left off.

She raised one bottle in her hand. "I think I'll take this and head to bed."

"I still wish she would've brought something more useful," I said. Something worth the interruption.

"Don't be ungrateful, Ladon. It doesn't look good on you."

Then she handed me my dosage, and I drank it in two gulps. At least we'd both have a restful night, void of nightmares and an aching cold.

Emilie and I were eating dinner one evening when Luther and Tristan came to retrieve us. I despised the evenings we were both called to entertain. I had my own coping mechanisms, but the thought of Emilie being paraded around for men and women alike to touch—it made me see red.

I was the only one who could touch her.

We were led down familiar paths to the large bathing chamber. They didn't even bother taking us in circles or trying to confuse us with complicated twists and turns. At this point, I'd already mentally mapped out many of the halls inside the mountain.

I snarled at the guard closest to me, who couldn't take his eyes off Emilie as she undressed and made her way into the basin full of steaming water. She crossed her arms over her chest and long brown curls fell over her shoulders.

I entered the water after her and she had the decency to look away, though I didn't care if she saw me. This was the first time we'd been expected to bathe together. The bath was large—it could've held twenty people—but it still felt intimate.

Emilie washed her hair, and I scrubbed my skin. A handmaiden was brought in who gave us each a concoction to lather on our bodies. She didn't bother to respond when I asked what it was.

It didn't take long to find out. I watched out of the corner of my eye as Emilie rubbed it over her skin like she'd done this before. So I followed suit.

I scowled as the hairs on my arms, legs and groin began to dissolve and muttered under my breath, "You've got to be fucking kidding me."

By the time I was finished, the only hair left was on my head. Even the stubble on my jaw had disappeared. I was disgusted.

I supposed it hadn't occurred to me how Emilie always seemed to have smooth legs. And the times I'd seen her naked...she'd been kept neatly trimmed.

Reyna had never done anything like this to me before. Which made me concerned that tonight might not be a normal night. What did she have in store for us this time?

We stepped out of the bath and dried off, but no clothes were provided. Instead, the handmaiden brought forward a bucket. She placed it on the ground and dipped both her hands inside. Then she smeared gold paint over Emilie's shoulders and chest.

Emilie's mouth opened in shock. The two guards standing in the corner snickered, and I shot them a deadly glare.

"What is this?" I asked the handmaiden.

She ignored me and continued to spread glimmering gold all over Emilie's body. Even in her hair, which she pulled back into a long braid. Once Emilie was covered head to toe, the handmaiden turned to me.

She dipped her hands in the bucket again and I stepped back before she could touch me.

"I'll do it myself."

She seemed to consider me for a moment before giving a curt nod, and I began to cover myself in the golden paint. My limbs and torso were easy enough. I covered my face and hair without any difficulty. But I did need help reaching certain spots on my back.

The handmaiden noticed, circling around me, but I stepped away.

"I can do it," Emilie volunteered.

Again, the handmaiden gave a small nod. I was thankful she didn't seem to be very confrontational.

Emilie dipped her hands into the paint and spread it along my spine. Then across the top of my back. I felt her cover the places I'd missed. My muscles tensed with anger.

"I'm sorry," she said quietly enough that only I could hear. She mistook my tension for anger with her. For touching me.

I pulled her by the hand until she was standing in front of me. My voice was hushed, mirroring hers. "Emilie, you have permission to touch me whenever you must."

If it weren't for the gold paint on her skin, she surely would've had rosy cheeks. Her eyes widened and mouth parted slightly. It was almost comical.

When she finally found her voice again, she simply said, "Likewise."

The guards led us to the dining room, where Reyna was waiting. She stood in the corner, directing servants on where to place table settings, bickering at the way they folded napkins and berating them for not lighting candles faster.

I looked at Emilie, and the dim candlelight made her skin look absolutely golden. Like she was truly made of gold and not just covered in it. It was breathtaking. *She* was breathtaking.

"Ah, good. You're here," Reyna said when she noticed us. She rubbed her hands together, then pointed toward the center of the long dining table. "I want you here."

"Beg your pardon?" It seemed like she might've pointed at one of the chairs, but I highly doubted she wanted us to get gold paint all over her emerald suede cushions.

"Right there. You'll be our grand centerpiece this evening. Honestly, I don't know why I haven't thought of it before. Here, Emilie, you lie down and then Ladon, if you would..." She paused as she realized we weren't moving.

"Well, don't just stand there."

Emilie crossed the room and crawled up on the table. She laid on her back and faced the ceiling, body prone and lifeless. She looked like a gilded statue.

"Knees up," Reyna said. "And then, Ladon, you'll be here between her legs."

I snorted. "You are delusional."

She had to be the sickest person I'd ever met. Not even a hint of acknowledgment that this whole idea was preposterous. To have us lathered in paint and set in the center of the table like some kind of décor. At least when she forced me to fuck her, I understood she got something out of it. But this? This was insanity.

"And you are going to be in trouble if you don't get on that table."

A blinding pain hit me like a flash of lightning traveling down my spine. It was over as quickly as it started, but the message was clear. Obey or prepare for a world of hurt.

I climbed on the table, kneeling between Emilie's legs. The sight of her laying in front of me, legs spread and pussy exposed to me, made my cock twitch.

"Good. That's good. Now pull her closer. Hands on her hips. And put your cock inside her."

Emilie gasped at the same time I froze with my hands on her hips, just about to pull her toward me as Reyna suggested.

Reyna patiently waited while my eyes flicked back and forth between her and Emilie. She was enjoying this too much. One day, I'd strangle her and watch the life drain out of those wicked eyes.

Emilie's hands rested on top of mine, drawing my attention to her. She nodded. "Just do it."

Reyna cackled, and I ground my teeth.

It didn't take much to get myself hard. Emilie's naked body had me halfway there already. I stroked myself a couple times and pulled her closer, tilting her hips up toward me.

My fingers trailed her thighs, leaving gold smudges in their wake. I pressed a thumb to her clit, and she gasped. She needed to be aroused too if I didn't want to hurt her.

Her bottom lip trembled, and I knew how scared she was. How humiliated she was. Reyna stood watching, eagerly waiting for her *playthings* to perform. Tears welled in Emilie's eyes.

"Hey," I said softly. "Look at me, Emilie. Look at me."

Her chest rose and fell with each strained breath, and I lined the tip of my cock with her entrance. I slowly nudged forward, maintaining a steady swirling pattern on her clit.

I no more than had the tip inside when she hissed and I pulled back. She was anxious and tense.

Reyna sighed. "Sometime today would be great. The guests are going to arrive any minute."

I snarled at her. I would take as much time as I needed. As much time as *Emilie* needed. I dragged my finger down her slit, gently pressing inside her and covering my finger in her arousal.

"Trust me," I said, moving my finger in and out of her. "I've got you."

She nodded, and I noticed the small rock of her hips as I moved my finger inside her. I felt her slowly relax. I removed my finger and slid my cock over her folds, then lined up again.

This time, she didn't tense as much. She whimpered when I slid into her tight cunt and I stopped breathing.

Oh fuck, she felt good.

I held her hips tightly and drove inside her as deep as I could go, only remembering to breathe when I pulled back an inch.

"Stay like that," Reyna said, after I'd pushed in again.

My mind was spinning, and I assumed I'd heard her incorrectly.

"Like what?" I asked, breathing like I'd just run a mile.

"Inside her. It's perfect. My guests will love it." She clasped her hands together and then left the room.

"What the fuck?"

"Ladon." Emilie sounded frantic, and my only instinct was to comfort her.

"It's going to be okay. I promise."

"I don't want to do this." She covered her breasts with her arms. "I'm so—"

I pulled back, but she grabbed me by the wrist, her inner walls clenching around my cock. My vision went black.

"Don't," she said. "It's not you. It's *this*. This display. I don't like this. I don't like them watching me. I hate it. Ladon, I—"

"Shh." I took her hand in mine and rubbed the back of her hand with my thumb. "Just keep looking at me, okay. No one else exists. Just me."

She clenched again, and I gritted my teeth.

"Please, try not to do that," I hissed.

She nodded, but as Reyna's guests filed in, she squeezed my cock again and my balls tightened. It was going to be a long night.

Guests ate their dinner and chatted as if Emilie and I didn't exist. As if we were merely a floral arrangement or some other decorative object and not actual humans. I understood why Emilie hated this part the most. It was dehumanizing.

I tried not to think of the throbbing ache in my knees. They'd been tucked underneath me against the hard surface for so long. It was nothing compared to the throbbing ache and need for release in my lower stomach.

Emilie did her best to keep her eyes on me, even letting them flutter closed every once in a while. I did my best not to combust every time she involuntarily clenched around my cock.

After dessert was cleared, the servants brought out more wine. A few of the men around the table lit cigarettes, and the air began to fill with smoke. I was beginning to think the night would never end when one woman finally turned her attention toward us.

"Reyna, you've outdone yourself with this masterpiece." Her voice was slippery while spoke about us as if we were art. I locked my gaze on Emilie to avoid giving the woman the attention she sought.

"Isn't it an elegant touch, Clarise? I thought since today was a special day, it deserved a special celebration."

It felt like she was taunting me, but I didn't care about what made today special. It was inconsequential. Her next words, though, fueled the rage inside me.

"You can touch if you'd like."

The woman giggled and reached toward us. I wanted to rip her arm off, but I found my limbs incapable of moving, locked in place at Reyna's will. Fuck these vines and the magic within them.

The woman—who I now recognized as the blonde woman who always took a liking to me—reached between our bodies and touched Emilie's clit.

Emilie jolted, her pussy tightening around me, and my eyes fluttered closed. A low grumble escaped my lips. It was the most exhilarating feeling I'd ever experienced. The crowd seemed to know this too. I caught Reyna smirking behind her glass of wine.

The woman played with Emilie's sensitive bud and another male guest leaned over to squeeze her breast. Her breaths quickened, and I knew by the pulsing around my cock—by the way she squirmed against me—she was going to come undone.

I focused all my energy on trying not to come inside her, but gods, it was difficult. Between the rocking of her hips and her pulsating pussy, I didn't know how much more I could take. I dug my fingers into her thighs, trying to hold her still. There would be bruises there in the morning.

"That's enough," Reyna said, leaning back in her chair as if tonight's entertainment bored her.

"Oh, come on, Reyna." I recognized the man who spoke as the one named Vero. I knew he liked to push Reyna's boundaries. I was surprised she hadn't killed him yet for testing her.

"What does it matter to you? Don't you enjoy seeing her tortured so?" Reyna tried to appeal to him but he eyed Emilie with a sick fascination.

"I want to see what she looks like when she comes." He laughed and several others around the table joined in, voicing their agreement.

Reyna was losing, and she knew it. Rather than embarrass herself further, she coyly changed her stance. "I suppose it could be fun just this once." She nodded toward the woman with her finger pressed to Emilie's clit and she began to circle again.

It didn't take long for Emilie's pleasure to peak. With a rapturous cry, she seized and shuddered, walls rapidly fluttering around me. She squeezed her eyes closed as waves and waves of pleasure flooded through her—and I felt each one.

"Oh, gods," she cried.

Oh, fuck.

I couldn't stop it. I'd tried so hard to keep it together, but Emilie was my undoing. The sounds she made, the way she moved, every bit of her spoke to some innate piece of me. She was designed to ruin me.

I clenched my jaw as pleasure seared down my spine. My balls tightened, and I spilled into her. Ecstasy ran through my veins—my bones—and twisted in my abdomen. I wondered briefly if she could feel my cock twitching as I had felt her orgasm.

She panted and her body quivered. The woman still had two fingers pressed against her clit, torturing her past the point of pleasure.

I released an animalistic growl at the woman, and she finally let up. She turned to Reyna to express her delight. "That was quite the display. I'd love to see what else you have in store for us tonight."

Chapter Thirty-Three

Emilie

I STOOD AND WATCHED as the room cleared of guests. The gold paint on my skin was a mess from all the places I'd been touched. In some places, the paint was missing entirely.

I didn't allow myself to look at Ladon, but I was confident he was the same. We'd been inseparable all night. I couldn't count the number of ways Reyna and her cohorts used us for their entertainment. I didn't think it would ever end.

I was tired...and cold.

Reyna dismissed Ladon and me, and the usual guards escorted us back to our room. We walked the halls in nothing but gold paint. Just another way to add to the humiliation, I supposed.

I tried to let numbness sink in, so that I wouldn't feel completely and utterly devastated. But something else simmered inside me. Like an itch I couldn't ignore.

Anger.

I was *sick* of playing Reyna's games. And I was sick of allowing her so much control over my emotions. From now on, I vowed that my responses would be my own. I wouldn't let her get to me anymore.

"Are you okay?" Ladon asked as soon as the door to our room closed. He was looking at me—not with pity—but something a little more tentative. Like he could see the resolution I was coming to.

I stood tall. "I'm fine."

He quirked a brow, and then seemed to realize we were both still naked, save for the paint on our skin.

"Do you want to shower first, or shall I?"

I stared at him and, for once, I didn't avoid letting my eyes wonder over his body. From his broad shoulders to his toned abs. And the sizeable length of him on full display. He didn't try to shy away or hide himself. He stood tall, completely confident in his own skin.

No one was going to control me anymore. Not even my insecurities or my fears and doubts. What did I have to fear, anyway? We'd already been together. When...if we escaped, I'd deal with the repercussions then.

My betrothed was nowhere to be found. My mother wasn't here to criticize me. There was only me and Ladon. And through all our ups and downs, I was pretty certain I knew where he stood.

Reyna had stolen so much from us, but she couldn't have this. I didn't want to think of her when I looked at him. There was something igniting between us, and she had no right to claim it. It was ours.

I inched closer until I had to look up to meet his gaze. He watched me approach with intensity.

"Emilie?"

Standing on my tiptoes, I reached up and threaded my fingers through his hair, pulling him down to me. I hesitated at that last miniscule space between us, curious as to what he might do.

I could feel him breathing. The heat of it tickling my lips.

Slowly, he closed the distance and gently pressed his lips against mine. It was tender. Satisfying. So, so satisfying, and still left me wanting more. More of *him*.

His arm wrapped around my back, and he pulled me flush against his chest. I felt his cock pressed against my stomach and I wanted more of that, too.

He moaned, and the sound of it filled my stomach with molten desire. I gasped and pressed his lips against me harder.

I ran my hand over his chest, what little gold remained now distorted even further. His hand reached down toward my ass and gave it a tight squeeze, pressing me even closer to him.

There was enough room for me to slide a hand between us and I closed my palm around his length. He groaned again and bit his bottom lip. Teasing. Taunting.

It was getting harder to breathe. He broke the kiss, only to drag his mouth and tongue down my neck.

"Ladon," I whimpered.

Strong hands grabbed the backs of my thighs and he hoisted me up. I wrapped my legs around his core and gods, his cock was perfectly positioned to tantalize me. I rocked against him and he growled with pleasure.

His mouth found mine again, and when his lips crashed into mine, it was messy and frantic. His tongue slid into my mouth and I moaned at the taste of him.

I could tell we were moving, but I didn't care where or why. Ladon was all that existed. Faintly, I heard the sound of the shower as he turned it on. After a few moments, warm water fell down my back.

Ladon pinned me against the wall, my ankles still crossed behind his back. He looked me square in the eyes as he ran his hands up my stomach, pressed against my breasts and then down again, breathing heavily as he did.

Water and gold paint trailed down my body and then swirled toward the drain. We both watched as the gold began to rinse from our bodies. His wet bangs hung in front of his eyes and he looked like a man who'd been starved.

And I was dinner.

His hands ran over my breasts again, and his thumbs brushed over my sensitive nipples. I arched against the shower wall. Urgent need building in my belly.

His mouth was on my throat again and he whispered against my skin, "Do you know how badly I've wanted this? How badly I've wanted you?"

I shook my head, half in a daze. "You've had me."

"Not like this," he moaned. And I knew what he meant.

Not like this. *All ours.*

I ground against him, my patience wearing thin.

"Greedy princess," he whispered, voice hot against my ear.

I bit his shoulder in retaliation. "You know how much I hate that nickname."

He held me steady with one arm while he used the other hand to play with my folds, dragging along my slit and never pushing more than a fingernail inside me. "No, you don't."

No, I didn't.

He leaned forward and his lips closed over my nipple, sucking and swirling in a way that had me seeing stars. He trapped my nipple between his teeth ever so delicately and then plunged a finger inside my pussy.

I jerked, and the abrupt motion tugged at my nipple. The pain and pleasure mixed until I couldn't tell the difference. He worked his finger in and out of me and when I felt like I couldn't breathe, he added a second.

So much attention. He was so attuned to my every need. I wanted to give him the same devotion he showed me.

I found his cock and ran my hand along his shaft. What little gold paint remained melted and rinsed off his skin.

It was the first time I'd really gotten to *see* him. To study him without an audience. To take my time and explore him fully.

I ran my thumb over his sensitive tip, and he hissed. His abs clenched, and I wanted to touch those, too. Feel every ridge, every muscle in his body.

While he teased my pussy, I continued to stroke him lightly. It was only fair that I tortured him equally as much as he did me. I cupped his balls and caressed them, squeezing him gently. A bead of white was already glistening at the tip of his cock.

"I want you," I said breathlessly. "Inside me. Right now."

He nodded, removing his fingers quickly and then driving into me with one hard thrust.

My mouth opened in a silent cry. His mouth was on mine in seconds and his tongue danced with mine. He pounded into me, each thrust had my ass bumping against the shower wall. Each thrust so deliciously filling. Ladon didn't take me gently this time.

I kissed him like he was my life source, like I could never get enough. My legs began to shake and thank the gods he was holding me up.

My insides turned to liquid, and before I knew it, I was unraveling entirely. I came harder than I ever had in my life, including the times at my own hand. I came so hard, the stars in my eyes turned to blazing comets.

And when he grunted and stilled, I knew he was as thoroughly wrecked as I was.

Chapter Thirty-Four

Ladon

I RAN MY FINGERS through Emilie's wet hair, her cheek pressed against my chest. My heart pounded at the sight of her sleeping on top of me, one arm hugging me.

She looked...she looked like my entire world.

With everything stripped away—the titles, the riches, the duties and obligations—Emilie was my everything. I didn't know how it happened, but I was glad it did.

Emilie shivered, and I pulled the blanket up over her shoulder. She stirred and tilted her head back to meet my gaze.

"You're awake?" Her voice was soft and sleepy. "What time is it?"

"It's not morning yet. Sleep."

She yawned and then closed her eyes again. Her fingers trailed over my chest, drawing lazy circles. I listened to the steady rhythm of her breathing, letting it lull me into a state of peace.

"Tell me something honest," she said.

This game only ever went one way—with one of us, sometimes both, spilling our emotional baggage.

"Why don't you tell me something honest?"

"I asked you first."

Her tone was light, but I still felt uneasy about what was to come next. I inhaled deeply.

"I'm happy I met you."

She chuckled. "You don't think I'm an insufferable nuisance?"

"Oh no, I do," I teased. "I just think your more pleasant traits are worth suffering for."

She giggled and rolled on top of me, propping herself up with her hands planted on my chest. Her smile was bright as the morning sun. Almost bright enough to make me forget about the darkness surrounding us.

But then her smile faltered, and she looked pensive.

"It's your turn," I reminded her. I still wasn't sure if I wanted whatever truth was on her mind, but it was better to speak of it now than let it fester.

She didn't look at me when she spoke, instead staring at the spot on my chest that she traced with her fingertip. "I don't want to marry your brother."

My bones turned to ice. I didn't want to think about Cyrus, especially not while Emilie was naked and tangled in the sheets with me.

Thinking of my brother made me feel guilty. He would never forgive me for this betrayal. I didn't know how I would ever forgive myself. The only thing that kept me from spiraling into misery was the ability to push it off until we were far from Murvort and safe.

"What's going to happen if we return to Osavian?" she asked.

"When," I corrected. "*When* we return."

Her silence was staggering. Each day we spent trapped in this mountain etched away at our hope of getting out.

"*When* we return to Osavian, we will figure it out."

"Your mother will hate me. Your people will despise me. Cyrus's first wife, Isabella was so beloved by the kingdom. And I am every bit the traitorous whore you thought I was."

"Don't you *ever* say that again." The words stuck in my throat. I hated that I'd ever belittled her like that. How wrong I had been...

"I wanted to do something meaningful as queen and all I've done is make a mess. Your family—*my* family—will never forgive me. I've ruined everything."

I rolled over, pushing her to her back and placed both of my hands on her cheeks. "You haven't done anything that I haven't done with you. Whatever sins you've committed, I've committed too."

"What will we do?"

"First, we will get out of here. Then we will talk to Cyrus. Perhaps he can be convinced that this marriage isn't for the best."

She laughed, unamused. "Didn't you try that already?"

"I did. But that was before. We can try another angle. After everything you've been through, you're not in the right mind to be queen."

She laughed more earnestly. "So your plan is to tell him I'm unstable?"

I chuckled, too, and kissed her forehead. "We'll figure it out."

Emilie nodded, but she didn't look convinced. "And if I can't get out of it...do we tell him?"

"You would keep all of this from him?" I frowned.

"If it would save you from being dishonored. If it would save both of us, I would."

I didn't like the thought of it, but deep down, I knew there was a chance it would come to that. There was a chance that one day I'd have to bury my feelings for Emilie, to forget I'd ever cared for her and watch as she lived the rest of her days with my brother.

That guilt rose inside of me once more. How dare I be so self-absorbed? To think only of my own feelings when Cyrus was the one who should feel hurt?

I held Emilie tight, not wanting to let her go. Not wanting to close my eyes in case she slipped from my grasp while I wasn't looking. "I don't want to imagine a day when I can't call you mine."

I spent several days wondering if I was self-sabotaging. If the thought of what awaited us in Osavian wasn't so dreadful, would we have found a way to leave sooner? I was constantly reminding myself that we were doing everything we could.

Find the tunnels—check.

Obtain Reyna's blood—check.

Bust down the door and navigate our way through the tunnels...pending.

We'd been right about the unlikelihood of returning to the Scholars' Cavern. It had been a week since Reyna had found Emilie's book and we hadn't seen the library since.

Instead, Emilie had the pleasure of cleaning toilets while I scrubbed kitchen floors. There were two other slaves cleaning with me, the first I'd seen since our arrival. Were there others we didn't know about?

They looked so similar; I wondered if they might be siblings. Both appeared to be teenagers, not yet adults. The boy had dirty blonde hair that was shaggy and in desperate need of a haircut. He was tall and lanky, not yet grown into his long limbs. The girl had the same dirty blonde hair, but even in a braid, it was down to her waist. She was tall too, though not as tall as him.

I didn't pay them much attention, and they kept to themselves on the opposite side of the room. When lunch rolled around, I ate by myself and they sat on empty buckets, quietly conversing.

At least I knew Reyna hadn't removed their tongues.

When our break was almost over, a loud noise came from right outside the kitchen. My head whipped toward the door while the two servants jumped to their feet.

An angry screech echoed through the room before Reyna burst in. I stood to my feet as well and assumed a defensive position. I didn't know what set her off this time, but whatever it was, it was bad.

She was blind in her rage and didn't even notice me. Something that I'd usually be thankful for, but it only highlighted the level of her fury. She strode straight for the siblings and I watched as they inched closer together, holding hands like they knew suffering—and possibly death—were imminent.

"What did you do?" Reyna seethed.

The girl looked at her brother with tears in her eyes. She pressed her lips into a thin line, like that might keep their secret inside.

I moved around a metal fixture that held several platters of half-pre-pared food to get a better view.

The boy took a step in front of his sister and I was impressed with the level of courage he displayed. Older men would've quaked in the shadow of her wrath.

"It was me. She had nothing to do with it."

Reyna faked a laugh. "I wasn't born yesterday. You couldn't have killed Nox on your own. She would've torn you to pieces."

I stifled a gasp of surprise. A *child* had killed one of her dogs? I admired his bravery, but it was foolish to act without a plan to escape... I shook my head.

Reyna stepped around him and grabbed the girl by the arm. Then she ripped her blouse open. From several feet away, I could see the scratches and bite marks on her chest. Defensive wounds. Evidence that he had, in fact, not worked alone.

The girl stumbled back when Reyna released her, turning again to the boy. I inched closer, as I feared this was headed in a very bad direction. They were only kids, for gods' sake.

Reyna raised her hand in the air and as she brought it down, strikes of lightning burst all around us. I closed my eyes to block out the blinding light. When I opened them again, the boy was pinned to the wall, ropes of electricity holding him in place.

He screamed and writhed, but was powerless against her magic. Smoke began to rise and I could smell his burning flesh. His sister held her hands to her mouth as she watched in horror.

Gagging, I took a step forward to intervene. I didn't know how, but I knew I couldn't sit back and watch as Reyna tortured this boy.

Her undivided attention to the boy allowed me to sneak up without her noticing. When I grabbed her arm, my palm instantly burned. I snatched it back and stared at the angry red flesh and blisters forming on my skin. Reyna was radiating with electric heat.

She momentarily turned from the boy, long enough to shoot me daggers with her eyes. Her orange eyes were so bright; the centers had turned almost white. It was like staring into the sun. "Stay out of it," she hissed.

I felt an invisible leash pull me back, pinning my arms to my sides. I couldn't blink as I watched the boy burn from the inside. His clothes caught fire and his skin bubbled. His screams went silent as the electrical current devoured him. Singed flesh turned to charred skin and when Reyna finally released him, he was nothing more than ashes and bone.

His sister screamed and fell to the floor, reaching out to the space her brother had just occupied. Reaching out for what had been taken from her. She wept with her face buried in her hands.

"Pretty girl," Reyna said, moving closer to brush the girl's hair. She shivered and skittered across the floor, stifling her pained howling.

"Please," the girl cried. "I don't want to die."

Death should've been the least of her concerns. There were worse ways to torment a person.

Reyna toyed with the girl like an animal with its prey. The girl continued to retreat, shuffling over the floor until she was backed into a corner between two counters. She held her arms over her face as Reyna towered above her, waiting for the inevitable strike.

The sinister smile that crept over her face sent chills up my spine.

Just then, I felt something move beside me. I looked to my right and my heart pounded as Vessina slithered through the kitchen. There was hardly enough space for the massive serpent to move. She bumped into a table and it scraped over the hard floor, drawing the girl's attention.

"No, no. I didn't do anything. Please...I...I'll do whatever you ask. I won't cause any trouble. Please."

Vessina hissed and Reyna stepped aside, no longer standing between the snake and the girl.

She screamed again and her feet kicked against the floor, trying to move back, but there was nowhere to go.

Vessina's head reared back, and she struck once, sharp fangs piercing the girl's chest. Then the snake sank back to the floor, moving to the left and then the right. Waiting. Taunting.

Streaks of blood ran down the girl's body, and she grimaced. I knew that pain all too well. I'd watched as Emilie had endured the same agony. I didn't think this girl would be so lucky as to receive the antidote.

She held her hand over the wound, but blood continued to ooze. She held her other hand up, surrendering to Reyna. "Make it stop. I'm so sorry. I didn't mean to...I didn't want to."

Reyna crossed her arms and shook her head. "My darling, if you're going to resist, you should've had the fortitude to stand by your actions. All this blubbering and pleading is quite pathetic."

The girl sobbed; her face scrunched in knowing anguish. She knew she wasn't going to make it out of this room alive. She knew that the end was near for her.

I knew it too. And yet I still couldn't move from the spot I was anchored to. I could only watch and hope the end would come swiftly. Let her suffering end now.

"What would you give me in exchange for your life?" Reyna asked.

The girl sighed with relief. "Anything. Whatever you ask of me. My family...we have money. I'll give it all to you."

Reyna twirled a strand of her black hair. "You don't have the ability to keep that promise. Your family's money is almost drained. They've spent the lot of it looking for their precious twins. And even with their riches and a decade on their side, they still couldn't rescue you."

Her shoulders shook as she laughed at the girl's pain.

A decade? How old were they when they'd been stolen? They must've come from one of the other continents—maybe Moridia or Wyland—because I hadn't heard of any missing twins. And with money, I was certain I would've known if they'd come from one of Osavian's families.

"What can I offer you instead?"

Reyna tilted her head to the side. The whole thing was a ruse. Just another way to torment the poor girl. Give her a glimmer of hope before taking it all away. The girl couldn't see it.

Nor did she see Vessina rise to strike again. The serpent lashed out, digging her fangs into the girl's other shoulder. And then her abdomen. Her thigh. Her chest.

Over and over again, she struck while the girl screamed. The sound was so piercing my head began to ache. I don't know how long it lasted, but it seemed to go on forever as Vessina ripped the girl to pieces.

When her lifeless body slumped to the floor, the ringing in my ears finally ceased. She was silent, but I would never forget the sounds she'd made in her last moments.

I watched as Vessina swallowed the fragments of her body and then followed Reyna through the room. Before she left the kitchen, Reyna turned back to me.

"Ladon, I think you have more cleaning to do."

Indeed. Red stains covered the floor, and so did a pile of ash. It was all that remained of the two twins, except for a small ring I found amid the ashes. A silver band with a family crest bearing the letter 'M.'

I worked too late into the evening to be called for Reyna's services that evening. When I returned to our bedroom, Emilie rushed over to me and flung her arms around my neck.

I paused, momentarily stunned by her actions, and then I wrapped my arms around her back and held her close. Images of the girl being torn to shreds haunted me when I closed my eyes. Images that could've just as easily been Emilie, had she not been given an antidote on our first day.

She pulled back far enough to look at my face. "Where were you? I was starting to worry."

I smirked, though it felt more forced than usual. "Feeling lost without me, princess?"

From the way she tilted her head, I could tell she wasn't in a playful mood.

I sighed and then locked eyes with her. "We need to get out. Now."

Chapter Thirty-Five

Ladon

Emilie was properly horrified as I recounted the events of that night. Our sense of urgency was renewed, and we began to train every day and night. Every moment of free time was spent with her learning to fight and defend herself while I pulled the magic from her tattoos and stored it for the right moment.

The problem was, neither of us knew when that moment might be. Emilie had the harpy looking for other entrances to the tunnel, but so far she'd hadn't come up with anything.

We couldn't risk waiting any longer. Ultimately, we decided that the harpy would have to unlock our room, and we'd escape through the Scholars' Cavern. The harpy understood the risk, and only agreed to the plan when we compromised and agreed to wait until a day when Reyna had left the mountain. That way, the harpy wouldn't risk getting caught.

Waiting was torture in and of itself. After witnessing the twins' death, I couldn't wait to get out of the mountain and far, far away from Reyna's clutches. I didn't want to think of the possible demises she had planned for Emilie and me.

My thoughts were interrupted when Emilie huffed in frustration. "You've got to be kidding me."

Her source of frustration was immediately apparent. She'd been working through a course of exercises I'd given her when snow began to fall through the crate in the ceiling.

I snorted. "If you work faster, you'll hardly notice the cold."

She narrowed her eyes at me, but she took my advice and quickened her pace, jogging while bringing her knees to waist level.

"Higher," I said and laughed when she scowled. She'd shown immense progress in a short period of time. While I still didn't think a textbook was a sufficient way to learn, Emilie seemed to absorb the information faster with its help. When we weren't practicing tactics, her nose was buried in that book, memorizing the illustrations. If I had to guess, I'd say she'd surpassed some of my novice soldiers already.

"Why aren't you training?" she asked between heavy breaths.

"Because I'm already in shape."

"So you're just going to watch me instead? You could be doing anything else. Anything other than monitoring me."

I shrugged my shoulders. "I prefer to watch you."

I could've sworn the pink that stained her cheeks was from more than the physical exertion. It was true. I could've watched her all day and never gotten bored.

But my plans to do just that were interrupted when the door to our room opened. Emilie quickly stopped her exercises, and I stood up beside her.

"Reyna requests both of you this evening," Luther announced as he stepped into the room, wearing his typical black uniform and face paint.

Requests. As if it were something we could say no to.

We were too close to our escape to cause trouble now, so I followed without resistance, and so did Emilie.

But as we walked through the halls, I couldn't help but notice something different about Emilie. The usual look of dread on her face had been replaced by something else. Something wild and ruthless. It reminded me of that day in Osavian. Of how she looked at me right before throwing a dagger at my head.

"Emilie?"

She turned toward me and the fire in her eyes was raging. "She can't keep doing this."

It was another evening without guests. We were taken to Reyna's bedroom again, rather than the dining room or the drawing room. I silently thanked the gods for Emilie's sake, knowing it was easier on her when there wasn't a crowd.

Inhaling sharply, I steeled myself for what I would need to do. Serving Reyna like this made me sick to my stomach, but I would do it a hundred times if it meant saving Emilie from the hands of strangers.

The bedroom door thudded loudly as it closed, sealing us in with Reyna.

As usual, she was sipping a glass of wine in front of the fireplace. Her eyes were glazed over and I wondered how many glasses—or bottles—she'd had before our arrival.

"Well, don't just stand there," she said. "Get on the bed."

Emilie and I exchanged a look before moving toward the canopy bed.

"Not you. Just Ladon," Reyna said.

Emilie nervously looked from Reyna to me. I only gave her a curt nod, letting her know it was fine.

Of course it wasn't fine. But I refused to anger Reyna right now. Not when I had seen her temper reach its breaking point. Certainly not when we were going to escape any day now.

Before I could lie on the bed, Reyna shouted again. "Clothes off."

I stripped silently and sat on the end of the bed. Reyna stared at the fire a while longer, finishing her glass of wine while I waited, and Emilie shifted nervously.

I wished she wasn't there at all. If Reyna was just going to make her watch...I wished she didn't have to see. I didn't want her to watch as I fucked someone else when the only person I wanted to fuck was Emilie.

Hopefully, she would look away once Reyna got started.

Setting her glass down, Reyna rose from her chair and made her way over to me. She was wearing a black robe similar to the ones she'd worn before. The only difference was this one had lace panels that allowed me to see her bare skin.

She pushed my shoulder, and I fell flat on my back, not bothering to resist. It was better if I didn't. It would be over faster.

Climbing on top of me, she began to untie the silk ribbon around her waist, letting the robe fall open. From somewhere to my right, I heard Emilie inhale sharply.

Look away.

Reyna bent down, peppering my chest with kisses. Her hips gyrated against my cock, only the thin fabric of her panties separating us. I could already feel she was wet and yearning for me.

I felt nothing.

After the first few times she'd assaulted me, I'd forgiven myself for my body's reaction. There was only so much I could do to resist the natural response to stimulation.

But today I felt nothing.

She ground against me, but I remained limp. Not even a single twitch, and I began to sense her frustration.

She sighed and spoke against my skin. "What's wrong, Ladon? Don't you want to have some fun?"

Her fingers wrapped around my shaft and even then, I didn't give her the reaction she desired. Not as her fingernails gently scraped down my length. And not as she ran her tongue down my abdomen.

Huffing in annoyance, she sat up and stared down at me. "What is your problem today? What am I supposed to do with you if you can't even get it up?"

I ignored my impulse to roll my eyes. As if the lack of arousal were *my* fault.

Beside me, I thought I heard Emilie chuckle. Reyna's head snapped in her direction.

"And what are you laughing at?"

"Nothing," Emilie responded.

Reyna's claws sank into me and I gritted my teeth. *Careful, Emilie.*

"Obviously, you find something to be amusing. Go ahead. Share with us."

The air in the room was toxic, filled with a flammable hatred that was sure to catch fire if we weren't careful.

"I'm just...surprised."

"Surprised," Reyna repeated, a hint of suspicion in her tone.

"Yes. That a *beautiful* woman like yourself wouldn't succeed in arousing her partner."

I didn't have to look at Emilie to hear the smile in her voice. The mocking manner in which she addressed Reyna. Fearful of what she might do, I gripped Reyna's hips.

"She didn't mean—"

Reyna swatted my hands away and crawled off of me. "You despicable little bitch. You're so full of yourself. I bet you think you could do better than me, hmm? Is that it? Conceited little Emilie is *so* irresistible."

Emilie had clearly stricken a nerve. Reyna was fuming, and I was afraid she might combust.

"If you think you're so seductive, why don't you try it, then. Go on. Let's see what you've got."

I softly cursed. We were going to ignite that flammable loathing in seconds if we weren't careful. Unfortunately, I didn't think Emilie was of the same mindset.

She sauntered toward me, removing her shirt without being commanded to do so. As she stood between my legs at the end of the bed, our eyes locked and she undid the buttons on her pants, letting them drop so she was only in her bra and underwear.

She crawled on top of me, much like Reyna had, and I swallowed roughly. I tried to convey with my eyes the dangerous territory we were entering, but her returning gaze said to trust her.

So I did.

I melted as the weight of her pressed on my groin. Even before she made a move, I already felt a warm longing swirling in my belly. She pressed her chest against mine and her lips trailed my jawline.

Before I could tell her to take it easy, she rolled her hips and my cock twitched.

Shit.

Emilie wasn't exactly an expert in seduction. But that didn't matter. Not when I was so enchanted by her. So bewitched by every sound and enraptured by every touch. My body was attuned to hers.

Her panties were damp against my cock, and I was desperate to remove them altogether. To feel her wet pussy sliding against me. I wanted her bra off, too. Wanted to feel her breasts in my palms. In my mouth.

She whimpered softly in my ear, and I knew she could sense my thickening length. She was succeeding where Reyna had failed, and a sick part of me enjoyed it just as much as Emilie did.

It was our own little way of getting back at her. Even if it wasn't the wisest decision.

Emilie licked the shell of my ear, and my hands snapped to her waist. I pushed them around to her backside and cupped her ass, squeezing her tight against my throbbing dick.

I was writhing now, desperate for more friction. More of her. Emilie's hair fell over my shoulder, and I shivered at the tantalizing touch.

Needing more, I nudged her cheek with my nose and when she faced me, our lips met. I sucked on her bottom lip, pulling it into my mouth while she released an exhilarated moan.

She kissed me feverishly, still grinding that perfect cunt along my cock. Fuck those panties. They needed to come off.

In a smooth motion, I rolled on top of her, panting and rubbing my length between her legs. The feel of her wet panties against me was mind blowing. I shoved my hands under her bra to feel her bare skin and her head fell back in delight. I nipped at the bit of neck she exposed to me and then searched for her lips so I could tangle with her tongue, too.

"Enough!" I froze at Reyna's voice. "That. Is. Enough."

Emilie was still panting, with her legs wrapped around my hips. I eased back, shifting my weight to my knees.

Reyna approached the bed, eyes darting between Emilie and me. I could tell she was putting together pieces like a puzzle. Figuring out what had developed between Emilie and me in the months we'd spent in the mountain. And she didn't like what she uncovered.

"Get up," she spat.

I hesitated, still thinking of the way she'd decimated the twins. That same electric fire was growing in her eyes now, but this time, it was directed toward Emilie.

"Reyna," I said her name softly, soothingly. She hardly heard me.

She spoke without looking at me. "Against the wall, Ladon."

Wrestling against that magical pull, I found myself moving away from the bed. Away from Emilie.

The lump in my throat was impossible to swallow.

Emilie sat up, and the look she gave Reyna was awe-inspiring. There was no fear. No remorse for what she'd done, even if she was about to pay for it. The fire in Emilie's eyes rivaled Reyna's.

Emilie smirked, and Reyna smacked her across the face. The sound was sharp and lingered in the air, sending Emilie's head twisting. When she turned back to face Reyna, her smirk only grew.

I felt something swell in my chest. Something stronger than anything I'd ever felt. A need to fight, not protect. I knew Emilie could do that now for herself. No, I wanted to fight beside her. I wanted to be her biggest supporter, her comfort when the fight was won, her sanctuary where she would find peace. I wanted her love.

Because I was in love with her.

When Reyna hit her again, my anger was untamable. I thrashed against the vines that bound me, desperate to break them.

Raising a hand, Reyna expelled a magical blast that had Emilie soaring through the air and landing against the wall opposite me. Her head cracked against the stone wall and she went limp.

"No!" I roared. "I'll kill you! I'll rip your head from your worthless body!"

Reyna didn't even so much as throw me a single glance. She extended her hand, and a whip appeared, glowing bright as the sun. Bright as lightning.

Upon closer inspection, I realized it was actual lightning. How she learned to wield her magic like that, I'd never know. I'd never seen anything like it in my life. To shape something as powerful and unpredictable as lightning was not a simple task.

She cracked the whip, and thunder boomed. With another flick of her wrist, Emilie was strung up on the wall, bands of lightning holding her up by the wrists with her back facing us.

Panic coursed through me. So similar...they were so similar to the electric ropes that bound the young boy. I threw all my weight against those magical vines that controlled me. I hardly moved an inch.

Reyna cracked the whip again, this time contacting Emilie's back. Her body jerked and a bright red line branded her skin. Blood trickled momentarily, but the heat of the lightning quickly cauterized her wound.

Over and over and over again, that whip of lightning connected with Emilie's flesh. Searing and slicing. Emilie moved in and out of consciousness, screaming when she woke and dangling lifelessly when she passed out.

The vines on my skin were relentless. Unyielding and infuriating. Panting and sweating, I looked down to find I'd only moved a foot away from the wall where I'd started. At this rate, I'd never reach Emilie. At least not in time to save her.

"Stop," I growled. "Stop or I'll skin you alive, Reyna."

My voice wasn't loud enough to drown out the sounds of thunder. Non-stop flashes of lightning and deafening booms filled the room. I wasn't sure how much longer Emilie could hold on during the relentless siege on her body.

Reyna took a break, twirling her wrist like she had a cramp. During the pause, I could see Emilie's mangled skin, full of deep, harsh lines that were already shiny red and scarred.

I stumbled two steps forward. It seemed Reyna's leash on me had faltered a bit. I was still too far to get my hands on her. The need to strangle her motivated me to keep pushing, keep dragging across the room.

Just a few more steps. Just a few more and I'd be able to reach her.

As if she sensed me, Reyna spun to face me. Her brows pinched together.

"And you...what will I do with you?"

Raising my arm, I begged her to stop. "Let her go. You don't need to do this."

She scoffed. "I don't *need* to do anything, you fool. I *choose* to."

"Then choose me. Choose to torture me. She doesn't deserve this."

"You pathetic excuse for a man. What has she done to you? The Ladon I knew would never beg. Never plead. What happened to the strong warrior revered by all of Lourova? What happened to the powerful commander whose armies would've followed to their death? Surely, this miserable man before me isn't *that* Ladon Castelli."

I didn't have a retort for her. I didn't know what spell Emilie had cast on me. But I didn't regret it. I could be both a loving companion and a fierce warrior. She hadn't made me weaker. She made me stronger.

I took another step and grunted with the effort it took. Reyna laughed before raising her whip and slicing down my chest.

Searing hot pain erupted as a gash appeared right in the center of my chest. One long line from my sternum to right above my belly button. Like the lashes she'd given Emilie, the heat of the lightning sealed the wound, but the pain remained.

It took my breath away. It was like little bolts of lightning were still traveling beneath my skin, burning my insides even though they could not be seen. They spread from the initial gash, coursing through my muscles and bone until they fizzled out. Even then, my whole body ached and trembled in the aftermath. And that was only one lash. If this was what Emilie had felt...gods, my heart split in two for her.

Reyna snapped her fingers, and the door to her room opened, allowing her two guards to enter. I was too dazed to hear her speak, but I found myself being dragged out of the room by one of them, while the other picked up Emilie's limp form.

I reached out for her. I even attempted to pull at my magic, but I was too weak. It wasn't enough to save her. My lips moved, but I was unable to make a sound. "Emilie."

Chapter Thirty-Six

Emilie

My eyes were swollen and heavy, but I managed to open them. I blinked a few times before truly seeing. I didn't recognize my surroundings. The ceiling hung low and was covered in stalactites. I was almost certain if I stood, I could touch it. Looking around, I only noticed one light hanging aside the door. It was so dim; it didn't even reach the far corners of the room.

I tried to sit up, but my body revolted. Every nerve in my body was on fire, simmering while my blood boiled. I couldn't fight the exhaustion, so I sank to the floor again. The pain lingering on my back reminded me of how I got here.

Reyna had attacked me. Viciously and repeatedly. I could only remember bits and flashes. I'd been unconscious for much of it, but what I did remember was vivid and terrifying.

I'd thought I was going to die. The pain was all-consuming. And the anger in her eyes—I thought she might burn a hole through me just from the look alone.

One thing I didn't remember, however, was how I'd gotten to this room.

I looked around again, head falling to either side as I lay prone. There was nothing in this room. No mattress. No connecting bathroom. No windows or even a dripping grate in the ceiling. Only a dark room with four dark black stone walls carved right into the mountain itself.

The air was freezing. It chilled me right to the bone, and I assumed we had to be deep into the mountain. A shiver rippled through my body, but I didn't have the energy to rub my arms and try to restore some of the warmth I was so desperately missing.

I groaned. My tongue was dry and swollen. Like I hadn't had anything to drink in quite some time. How long had I been out? Hours? Days? There was no way of knowing. I needed water. And probably food too, though I had no appetite. My stomach was so knotted; I couldn't dream of eating anything at that moment.

Once again, I tried to sit, but my arm gave out and I slammed back into the floor. Closing my eyes, I let exhaustion overwhelm me.

The sound of stone scraping against stone tore me from my deep sleep. I looked to my left just as the heavy door slammed shut.

"Wait," I rasped, but there was no point. Whoever it was wouldn't be able to hear me through the thick barrier. I sighed and let my head fall to the side.

That's when I noticed a small platter sitting on the floor. With much difficulty, I managed to sit up and crawl on my hands and knees to the meal I'd been given.

My shoulders slumped when I saw what awaited me. A small cup of broth, which was room temperature at best, and a glass of water that I was able to drink in three gulps. By the time I'd finished, I was hungrier and thirstier than I had been to begin with.

I leaned against the wall and hissed as the cool stone met my back. More flashbacks hit me, and I remembered that I hadn't been wearing my clothes during Reyna's assault. But now I was wearing a thin white cotton shirt and black leggings. I hadn't been given socks though and my feet were freezing against the icy floor.

Reaching around, I tried to feel the wounds on my back. My fingertips met smooth skin, like it had been melted and solidified without pores or wrinkles. I couldn't find the mole on my shoulder that I'd had all my life. Every small mark that made me human was gone, leaving behind deep ridges and shiny skin.

I felt dizzy and sank to the floor again before I passed out.

Each time I closed my eyes, my dreams were worse than the last. They started off normal enough. Usually with Ladon in some compromising position. Ladon with his hands in my hair. Ladon with his head between my legs. Ladon whispering naughty things in my ear...

But then they abruptly shifted to uncomfortable territory. A crowd gathered around us. Strangers watching me. Unfamiliar hands touching me.

Cyrus appeared too, his eyes lingering on his brother before turning to me. My cheeks flushed, and I threw him an apologetic look. I whispered, *I'm sorry*, but he shook his head and walked off into the shadows of my mind.

My mother appeared too, and I asked her to save me. I begged her, but she looked at me with such disappointment. She seemed to say that this was the punishment I deserved for letting her down. For not living up to her expectations.

I sobbed and tried to crawl away from rogue hands and prying eyes, but I was tied to the ground with strands of fiery lightning. I screamed in agony, and the ropes only cut deeper. Then Reyna appeared, handing her whip to Ladon. She didn't have to speak for me to understand her command. Ladon understood just as well, grabbing the whip and holding it high above his head.

I avoided his gaze as he brought it down. I didn't think I could handle the wrath I saw in his silver eyes. Wrath that wasn't his own, but a mere figment of my twisted imagination. I screamed again as lightning ripped through my body, burning me alive from the inside out.

I thrashed, body arching off the floor while I begged for it to stop. Another blinding flash of lightning jolted me awake, but it wasn't immediately clear if it had been a dream. It might've been a hallucination.

My panic slowly subsided while the room came into focus. It took several more minutes for my heart to stop pounding and my hands to stop trembling. Shadows of the horrifying pain lingered, but they were slowly fading.

When I had finally calmed down, an urgent need pressed on my bladder. I needed to relieve myself, but there was no bathroom to use. Not even a portable chamber pot. I rose on shaky legs and slid my leggings down, hovering over the bowl that had held my broth.

Since I was so dehydrated, it was able to hold the contents of my bladder without overflowing. I hovered a few extra moments before pulling my leggings back on. Then I sniffled, wishing I'd been given toilet paper.

And socks. My feet were so fucking cold, it was unbearable. My shoulders ached, and I thought it was from the incessant shivering. Not to mention the ever-present sting on my back. Like a sunburn but ten times worse.

I moved toward the door and ran my hands along the crease. I'm not sure what I was hoping to find. Some magical opening that would allow me to free myself. But all I found was a tight seal.

Resting my forehead against the door, I closed my eyes and wished I still had my magic. I'm not sure how I would've used it in this specific situation, but at least I wouldn't have felt so hopeless. And trapped.

Desperate for something to hold on to, some ounce of resilience, I began to walk the exterior of the room. I ran my hand along the rough and uneven stone, still not quite certain what I was searching for. I'd made it halfway around the room when I heard the door shift.

I made a quick lunge for it, forgetting that I was still healing. My jaw clenched, and I doubled over in pain. When I heard the sound of laughter, I looked up.

Luther was standing above me, his figure dark and contrasting with the light coming from behind him. He sat a new tray on the ground before picking up the old one. Noticing the bowl of urine, he shot me an unamused glare.

I shot it right back.

"If you bothered to give me a chamber pot, I wouldn't have to use the dishes."

He narrowed his eyes, but I thought I detected a subtle nod, and hoped the next time he returned would be with a proper basin and maybe something to wipe with, if I was lucky.

Still aching all over, I shuffled toward the meal I'd been brought. Broth and a tiny cup of water again. I stared at it, hoping if I glared long enough, then it might turn into a full feast of roasted chicken, vegetables, and pie.

Unsurprisingly, it did not.

It took all of ten minutes to finish devouring the soup and glass of water. With nothing else to do, I laid down and curled into a ball. Despite the cold and the pain I still felt all over my body, I managed to fall asleep in minutes.

I was certain I'd been in this cell for days. Maybe even more than a week. I attempted to count the days using meals as a marker, but they were brought intermittently. Sometimes it felt like four or five hours, and other times it felt as if a whole day had gone by before I got another feeding of broth.

It was always night inside the cell. Always dark with the smallest flicker of light emitting from a single lamp. And it was always quiet. So disturbingly quiet that I could hear my own thoughts. I even wondered sometimes if I was talking aloud. If I was going mad inside these four walls.

On the bright side, I was given a chamber pot after the unfortunate incident with the soup bowl. However, I was not given anything to clean myself with and the basin wasn't taken frequently, so I pushed it to one corner of the room while I did my best to stay on the other side.

As I lay on my side on the floor, drawing circles in the dust, I wondered how long Reyna intended to keep me in here. Forever? Until she was no longer angry at my actions? She didn't seem like the type to forgive and forget. If I had to guess; I was going to die in this cell.

I recalled the reason I was thrown in here to begin with. It was stupid to bait her like that. I knew perfectly well that she would react poorly to the obvious chemistry between Ladon and me. I knew it would turn her into a jealous, raging bitch. But I couldn't help myself.

I smiled while writing his name with my finger. Did I regret it? Maybe a little. Not because I didn't want to feel his body against mine. But because I was afraid I never would again. Not while I was locked far away from him.

Did he think I was dead? Was he dead? I squeezed my eyes shut, attempting to blink away the thought. What had she done to him after I'd passed out? I convinced myself that she wouldn't kill him. She enjoyed toying with him too much to get rid of him.

Tears welled in my eyes, and I erased his name.

I don't know how long I'd been staring at the wall. Everything seemed to blend together. Every glistening pane of rock. Every shadow and crevice. It all danced and swirled in my tear-filled eyes.

My eyes traveled along the lines and ridges of the jagged rocks. It was like a city map. Full of crossing paths and open spaces. One crack in the rock looked vaguely familiar. I continued following the lines, but something tugged on my mind, bringing me back to that crack.

I sat upright. I wasn't as sore as when I'd arrived days ago, but I was severely dehydrated and on the verge of starving. Every movement took more effort than it should've.

I crawled over to the familiar-looking mark in the rock. Not a crack at all. It was etched into the surface. I recognized it, along with the series of runes next to it.

I ran my fingers across them. The runes were old and disintegrating, almost completely eroded and flush with the mountain wall. Aside from the first one, they were almost invisible unless you knew what you were looking at.

And I did know.

I was looking at a set of runes that marked the opening to the tunnels.

Chapter Thirty-Seven

Ladon

WHEN EMILIE DIDN'T RETURN to our room the first night, I panicked. When she didn't return for a week and then another, I went mad.

I tore our room apart, throwing that damn bucket against every wall. Ripping the pillows and thin blanket to shreds. I lifted the mattress and tossed it across the room. I punched the door until my knuckles bled.

And none of it helped.

She haunted my every thought. Where had they taken her? She'd been so broken when I'd been dragged out of Reyna's room. But I was certain she was alive. I had no evidence, but I *felt* it in my soul.

One morning, on the way to begin my chores for the day, I managed to trick Luther into admitting that Emilie was still alive and being held in an isolated cell. He didn't realize that I didn't have any details on her whereabouts, but he confessed that he had been tasked with not only bringing me meals, but also bringing them to her. An extra duty that he was not happy about.

I smiled at his displeasure.

My evenings with Reyna alternated between boring and dreadful. I assessed her mood each night, wondering if I should play the obedient slave or press her for information regarding Emilie. The last thing I wanted to do was cause more harm by upsetting Reyna. I tiptoed carefully where she was concerned. Perhaps if I played my part well enough, she'd return Emilie to me.

Doubtful, but I had to try.

I had just returned to my room one night and was standing in the shower when I thought I felt the ground rumble. I paused and frowned at the floor, water running between my bare feet and down the silver drain. After waiting for several minutes, I assumed it was my imagination. Maybe I hadn't eaten enough that day and was hallucinating.

I continued to scrub my skin, attempting to remove all traces of Reyna's hands on me. The water and soap were never enough to completely erase her, but it was all I could do.

The ground shook again and this time, I reached for the wall to hold myself steady. I had *not* imagined that. Quickly rinsing my hair, I jumped from the shower and dressed.

A loud boom accompanied the next ground-rattling event, and I looked around the room helplessly. Quakes weren't common in Osavian but I'd learned enough about them in books. They were common in the mountain ranges but I couldn't recall ever reading about that loud noise that kept repeating.

Boom. Boom.

Two more explosive sounds.

"What the hell?" I whispered for no one to hear.

The next tremor had me stumbling for the wall. The mountain shook so ferociously; tiny rocks fell from the ceiling. I shielded my head with my arms and searched for some place to take cover. There was nothing. Our little room was bare of any place to hide.

Those booms grew louder and more frequent and I ran toward the door, pounding my fists for someone's attention.

"Help!" I roared. "Get me out of here!"

Unsurprisingly, my plea for assistance went unanswered. I listened for the sound of footsteps running down the hall. Or the sound of frantic chatter. Any sign of life beyond my door. But it was silent aside from the rumbling rock.

More rocks tumbled from above my head, crashing to the floor and covering the mattress in dust.

Running my hands through my hair, I went into problem-solving mode. If I didn't do something, there was a good chance I might be buried alive in this room. There was nowhere to take cover. No one was coming to rescue me.

The door was thick, solid wood. It was unlikely I'd be able to force it open, but I had to try something. I slammed my shoulder into the door, testing its strength. Then I backed up and shook out my limbs.

This might've been one of the stupidest ideas I'd ever had, but I was desperate.

I took a deep breath and, just as I was about to blast through the door, it swung open. It took a moment to realize what I was looking at. The harpy appeared before me, slightly alarmed at my fighting stance.

She blinked at me a few times. Then she waved at me as if to say, *follow me.*

I didn't hesitate. The harpy had proven herself to be trustworthy, even if I found her a bit odd. There had been more than one occasion during which she'd proved herself useful. She moved with more haste than I would've thought her capable. She didn't even falter as the mountain shook, throwing me off balance again.

"What is that?" I asked, knowing damn well she couldn't answer. At least not with words. "Is it a quake?"

She shook her head.

If it wasn't a natural quake...

"Explosion?" I asked.

She nodded at me before twisting to the right and shuffling down a spiral staircase. The mountain shook again and rock fell, nearly blocking the path ahead of us. We were barely able to scoot by. Of all the places I'd been in the mountain, this area was unfamiliar to me. I did my best to keep up despite all the questions running through my mind.

"How?" I asked. "Was it an accident? Or an attack?"

And if it *was* an attack, were they friend or foe to me? Everyone was well aware of the unrest in Murvort. Osavian's forces would love to take down Reyna, but so would half of her kingdom.

The harpy ignored me and continued running down the hall. The mountain shook again, and the lights flickered.

Fuck. We needed to get out of the mountain. Before it came down on top of us.

We rounded another corner and skidded to a halt. Two of Reyna's guards were headed right in our direction. They drew their swords when they saw us coming.

With nothing but my bare hands, I prepared to fight. I expected the harpy to hide behind me, but she stepped beside me, her claws seemed to grow before my eyes. Claws as sharp as knives and glistening in the warm light of the flickering lamps.

All this time, she'd been hiding her lethal advantages. She chose the perfect moment to reveal them.

The guards faltered for a moment, but ultimately charged toward us with the blades held high. I skillfully dodged the first attempt to strike, and I heard the other guard yell in agony. I assumed he'd met the harpy's talons.

An animalistic cry that sounded like a hawk reverberated in the air. I didn't chance a look to see if the harpy had been struck. Instead, I jammed my elbow into the guard's back and he grunted as he fell forward on his face.

I didn't give him a chance to regain his footing before I jumped on his back and grabbed him by the back of his head. Pulling his hair, I brought his head up and smashed it against the cold, dark stone. I repeated the motion several more times until his body went limp and blood splattered the floor.

Glancing up, I noticed the harpy was still engaged in battle with the second guard. She was putting up one hell of a fight, but she wasn't as big or strong as the guard, and I could tell her stamina was fading.

I grabbed the sword of the fallen guard. I hadn't held a weapon in months, but it felt so *right*. So natural. I deeply missed the feeling of power I experienced when I wielded a blade.

The harpy saw me out of the corner of her eye and skillfully maneuvered out of my way. When the guard noticed my advance, he turned his blade to me instead. He was panting and blood ran down the side of his face. The harpy had landed several deep punctures to his arms, shoulders and head.

And while I held his attention, she landed one more to his spine. His body arched, and he shrieked. I didn't even get the chance to duel with him before his lifeless body fell to the floor.

"Damn," I said, a bit speechless. "Where did that come from?"

She didn't respond. She simply brushed her feathers and waltzed away. I snorted, staring at where she had just stood in shock. When I regained my senses, I ran to catch up with the harpy, who was now several strides in front of me. But not before stealing the guard's belt to sheath my new sword. "Hang on," I said breathlessly. "We need to get out."

She nodded and flicked her eyes to the ceiling like that much was obvious.

"But we can't leave behind—"

I froze as the harpy flung open another large stone door, and I caught sight of the woman lying on the floor.

"Emilie."

She moved slowly, like she was still in a lot of pain and not quite aware of her surroundings. I rushed to kneel beside her.

Glassy eyes peered back at me as I held her face, stroking the stray hairs from her forehead. I wasn't sure she recognized me. Or maybe she didn't think I was real. "It's me, Emilie. I'm here. You're okay."

Gentle fingers brushed my jaw, and she mouthed my name. "Ladon?"

"Your hands are freezing." I held her hand between mine, rubbing her skin until it turned warm. Her eyes fluttered closed and I hated not being able to see her brown pupils.

"Stay with me, Emilie. We're going to get you someplace safe."

"Safe?"

"Yes, princess. Safe."

She grunted as I picked her up, one arm under her knees and the other around her shoulders. I started to walk toward the door when she began to cry, hand flailing to the side.

"Shh, I know. I know. I'm not going to let them hurt you again."

Emilie tried to speak, but her lips were so dry; I couldn't make out any of what she said. The harpy appeared on her other side and held her hand, the one that had been flailing. She pressed a small bottle into Emilie's hand and, as she brought it to her lips, I could see the clear substance.

I waited patiently while Emilie drank the water. Once she finished, she licked her lips and returned her gaze to me.

"Tunnels," she whispered. Her voice was still weak.

I nodded, happily giving her anything she asked for. "Of course. We can go to the cavern and use the tunnels. Excellent idea, princess."

The mountain shook again, and I looked toward the door. I was eager to leave, but Emilie was still struggling in my arms. She swung her arm again, back to the corner of the room she'd been lying in.

Pointing. She was pointing.

"What is it?" I asked.

"Tunnels," she repeated. "There."

I slowly stood her on her feet where she wobbled but remained upright. Then I strode for the corner of the room to investigate. It took a few moments before I realized what she wanted me to see.

"My gods," I said, running a hand along the faint traces of runes. Ancient markings that had faded over centuries. I recognized them as the same ones from the Scholar's Cavern.

I peered behind me to find her faintly smiling. We were getting out of here.

Digging in my pocket, I wrapped my fingers around the tiny vial of Reyna's blood. I felt Emilie move closer to watch.

"I just have to cover the runes with it?" I had to double check. We couldn't get it wrong with so little blood to work with.

Emilie nodded. "Yes. Make sure you fill them all in."

I carefully wetted my index finger and traced each and every rune, ensuring all of them were sufficiently covered. Once I finished, I sat back, waiting for a sign that it had worked.

The runes turned dark, somehow even darker than the walls of the mountain already were. They crackled as thin lines began to spread in the wall like shattered glass. The cracking continued until the entire wall seemed to rumble and the fissures expanded to outline the shape of an arched doorway. More and more tiny crevices appeared until, finally, the wall fell like rubble to the floor.

The room descended into silence, and I stared into the black depths of the hole in front of us.

Emilie appeared at my side, linking her arm in mine and sighing in relief. "You did it."

She rubbed her throat, and I had the impulse to check her for injuries. Her back had been nothing but blood and harsh scars when I'd last seen her. I gently touched her back, and she didn't flinch. "Are you...alright?"

She nodded. "Yes, I'm...I'm feeling much better." She glanced toward the harpy and I followed her gaze.

"That wasn't just water, was it?" I asked.

The harpy responded with a soft smile.

We didn't have time to question how the harpy had access to such magical remedies. Perhaps she worked with the healers and had access to their storerooms. Regardless, I was thankful she had come to our rescue.

"I'll walk," Emilie said as I went to carry her again.

"Are you sure?"

She nodded. "Yes. I think I'll feel more like myself if I do."

I looked down at her feet. Bare. In my haste to leave the room, I hadn't grabbed any of her clothes.

"At least take my socks," I told her. The shoes wouldn't fit, but at least the thick socks would give her feet some protection. I sat and removed them, lifting her foot by the ankle to slide the first sock on.

Gods, I missed the feel of her. As hard as I'd tried to fight the thoughts, there were moments I wasn't sure if I'd see her again. Feel her again. Hear or smell her again.

During that time of separation, I'd thought nonstop of a world where she didn't exist. When I wasn't thinking of her writhing in pain, of course.

My brows furrowed as I put the second sock on her other foot. Something burned in my sinuses and I sniffed. Suddenly, I felt Emilie's hand cupping my face, and I leaned into it.

"What's wrong?" she asked. So softly.

After I dropped her foot to the ground, I held her around her waist, letting my forehead rest against her stomach. My voice cracked as I spoke. "Don't ever leave me again."

She ran her fingers through my hair over and over again. "I don't plan to."

Chapter Thirty-Eight

Ladon

I YANKED THE TORCH from the wall. The tunnels were pitch black and slick with fresh water. They were also eerily quiet. Not even the flutter of bat wings.

The mountain rumbled again, and I looked at my traveling companions. "It's now or never, I suppose. Are you ready?"

The harpy only looked at Emilie, who straightened and gave me a curt nod. "This is our only option."

I held her hand as we took our first few steps into the tunnel. It took a minute for my eyes to adjust to the overwhelming darkness. My first few steps were tentative, but then stones fell from the ceiling with another boom in the distance. We needed to move quickly.

The floor of the tunnel was uneven and rocky. Clearly, they hadn't been used in years. They'd long been forgotten by Reyna's people, after being sealed by her ancestor.

We came upon our first split. Two identical paths lay before us, with no indication as to which was the right one to lead us out.

Emilie squeezed my hand. "I suppose we just pick one?"

"What does your gut tell you?"

"Right feels...right. But maybe it's *too* right. Maybe we should go left."

"You're overthinking. You're an air wielder, Emilie."

"Well, yes. But I can't use my magic right now. You know that."

"Sure. But which way *feels* right. Does the air not call to you? Can you not feel it in your bones? Which way does the air flow?"

"I...I've never tried that."

She looked at me like I'd spoken a foreign language. But I'd always felt one with the earth. A kindred spirit that never left my side. An extension of *me*. I'd seen enough of her magical abilities to believe she was capable of that same intuitive sense.

"Just breathe. Close your eyes and *feel*."

Emilie closed her eyes and stood tall, strikingly beautiful and radiating strength, even after being tormented and starved for weeks. Her skin glowed in the firelight and it was hard to take my eyes off her.

I watched as she inhaled deeply and then exhaled slowly through her mouth. After a few moments, she opened her eyes again. "Right."

I smiled, waving my hand in that direction. "Let's carry on then."

I had the sense that we were moving deeper into the mountain, but further from the inhabited areas. The sounds of explosions softened until they were nothing but a faint rumble.

It was hard to tell if the growing distance was a good thing or a bad thing, but I trusted Emilie's judgement. At each fork in the path, she paused and listened to the quiet, waiting for the air to guide her in the right direction. Each time, she was sure of herself as she led the way.

We were traveling down a particularly long and narrow path when she stopped abruptly. I nearly toppled her over, and the harpy bumped into my back as well.

"What is it?"

She held the torch higher, staring into the dark abyss in front of us. "Something isn't right."

I stiffened, feeling for the sword tucked away at my hip. "Murvort soldiers?"

She shook her head. "No. The air feels...different. Before it felt hopeful. Bright and optimistic. Now it feels...wrong."

"Did we go the wrong way?"

"No. I'm positive we went the right way. It feels...deceptive."

Gods only knew what lurked in these tunnels. Maybe she was sensing some other magic. Something up ahead that we didn't want to run into. I weighed our options. Go back and find another route or charge ahead and deal with whatever monstrosities awaited us. I was debating which would be worse when Emilie gasped.

"The tunnels—they change directions, magically appearing and disappearing at will. The path has changed."

That certainly beat the imaginary beast I was picturing in my head. We could deal with clever tunnels.

"Do we go back or keep moving forward?" I asked.

She tugged on my hand and replied, "We keep going this way. Turning around won't do any good if the tunnels are going to change at random. We'll keep moving forward and get straightened out at the next divide."

There was something admirable about her certainty and the way she took charge. While I had hated that arrogance when I'd first met her in Renoa, I now respected her confidence. It was well deserved. What she lacked in physical strength, she made up for with her intelligence and composure in a tough situation.

She led us through wandering paths and decidedly chose which turns to take. I followed closely, still holding her hand tightly. The harpy was so quiet; I almost forgot she was with us until she occasionally stumbled on loose rock.

"Careful," I said to her, and she responded with a wide-eyed gaze. She relaxed ever so slightly. There—we were making progress. I went as far as reaching my hand out to her to help her over the rocky pass. It looked as if part of the tunnel had caved in at one point and massive boulders were strewn about the path. She stared at the treacherous terrain for a moment and then opted to take my assistance.

As I was helping her cross that difficult section, I heard a noise ahead. It sounded like crumbling, and the mountain shook again. Gods, what would we do if the mountain caved in on us?

The rumbling subsided, and our surroundings went silent. Emilie raised the torch to check on us. "Are you both okay?"

"Yes, just a few more steps." The harpy was almost across the fallen rock when suddenly, Emilie was screaming, and then there was a splash.

"Emilie!" I shouted, turning to find a massive hole where she had been standing. The light she'd been carrying was lying on the ground, and I quickly picked it up before the damp stone could extinguish it.

"Emilie," I called again. I got as close to the hole as I could without falling in myself. These tunnels were so delicate. One wrong step could send us plummeting into the unknown. "If you can hear me, I need you to respond."

"I'm alright." Her voice sounded far away. Far *down*. "I...I landed in a bit of a lake."

She also sounded like she was spitting out water, treading to stay afloat.

"Can you see anything?"

"No. Well, there's a bit of glowing moss down here. It's not far away. I can swim to it."

The sound of wading water drifted up to me, and I breathed a sigh of relief. But then a fresh wave of worries hit me. How in the hell were we going to get her back up?

"What else do you see, Emilie? Are there more tunnels? A staircase? A...rope?" I doubted she had the strength to pull herself up. Even with her training, she'd lost a lot of muscle while being held in isolation. But I could pull her up if she got the rope to me.

"No, I don't see any stairs or *rope*." She laughed at the last word. At least she hadn't lost her sense of humor. "I can't see the other side of the water from here. I could swim and try to—"

"Don't," I said. "Who knows how far away the other shore is? If you're safe where you are, don't move."

Shit. If she couldn't come up, then we were going to have to follow her down.

I turned to the harpy. "We need to go down there."

She blinked once.

"Emilie needs us."

She blinked again, then nodded.

"Ladon?" Emilie's voice echoed in the hole.

I kept my attention on the harpy. "I'll jump first and then, when it's clear, I'll yell for you to follow. Understand?"

She nodded again.

"You're going to jump, aren't you?" Emilie asked.

I grinned. "Yes, princess. We're coming."

Placing the torch on the ground, I readied myself to jump. I gave myself to the count of three, and then I was plunging into darkness, eyes and mouth pressed shut as I waited for the water to hit.

It felt like I'd been slammed into a block of ice. The water was freezing cold, something Emilie had failed to mention. I kicked my feet and reached up, gulping for air, when my head breached the surface.

Glancing around, I wiped the water from my face. After a few seconds, I found Emilie standing on a rocky shore with glowing moss covering the walls and ceiling. It would've been beautiful if our lives weren't in danger.

I paddled until I reached a point where I could stand on the rocks. They were slippery and covered in algae that was also glowing, though not as bright as the walls up ahead.

Shaking the water from my hair and wringing my shirt, I called up to the harpy. "You can jump now!"

We waited. And waited. And waited.

I turned to Emilie. "Do you think I should've made her jump first?"

"I don't think she would've liked you forcing her into it."

We waited a few seconds more and then I heard *fluttering*. The beating of wings.

An orangish glow descended from the ceiling where we'd fallen, and the harpy burst through the opening with the torch in her hand as she floated gracefully down to us.

Not a drop of water on her.

I gritted my teeth. "I don't suppose you could've mentioned that *before* I jumped into a lake of freezing water."

Emilie elbowed me.

After they shared a grin at my expense, Emilie took the light and continued toward another tunnel. The one benefit of following the air stream was that we couldn't ever be truly lost. We could never be thrown off track. So Emilie continued as our guide, feeling her way through the tunnels.

At last, the path began to open up. The ceiling arched upward, and the walls expanded. We no longer had to walk in a single file. My spirits lifted at the sight of white light ahead.

"Is that—"

"The exit. Yes, I think so."

I stood next to her, and she beamed up at me. Those beautiful hazel eyes lit up, reflecting the glow from outside. I couldn't help but smile back down at her, pressing a hand to her cheek. Her throat bobbed as she swallowed.

Hand in hand, we walked toward the exit together while the harpy followed in our footsteps. Emilie even laughed a little, both of us full to the brim with excitement. We were eager to see the outside world again. And eager to no longer be Reyna's prisoners. Her playthings. Freedom was only footsteps away.

"Stop right there," a burly voice commanded. His figure was dark and unrecognizable against the blinding light coming from behind him. I tried to shade my eyes so I could see, but it wasn't effective.

Two more figures appeared at his side and together they moved toward us. Instinctively, I moved to protect Emilie, pulling her behind me while my free hand reached for my sword.

"I wouldn't do that if I were you." A fourth figure emerged. A voice I recognized. Slowly, the group moved close enough to see in the glow of our torch. "Mother always hated it when we fought."

I could hardly breathe. "Cyrus."

He smiled at me, and in the dim light I could see tears glistening in his eyes. "It's good to see you, Brother. I wasn't sure if I'd ever see you again."

It felt like a dream. Or like waking up from one. I'd been in an alternate reality for so long, the vision of him didn't feel real. I had to touch him. Had to feel with my own hands that he wasn't a figment of my imagination.

My hands...I quickly dropped Emilie's hand, and I heard her gasp behind me. I mourned the loss of her touch immediately, but Cyrus was staring, waiting for me to say or do something.

I stepped forward slowly, as if I might chase him away by making a sudden move. When I was close enough to touch him, I reached for his hand.

He looked down at my hand, posed to shake, and scoffed. "Get in here, Ladon." He wrapped his arms around my shoulders and pulled me in for a hug. I flinched at the sudden feeling of hands on me but eased into it, clapping my hands on his back too.

"I've missed you, you fool. Do you know how long we've been searching for you? How long we've been fighting with Reyna's forces on the border? She's amassed quite the army, huh? When were you going to tell me about that?"

He released me and gave me a once over. "Are you okay? Gods, you've been missing for ages. I'm sorry we couldn't get to you sooner. We better get you cleaned up before taking you home. Mother won't let me hear the end of it if I show up with you looking like that."

I allowed a small grin to take form, still feeling as if this were a dream. "I still look better than you."

His laughter was warm and comforting. I hadn't realized how much I missed him. I'd tried not to think too much about life outside of the mountain, for fear that it would hurt too badly. Now it felt as though my heart were being squeezed inside my chest.

He clapped me on the shoulders again and then looked behind me. "Emilie?"

Hearing her name on his lips? My heart sank. I turned in time to see Emilie walking forward.

"Hello, Cyrus," she said. There was a formality there that I didn't recognize. It'd been easy to forget that they hardly knew each other. They weren't nearly as familiar as she and I were...not by a long shot.

And yet, she was going to marry him. Unless I could find a way to stop it. My concerns only grew when he wrapped her in a warm embrace, resting his cheek on top of her head.

Something roiled in my chest, and I wanted to drag him away from her. My lip curved in a snarl, and I caught Emilie's gaze. She was staring at me with a placating look. I could almost hear her voice in my head, telling me that now wasn't the time.

Cyrus pulled away, and I grumbled when he placed a chaste kiss on her forehead. It was a battle to keep my anger at bay as my brother treated Emilie as if she was already his wife.

The gods had a sick sense of humor. Not long ago, I'd been adamant about keeping Emilie away from Cyrus. Now I wanted to keep Cyrus away from her.

She was *mine.*

"I'm glad to see you're both alive and...well, I guess you're not quite healthy, are you? Better than I had expected, though. We can clean up these wounds and nurse you both back to good health."

He didn't see the wounds beneath the flesh. The distress when Emilie was in a crowd. The dread when someone other than her touched me. Our scars were plentiful, even if they weren't all visible.

"Are you sure you're both okay? We got here as soon as we could. I know that'll never be enough but I swear we tried our hardest." I could hear the pain in his voice and knew he was sincere. My brother would do anything for me, just as I would for him.

"And who is this?" he asked.

I turned to see the harpy standing rigid, looking completely unnatural and entirely out of place. I couldn't help but roll my eyes.

Emilie jumped in. "This is our friend. She's helped us numerous times, including helping us escape. We owe her our life."

I couldn't deny that was true, so I gave the harpy a small nod of gratitude. "She comes with us."

He looked her up and down, seeming to find no reason to deny us. "Understood."

From a distance, I heard another sound of explosives shaking the ground, and a soldier in the back spoke up. "Sir, we need to move."

Cyrus was still looking us over as if we might crumble but he agreed. "Let's get moving. Unless Ladon here can use his magic to keep the mountain from caving in.

I gave my brother a pained look. "That won't be happening."

"Why not?" His expression was a mixture of confusion and defeat.

Raising my hands, I showed him the black vines around my wrists. "My magic is bound. I...we"—I glanced at Emilie—"are under Reyna's control. My magic is useless. I am useless."

I felt Emilie bristle behind me, but she didn't interrupt.

Cyrus studied the marks with a sick sort of fascination. And then disgust. And then determination. "I should've listened to you. You were right all along about her. I'm sorry, Ladon. I hope you can forgive me."

"Already forgiven." Guilt washed over me as I considered how I'd wronged him far worse than he had wronged me.

He sighed. "Let's head to the healers' tent first. We'll see what they can do about those restraints."

I nodded. "Lead the way."

Chapter Thirty-Nine

Emilie

"Can you remove them?" Cyrus asked the healing mage, who was examining my vine tattoos. Beside me, Ladon waited to be seen by the mage as well. We had a private room in the tent, but on the other side of the thin flap of fabric, I could hear the cries of wounded soldiers. Fighting had ceased for the night and the healers were working non-stop to treat the injured and comfort the dying.

"I haven't seen magic like this before," she said, holding my wrist up and prodding the marks with her fingers. "How did you say you received them?"

"I don't know. We were knocked out and woke up with them."

"Hmm. Not good," she murmured.

I exchanged a worried look with Ladon. If we couldn't remove them, would we ever truly be free?

"And what are your symptoms? Aside from the loss of magic?"

Ladon went on to explain the excruciating headaches and impulse to obey Reyna's command. Across the room, I watched as the harpy browsed through medical supplies and ingredients.

I was glad we were able to rescue her, or rather, she rescued us. She was far too pure to be kept under the mountain. She picked up a glass jar with a blue substance that I couldn't name, inspecting it before pulling out a second.

The healer was too preoccupied in conversation with Cyrus and Ladon to notice the harpy scavenging through her belongings. I watched with curiosity as she gathered more ingredients.

Then she grabbed a small ceramic bowl and began to crush some type of plant. She worked diligently, completely uninterested in the conversation happening in the room. In fact, when the healer finally realized, she shouted, but the harpy ignored her entirely.

"What do you think you're doing? You can't just go dabbling in those stocks. That's not for you. Get out of there." She moved to swat at the harpy, but I stood from the examination cot.

"Don't." I held out an arm to stop the healer. "Let her work."

We were all watching as she completed the finishing touches and presented a salve. She dipped her fingers into the mixture and stared pointedly at my vines.

I nodded, permission to touch me.

As she spread the salve over my wrists, I felt a tingling sensation. Then, as the ointment began to sink into my skin, I felt like I was on fire. I dropped to my knees, clutching my burning wrists to my chest. The pain took my breath away, and the room spun. I was faintly aware of the healer, Ladon, and Cyrus, all surrounding me. Shouting at the harpy. Demanding the healer make it stop. Begging me to let them know what was wrong.

Slowly, the pain began to subside. Unfurling myself, I looked down at my wrists, expecting to see inflamed skin. It felt as if my flesh had been seared off. But when I looked, the black ink had disappeared. I found my skin to be perfectly intact.

No. Not quite.

Where those black vines had once been was now marked with light scars. Unnoticeable from a distance, but I could see the difference in my skin tone.

I laughed softly. And then sobbed.

"Emilie, are you—"

"What did—"

My onlookers crowded around me and watched as I stood. Stretching my arms out, I showed them what the harpy had done. "They're gone," I said, crying tears of joy.

I looked at the harpy, who was smiling warmly. "Thank you."

She nodded and then pointed at my ankles.

Knowing the pain that was coming—and knowing it would stop relatively quickly—made it easier to face. I laid down on the cot and took a deep breath. Cyrus took my hand in his and gave it a soft squeeze.

I tried to smile up at him, but my attention was focused on Ladon. He stood behind his brother, visible over Cyrus's shoulder. His head drooped, and he swallowed hard. I wanted to hold *his* hand. I wanted *him* beside me.

The harpy rolled my pants to reveal my ankles and then proceeded to spread the salve over those tattoos, too. I squeezed my eyes shut as the fire set in, gritting my teeth and counting upwards. I knew the pain had an end. I just needed to make it through.

When it had passed, I looked down at my feet. The same faint white scars that were on my wrists now marred my ankles, too. I didn't expect to ever forget my experience in Murvort, but now I'd have a constant reminder.

Ladon took my place on the cot, and to my shock, he allowed the harpy to cover his wrists and ankles in the salve. He handled the pain better than I had the first time. The only signs of suffering he showed were the ripple of his jaw as he ground his teeth and the white knuckles gripping the edge of the cot.

"Your magic?" Cyrus inquired.

I felt the tingle immediately and was surprised by how easily it all came back to me. A gust of wind rippled through the curtain separating us from the rest of the tent and I sighed with relief as it blew through my hair.

Ladon displayed a similarly simple demonstration of his magic, molding a lump of clay into a ball and catching it in his right hand. He tossed it to Cyrus, who snatched it out of the air.

"Fantastic. Why don't the two of you get some rest. Maybe some food too. You're looking a little thin and I'm sure you're both exhausted and hungry. What else can we get you?"

An actual meal and some sleep sounded amazing, but Ladon spoke first. "What about the battle? I want to see Xavier and talk about our next steps. I'll need replacements for my weapons."

"Slow down, Ladon. You've been missing for months. You don't need to jump back into things so quickly."

"Yes, I do. For one, it's my job and two...I just...need this."

I could hear the words he wasn't saying because I felt them myself. I wanted some reassurance that my life still existed outside of Murvort. That after everything we'd been through, I was still *me*.

Cyrus seemed to hear the unspoken plea as well because he studied Ladon with careful consideration. "You're sure you're okay?"

"Yes."

"Alright. I'll take you to Xavier's tent. But I'm having someone bring food. I won't take no for an answer."

Ladon nodded. "Thank you."

I accompanied Cyrus and Ladon to a separate tent that had been set up for strategy meetings. They droned on for what felt like hours until I could no longer keep my eyes open.

"Why don't you head back to my tent, Emilie. Hudson can take you there."

It was impossible not to look at Ladon after Cyrus's suggestion that I stay the night in his tent. Ladon pointedly kept his eyes fixated on the map covering a sturdy wooden table. I felt slighted, but what was he supposed to do? Suggest I stay with him instead? I would've said yes.

"Okay," I told Cyrus. "I'll see you soon."

Hudson led me to the largest tent in the camp, and when I stepped inside, I found a small blue fire contained in the center. A magical making of Cyrus's, I presumed. Overwhelmed with warmth and weariness, I took off the shoes I'd borrowed from the healer and sat on the edge of the bed.

I rested my head on the firm pillow, but it smelled all wrong. I wrapped my arms around my body, wishing they were someone else's. Outside the tent, I could still hear soldiers moving and chattering. It was difficult to sleep, having been kept in silence for so long.

I wasn't sure how long I'd been tossing and turning when the flap of the tent opened and Cyrus came in. I started to sit, but he held up a hand.

"Don't get up. I didn't mean to disturb you. I'm surprised you're still awake."

"I was having a hard time falling asleep," I admitted.

He unclasped the buckles on his coat and pulled it off, setting it aside on top of a chair. He looked as uncomfortable as I felt, running a hand over the scruff on his chin.

"I can sleep on the floor if you'd like. I know this is all very sudden. We didn't have much time together before...and now...well, I'd understand if you're not comfortable sharing a bed tonight."

It would've been easier if Cyrus was a horrible man. But he was gentle and kind. He deserved someone who loved him. My heart pounded in my chest, knowing that could never be me. My heart belonged to someone else. To his brother.

"I'm sorry. I don't think I'm ready for that yet." My throat was so dry, it was nearly impossible to swallow.

Cyrus was full of understanding. "Don't worry about it. I can prepare a spot on the ground for myself. I want you to be comfortable." He reached out to touch me, but then must've thought better of it. "You're safe now, Emilie."

"Thank you."

"Um, I'm going to change first. I actually brought some of your items as well, if you'd like fresh clothes."

I felt genuinely delighted by that. He handed me a bag, and I pulled out a few items of clothing. A long sleeve shirt and loose pants to sleep in. We both changed with our backs to each other and then I returned to the cot. Cyrus dimmed the fire until it was only a subtle flicker and then he laid down on a sleeping pad beside my cot.

A king sleeping on the ground. I wondered if he'd be so kind to offer me the cot if he knew everything that happened between Ladon and I.

I turned to my side, facing away from him. As I listened to the sound of his rhythmic breathing, tears filled my eyes. I bit back a sob and covered my mouth with one hand. I'd never felt so alone in the presence of another.

After an entirely unrestful evening, the camp sprang to life again. I woke up to find Cyrus slipping out of the tent.

"Where are you going?" I asked before the flap could close behind him.

He reentered, and I noted that he appeared to be full of energy.

"To meet with Ladon and the other squadron leaders."

"I'm coming with you," I said, flinging back the blanket and leaping to my feet. I grabbed my bag and searched for appropriate attire. Comfortable and practical. Something I could easily move in.

"I'm not sure that's the best idea, Emilie."

"Why not?" I asked, still rummaging for something to wear. I sighed with relief when I also found a pair of sensible boots.

"I just don't think you should be fighting."

"Ladon is fighting," I said, motioning for him to turn around so I could change.

He did, facing the wall of the tent. "Yes, but Ladon has had extensive training. This is his *job*."

I finished swapping clothes at record speed and headed toward the tent's exit. I glanced up at Cyrus. "Well, then I had an excellent teacher."

He frowned but seemed to realize I wasn't going to take no for an answer. He pushed aside the tent, allowing me to step outside.

We met the leaders of Osavian's army in the same tent we'd been in last night. Ladon was the first thing that caught my eye as I stepped inside, pointing to the map and talking to another soldier.

He was dressed in black fighting leathers, his muscles tense underneath. Gods, had he always been that hot when he was in leader mode? I shivered and hoped Cyrus hadn't noticed.

"Good morning," he greeted the room.

Ladon briefly glanced up at his brother and then did a double take when he noticed me. He straightened, and I was in awe of the way he commanded a room. Even with his brother, the king, Ladon was the most striking person with his shimmering silver eyes and skillfully brushed-back white hair. I wanted to run my fingers through those locks, just to tousle them the way I'd grown accustomed to seeing.

He tilted his head in a formal greeting. "Your Highness. Miss Emilie."

I flushed at the sound of my name and I could've sworn I saw a smirk on his face.

"At ease, Brother. Any news from the night scouts?"

Ladon filled in Cyrus, glancing over at me every now and then. I busied myself talking to another soldier, who identified herself as Lucia, the only female captain in the room. Most of what she said went in one ear and out the other. I was too preoccupied with watching Ladon in his prime.

His confidence mixed with the sheaths of weapons was sexier than anything I'd ever witnessed.

"Don't you think?"

Shit. Lucia had asked me a question. "Uh, I agree." I had no idea what I had just agreed to.

A hand on my back saved me from continuing the conversation. "May I steal you for a second?" Ladon asked.

Lucia gave her commander a polite nod and turned away.

Ladon leaned in close, closer than should've been appropriate, but I didn't have the strength to retreat. "Come with me."

I followed him out of the tent, the chilly air stinging my cheeks as we walked.

"Where are we going?"

"If you're going to fight, you need proper weapons." He said it loud enough for passersby to hear. Nothing suspicious going on here.

As he dipped into a tent, I half expected him to wrap me in a tight embrace. This was the first night we'd voluntarily spent apart, and I was dying to have my hands on him.

To my surprise, the tent was actually filled with weapons. I scoffed, but he didn't notice.

First, he tossed me a small leather jacket, which I pulled on. The hide looked to be dragon—flexible and difficult to puncture. Then he grabbed a black belt and a variety of knives. Then he picked up a slender sword and turned to face me. "This one should work best for you. It's lightweight, but the blade is freshly sharpened. It's a suitable length for your height as well."

I was still staring at the sword when he wrapped the belt around my waist. I smiled as he tightened it and sheathed the knives.

"This isn't practice," he warned me. "Use your magic freely. Your powers work well at a distance. Only engage in direct combat if you must."

He was so serious. I grinned. "You're not going to tell me to stay behind?"

"No," he said with a tone of indignation. "I believe in you."

His answer surprised me. "Oh."

"If that's all then, let's get going."

"Hang on," I said, grabbing his arm as he strode past. He looked where my hand held his jacket, but he didn't pull away. "Is that it? You don't want to say anything else?"

His throat bobbed as he swallowed. Then he released a heavy sigh. "I think it's better if I don't."

I let go, feeling a bit dejected. Maybe he could leave his feelings behind in the depths of Murvort's mountains, but I couldn't. I couldn't forget the way he'd opened up to me, nor the way his touch made my stomach twist with desire.

He took three steps toward the door before I shouted his name. "Ladon!"

He turned around with a look of sorrow and longing. Before he could open his mouth, I ran and leapt into his arms, wrapping mine behind his neck. His lips parted for me and I licked the inside of his mouth, tasting him for what might be the last time.

I felt him reach behind me, gripping my thighs and hoisting me up. Then he slammed me against a tent post and devoured me, moaning and panting between frantic kisses.

I clung to his hair while he licked his way down my neck and to my chest. His hips writhed against mine, creating a friction that was sweet as sin. His hand roamed my body, cupping my breasts over top of my leather jacket.

More. I wanted more of him.

But suddenly he was dropping me to my feet, putting a small amount of space between us that might as well have been infinite. He held my cheeks and dropped his forehead to mine, still breathing heavily.

"I...I think I love—"

"Don't," I said abruptly, interrupting what sounded like a goodbye. "Don't say it. After. Tell me after."

Chapter Forty

Emilie

If Cyrus would've had his way, I would've been in the back of the infantry, kept out of the main altercation. Ladon managed to convince him I'd be better suited in one of the trenches, protected from projectiles while still able to use my magic.

In the end, Cyrus agreed, and I found myself under Lucia's command, waiting for war cries to signal the battle had begun.

The longer we waited, the more my anxiety rose. I began to doubt my abilities, thinking I'd made a mistake insisting on fighting.

"You hanging in there?" Lucia asked.

"Sorry?"

"You look like you're about to pass out."

I forced a laugh. "I'm alright. Is this normal? The waiting I mean?"

She shrugged. "Sometimes yes. Sometimes no. Honestly, this is the first large battle of its kind that I've been in. Usually our skirmishes at the border are just that—skirmishes."

"You don't seem nervous at all."

"I'm not. A battle is a battle. The size of the battle—we'll be fighting a lot longer than usual. That's all."

That was one way of looking at it.

"Can I offer you a bit of advice?" she asked.

I nodded. "Yes, please."

"Just focus on one thing at a time. Back here in the trenches, you'll have the advantage of not having to multitask. Keep an eye out for aerial attacks, but otherwise, focus on striking individuals or small groups. You're an air wielder, right?"

I nodded again.

She stood and looked out over the top of the trench, and motioned for me to follow suit. We were halfway up a hillside, the Osavian troops visible in the valley below and in the distance, I could see Murvort's armies.

My mouth fell open. "I didn't realize there were so many."

She frowned. "Neither did we. I'm fairly certain Xavier expected the battle to be finished days ago."

I shook my head. During the initial meeting upon our return to camp, we'd learned that war had been raging for almost a week. Hordes poured out of the mountains and they'd kept coming. After suffering so many losses, Xavier and Cyrus agreed to begin siege on the mountain itself, hoping to cut off any others from joining the fight.

They were ready to risk Ladon's and my life, hoping they'd rescue us before the mountain crumbled.

Now it looked as though our forces were nearly even in numbers.

Lucia pointed to the center of the enemy armies. "Focus your magic on the far side. You don't want to accidentally cause any casualties on our side. And Emilie?"

I gave her my full attention. "Yes?"

"Aim to kill."

It took another thirty minutes before we heard the roars signaling the fighting had begun. I watched as the front lines clashed, searching for Ladon and Cyrus. Once I spotted them, I turned my attention to my own task.

I did as Lucia instructed and searched for the farthest soldiers, focusing my attention on a cluster in the back. Inhaling deeply, I let magic fill my body, swirling and blossoming with each breath. When I felt it reach its peak, I expelled it toward those small dots in the distance and grinned as a cyclone of wind began to sweep through.

It blasted through dozens of confused soldiers. They couldn't figure out where the mysterious power was coming from. Until a band of archers spotted our trench and began to rain down on us with arrows.

"Down!" Lucia cried, and our squad ducked below ground level. One of my fellow soldiers conjured a thick wall of ice and the arrows bounced off it without even cracking the barrier. "Well done, Bianca."

A second wave of arrows hit, but they were no more effective than the first. Once Lucia was sure we were in the clear, she signaled for us to rise again, throwing our magic at the Murvort legions.

Everyone in the trench had a magical ability that was able to be wielded from afar. One soldier could create shields of stone. Another created bursts of light, like a star exploding. When her blasts appeared out of thin air, the ground shook and the sound echoed through the valley. It was clear hers were the explosions we'd heard under the mountain.

We hurled strike after strike at our enemies. Before long, their troops and ours were so commingled, it was difficult to aim without maiming our own.

Lucia sighed. "Well done everyone, but the fight isn't won yet. Follow me to the battlefield!"

Ladon had told me to keep my distance, but I couldn't abandon my squadron now. It felt like I was already a part of their group. And I wanted to have their backs, the same way I knew they'd have mine.

So I stood and double checked my weapons—all in place and accounted for. Then we began our descent down the steep mountainside, back to the valley where the battle was raging on.

I second guessed my decision to join the battle when a soldier charged at me within seconds of reaching the fight. Side-stepping him, I drew my sword and slashed across his back. The tip of my sword barely grazed him, but it was enough to anger him.

He spun around and prepared to charge again, but this time, I was ready for him. I called on the wind and he propelled toward me as I sliced my sword through the air again. His head fell to the ground.

"Remind me to never get on your bad side," Lucia said with a smile.

I gave her a tentative grin in return. I could do this.

Remember what they did to you. What they did to Ladon. Remember everything they took from you. Show no mercy.

I sent a blast of wind into a pack of Murvort soldiers, knocking six or seven to the ground. Bianca came up beside me, and icicles rained down, impaling our enemies in a matter of seconds.

A man with a long, black braid spotted us and threw a pair of daggers in our direction. With a powerful gale, I halted the blades in mid-flight and sent them soaring back in his direction. One hit his thigh while the other landed right between his eyes. He collapsed right next to his fallen comrades.

Most of our soldiers seemed to be fighting two against one, so I stepped in wherever I could, taking out assailants left and right with a lethal mix of magic and steel.

The ground was littered with bodies and reeked of metallic blood. I tried not to look at their faces, frozen in time. I didn't want to know which ones belonged to Osavian, though it was hard to miss the insignia embroidered on their sleeves.

While I was blocking blows from a soldier with black eyes and blood soaked, tangled hair, I felt something wrap around my ankle. I lost my balance and fell forward, hitting my face on the ground and possibly breaking my nose. I could feel liquid dripping down my face and winced as I brushed the tip of my nose. Ignoring the pain, I turned over quickly before the man could stab me in the back.

He smiled, knowing that I was at a disadvantage, and took his time playing with his prey. Gods, I was sick of people using me for their entertainment.

That thing around my ankle tightened, and I realized in horror that someone had a hold of me. A soldier who had fallen but wasn't dead yet. Their eyes were hungry for destruction and I kicked at them, hoping to loosen their hold, all while still thwarting the other soldier's slashes.

Sweat rolled down my neck, and I prayed to the gods. My magic was strained; I'd been without it for so long and the expenditure earlier in the battle had nearly drained me. It was getting harder and harder to summon. I'd have to choose my next moves wisely.

I tried not to panic, but I wasn't prepared for this. A voice in my head told me I was a stupid girl for getting myself into this predicament. But I shut her out. I was smart and strategic and completely capable of fending for myself.

Mustering what little magic I had left, I thrust it down toward my feet, blasting that half-dead soldier away from me. He roared and then fell limp a few feet away. With my full attention on the other soldier, I thwarted a few more blows and looked for an opening in his attacks. A place where I could rise to my feet once more.

I reached deep inside, summoning another blast of wind that hit him square in the chest. He stumbled backward, and I was on my feet in record speed, thrusting one of my daggers into the soft part where his jaw and neck met. Blood squirted as he struggled for breath and then his eyes went dull.

There was hardly time to recompose myself before another one of Murvort's warriors was headed my way. It seemed like they were coming from every direction. My muscles were throbbing already, but I held the sword up, prepared to take the first strike.

It landed with a ringing clamor. I dodged each of his attacks as quickly as I could, but he moved fast and with lethal precision. Just when I thought I might get a blow in, he sliced the back of my arm and my sword fell out of my hand.

Shit.

I still had my shield, and I lunged ahead, trying to drive into him with the weight of the round metal armor. We clashed, but he was stronger than me. Bigger than me. He forced me backward, and I tried not to trip over the lifeless bodies at our feet.

I shook the sweaty hair out of my face and from the corner of my eye, I spotted another soldier lining up an arrow to send toward one of ours. I gritted my teeth and focused my magic on that arrow, pulling it from its path and driving it into my assailant's back. He grunted before slumping to the side.

I heard the sound of horses stampeding behind me. Spotting a boulder a few feet away, I ran and dove behind it just in time to avoid being trampled. I wasn't the only one who sought refuge. A blonde woman with a massive bloody gash fell down on top of me.

She screamed when she noticed me, lashing out and trying to wrap her hands around my neck. I used the move Ladon taught me, forcing my hips up into the air and knocking her off with ease.

We both stood, assessing each other. She looked wild, rabid even. I wasn't sure there was an ounce of humanity left in her.

She crouched to leap forward, but then, a horse came out of nowhere and its rider sliced the girl's head clean off. It rolled to a stop in front of me and I could see her face frozen with hatred.

Meanwhile, the rider turned around and trotted back to me, reaching out a hand.

"Need some help?" Cyrus asked.

It was a very heroic move—if I had needed a hero. Still, I weighed my options and decided it would be better to ride with him than try to make it on my own.

Not to mention it would've been very rude to decline the King of Osavian, my betrothed.

I swallowed hard and took his hand as he pulled me up. Once I'd wrapped my arms around his waist, the horse began to move and together we jabbed our swords at any enemy fighters within our reach.

Around us, I could see their numbers dwindling. It was clear that we were winning. The spirits of Osavian's soldiers were high as they fought valiantly. I even chanced a smile myself, feeling more protected atop Cyrus's stallion.

Premature roars of victory rang through the air. The excitement was tangible. My gaze roamed the crowd, looking for one fighter in particular. My uneasiness grew the longer I did not find him.

He couldn't be dead. Cyrus would've said something. Wouldn't he? Maybe not. He didn't know what Ladon meant to me. He probably still assumed we were enemies and had spent the past few months biting each other's heads off.

Dread settled in my belly. *Where was he?*

While my attention was elsewhere, I missed the spear headed toward us. Our horse toppled forward as the spiked tip pierced its side, tossing Cyrus and me off. I tumbled, coming to a stop several feet away.

I groaned as I twisted to my side. Every bone in my body ached, and as much as I wanted to give in and rest, I knew there was still work to be done. I searched for Cyrus, spotting him a few yards away.

I gasped in horror at the sight before me.

Cyrus was kneeling, his eyes zeroed in on me. Behind him, a soldier held him by the hair with a knife pressed to his neck.

"Don't," I cried, reaching hopelessly for them.

A sinister smile erupted on that treacherous face.

"Please." My voice broke. I didn't dare look around for help. I couldn't take my eyes off of them. But it seemed no one else was aware that their king was about to be slaughtered.

I opened my mouth to scream for help, but the soldier cut me off.

"Don't you dare. I'll kill him."

The blade on Cyrus's neck tightened. He'd kill him anyway. Wouldn't he? Or did he have plans to capture him for Reyna, like she'd meant to do all along?

"What do you want?" I asked.

He scoffed. "I don't want—"

His sentence was cut off with a swift blow to the head. He stumbled but kept his hold on Cyrus, though now he also had to defend himself against one of Osavian's fighters.

His silver blade flashed as he swung it wildly through the air, desperate to kill his attacker. While he was distracted, Cyrus was able to free himself and he scrambled for his sword that had fallen a few feet away.

It all happened so fast. One second the Murvort soldier was slicing through the abdomen of his foe, spilling his guts, and the next he was clashing with Cyrus. This time, Cyrus was equipped to engage in a proper fight.

Still frozen in shock, I watched as our enemy drew his sword while keeping the knife in his other. He snarled and dove toward Cyrus, who sidestepped just in time to dodge the man.

Cyrus struck the man with the dull edge of his blade right in the center of his back. He scoffed and I could tell he wanted to take his time. Wanted to punish the soldier for thinking he could kill the king.

They sparred—swords clanging and sweat falling as they circled each other like ravenous beasts. The Murvort soldier struggled to breathe and even Cyrus appeared to be losing steam.

More soldiers gathered until Cyrus was completely surrounded. I moved toward him to help, but suddenly his blade went up in flames. He swung it around in a large circle, taking out multiple enemies with one swoop. I had to block my face from the heat of it. The Murvort soldiers screamed and I could smell their burning flesh as Cyrus took their lives. As the fire cooled, I peeked beyond my arm to see a mass of ash that vaguely resembled human figures lying at his feet.

He gave me a casual smile, like the massacre was a just a small feat. Suddenly, his eyes went wide, and he reached for me. "Emilie!"

I spun around, swinging my sword into a defensive position. I'd been so captivated by their ongoing quarrel that I didn't notice the soldier sneaking up behind me. His weapon clashed with mine, and I felt his power ripple through my arm.

Speed and agility. Those were my two strengths when it came to physical fights. I needed to be quick and take advantage of any careless moves he made. And he made a lot of them.

Over and over, he lashed at me. He wielded his heavy blade like a reckless child, showing little concern for where or how he struck—just as long as he did. He managed to get one lash in against my calf and I screamed as the hot searing pain ran through me.

But he foolishly gloated over his one small victory, allowing his sword to fall slack, and I seized the opportunity to drive my blade straight into his belly. His face morphed from triumph to confusion as blood began to spill from his mouth. He sputtered before falling to the floor, and I forcefully removed my blade from his lifeless body.

I turned back in time to see Cyrus vanquish another foe as well. They'd both been scrambling on the ground, but Cyrus dealt a fatal blow to his chest, driving a small knife into his heart.

The soldier went still and Cyrus's face paled. He was covered in blood. His face was splattered with it and his shirt was soaked in it. In fact, it seemed to grow redder by the second. He slumped and clutched his hand to his side.

"Cyrus!" I yelled, dropping to the ground beside him.

It wasn't just the blood of our enemies on him—it was his blood. I could see through a gaping hole in his shirt that he'd been pierced and dark red flowed freely over his hand...over my hand as I tried to stop the bleeding.

I looked around for a piece of fabric to cover the wound. I looked for someone to help, but all I saw was a blur of unrecognizable faces. The world moved on while I held Cyrus's head in my lap.

"Help!" I cried, but no one paid me any attention. They were too preoccupied to stop and listen.

"Emilie," Cyrus said. "It's okay. It's barely a scratch."

I could tell he was lying. There was so much blood. I pulled his shirt back to get a good look at the wound. It was a clean cut and even as I watched, the flow of blood seemed to slow. But the edges...the surrounding skin was turning dark like a bruise. Something wasn't right. I quickly covered the wound and applied more pressure. "You're right. It's fine. We just...we just need to get you help. We need a healer."

He saw the concern in my eyes. "What's wrong?"

I searched the battlefields, looking for someone strong enough to carry Cyrus back to the healers' tent. When I finally caught another soldier's eye, I waved him over frantically. He nodded and began to run in our direction.

"It's okay, Cyrus. You're going to be alright."

"Emilie?"

Chapter Forty-One

Ladon

I WALKED THROUGH THE raging battle and roaring chaos focused on one mission—kill Reyna. It was by the grace of the gods that very few chose to approach me. Each soldier that did met a swift end.

I scoured the battlefield for her, but she was nowhere to be found. I don't know why I expected anything different. She was a coward. She only put on a brave face when there were others to do her bidding.

Stepping over dead bodies and crimson puddles, I headed toward a familiar landscape. Among a dark and dreary valley nestled between onyx mountains stood a tall wall of hedges. The rare sight of greenery was a stark contrast against the ominous mountain range.

I knew what lay on the other side of that maze of hedges. I entered with my back straight and my chin held high.

I made it halfway through before I ran into the first trial—Reyna's surviving hound, Nova. Immediately, I knew I was on the right track to find her. She wouldn't have let her precious pup behind if she were anywhere else, especially since the first had already been slaughtered.

The dog slobbered and growled, pawing at the ground as it prepared to pounce. Taking a step forward, I twirled my blade in a circle as a grim smile appeared on my face. Nova faltered and took a step back. I guess it was a bit more timid without its twin.

"Not so scary now, are you? Come on. Don't you want to play?"

It leapt into the air, and within two steps, was snapping at my face. I grazed its belly with my sword and the hound yelped, retreating only for a moment before it dashed around me to attack my other side. I whirled on my heel and slashed across its snout. The dog's mouth, which had been open, snapped shut as it retreated in pain.

It circled me, looking for a weak point to attack, finding none. I made the first move this time, sending a seismic wave through the earth. It stumbled, and I lurched forward, striking its hind leg. It tumbled to the ground, but not before it whipped a heavy paw in my direction. I was able to dodge it, barely missing those sharp claws. I struck again, and this time, my blade pierced the hound's eye. It shrieked in horror—both at the pain and the loss of sight.

I almost felt sorry for the creature. It was only a product of its environment, never standing a chance with Reyna as its master.

It howled again before limping off through the hedges. I drew a small knife from my belt and flung it through the air. The blade hit its target—right at the base of the hound's skull. It fell to the ground, legs still twitching as its spirit left this world.

After allowing myself a second to catch my breath, I approached the beast and retrieved my knife. I kept it drawn in case another one of Reyna's abominations appeared.

Mist hung over the hedge maze, cooling me to the bone. It somehow tuned out the din of battle beyond the tall green borders, leaving me feeling incredibly isolated. I might've felt lost with terror if I hadn't spent so much time in these hedges. I knew my way around now.

Once I found a recognizable landmark, it was easy to find my way toward Reyna's stage.

I didn't run into any other obstacles on my way out, and when I finally reached the clearing Emilie and I had been dragged to on our first night in Murvort, Reyna stood waiting, flanked by her two loyal guards, Luther and Tristan.

She seemed a bit surprised to see me. No doubt she'd expected her hound to walk out of the maze instead of me. Too bad she'd never see it again.

I smirked. Vengeance would taste sweet.

She folded her hands in front of her while her two guards stood at attention, waiting for her command to kill or otherwise disarm me.

Reyna's eyes narrowed, and we stood staring each other down for several long moments. She tilted her head with an irked expression and my grin only grew.

I'd expected this. I knew if I confronted Reyna, she'd rely on her magical influence. I suspected she was now realizing those chains tying me to her were now gone.

"Something the matter?" I taunted.

Her face twitched with irritation, but she masked it with practiced ease. "Of course not. I'm so delighted that you've returned to me. Couldn't stay away for too long, could you?"

I matched her insidious energy. "We were having so much fun out on the battlefield, Reyna. I thought you might like to join us. I wouldn't want you to miss out on all that bloodshed. You should see the way your soldiers scream—beg for mercy in their last moments."

"Thank you for the courteous invitation, but I'm afraid I'll have to decline. I wouldn't want to get my gown dirty. It's far too pretty for that, don't you think?"

"The dress is beautiful," I said, and her eyes brightened. "You'll make a lovely corpse."

Her friendly façade melted into rage, and lightning cracked above our heads. "I will have your head on a platter, you inferior lordling."

Her right hand twitched, and I caught sight of Luther readying a knife. I was too fast for him and threw mine with pinpoint accuracy. It lodged in his palm and he dropped his blade with a sharp outcry.

"Don't be a useless imbecile," she seethed. "Grab him!"

Tristan moved swiftly to the edge of the platform and jumped down, sword in hand. I took a fighting stance, ready to take him on. His first strike was met with clanging steel, and sparks flew as our blades clashed and skidded. He was strong and I could tell he'd had a substantial amount of training. If I hadn't spent the past few months imprisoned, he would've been no match for me. But since I had, I struggled to match his power.

As I was engaged in a fight with Tristan, Luther came up behind me. I saw him out of the corner of my eye and sent a blast of dirt his way, blinding him in the process. He roared again, and his anger fueled me forward.

I skillfully maneuvered a move that I'd mastered as a child. My trainer back then had been so impressed that I was able to perfect the move so young. I spent three whole months showing off to anyone who would watch.

Now the muscle memory took over. My sword connected with Tristan's and I slid the blade along his until it almost reached his hand. I flicked it, and his wrist twisted unnaturally and he dropped his weapon as I swirled mine in a large circle.

He didn't miss a beat, though. He punched my jaw, and I heard what sounded like a bone cracking. Gods, that fucking hurt. I didn't have time to think about the burning pain, though. I dodged his next punch and when he swung his fist again, I swung my sword, completely severing his arm from his body.

He screamed as blood sprayed, drenching his shirt and mine. While he was distracted by his missing limb, I raised my weapon again and sliced across his shoulders, splitting his neck open until his head rolled off and fell back. Tristan's body hit the ground with a booming thud.

Thunder echoed in the skies, mirroring the sound of his lifeless figure collapsing. I caught a glimpse of Reyna, and her eyes were sparkling red and orange. Defeating one guard was blissful, but seeing Reyna in such a fit—that was ecstasy.

Luther had managed to clear the dirt from his eyes and rounded on me with a renewed sense of fury. His hands rose and with them, the misty fog that lingered over the hedges seemed to grow, moving closer toward us and thickening until I could hardly see a thing.

I squinted, barely catching a flicker of his black clothing before he dove forward. I threw up a wall of solid earth to block his attack, but he shattered through it with a roar.

His hands wrapped around my waist, sending us both flying to the ground. We tumbled until we came to a stop—him underneath me. I landed a good punch and then a second before I squeezed my hands around his neck, watching as his eyes bulged in fear. I could feel his pulse throbbing beneath my fingers.

Lightning cracked through the mist, and Reyna descended from her safety on the platform. The air around her cracked with electric energy and I could feel it surrounding me. One look into her eyes and I knew she was about to unleash everything she had.

I stood as quickly as I could and began to run. Strikes of lightning *rained* down, illuminating the misty area. It was the most eerie, unsettling phenomenon I'd ever witnessed. It was incredibly difficult to dodge each of her strikes. I used my power to send up shields of dirt wherever I could, but they quickly crumbled as soon as the lightning struck them.

With a quick glance, I tossed my last dagger in Reyna's direction. It struck her right arm, and she screamed with dangerous rage. She snarled at the sight of blood staining her fine gown. She was distracted, and it was exactly what I needed. I spun and ran toward her with my sword extended. It was now or never.

Before I could get too close, she spotted me and sent another bolt of lightning right toward my chest. I ducked and sent a mass of dirt in her direction. It rose up like the waves in the sea and crested over top of her. She screamed again as she tried to shield herself from the falling ground.

I was close enough to strike now, so I swung my sword at her throat. She dodged it just in time and I was only able to nick her chest. Even the smallest amount of ruby red blood on her skin made her glow with fury.

We danced in a sphere of lightning and clumps of earth, masterfully attacking and blocking each other. I hated to admit that I was surprised by her skill set. I hadn't expected her to be so competent.

But I was better.

I was made for this. I spent my whole life training for this.

She didn't make many mistakes, but each time she did, I used it to my advantage. An elbow in the back. A cut across the bicep. A kick to the shin. Over and over again, I took whatever small win she would give me, until she was panting and hanging on by a thread.

Fighting at close range made it difficult for her to use her magic. She could strike herself just as easily as she'd hit me. So when she sent another bolt, I knew she was getting desperate.

I barely managed to evade it and she slipped out of my reach. When I straightened and found her again, she looked even more rabid than usual—hair tussled and clothing shredded. She was a madwoman. I didn't want to know what it was like to be in her head.

"Give it up, Reyna. It's over."

"My sweet Ladon. It is so far from being over."

I tilted my head and shrugged my shoulders. "Then let's carry on. Shall we?"

She was breathing so heavily, and I'd struck her chest harder than I'd thought. A bright line of red stretched from shoulder to shoulder and blood dripped down the top of her dress. On the other hand, I was doing quite well. I had injuries, of course, but I was used to fighting through the pain. I'd mentally blocked it all out.

I smiled, knowing she was close to giving up. I could sense it.

But then she smiled back at me.

"Luther," Reyna shouted. "It's time."

Time for what? I let my gaze bounce back to her guard and only caught sight of him for a moment.

Then he was gone. One second, he was standing in front of me and the next he'd completely disappeared. I heard what sounded like a light breeze, and I turned to find him standing next to Reyna.

She winked as Luther wrapped a hand around her upper arm. My insides screamed for me to make a killing blow. Screamed for me to leap through the air and close the distance between us so that I could drive my sword into her cold, black heart.

"No!" I shouted.

I never got the chance to make that killing blow. Just as fast as he'd appeared next to her, they were both gone.

My jaw went slack, and the silence and emptiness surrounding me sank in. They were gone.

Luther was a traveler—a type of magic even more rare than my siphoning abilities. I wracked my brain for any hint that he'd shown—any sign that I should've known—but there were none. As I looked at the dead guard on the ground, I wondered if he'd had any special talents as well.

I ran a hand over my face, smeared with blood and sweat, and I dropped to my knees. I looked up toward the sky and the gods who should've been on my side, and I screamed.

By the time I'd left the maze behind, the battle was swaying largely in our favor. Most of Reyna's forces had been defeated. Some were fleeing, and I wondered if they knew their master had abandoned them.

As I walked through hordes of my men celebrating, one of my generals approached.

"Sir, what should we do with the living?"

Without Reyna, there was no one to officially surrender. Coward. "Take them prisoner. Kill anyone who resists."

He nodded and moved to relay the message to the other generals while I continued back to the camp. Up ahead, I noticed a swarm of bodies gathered in a circle. Curiosity got the best of me and I moved my way through the crowd to see what the spectacle was. I couldn't help but notice the way all conversation ceased as I weaved my way through the bodies.

My heart began to beat faster. Then it stopped entirely as the crowd parted and I found myself in a small clearing. Emilie knelt on the ground with my brother's head cradled in her lap.

He looked so peaceful with his eyes pressed shut. A peace I hadn't seen on my brother in years. I swallowed hard and Emilie looked up with tears in her eyes. She gasped at the sight of me. Her bottom lip trembled as she said my name.

I could hardly hear her though as I collapsed. There was a ringing in my ears that blocked out all other noise. I pressed my hand to Cyrus's cheek, choking back a sob when I felt how cold his skin was.

A haggard breath escaped his lips, and I almost lost it. He was still alive, thank the gods.

"What happened?"

Before Emilie could fill me in on the details, two healers barged through the crowd and knelt beside us. They began to work with such focus and determination, drowning out the din of onlookers. They swatted away my hand without an ounce of remorse, but I didn't mind in the slightest. I'd allow them to punch me in the face if it would save my brother.

"Will he be alright?" I heard Emilie ask quietly. I was thankful she had the energy to speak because I couldn't muster any. My mind was numb as I reached to hold my brother's hand. His cold, blood-soaked hand.

"He's lost a lot of blood—which we can replace—but this wound appears to be resistant to our healing methods. It isn't closing properly." Indeed, when I looked at his midsection, I could still see more blood oozing from the wound. With their healing ointments, it should've been closed by now. "Let's get him back to camp and try some other remedies."

"You can save him, right?" I asked. In all that chatter, I hadn't heard the healer confirm that my brother would be okay. They still seemed to be lost in their work. I raised my voice. "You can save him. Can't you?"

"We will do everything we can."

Chapter Forty-Two

Ladon

THE FULL MOON LIT the night sky and shimmered on the smooth sea waters. It was a calm night, barely a breeze coming off the coast. I'd missed this view so much during the past few months. There were times I wondered if I'd ever see Renoa again, and it hardly seemed real now.

We arrived back home two days ago, after rounding up the last of Reyna's armies. Many were killed. Some we kept for questioning. And then there were those that managed to escape and flee the battleground. We'd have to address the unrest in Murvort soon. With Reyna on the run, a new leader would come to rise soon and it was in our best interest to throw our support behind someone more agreeable, and not one of her minions.

The city had planned a reception for our arrival, but the party quickly sobered when they learned of Cyrus's injury. He wasn't the only one with a mysterious infection. At least a dozen others had been poisoned on the battlefield and, so far, our healers had yet to find a cure. I was just grateful it hadn't been more.

Clouds began to fill the sky, and I felt a sprinkle of rain on my skin. I sighed, knowing it was time to head back inside, even if I would've preferred staying out all night. There was something so comforting about the open sky after being caged under a mountain for months.

The halls were quiet. I wasn't even sure what time it was. I only knew I had difficulty sleeping alone in my enormous bed. It felt *wrong* somehow. I'd always had trouble sleeping, but now it was like I didn't *belong* anymore. The man who used to sleep in that bed was gone, and I was searching empty halls to find a trace of him again.

I passed the training grounds and then the hall that led down to the dungeons. I was about to pass the library when I heard what sounded like a book hitting the floor. I kept moving, intent on going back to my room, but then I paused. There were few people who would be up so late, and even fewer who would be in the library.

Quietly, I entered and followed the sound of scuffling shoes. I only had to look through three aisles before I found Emilie attempting to balance a stack of books in her arms.

I leaned against the bookshelf and crossed my arms. She tried to pull another tome from the shelf and place it on the already-too-tall stack of books. It swayed, and I thought for sure they were going to tumble out of her hands.

"Need some help?"

Emilie nearly jumped out of her skin and the stack of books crashed to the floor. She placed her hand on her chest like it might settle her pounding heart and let out an exaggerated sigh.

"You scared me half to death."

"Sorry about that. Reading anything interesting?" I asked, stepping forward and reaching for one of the books at her feet. It was a book dedicated to the theory of experimental healing. "Oh, just a bit of light reading, I see."

She smiled as she took the book from me. "I feel like I should be doing something...for Cyrus and the others."

I knew better than to tell her to leave it alone. In fact, if anyone could solve the mystery, it would be Emilie and her passion for knowledge.

"Has there been any progress?" she asked, sounding hopeful.

"The healers have already gone through a list of a hundred possible poisons and their antidotes. None of them have been successful so far. We've sent communication to the healers in Moridia. The harpy seemed to think that was a good idea. Given Reyna's affinity for the creatures of Moridia, it's possible the poison also originated on their continent."

She nodded. "That would make sense. I hope they're able to identify it for you. And where is Reyna now?"

"Still working on that, too. Though, I think we're closing in on a lead." We were closer than that. We knew Reyna had a getaway ship in Sage Harbor, manned at all times in case of an emergency, and was likely headed for the continent of Wyland. But I didn't want to tell Emilie about the bloodied soldiers in the dungeons who'd been tortured for that information. I'd tell her when we knew for certain what our next steps were.

Her half smile was missing the familiar sparkle as she bent to collect the rest of her books. She placed them one by one on an empty shelf, and I made a mental note to have them delivered to her room first thing in the morning.

"Emilie?" I whispered.

"Yes?"

"Tell me something honest."

She thought for a moment. "I feel like a stranger in my own skin. I feel this pressure to jump back into life before Murvort, but I don't know how to do that. And I don't know that I want to."

I knew exactly what she meant. I was having a hard time falling back into place, too. "It's only been a couple of days. Give it some time."

"The truth is, I've never felt more *me* than when I'm with you."

My heart hammered against my chest while she spoke. The level of honesty that she was comfortable sharing was exhilarating, if not terrifying sometimes. It was a high that I'd never get used to.

I moved closer, desperate to touch her. To wrap my arms around her and kiss her. To be engulfed in her scent. She'd taken something from me during those months of captivity. Piece by piece, she stole my soul and I'd never get it back. But I didn't want it back, because it belonged to her.

I belonged to her.

She stepped back until she collided with the shelf behind her, and I covered her body with mine. She sucked in a breath as my chest pressed into hers. Her brows shot up as she swallowed, and I couldn't help but note the way she looked at my lips. So tantalizingly close. I leaned in, grinding my hips against hers while she took hold of my waist.

"What are you doing?" she asked, licking her bottom lip.

"I'm thinking about how much I'd like to kiss you, Emilie."

I inched closer, eyeing her soft and delectable lips. I wanted to brush my tongue across the seam of them and feel her open for me.

"I...I want to kiss you too."

I moaned and rolled my hips against her, feeling her body melt into mine. I'd missed her touch so much. A few days apart felt like an eternity when it came to her. It was more than I could bear.

"I can't stop thinking about you," I said, brushing her hair behind her ear. Her eyes met mine, and I found a mix of longing and sorrow. "What is it?"

"Cyrus..."

A low growl rumbled in my throat and I leaned back. I hated hearing his name on her lips, especially right as I was about to kiss them.

Emilie sighed. "I'm sorry."

"Don't be sorry," I said, cupping her cheeks and tilting her head to look up at me. "You're a better person than I am."

She rolled her eyes, but her smile told me she appreciated the sentiment. "You're a good person too, Ladon. I know you are. Which is why I think we should do this the right way."

"And what is the *right* way?" I already despised the sound of it.

"We stay strictly platonic."

I chuckled. *Unlikely.*

She gave me a stern look before continuing. "No kissing. No lingering touches. No sex. No...improper comments."

"Improper comments? Such as..." I smirked.

"Stop it."

"I can't tell you how beautiful you look tonight?"

"No."

"Or tell you how much I miss you? And how badly I want to sleep next to you tonight?"

"Certainly not."

"What if I want to ask you if your pussy is as wet as my cock is hard?"

She shuddered a breath before her eyes flickered down to my groin. I could practically feel the heat radiating from her body. "Also...*very* inappropriate."

"Mmhmm."

"Trust me, I hate it as much as you do. But I think it's the right thing to do."

Even as she spoke, her hands traced a path up my chest, testing my restraint. But I knew she was right. I wanted to spend forever with her, and the only way we'd get that chance was with the approval of our families. Waiting was the right call, and I'd wait an eternity for her.

"One last kiss. One more until Cyrus wakes. Then we'll talk to him and we won't have to hide anymore. One more kiss, Emilie. I didn't know that the last one would be my last. I would've savored it more."

She smiled and pulled my face down to meet hers. "One more," she whispered against my lips. "Make it good."

I pressed my entire body against hers before my lips followed suit, capturing her moan in my mouth. I pulled at the fabric of her skirt until I could slip my hands beneath, clawing at her thighs while she squeezed my ass. Her back arched and her chest swelled as I explored her mouth with my tongue, tasting her like she was my last meal.

I wanted that kiss to last forever. I wanted our bodies to be permanently intertwined. Our souls to form an unbreakable bond.

Emilie ran a hand over my cock, and I released a ravenous moan. We were getting carried away in the privacy of the library, but I couldn't find it in me to stop.

All too soon, Emilie pulled back, breathing heavily and looking at me with lust-filled eyes. "We should stop."

I merely nodded, unable to speak. Slowly, I backed away, creating an unbearable amount of space between us.

Emilie took one look at the disappointment on my face and gave me a breathtaking smile. "This isn't the end for us, Ladon. You and I—we're meant to be together. I feel it in my soul." She placed a hand over her heart and I felt that same aching tug in mine.

She turned to walk away and right as she was about to round the corner, I found my voice again. "Emilie."

She paused and looked back at me. "Yes?"

"Falling for you might be the most foolish thing I've ever done." I hesitated. "But I love you."

Her cheeks flushed the most beautiful shade of pink as she smiled. She bit her lip, looking a bit flustered. "Then I must be a fool as well, because I love you too, Ladon."

As Emilie left the library, I leaned against one of the old shelves with a love-drunk smile on my face. Hearing her say those words...I wanted to hear them over and over again until the sound was permanently etched in my brain.

After a few more moments of paralyzing bliss, I moved toward the exit. I needed to at least attempt to get some sleep before sunrise. I rounded the corner of the aisle, and a figure in a dark cloak and light blonde hair stopped me in my tracks. From the look on her face, there was no doubt in my mind that my mother had heard at least part of the conversation between Emilie and me.

She stared at me with a mixture of empathy and frustration.

"We need to talk."

Shit.

Acknowledgements

It feels wrong to *not* acknowledge the Dramione fandom. It's where my love for writing originated and it's what inspired this story in the first place. Without the fandom and AO3, I never would've had the confidence to write my own stories so thank you to anyone and everyone who ever supported my fics or interacted with me on the Dramione subreddit!

I also want to thank my friends, fellow authors and readers for always being there to listen and pump me up. And to Frankie and my street team – you all have made such a difference in my life! I hope one day the imposter syndrome will disappear but until then, I know I can rely on you guys!

Lastly I'd like to thank my beta readers, editors, and artist friends who helped bring this book to life! I couldn't do it without you!

For a list of titles by Rachel Mays, please visit
www.authorrachelmays.com

Printed in Great Britain
by Amazon

43326738R00223